SARAH'S LEGACY LIVED

Book Four

DAISY BEILER TOWNSEND

Other Books
by
Daisy Beiler Townsend

Homespun Faith

Sarah's Legacy Series

Sarah's Legacy
Sarah's Legacy Shared
Sarah's Legacy Tested

Dedication

This book is dedicated to our much-loved daughter, Jennifer Hawthorne, a special gift from God given to us when she was eighteen years old. We're so proud of the legacy Jennifer has chosen to live.

Acknowledgements

I want to thank my husband, Donn, for all the ways he supports my writing ministry, especially with the Sarah's Legacy series. He did research, proofread, partnered with me in the enormous undertaking of publishing, made bookmarks, drove me to and from, as well as set up for, my book events, catered my book launch, and steadfastly prayed for me. I couldn't have done it without him.

Thanks to my readers who gave me incentive to finish this series! I thank God for all of you. What a blessing you are!

Ongoing thanks to the American Christian Fiction Writers Scribes who walked with me through the critique process of the first three books of this series. Continuing gratitude to Laurie Germaine who critiqued every chapter of the first book of the Sarah's Legacy series and to Carrie who critiqued every chapter of this final book. I'm so blessed that God connected me to each of you. Thanks also to Don McNair, whom I've never met, but whose book *Editor-Proof Your Writing* taught me so much.

Thanks again to my faithful prayer partners who continue to encourage me and pray for me: Angelyn Trumbull, Bonnie Prugh, Cherri McAnallen, DeVonne White, MaryElla Young, and Stacey Pardoe.

Great appreciation to my beta readers for this book, Rebekah Crane, Stacey Pardoe and Mary Ella Young, who read all the previous books in this series and gave me input before publication.

I want to continue to express gratitude to Isabel Dye, the wife of George Dye, without whom these books would not have been written.

Disclaimer

Sarah's Legacy Lived was inspired by the Thomas and Sarah Davis family and the Robert and Margaret Dye family. They lived at 259 Broad Street (now 81 Broad Street) in Sandy Lake, Pennsylvania, in the late 1800's and early 1900's—our home from 1988 to 2008. You will also encounter other professionals and residents who lived in Sandy Lake and Stoneboro during that era.

In spite of the fact that the Davis family, the Dye family, and several other characters were real people and that some of the events in this book actually happened, the characters I've created and the story I've written are a work of fiction.

Chapter 1

Broad Street
Sandy Lake, PA

February 4, 1921

Polly startled awake, then lay listening. What had awakened her? She rolled over and reached for Will, but found only empty space. She groaned. How she hated the nights when his job as a brakeman for the New York Central Railroad kept him in another city. He wouldn't be home until tomorrow night.

She sat up, pushing her tangled tresses behind her ear. Had she heard something, or was she imagining things? With another groan, she swung her legs over the edge of the bed. Her toes touched the cold, bare floor, and she scurried to move the loose board where she'd found Sarah's diary many years ago. Getting down on her hands and knees, she lowered her ear into the opening as far as possible.

There it was again. Maybe muffled sobs? She hadn't imagined the sound. Who could it be? Certainly not George or Beth. They would graduate from high school in June and weren't given to tears. Elsie and Twila, her youngest sisters, seldom went downstairs in the middle of the night.

Polly stood and pulled on her robe, then added thick woolen socks she'd grabbed from a bureau drawer. She started through the former nursery they had turned into a sitting room, stumbling over a shoe before reaching the hall.

A small amount of light filtered up from the gas lamp downstairs, and Polly headed for the steps. Apparently, Father hadn't returned from his meeting or he would have extinguished the lamp.

The sobs grew louder as Polly neared the bottom of the stairs. When she crossed the landing and stepped into the living room, her jaw dropped. Lydia Wilds, her father's former girl friend, sat on the davenport, head bowed and shoulders shaking, as though she had every right to be there. No one in Sandy Lake locked their doors but still…

"Mrs. Wilds?" Polly took another step into the room. "What are you doing here?"

The distraught woman raised her tear-streaked face to meet Polly's gaze. How did she manage to keep every hair in place at a time like this? "I'm waiting for your father. I heard Dorothy tell someone at Young's Insurance Agency that Bob had a late meeting in Stoneboro tonight."

"You came into our house without knocking at this time of night?"

"Oh, I knocked but nobody answered."

Maybe that's what had awakened Polly.

"You wouldn't expect me to wait on the porch, would you? It's cold out there."

Shaking her head in disbelief, Polly went to stand in front of Mrs. Wilds, torn between speaking her mind and concern for the woman's obvious distress. She peered at Mrs. Wilds' hands, looking for the engagement ring Mr. Chesterfield had given her. "Why do you need to see my father?"

"It's a private matter. I have no one else to turn to." Mrs. Wilds lifted her left hand to wipe tears from her eyes.

Polly's stomach dropped and a sick feeling rose in her throat. Lydia Wilds' left ring finger was bare.

♠

Bob pulled his Model T into the parking space in front of his house. He turned off the automobile and scrubbed both hands over his face, fighting to keep his eyes open. If he knew how to do anything besides being a coal mine operator, he'd be tempted to sell his part of the mining company. His father had passed it along to him and his brothers some years ago.

The miners refused to believe that the decline in demand for coal since the end of the war made cuts in wages essential. Constant talk of strikes hung over the owners.

He lifted his head. Nothing he could do about it. His bed lured him while his mind refused to relax. Florence had left a light burning, but why was the outside door open? It was difficult enough to keep the house warm in the winter. Bob opened the car door as he peered at the shadowy figure standing in the doorway, then leapt out of the car. Was one of the children sick?

A frown puckered his forehead as he caught a glimpse of Florence gazing through the leaded window beside the door. So who was the shadowy figure? He bounded up the steps to the porch. It looked like… It couldn't be…

Bob stopped and stared. "Lydia?" He advanced several more steps. "What are you doing here?"

Lydia dropped her head to her chest and wailed. "You're not happy to see me. I knew I shouldn't have come."

"I'm just—surprised. It's late." Bob stopped in front of Lydia and pulled the door open wider. He placed his hands on her shoulders and gently turned her around. "Let's go inside."

As they entered the living room, he caught Florence's eye and telegraphed a question with raised eyebrows.

She shrugged. "Mrs. Wilds said it was a private matter."

"You can go back to bed then." He smiled at his unhappy daughter. It was unlikely she would have much sympathy for Lydia regardless of why she was here.

Florence sighed and took a reluctant step backward, then another. It was obvious she didn't want to leave him alone with Lydia.

When she finally turned and stepped onto the landing, he turned back to Lydia. He had never seen her so despondent. She stared at the floor. Why had she turned to him instead of her fiancé? He gently helped remove her coat, his weariness forgotten. She needed him.

After throwing her coat over Margaret's chair, he guided Lydia to the davenport. "Sit down and tell me what's wrong."

Chapter 2

Polly stood out of sight on the landing, straining to hear what Mrs. Wilds said. She shouldn't listen. Her conscience won in the end. She sped up the stairs, jumped into bed and pulled the warm quilt and blankets over her trembling body. Was she cold or frightened? Probably both.

Mrs. Wilds' bare ring finger haunted her. Had she and Mr. Chesterfield broken up? Or maybe she had taken her engagement ring off for some other reason. Polly stared into the darkness, then closed her eyes and tried to coax sleep to come. Her mind wouldn't stop racing.

What would she do if Father *married* Mrs. Wilds? What would Will think they should do? He had chosen to live with her family so she could help raise the children as she'd promised her mother. But if Father remarried, that changed everything.

She squeezed her eyes shut even tighter. Somehow she had to rid herself of the vision of what life would be like with Mrs. Wilds. It didn't help. Polly's vivid imagination pictured the woman sitting in Mother's chair, telling everyone what to do, giving orders like the Queen of England herself.

In desperation, she climbed back out of bed and put her ear over the cavity in the floor. Nothing except muffled voices. If only Will were here. He would know what to say to dispel her fears.

I will never leave you nor forsake you.

Polly sat straight up. She turned on the gas lamp beside the bed and reached for her Bible and journal. How quickly she'd gone from depending on God to depending on Will. She had done the same thing for years with her mother, but somehow she hadn't been prepared for how easily she could fall into this trap again.

She opened her journal and grabbed Chartreuse, her green fountain pen, to write the date. *February 4, 1921.* Two months ago today she had become Mrs. William Rieser. It had taken only two months to transfer her dependence from God to Will. She nibbled the tip of her pen. Weren't wives supposed to rely on their husbands?

Beside the date, she wrote the words she'd just heard—*I will never leave you nor forsake you*—then continued writing. *No one else can make that promise can they, Father? Not even my husband...*

Her husband, who had to be away whenever his job required. Her husband, who ran over the tops of slippery train cars when the brakes failed. Her husband, who had one of the most dangerous jobs in the world according to his railroad magazines. Her breath became quick and shallow.

Polly picked up her Bible. It opened to the marker she'd put in this morning. A verse she'd marked lightly in Isaiah leapt out at her. *So do not fear, for I am with you; do not be dismayed, for I am your God.*

Painstakingly, she copied the words into her journal. As she wrote them, she reminded herself that God wasn't promising that nothing bad would happen. He was only promising that whatever happened, He would be with her. He was her God. He would never leave her or forsake her.

♠

Bob sat beside Lydia on the davenport, allowing a fair amount of space between them. She was engaged. Why was she here? When she'd come to him the night before the wrap up of his court case, he had tried to ask Lydia about her relationship with Byron but received no answer. He wouldn't make that mistake again.

He cleared his throat. "What about Byron Chesterfield?"

Lydia showed him her left hand. Her ring finger was bare, the large diamond absent.

Bob waited. He needed to hear her say the engagement was broken. When she said nothing, he stood up. "Lydia, I can't help you if you won't talk to me."

Sobs exploded from her mouth and tears gushed down her cheeks. He could barely understand her words. "I ca…can't ta…talk about it."

"Take your time." Bob longed to gather her in his arms and comfort her, but he wouldn't until he knew she was free.

He dug a clean handkerchief from his pocket and handed it to her. The sobs became softer and the tears slowed as she wiped her face and blew her nose.

"I'm sorry." Lydia's words were barely a whisper.

"Tell me what happened." Bob restrained his urge to touch her and moved a bit further away.

"Byron broke our engagement." Lydia gulped. "He made me give back his ring tonight."

Bob expelled the breath he didn't know he'd been holding. "Why?"

"He said he didn't think I loved him."

"Do you love him?" Bob reached out, intending to tilt Lydia's chin so he could see her eyes.

Instead she threw herself toward him, clasping her arms around his neck in a strangle hold. "No, Bob. It's you I love. It's always been you."

Chapter 3

Bob gasped, trying to draw back from Lydia's clinging arms. Her grasp loosened and her lips found his. Her lily of the valley perfume clouded his brain. All the questions he wanted to ask fled.

"Oh Lydia, I love you too. I've missed you so much. I thought I'd lost you forever."

"I've missed you too. Since Kathleen got married last fall and moved to Cleveland, I've been so lonely."

"I'm sure it's been lonely in that house without your daughter." Bob kissed Lydia again. Then he drew back, shook his head. "Why did you accept Byron's proposal if you were in love with me?"

Lydia gazed into his eyes. "Remember when you invited me to go to the cottage with you and some of your family five years ago?"

"Of course I remember. It was a wonderful week." Why had he ever let Lydia get away?

"That's when I first fell in love with you. But then you decided we could only be friends. You hurt my feelings, and I just couldn't forgive you. That's why I agreed when Byron wanted to court me."

Bob tilted his head, processing her words. "I'm so sorry. My older children weren't ready for me to remarry. I promised Florence I wouldn't make any definite plans with you until she and I came to some agreement."

"She got married, didn't she? Why should she care if you do the same?" The corners of Lydia's mouth drooped.

"Florence and Will are living here so she can help raise the children. It was very unselfish of them." Bob sighed. "I can't make a decision to marry until I talk to them."

Lydia gave a little huff and moved further away. "That's ridiculous. A father shouldn't have to ask his daughter's permission to marry."

"I'm not asking permission. I'm keeping a promise. Wouldn't you want me to be a man of my word?"

As the silence stretched on, his question unanswered, Bob got up to check the fire. The fragrance of burning wood permeated the room. As he picked up the poker and moved the coals around, it stirred up the flames just as Lydia's kisses had stirred up his feelings for her. He couldn't allow anything to come between them this time.

He returned to the davenport and pulled Lydia into his arms, ignoring the disquiet in his spirit. "We'll find a way. Things will work out. You'll see."

♠

"Garrett, are you having trouble sleeping?" Savannah's husband sat at the dining room table, head bowed over his Bible. The yellow glow of the gas lamp beside him brought out the highlights of his hair, making it look like burnished gold.

He looked up, stretched out his hand and pushed a chair toward her with his foot. "It's been five months since Jim moved away."

Savannah slid into the chair and nodded. It seemed impossible that five months had already passed since their friend had gone to pastor a church in Akron, Ohio. "Are you missing his friendship or do you have a problem you can't solve?"

"I do miss him but he can't solve this problem." He groaned and bowed his head again.

Savannah moved her chair closer and stroked his thick hair. "Remember when I worried that Mrs. Greely would interfere with you being hired as the circuit riding preacher?"

Raising his head, Garrett lifted a puzzled eyebrow.

"You said nothing was too difficult for God. Maybe Jim can't solve your problem but God can."

Garrett gave a deep sigh but didn't respond.

She reached for his hand. "Tell me what's troubling you."

"Before he left, Jim asked me if I'd visit George Burns in jail. I told him I would if God helped me forgive George for kidnapping you."

"I remember."

"So far that hasn't happened."

Savannah bit her lip. "Your mother told me once that forgiveness is a decision, not a feeling."

Garrett frowned. "What does that mean, really?"

"I think it means we can decide to forgive, trusting God to change our hearts, rather than waiting until we *feel* like forgiving." Savannah squeezed his hand.

"So I can *choose* to forgive George." Garrett's words were slow and deliberate. "Then I can set up a time to visit him, trusting God to change my feelings?"

She nodded.

"Sounds risky. What if I get to the prison, and I still hate his guts?"

"The real question is, are you going to trust God or not?"

A long silence followed. "The truth is..." Garrett swallowed convulsively, then tried again. "The truth is, I don't *want* to forgive George. I hate him. He doesn't deserve my forgiveness."

Savannah released Garrett's hand and picked up his Bible. She flipped some pages, cleared her throat and began to read the parable of the unmerciful servant in Matthew. He had been forgiven a debt he couldn't repay but would not forgive a much smaller debt owed to him.

When she finished, she cleared her throat. "So Jesus said the king turned the unmerciful servant over to the tormentors, and He said God will do the same with us if we don't forgive."

Garrett took the Bible and read again the last verse of the

eighteenth chapter of Matthew. "No wonder I've felt so unsettled since Jim left. I was beginning to wonder if I'd made a mistake taking this position, but maybe my refusal to forgive has prevented me from experiencing God's peace."

After pressing a kiss to Garrett's forehead, Savannah stood and smiled at him. "Is holding on to your anger worth losing your peace?"

Chapter 4

Despite the lack of sun on Saturday morning, Polly's spirits lifted as she sat up in bed and raised her arms over her head. Will would be home by noon today. Nothing brought a smile to her face more quickly than that—a smile that left just as quickly when the events of the previous night closed in on her.

Mrs. Wilds was no longer engaged. Polly's hands grew clammy and her pulse raced. Ugh. What had that woman wanted with Father? No matter how Polly tried, she had never trusted her since the day Father came home whistling *Down by the Old Mill Stream.*

Polly slid back under the covers and pulled them up to her chin. No need to rush. It was every man for himself at breakfast on Saturdays. Father had suggested it recently to give Polly a morning off. Twila and Elsie were eleven and thirteen, old enough to fend for themselves once a week.

Maybe if she went back to sleep, she would awaken to discover last night had been a bad dream. A light tap on the upstairs sitting room door startled her. So much for escaping back into slumber. "Who is it?"

"It's me." Twila's attempt at whispering left a lot to be desired.

"Come in. Thanks for knocking." The girls were finally adapting to Polly's desire for some privacy with her new husband.

The door burst open and Twila's feet, even though bare,

made a substantial amount of noise racing through the sitting room into their bedroom. "Ouch!" Twila dropped to the floor. "Ouch! Ouch!"

Polly sprang out of bed. "What? What happened?"

Nursing her big toe, tears rolled down Twila's cheeks. Beside her lay the board Polly had loosened during her eavesdropping efforts the night before.

"I'm so sorry." Polly plopped down beside Twila and pulled her close. Who would comfort her if Father married Mrs. Wilds and Polly and Will moved out? *Stop it, Polly.* She reined in her imagination.

Twila wriggled out of her grasp and glared, first at the board, then at Polly. "What did you think you were doing, pulling out that board and leaving it in the middle of the floor? I could have stepped into that hole and broken my ankle or my leg."

Polly sighed. "It's a long story…" Her cheeks warmed as Twila's gaze bounced from the floorboard to Polly. She might as well confess. Twila was a regular bloodhound when it came to sniffing out the truth. "You really want to know? I was eavesdropping—trying to."

"Eavesdropping?" Twila stared at the cavity in the floor, her eyebrows raised in a puzzled frown. "On who?"

"Did you hear noises downstairs late last night?"

"Not a thing."

Polly hesitated. How much to tell? "Father had a visitor, and I wanted to hear what they were saying."

"But you told me—"

"I know. I told you and Elsie never to eavesdrop. It's bad manners and it's rude."

"Then why—"

"Why was I eavesdropping?" Polly sighed. "Because I didn't trust Father's visitor and their conversation might affect my life."

Twila stared off into space, squinting her big brown eyes. Suddenly her forehead relaxed. "Father was talking to Mrs.

Wilds wasn't he?"

Polly couldn't keep from laughing. "How did you know that? Do you have ESP?"

"ES what?"

"Extrasensory perception. It's what some people call it when a person knows things they have no way of knowing."

"I don't have ESP. Papa says I'm good at figuring out what makes people tick—why they do the things they do."

"That you are, Twila. I'm not sure I like being known that well."

"Why didn't you just say Father was talking to Mrs. Wilds?"

"Because I don't want to influence your opinion." Polly shrugged. "Maybe I'm wrong."

Twila reached out and tilted Polly's chin, forcing her to meet Twila's eyes. "You don't really think so, do you?"

Polly scrambled to her feet. "Come on. We've got to get dressed. Will is coming home today."

She glanced out the window at the mixture of snow and rain falling, thankful that Will should be on his way home. All throughout the month of January, she had thanked the Lord over and over for the warmest January in years. Each of the twenty sunny days meant one less day for Polly to worry and fret about Will running on the tops of slippery train cars.

Will I ever learn to trust you, Lord?

Be anxious in nothing; but in everything by prayer and supplication let your requests be made known to God... So much easier said than done.

Chapter 5

George's bedroom was empty by the time Polly finished dressing. He had agreed to help out at the mines today. She paused outside the room he previously shared with their brother, Robert.

Robert, who had vowed never to work underground, had gotten a job at Goodyear Tire and Rubber Company in Akron right after graduation. Less than a year later, he'd married a girl there. They had a son and moved in with her father.

The few times they'd come home to visit had shown the marriage was rocky. Polly sighed. It was hard being a substitute long-distance, mother-in-law to someone only six years younger than she.

Disgruntled comments from Robert when he called told her all was not well with their marriage.

Another situation beyond her control. She headed for the steps.

The door to the girls' room remained closed, and her father's room was empty. She narrowed her eyes. He said he wasn't working today. Where was he?

As soon as she entered the living room, a note propped up against the unlit gas lamp caught her eye. Her father's handwriting. *Lydia and I are going to Aunt Adda's restaurant for breakfast.*

Polly swiped the paper and crumpled it into a ball just as a car pulled up in front of the house. Will. She grabbed her coat from its hook, shoved her arms into the sleeves and dashed out the door. Before he could get out of the car, she jumped in from the passenger's side.

"What is it, Lass? Are we late for an appointment?"

"No, no. Nothing like that. I couldn't wait another second to see you." Polly scooted as close to him as possible.

Will put his arm around her and drew her closer still. "There, there, Lass." He peered at her, then leaned in for a warm kiss. "I'm thinkin' something is troublin' you, Love."

"You know me too well." Polly sighed and closed her eyes, leaning in for another kiss.

"Is it warm enough ya are? We can go up to our sittin' room to be alone."

"I'm fine. Truly I am." She tilted her head against his shoulder and told him about Mrs. Wilds' visit the night before. He listened, his cheek against her hair, his left hand stroking hers.

"Oh Will, did we do the wrong thing in getting married?"

Will put a finger to her lips. "Nay, nay. Don't ever be sayin' that, Lass. Whatever happens, we'll face it together. If your father remarries, perhaps we can live with me mam."

"Ah, Will, we can't do that. You know she doesn't like me."

"Don't be sayin' that, Love. She barely knows ya."

Polly hung her head, and a tear trickled off her chin onto Will's hand.

"Don't cry, Lassie. Don't cry. The Lord will make a way for us."

♠

The next day, Twila and Elsie squeezed into Will and Polly's car while Beth and George rode with Father on the short trip to church. Polly had gone to Mass with Will and his mother last Sunday, so today it was his turn to go with her. Neither of them felt completely comfortable in the other's church, but they weren't willing to go their separate ways on a Sunday morning. A familiar setting would never win over being with Will, and he felt the same.

Will parked among the other vehicles, horses and buggies outside the Presbyterian Church. After scrambling from the car, he hurried to open the passenger door and helped Polly down from the running board. Today he assisted each of the three ladies with the utmost care. Polly's heart warmed. Her husband had such good manners and showed such kindness to her younger sisters. She prayed his behavior would be a model for what Elsie and Twila should expect in a gentleman. With her hand tucked in his arm, they started toward the church.

"Polly."

She looked up, then her eyes widened to see Savannah waiting for her on the church steps. "What are you doing here? I mean, I'm happy to see you, but you didn't mention… Is Garrett preaching today?"

"Yes, it was unexpected. Reverend Lawrence came down with something in the night. His wife called this morning to find out if Garrett could fill in."

"This will be our first time to hear Garrett preach." She smiled at Savannah. "Has he been busy?"

"Quite busy, in spite of a few whispering campaigns. Mrs. Greely is trying to cause trouble. So far no one seems to believe her." Savannah started up the steps. "May I sit with you today? I try to stay in the background when Garrett's preaching."

"Of course. You know you're family."

Twila bounded up the steps to ensure getting a seat beside Savannah, whom she idolized, and Elsie sidled up close to Will with an adoring smile. She'd become his friend for life after he took an interest in her art work. Polly repressed a smile. At one time, she might have been jealous when her sisters showed a preference for other people. Now, it delighted her to see them connecting with other grown-ups.

What about Mrs. Wilds?

She frowned and followed Twila and Savannah down the aisle. What would she do if her sisters showed a preference for Lydia Wilds?

Chapter 6

Will settled into the pew, trying to prepare his heart for worship. It would be interestin' to hear someone Garrett's age deliver a sermon. Reverend Lawrence and Father Craig were a great deal older. He stared at the hymnbook Elsie and Polly held on either side of him, makin' sure he could see the words. It didn't really matter since the song wasn't one he knew.

What a friend we have in Jesus all our sins and griefs to bear.

What a privilege to carry everything to God in prayer.

The words reminded him that his wife didn't believe it necessary to confess her sins to anyone except God. The muscles in his neck tensed, but he rolled his shoulders. She probably worried because he didn't feel forgiven unless he confessed to his priest. They never argued about the differences in their beliefs but sometimes he did worry. And undoubtedly, it troubled Mam.

When the song ended, Polly closed the hymnbook and placed it in the rack on the back of the pew in front of them. Garrett walked up the steps to the pulpit. She had once fancied herself in to be in love with this man. Did she still have feelings for him? He glanced at the rapt expression on her face, then blew out a breath. That was a long time ago.

Garrett cleared his throat, then greeted the congregation with a smile. "Thank you for inviting me to fill the pulpit this morning in Reverend Lawrence's absence. I count it a high privilege."

After opening his Bible, Garrett flipped a couple pages. "This morning I'd like to preach on one of my favorite Bible passages, Psalm 107."

Did protestant ministers just preach on any Scripture they wanted? Didn't they have a Sunday Missal that had a yearly cycle of readings laid out?

Polly opened her Bible and found the place in less than ten seconds. Will envied how easily she and Garrett located the text. The Bible readings in his church were in Latin, so he'd never carried a Bible to church.

She leaned over and put her mouth close to his ear. "This was one of Mother's favorite chapters, too."

Will glanced at her Bible, then pulled a Bible from the rack in front of him and began turning pages. How would he become adept at locatin' scriptures if he didn't try?

"This chapter of Psalms contains basically four scenarios of people experiencing hardships and trouble…some brought about through no fault of their own, some because of their rebellion and sin." Garrett paused. "However, in every situation, the result was the same. When they cried out to the Lord in their trouble, He delivered, saved or brought them out of their distresses, regardless of the cause.

"Each time this truth is recorded, the psalmist goes on to say, *Oh that men would praise the Lord for His goodness, and for His wonderful works to the children of men!* What does this tell us? Perhaps that the Children of Israel are a great deal like us. When God rescued them, they quickly moved on, forgetting to give Him the credit and the praise."

♠

Polly eyed Will as he fumbled through the pages of the Bible. She smiled and leaned over to assist him. Even as she flipped pages, she processed Garrett's words. The situation she and Will would find themselves in if Father married Mrs. Wilds was through no fault of their own. They wouldn't have moved in with her family if they'd known this was a possibility. However, Garrett said even if it had been their fault, God would still rescue them if they cried out to Him. She pointed out chapter 107 to Will and returned her gaze to Garrett.

"The Lord responded in the way that best suited the situation in every circumstance. Look at verse seven. 'And He led them forth by the *right* way, that they might go to a city of habitation.' God had removed this group of people from the places they lived, and when they cried out to Him, He gave them a new place to live. God's deliverances are abundantly practical."

Polly glanced at Will and reached for his hand. Had God sent Garrett with this message for them today? If Father married Mrs. Wilds, God had a plan for them. As her gaze lingered on Will, her smile faded. What if he thought the new place God had for them was with his mother? It might be practical, but it could also be like jumping out of the frying pan into the fire.

After the last hymn and the benediction, Savannah reached out to hug Polly. "Is everything okay? You look worried."

Savannah knew her so well. Polly chewed her lower lip and peered at Father on the other side of Savannah. He wouldn't hear her over the friendly chatter. "I think Mr. Chesterfield and Mrs. Wilds broke up."

Raising one eyebrow, Savannah whispered, "Why?"

Polly shrugged and told Savannah what had happened the night before.

"You found her sitting in your living room late last night?" In her astonishment, Savannah forgot to whisper.

"Shhh. I don't want Father to hear us discussing this. But yes, I did."

Savannah frowned. "Unbelievable. What did she want?"

"She said it was personal, and Father hasn't told me."

Will edged out of the pew and Polly followed with

Savannah close behind. Polly stopped and faced her. "Aren't you going back to shake hands with folks? The wives of visiting pastors often do."

Looking away, Savannah shook her head. "Garrett wants me to but I don't want to remind the people of who he married. I'm sure they haven't forgotten my past. To be honest, there might be people who would snub me."

Now it was Polly's turn to frown. "But Savannah…"

Just then they reached Garrett and he took Polly's hand. "Hello Polly. How are you doing?"

"I'm all right." She clung to his hand. "That was our first time to hear you preach, Garrett. A wonderful message, wasn't it, Will?" She turned to Will. His gaze met hers, a guarded expression on his face.

Then he smiled at Garrett. "A wonderful message, indeed. I wish I understood the Bible as well as you do."

"I have Reverend Caldwell to thank for all the years he trained me and helped me study God's Word. I miss him and our Bible studies." His eyes lit. "Say, Will, would you be interested in studying the Bible together?"

"I…I don't know. Mam…" He stopped and looked at Polly. "I'm Catholic, you know… We're not encouraged to interpret the Bible ourselves." His voice trailed away. "Maybe… I'll let you know."

Chapter 7

Polly slumped into the deep maroon cushion on the loveseat she and Will had bought to furnish their sitting room. He was away on one of his longer runs, so she sat alone. Everyone else except Father was already in bed. She picked up her journal and smoothed her fingers over the raised, gold lettering, then opened it and grabbed Druscilla.

February 11, 1921 Father has gone to see Mrs. Wilds after supper every day and hasn't come home until after I was in bed. There's been no opportunity to talk to him about her. Savannah said Dorothy told her Mr. Chesterfield broke up with Lydia because he didn't believe she loved him, said she just loved his money. Maybe tomorrow I can talk to Father since he rarely works at the mines on Saturdays. He'll be upset if he thinks I've been listening to gossip.

She paused and nibbled the tip of her pen. Did she really want to talk to Father? Maybe it would be better to pretend nothing had happened. He had promised her a few years ago that he wouldn't make plans with Mrs. Wilds until he and Polly had reached an agreement.

Sighing, she bent over her journal. *Last Sunday afternoon, I asked Will if he thought God was speaking to us through Garrett's sermon, if He'd been saying He'd provide a place for us to live if Father and Mrs. Wilds married. He looked bewildered and said he thought it presumptuous to think God had a message especially for us in Garrett's sermon. Maybe*

Catholics don't believe God speaks to them. Actually, maybe lots of Christians don't believe that either.

By unspoken mutual agreement, she and Will had dropped the subject. Polly closed her eyes and leaned her head on her hand. "Father, I've never heard an audible voice but I know you've spoken to me many times through Scripture and through my thoughts."

After a few moments of silence, she opened her eyes and began a new paragraph.

Were you speaking to us through Garrett's message, Father?

Words from the fourteenth chapter of John came gently to her mind, and she wrote them in large letters. *I go to prepare a place for you…*

Peace settled over her. "Thank you, Father." Perhaps now she could sleep.

♠

Garrett awakened and stretched, then sniffed. The tantalizing smell of bacon was in the air. He sat up and rubbed his eyes. It wasn't like him to sleep later than Savannah on a Saturday morning, but all week he'd lain sleepless for hours as he wrestled with forgiving George Burns.

Despite Savannah's counsel that it was as simple as making a decision to forgive, he couldn't quite bring himself to believe it was that easy. Swinging his legs out of bed, he shivered and made a dash to grab some clothes. It was a non-work day, so he made quick work of his toilette.

A few minutes later, he snuck up behind Savannah and kissed her cheek as she stood at the stove. "Good morning, beautiful wife. I don't know which smells better—you or the bacon."

She turned and gave him his favorite *I love you more than anything* smile with a twinkle in her eye. "Good morning, handsome husband. I'll bet it was the smell of the bacon that got you out of bed."

"You're right. I can't believe I slept so late. I have sermon preparations to do for the Methodist Church in Jackson Center tomorrow."

"I didn't want to wake you because I know you haven't slept well this week." Savannah placed a tender kiss on his lips and slid the bacon on a plate.

Garrett bowed his head. "I'm still wrestling with forgiving *you know who*. I have to make a decision by Monday if I'm going to set up a visit with him next week."

"I'm sorry, darling."

Before Savannah could say more, he asked, "Do you want me to toast some bread?"

"That would be wonderful. Maybe when we get electricity in Sandy Lake, we can buy one of those pop-up toasters." She began scooping scrambled eggs from the iron skillet, then reached to pat his arm. "I'm praying for you."

"Thank you. This is one of the hardest things God has ever asked of me." He inserted the long-handled toasting fork into two pieces of bread. "If only there were such a thing as pop-up forgiveness."

Savannah smiled. "The same Spirit that raised Christ Jesus from the dead now lives in you. The power lines for electricity in Sandy Lake and Stoneboro won't be ready for a month or two, but God's power is available to you now."

"My head knows that but I can't seem to get my heart to believe it. How can I preach to others when I have unforgiveness toward Mr. Burns?"

♠

The next morning, a tap on their upstairs sitting-room door roused Polly from her sleep. She sat up and stretched. Had she overslept? "Who is it?"

"Your father. Can I come in?"

"Just a minute." Polly jumped out of bed, grabbed her robe, and rushed to open the hall door. "Is something wrong?"

"Just wondering if you'd like to have breakfast with me at Aunt Adda's?" Father's smile was tentative.

Father had never invited her to go to breakfast with him at a restaurant. She took a deep breath. Was he setting the stage to tell her he was marrying Mrs. Wilds?

Chapter 8

Bob went to hitch up Jupiter while he waited for Florence. It was easier than starting his car on a cold morning. He could see Jupiter's breath as he snorted and stomped his feet, showing his displeasure at leaving the comparative warmth of his stall.

"Sorry, old friend, but it's important. I'm walking into territory infested with land mines this morning. Maybe some good food and a pleasant atmosphere will help improve my chances of avoiding an explosion."

He hitched Jupiter to the buggy and jumped in just as the door to the house slammed. After a gentle tap with the reins, he added in an undertone, "Wish me luck."

Florence stepped into the buggy as soon as it stopped moving, and Bob tucked a blanket around her. "Maybe some day someone will invent something to help cars start better in the winter."

"It's okay. It's not far to the restaurant." Florence rubbed her mittened hands together.

Bob chewed the inside of his cheek and eyed his daughter. She stared straight ahead. He couldn't start the discussion here. The silence between them grew awkward.

When Jupiter stopped at Lake Street to allow a buggy and an automobile to pass, Bob glanced at Florence again and found her looking at him. "Thank you—"

"Thank you—" They both started to speak at the same time.

He smiled at her. "Ladies first."

"I was going to say thank you for inviting me to breakfast." Florence didn't quite meet his eyes.

"You're welcome. I was going to say thank you for coming."

"You're welcome."

Bob breathed a sigh of relief as they entered the parking area. There were plenty of hitching posts available, so he stopped at the closest one and tied up Jupiter. Florence slipped down from the buggy before he could help her and waited for him at the restaurant door.

When they entered Aunt Adda's establishment, Bob's brother's wife noticed them almost immediately. She waved them over to a table near the wood stove. "Only the best for family." Her voice was low enough that only they could hear, but no one could miss her beaming smile.

"Thank you, Adda." Bob greeted his sister-in-law. "We appreciate it. What's good this morning?"

"Everything, of course. You might like the waffles. They're especially tasty today."

"Were you sampling the food, Aunt Adda?"

It was the first time Bob had seen Florence smile this morning.

"Just a small one, child." Adda was the only one who called twenty-nine-year-old Florence "child," but it brought another smile to his daughter's face.

"I'll take a waffle. Would you like one, too, Florence, or does something else sound better to you?"

"A waffle is fine."

"Two waffles coming up." Adda started to leave, then turned back. "Would you like some sausage or bacon with that?"

"I'll take some bacon." Bob waved at his daughter. "How about you, Florence?"

"Bacon is fine." Florence's smile was for her aunt.

Adda never wrote anything down. Today was no exception as she wound her way between oak tables toward the kitchen. The moment of truth had come. Bob's stomach clenched and he cleared his throat. Before he could open his mouth, Florence beat him to it.

"I know you didn't bring me here just to enjoy Aunt Adda's cooking, Father. I've been waiting all week to hear what Mrs. Wilds had to say last Friday."

Bob choked a little and took a long swallow of water one of the waitresses had just brought them. "You get right to the point, don't you?"

"As I said, I've been waiting all week." She opened her mouth as if to say more, then closed it again.

"All right." Bob gazed at his glass for a long time before looking at Florence. "Byron Chesterfield broke up with Lydia last week."

Florence tapped her fingers on the table. "Did she say why they broke up?"

Bob took another long swallow of water. "I don't know if Lydia would want me telling that around."

"I don't plan on 'telling it around,' but I'd like to know what she told you."

"All right." Bob sighed. "I'll trust you to keep this confidential. She said he doesn't believe she loves him."

"Is that all she said?"

How much to tell? After a long pause, Bob blew out a long breath. "She said I'm the one she loves and always has."

Water spewed out of Florence's mouth. She grabbed a napkin. "And you believed her? You fell for that. Maybe you should ask Mr. Chesterfield to tell you the whole story."

Bob scowled. "Did you talk to Byron?"

Florence scowled back. Then told him what Savannah had said the day before.

"You know I hate gossip, Florence. Your mother used to say *Love always believes the best*, and I'm choosing to believe the best of Lydia."

Staring at him, Florence shook her head. She spoke slowly as though thinking aloud. "I believe we need to be led by the Holy Spirit in everything we do. We're being gullible if we think God wants us to 'believe the best' when there is plenty of evidence someone isn't telling the truth."

"I guess we'll have to agree to disagree on this, Florence. When Lydia became engaged to Byron, I thought I'd lost her forever. I won't let that happen again."

Chapter 9

Polly sat very still, willing herself to calm down as the short, pretty waitress placed their food in front of them. If only Will were here…

God is our refuge and strength, a very present help in time of trouble.

I'm sorry, Father. I'm doing it again. Help me rely on you.

Be quick to listen, slow to speak and slow to get angry.

She took slow, deep breaths and focused on her hands folded in her lap until her pulse slowed. "So are you saying you plan to marry Mrs. Wilds?"

"I am. I love her and she loves me."

"Have you set a date?" Polly forced herself to meet her father's eyes.

"We didn't because I needed to talk to you first." He poured a generous amount of maple syrup on his waffle. "I promised you a long time ago I wouldn't marry Lydia until you and I came to an agreement. That's especially important since you and Will are living with me."

Polly nodded, continuing to take slow, deep breaths. She picked up the syrup, then set it down when her churning stomach objected.

"I'd like to marry her soon, and I have a plan that might allow that to happen." He picked up his knife and fork and began to cut up his waffle.

"What are you thinking?"

"You and Will could continue to live in our house at least until Beth and George graduate in June. Twila and Elsie could choose whether to live with Lydia and me in her house or stay with you and Will until you move." He put a bite of waffle into his mouth.

"And after Beth and George graduate?"

"I believe Beth wants to go to nurses' training and George says he wants to get a job and move out after graduation." Bob speared a piece of bacon. "If Lydia is interested, maybe you and Will could buy or rent from her, or there would probably be room for you to continue to live at our house with us."

Polly couldn't control the vehement shaking of her head when her father gave his final option. "No, no. I'm sure we won't want to live with you after June."

"But you think the first part of my plan might work?"

"Maybe. I have to talk with Will, find out what he wants to do." She played with her fork.

"All right. When will he be home?"

"Next week."

Father nodded. "Aren't you going to eat your waffle? Mine is delicious."

Polly shook her head. "I'm not hungry." She stood. "I think I'll walk home. The smell of food is making me nauseous."

♠

Garrett had come out early to make sure the car started since they needed to drive to the Methodist Church in Jackson Center. He held the door open for Savannah to get into the car. What a beautiful picture she made as a few lazy snowflakes fluttered onto her raven-black hair.

"Where's your red winter coat? It's one of my favorites." He leaned in to kiss her as she settled herself.

Savannah bit her lip. "It's getting old and maybe not appropriate to wear to church."

"You didn't wear that coat because of Mrs. Greely,

right?" Garrett slammed the car door and ran around to the other side.

She met his gaze as he jumped in. After a moment, she nodded. "If I'm honest, you're probably right. I don't want to give her any more reason to gossip. I'm amazed that Reverend Greeley invited us to come."

Garrett put the car into gear and grinned at his wife. "He's a brave man, isn't he?"

"I keep praying that God will enable me to continue choosing to forgive her for the trouble she's causing and also change her heart."

A grimace settled on Garrett's lips at her words. "Choosing to forgive. You had to remind me. I promised the Lord I wouldn't preach another sermon with unforgiveness in my heart."

Savannah twisted her head in his direction, her violet-blue eyes appearing almost black. "You did?"

"I did." He sighed. "If Jim hadn't asked me to go visit George Burns, I might not have realized how much I hated him. But since I know, I have no excuse for not forgiving."

"Your mother quoted this verse to me from Psalms, *If I regard iniquity in my heart, the Lord will not hear me.*" Savannah opened and closed her purse. "She said that means if I know the sin is there and I don't deal with it, God won't hear my prayers."

Garrett sighed again, longer and deeper. "Another good reason to forgive. All right, here goes. *Father, you know my heart. You know how angry I've been at George Burns, how much I've hated him. The only reason I want to forgive him is because that's what you're asking of me. Well, that and I want you to answer my prayers.*"

He glanced at his wife whose eyes were tightly closed. *Thank you for my wife, who has already forgiven George, although she has every reason to be bitter. I'm choosing to follow her example. I'm choosing to forgive and trusting you to work that forgiveness in my heart. Amen.*

Savannah's eyelids fluttered open as they pulled into the parking lot of the church. He parked and turned toward her. "I don't feel any different."

"You've done your part, Garrett. Now you have to trust God to do His."

Chapter 10

As Garrett climbed the church steps with Savannah beside him, the door burst open and Mrs. Greely appeared.

"I can't believe you came here today knowing how I feel about you." Her steely glare was centered on Savannah.

Garrett answered as though the words were directed at him. "Your husband asked me to preach today, Mrs. Greely. I believe he's expecting us." He gripped Savannah's hand and tried to squeeze through the doorway around Mrs. Greely's substantial bulk.

For a moment, it appeared she wouldn't allow them to enter, but at the last minute, she backed up. Mrs. Greely's fierce glare might have stopped many. Not him. Garrett gritted his teeth and sheltered his wife as they pushed past her.

Savannah said nothing, simply following her husband's lead. When she tried to smile at their opponent, the woman snorted and stormed off. Savannah's cheeks warmed and she pulled hard on Garrett's hand. "Maybe I shouldn't have come. I don't want to upset anyone."

"Do you want to encourage her unconscionable behavior? God forgave you long ago and she has no right to deny you access to this church. Take off your coat and I'll hang it over there." As he reached for her coat, Savannah's face was so pale, his heart thumped. "Are you okay?"

Savannah pressed her lips together, then gave a brief nod. Her pale face and pinched lips told him otherwise, but what else could she do? He was scheduled to preach so he couldn't very well leave.

Today he would insist she sit with him. He wouldn't leave her unguarded in this lions' den. As he stepped into the sanctuary, the smiling faces forced him to acknowledge there was only one lion in this den, one lion too many.

Reverend Greely stepped out of a door beside the pulpit and hurried down the aisle. "I intended to greet you at the front door. Sorry, I was detained. I hope everyone has made you welcome."

Garrett could barely hold his tongue. He didn't intend to lie, so he said nothing. Savannah reached a hand to the pastor. "Thank you for inviting us."

They had barely finished shaking hands when Mrs. Greely sailed past them and sat in her usual spot in the second pew on the left. Reverend Greely shook his head. "I'm so sorry. I hoped she had gotten over her…her…"

"Dislike of me?" Savannah filled in for him.

He closed his eyes. "I'm so sorry."

♠

That night Garrett tossed and turned, trying not to disturb Savannah. Not only was his heart heavy over Mrs. Greely's behavior, but he had to call the prison tomorrow. To set up a visit with George Burns this week. His stomach heaved and he leaped out of bed, fearing he would lose what little supper he'd managed to force down.

By the time he reached the bathroom, the urge to vomit eased. He turned to go back to bed and almost ran into Savannah. "I'm sorry, did I wake you?"

"It doesn't matter. Are you sick? You jumped out of bed so fast." Savannah laid a cool hand on his forehead.

"Just sick at the thought of visiting Mr. Burns." No use upsetting her by mentioning Mrs. Greely.

"Do you remember what Sarah said in her diary when she feared losing a child?" She turned on the gas lamp, then drew Garrett back to sit beside her on their bed.

He frowned as he tried to remember. "Not really."

"She wrote in her diary, *Only God could get me through the loss of a child.* If God could get her through the loss of a child, surely He can get you through a visit with Mr. Burns."

Garrett scrubbed his face with both hands. "Maybe I should wait another week before I call to set up a visit."

"That would just give Satan another week to make you doubt whether you can do this."

He dropped his hands from his face and stared at her. "How did you become so wise, Savannah Young?"

"A lot of credit goes to your mother and all the Monday evening Bible studies. She said when Satan tempted Jesus, He always answered with Scripture."

He frowned. "I don't know any scripture that says, 'Garrett Young has forgiven George Burns.'"

"No, but every time you doubt you've forgiven him, you could say, *The same Spirit that raised Christ Jesus from the dead now lives in me.* Or *I can do all things through Christ who strengthens me* is another strong affirmation when we doubt if we can do what God is asking."

Garrett nodded slowly. "I see what you're saying. I can't do it, but God can do it through me."

Savannah beamed. "Exactly. It's the Holy Spirit who changes our hearts and enables us to obey."

♠

"Hello. This is Garrett Young. I'm a friend of Reverend Jim Caldwell. He asked if I could visit, George Burns, one of the prisoners that he'd been visiting at the jail when he moved out of the area."

"We'll need some information, sir. What was your name again?"

"Garrett Young."

"And your occupation?"

"I'm an insurance agent and a circuit-riding preacher."

"Hmmm… Interesting combination." The person on the other end of the line chuckled. "Do you convince people they can buy insurance to escape hell, fire and brimstone?"

Garrett laughed. "No, that's not my goal. I want prisoners to know that even though their body is incarcerated, Jesus can free them from sin if they repent and believe in Him."

"All right, Pastor Young. Visiting hours are from 9:00 am to 5:00 pm daily. When would you like to come?"

"How about this Saturday afternoon at 2:00?"

"We'll put you on Mr. Burns' list of approved visitors—"

"Who else visits Mr. Burns?" Perhaps some other pastor had begun visiting George since Jim left.

"Let me check, sir." A minute or two passed. "Actually, I don't believe there've been any visitors for Mr. Burns since Reverend Caldwell stopped coming."

His heart sank to the pit of his stomach. Thanks to Garrett's procrastination, Mr. Burns hadn't had any visitors since September. Still, what would be worse, not having any visitors at all or having someone visit who hated you?

Chapter 11

Polly collected the dirty laundry from all the bedrooms and sorted it into piles on the upstairs sitting room floor. Best to start the whites this morning and have the laundry well underway before Will came home at noon. Today was Valentine's Day. If she hurried, they could spend the afternoon together before the family returned home. Later they would attend a Valentine's Day dance at the Opera House downtown.

An uneasy peace had settled between her and Father while they waited for her to have a conversation with Will about the future. Father continued to spend a lot of time at Mrs. Wilds' home. *I guess I should be thankful he isn't bringing her here.*

She piled a laundry basket high with white sheets and pillowcases, hoisted it onto her hip and started down the steps. A few backfires outside had her hustling downstairs to find out who had pulled up in front of the house.

Will was already out of the car and bounding up the porch steps with a single red rose in his hand. *He's early.* Her laundry basket dropped unheeded as she flew across the living room and threw open the door. He grabbed her and held her tight..

"Oh, Will, I miss you so much when you're away."

He closed the door, then handed her the rose with another kiss. "I miss you, too, Lass. But coming home is all the sweeter for havin' been away. Happy Valentine's Day."

How like him to look on the bright side of things. He

shucked out of his coat and she hung it on a hook by the door.

"I finished me work sooner than expected today. Did I interrupt somethin' you were doin'?"

"I was taking the laundry to the basement is all." Polly glanced at her overflowing basket.

"Then I'm just in time to be carryin' it for you. Good timin', indeed."

When Will grabbed the basket and headed for the basement door, Polly stepped in front of him. "That can wait. There's something we need to discuss."

"What is it, Lass? I thought it was troubled you were lookin'." He set down the basket.

"Let's go up to our sitting room." She took his hand and drew him across the living room and up the steps. "Even though we're alone here, I'd rather be in our private quarters."

When the door closed behind them and they were seated on the loveseat, Will turned and looked into her eyes. "Is this about your father and Mrs. Wilds?"

With a quick nod, Polly closed her eyes for a second. "He's going to marry her, Will. We have to decide what we want to do."

"When are they getting married?"

"Father won't set a date until we decide." Polly explained the options her father had suggested.

Will stood and began to pace. "What are ya thinkin' then, Lass?"

"I'm okay with staying here until school is out if they live in her house. It will make things easier for George and Beth if Mrs. Wilds doesn't move in until they're gone."

"What about your younger sisters? You'll miss them if they decide to live with your father."

"I will miss them, but they'll have to decide what they want to do." Polly massaged her forehead. "I don't think I want to buy or rent Mrs. Wilds' house. I don't want to live that close to her long term."

Will nodded. "All right, I understand. I know ya don't

want to live with me mam." He paused. "In a few years, we would have wanted our own place anyway. No reason we can't move things up a bit. I'll start lookin' for land—maybe in Stoneboro. Mam would be happy 'bout that."

Polly smiled. "Stoneboro is fine, but I'd rather not live on Chestnut Street. Please don't be offended. I'm just a little overwhelmed by so many of your family living so close together there. I'd like to have our own lives."

As Will pulled her closer, Polly snuggled against him. "We'll get through this, Lass. That we will. God will make a way."

♠

Polly gathered another stack of dirty dishes as the family left the table. "Does your mother remember you won't be visiting tonight, Will?" Will usually visited his mother on Monday evenings while Polly went to Bible study with Savannah.

"I hope so. I told her I'd be takin' me sweetheart to the dance."

"We'll have to talk to Father some time about our decision, but he's gone to see Mrs. Wilds, so we'll catch him some other time."   Polly headed for the kitchen with Will close behind.

She put the dishes in the sink and went to the foot of the stairs. "Twila and Elsie, I want you to wash and dry the dishes tonight."

No answer. The door to their room was closed so perhaps they hadn't heard her. She raised her voice a notch and repeated her instructions. The door opened and a groan resounded down the steps.

"Why do we have to do the dishes?" Elsie's whine preceded her.

"Because you're plenty old enough to do them together. You don't need my help. I made dinner and now I want to get ready for the dance."

Twila clomped down the stairs behind Elsie like a herd of elephants. How had she failed in teaching that child to walk down steps like a lady?

"Tread lightly, Twila. *Lightly.*"

"It's not fair that you and Will and Father get to go away, and Twila and me have to stay home." Elsie had definitely begun stomping after Polly told Twila to tread lightly.

Perhaps there would be some advantages to having Father and Mrs. Wilds deal with the girls' teen years.

Chapter 12

Polly spent a substantial amount of time arranging her hair in front of the mirror long after Will had finished his preparations and gone downstairs. Her naturally curly auburn hair resisted the smooth look she preferred. Finally, she allowed it to curl more naturally around her face and then pulled it to some semblance of order on top of her head. If only she had the courage to get her hair cut as some women were doing. She sighed. Truth was, she wasn't willing to risk the criticism that would follow.

After one last look at herself, she floated down the stairs, pale green skirt swirling around her. She crossed the landing into the living room just as the telephone rang. Will picked up the receiver. "Hello… Oh hello, Mam."

With an eyebrow raised, Polly joined him.

"I'm sorry, Mam. I didn't know you were plannin' for me to eat dinner with ya before the dance." He sent Polly a beseeching glance. "Maybe Polly 'n me can come for dinner tomorrow evenin'."

She nodded. Thank goodness she hadn't given in to the temptation to cut her hair. Will's mother would have disapproved, as did most older women.

Tuning in to Will's conversation, she found him still apologizing. "I'm so sorry for the misunderstandin', Mam. I thought you knew I wouldn't be comin' this evenin'."

Polly fought the temptation to groan. Will had told his

mother he wouldn't come by tonight. Pulling her coat from the hook, Polly stood by the door indicating it was time to leave. A few minutes later, Will hung up and took her coat. As he helped her put it on, he apologized. "I'm so sorry, Lass—"

She put her finger to his lips and kissed his cheek. "It's all right. No harm done. I know it's hard for your mother to share you after having you to herself for so many years. Now let's just focus on having a good time."

Swarms of people had turned out for the Valentine's Day dance. Will and Polly mingled with the crowd, speaking to people they knew. On the stage, the band tuned up and then began playing an energetic tune. Will took care of their coats, then grabbed her hand. "Come on, Lassie, let's do the Lindy Hop."

Will was a good dancer and Polly's cheeks were soon warm, and probably rosy, from the lively moves. All her concerns about the future seemed far away until Will spun her out to arm's length and she almost bumped into Mrs. Wilds. Where had she come from?

Polly stumbled sideways but Will maintained an iron grip on her hand which steadied her.

Mrs. Wilds looked over her shoulder. "Watch where you're going." Recognizing Polly, her brows drew together in a dark scowl. "You almost made me fall."

The encounter with Mrs. Wilds brought back all her fears about the future and wiped out her enjoyment of the present moment. Is this how a balloon feels when it deflates and all the air whooshes out?

"I'm sorry." Polly veered away from Father and his dance partner, but not before she heard his conciliatory words to Mrs. Wilds.

"Florence has always been a bit clumsy. I'm sure it was an accident."

Not a word of apology from either of them. Polly's cheeks heated. Had it really been her fault?

Will squeezed the hand he still held. "You're not to

blame, Polly. It was no more our fault than theirs. It could have happened to anyone."

Staring off into space, Polly didn't respond.

"What is it, Lassie?"

Polly shook herself as though coming from a trance. "I didn't know Father thought I was clumsy. Am I clumsy, Will?"

"Nay, you aren't clumsy. Your father was just tryin' to smooth Mrs. Wilds' feathers, me thinks." He tugged on her hand. "Come, let's get some punch and cool off a bit."

Savannah and Garrett arrived just as they reached the punch bowl. Savannah hugged Polly. "I was hoping you'd be here." She gave Polly a long look. "What's wrong?"

Garrett squinted at them. "How do you two do that?" He gave Will a sidelong glance. "They always seem to know if something is bothering the other one."

Polly and Savannah exchanged a look. "You wouldn't understand." Polly shrugged. "It's something girls do better than fellows."

Savannah took Polly's arm and motioned to Will and Garrett. "Let's get some punch. Then we can find a place where we can talk."

A few minutes later, they were all seated behind several tall, artificial ferns in a secluded corner of the large open room. Savannah touched Polly's arm. "All right, spill it. What's wrong?"

Tilting her cup, Polly took a long swallow. "Mrs. Wilds and I almost ran into each other on the dance floor. She wasn't exactly nice about it."

"Rude." Will spoke the word with relish. "She was rude."

"But the real problem is…" Polly took a deep breath. "Father is going to marry her."

"Did you tell him what Dorothy said about the reason Mr. Chesterfield broke up with her?"

"I told him." Polly shrugged. "I don't think he believed me."

Savannah sighed. "No wonder they say love is blind."

♠

Polly and Will found Father sprawled in Mother's gray chair when they entered the house after the dance. So much like when he used to wait up for her when she and Garrett were courting.

He scooted forward in his chair, his face somber, unsmiling. "We need to talk."

Will raised a questioning eyebrow at Polly when they turned to hang up their coats. She lifted one shoulder.

When they crossed the room and sat on the davenport, Father remained silent. Polly opened the conversation. "Did you want to talk about our plans after you and Mrs. Wilds marry?"

"If she even marries me." Father's tone was grim.

Polly maintained a level tone, not expressing any hopefulness. "Is she having second thoughts?"

"We overheard your conversation with Savannah and Garrett at the dance."

She gasped and covered her mouth.

"It's a little late to cover your mouth now. Apparently, all these years of warning you about gossip hasn't made a bit of difference."

Polly's temper flared. "I wasn't gossiping. Savannah could tell I was upset so I explained about the incident on the dance floor with Mrs. Wilds. That's not gossip."

"Certainly you can't deny that discussing what Dorothy told Savannah qualifies as gossip."

"Maybe." Polly sighed. "But Savannah is concerned about you and wanted to be sure you knew what Mr. Chesterfield said."

Father steepled his fingers on the arm of the chair, then looked at Polly. "Mrs. Wilds is very hurt that you would believe, let alone repeat, such a thing."

"We didn't even repeat what Mr. Chesterfield said. If Mrs. Wilds knew what he said, it must be true."

Father closed his eyes and rubbed his forehead, but said nothing.

Polly kept her tone firm. "If she had told you the truth in the first place, she wouldn't have needed to worry about you finding out from someone else."

Chapter 13

Will's early arrival on Monday had made it necessary for Polly to do her laundry on Tuesday this week. The sky hadn't fallen. Really, what was the magic of doing it on Mondays? She was a little behind with her ironing, but she'd catch up by the end of the week.

She met her brother and sisters at the door after school. "Good day today?"

Beth responded with a cheerful smile, but the other three just shrugged and headed for the kitchen. "Wait, I need to talk to you for a minute. Will and I are going to eat at his mother's house this evening."

They all looked at her as if she'd announced an excursion to the moon but said nothing.

"Beth, I'd like you to make dinner. You can have toasted cheese sandwiches and tomato soup. Elsie and Twila, I'd like you to do the dishes."

The outcry from Elsie and Twila was deafening. "But we just did the dishes last night." Twila scowled.

"What about George? It isn't fair that he doesn't have to help." Elsie, as usual, the expert on fairness.

"You're right, Elsie. George can set the table."

George frowned and opened his mouth. "Not a word, George, or I'll have you do it every night this week." It wasn't often she gave orders to George who stood some inches taller than she, but she was in a no-nonsense mood today.

"Thanks for not complaining, Beth."

"None of us should complain. You do so much for us." Beth threw an unaccustomed look of disapproval at her brother and sisters.

"I'm happy to do it, but then I need each of you to help when I ask you."

Polly gave them a big smile and headed for the staircase. If she were honest, she'd probably have rather stayed home to cook and wash dishes than go with Will this evening. He said it was her imagination that his mother didn't like her. Was that true? Was she being paranoid? She avoided going when she could, assuring Will his mother would prefer having time alone with him.

She glanced at the clock and a lightness filled her chest. Only an hour until Will should be home. Her spirits rose. His homecomings always had that effect on her. The weather in Franklin was to be fair and warmer today, so he shouldn't be delayed by bad weather.

An hour to get ready. She closed the sitting room door. Not that Will ever complained about how she looked. On the contrary, he nearly always complimented her, no matter what she wore. But she loved spending extra time making herself more attractive when his arrival was imminent. It was worth it seeing his eyes light up.

She removed her work dress, then slipped on one of Will's flannel shirts to wear while brushing her hair. He'd worn it for a few hours the previous day. What a pleasure to put on something that smelled of his Aqua Velva aftershave.

After pulling out her hair pins, Polly brushed her thick, curly hair with long, smooth strokes. It wasn't easy to get all the knots out but she tried. Sometimes when she brushed her hair at bedtime, Will begged her to let him do it. He never yanked on the snarls and tangles. Tears sprang to her eyes at the tenderness he always exhibited toward her.

He would make a wonderful father, even though she herself wasn't eager to raise more children. This year in August it would be ten years since her mother died. Ten years of raising children. She drew a deep breath. Having children was one of those issues she had to keep giving back to God. She couldn't discuss it with Savannah who longed for a child.

Polly sat on the loveseat and leaned over, allowing her hair to fall in front of her, curtaining her face as she brushed.

A soft click alerted her that the door to the hall had opened. Before she could move, Will knelt beside her, took the brush from her hand, and continued the long, smooth strokes she'd been making. She kept her head bowed, inviting him to continue. "What beautiful hair ya have, Lass." His musical voice caressed her. "The most beautiful color I ever did see."

At last he stopped brushing and entered from below the tent made by her hair. He found her lips and encircled her with his arms, holding her ever so close. When she straightened, he parted her hair gently so he could see her face and kissed her again.

After she caught her breath, she smiled. "You're early. I was going to put on a nice dress before you got home."

He smoothed his hand over the soft flannel covering her body. "Tisn't the clothes but you yourself that is beautiful, Lass." Love permeated his dark brown eyes, rendering them almost black. When he seated himself beside her and drew her close, all worries about the future dissolved.

♠

Mam waited for them at the door and Will pulled her close. "I've missed you, Mam. How have ya been keepin'?"

She touched his dark hair tenderly. "I've missed you, too, Lad. All me other children married and moved on but ya stayed so long, I'd come to believe ya might never leave."

"I know. It can be right jarrin' when a crusty, old bachelor decides to get married."

"You aren't crusty or old, Will." Polly smiled at him and his mother.

"Compared to the age of me brothers and sisters when they left home, I'm old." He drew Polly into the circle with them.

Polly leaned in and kissed Mam's cheek. "How's your health been, Mam?"

"As well as can be expected. I'm not a spring chicken, that's for sure." Mam started for the kitchen. "It's hungry that you must be then." She glanced at Polly. "I hope you can eat Irish cooking."

"Oh, of course, I can." Polly gave a long appreciative sniff. "It smells heavenly."

"Smellin' and tastin' can be two different things, ya know. I hope it won't be a different tune you're singin' after you've finished."

Chapter 14

Garrett opened one eye and peered out the window. Not a speck of light and much too early to get up on a Saturday. Saturday… the day he was to visit George Burns. Not too early to pray…

He scooted out of bed as gently as he could, making every effort not to disturb the beautiful woman beside him, still sound asleep. Making circles with his foot on the rug beside the bed, he discovered his slippers and crammed his cold feet into them. They were calling for snow tonight.

Creeping in the general direction of his bedside table, he located his Bible. He'd arm himself with the Sword of the Spirit today and every piece of armor the apostle Paul spoke of in Ephesians. How else could he expect to succeed on this mission?

The day before him weighed heavy on his shoulders. Visit George Burns? How could he do that? But God had made it clear. He didn't have to like what God had asked of him, he just needed to obey. Pretty sure Jim had told him that.

If you love me, keep my commandments. So easy to *say* he loved God, but this scripture seemed to more than imply *saying* it wasn't enough. Obedience was the acid test of love for God.

He dropped down beside the loveseat in the living room and bowed his head. *Father, I'm still waiting for you to change my heart toward Mr. Burns. I did my best to make a decision to forgive him like Savannah said I should. I'm trying to trust you but so far my heart is still hard toward him. I guess you know if you don't change it, I'm in a boatload of trouble. And a preacher at that.*

He stood, turned on the gas lamp and sat back down. After flipping open his Bible, he turned pages, not even knowing what he was looking for until he found it. *A new heart also will I give you, and a new spirit will I put within you: and I will take away the stony heart out of your flesh, and I will give you a heart of flesh.* He glanced at the top of the page. Ezekiel, not a book he read often.

That's what I need, Lord. I need you to take away my stony heart and give me a new heart like yours, a heart that loves and forgives unconditionally. No one can change my heart but you. Tears wet the pages of the Bible in front of him at the hardness of his heart. He returned to his knees and continued to pour out his heart to God.

♠

Savannah entered the living area, dressed in her fuzzy emerald green robe, ready to make breakfast. Her husband knelt by the loveseat, head bowed in prayer. How long had he been there? Making as little noise as possible, she prayed silently as she set the table and started water for coffee.

I don't know for sure why Garrett's on his knees, Father. Is he still wrestling with the forgiveness issue? How should I pray for him?

We wrestle not against flesh and blood but against principalities, against powers, against the rulers of the darkness of this world, against spiritual wickedness in high places.

Savannah put some eggs in a ceramic bowl and whipped them with a little milk. She had studied Ephesians six with Garrett's mother. *Why didn't I think of that, Lord. This battle is against Satan. He's the one who doesn't want Garrett to forgive Mr. Burns. He doesn't want him to minister to that man.*

As she got out her iron skillet, Savannah took authority over the enemy in an undertone. In the name of Jesus, she broke the power of unforgiveness over her husband. "You are a defeated foe, Satan, by the blood of Christ. You will not win this battle."

♠

Garrett cranked his car and then jumped into the driver's seat. Maybe the snow would hold off and he'd have decent weather for the trip to Mercer. He used to make this trip almost every day when he worked for Mr. Black at the clothing store. So long ago it seemed. About nine years.

Uninvited, vignettes of those days paraded through his mind—finding the picture of Savannah on Mr. Black's desk, the doubts and fears that Savannah could still be involved with his boss, the wilderness he'd wandered in for days.

Had he forgiven Mr. Black for trying to break up his relationship with Savannah? For trying to lure her back to her former profession, seeing gentlemen callers above the tavern? He sighed. Probably not. It seemed he was gifted at holding grudges without knowing it.

Are you concerned for his soul?

He cringed.

Years ago, he had asked Mr. Black if he was a Christian. The man seemed to think he might be since he'd been baptized as a baby and wasn't any other religion. Garrett's question about whether he'd asked Jesus to forgive his sins and come live in his heart had gone unanswered.

God's continual pursuit of people who didn't give Him the time of day amazed Garrett. But why should it? God had pursued him when he had no interest in spiritual things.

I guess I'm not concerned for Mr. Black's soul. It's still all about me, isn't it? All about Mr. Black trying to steal my girlfriend. I'm sorry, Father. Help me forgive him and pray for his soul.

Garrett allowed himself then, for a moment, to check his attitude toward Mr. Burns. He did it intermittently, as one might check one's pulse or temperature. Still nothing but animosity and hostility. He groaned as he swung into the parking lot at the jail. "We're running out of time, Lord."

After turning into a parking space, he stopped the car and pulled out his identification. He stared at it for a long time, then picked up his Bible, got out of the car and trudged toward the faded gray and black concrete jail. *I'm going to do what you asked me to do, Lord. The results are up to you.*

The officer at the desk looked at his ID, then motioned to the guard by the inner door. "Burns has a visitor."

"Zat right?" The green-uniformed guard patted Garrett down and opened the door. "Follow me. He's in a bear of a mood today."

As the door locked behind them with an audible click, Garrett swallowed. Even though he hadn't lived an exemplary life before becoming a Christian, he'd never seen the inside of a jail. He followed the guard down the hall and into a small, bare room with a table and two rickety folding chairs. Four walls closed in on him with no escape. No natural light. All his senses urged him to leave.

"Wait here." The guard gestured to one of the chairs. "I'll be right back."

Garrett sank into the chair, clutched his Bible with one hand and gripped the table with the other. What had he been thinking coming here? Why on earth would Jim ask him to come?

Chapter 15

"You took your mother to see the lot that's for sale in Stoneboro before you took me?" Polly's green eyes were shooting sparks. Will had made a big mistake. He chased her up the stairs which she was taking two at a time.

He'd gotten off the train in Stoneboro this morning in order to be on time to look at the land Clyde Truxell had for sale on Walnut Street. If he'd gone back to Franklin to get the car and then pick up Polly, he would have been late.

Will closed their sitting room door. He reached for Polly's hand, but she backed away. "I'm sorry, Lass. After I looked at the land, I decided to visit Mam while I waited for the next train to Franklin. When I mentioned the lot, she wanted to see it. How could I say no?"

Polly pulled a handkerchief out of her pocket and wiped her eyes.

"Ah Lass, is it cryin' ya are? Please don't cry."

Dropping down on the loveseat, Polly shook her head. "I'm sorry. I shouldn't make such a fuss. It's just that…"

"Just that what?" Will sat beside her.

"Sometimes it feels like there's a tug-of-war going on between me and your mother. I'm not sure if it's my fault or hers. If we move to Stoneboro, I'm afraid it will get worse."

"I guess I could look for land in Sandy Lake. Is that what you want?"

"No, that could cause trouble since you've already

showed your mam the lot in Stoneboro." Polly swiped another tear. "Do you think it will be suitable for us?'

"Let's go look at it." Will jumped to his feet, pulling Polly up behind him. "Come on."

"Wait." Polly scrubbed her face with her handkerchief, and then blew her nose.

Will tilted her face to his. "I'm truly sorry I disappointed you."

Polly nodded. "It just feels like I'm second best."

"Never, Lass. You could never be anythin' but first with me."

He kissed her nose, then her lips, before drawing her with him to go downstairs.

Beth looked up from dusting the window seat in the living room when they stepped off the landing. "You two sure make a lot of noise. Almost as much as Twila."

"Hey," Twila appeared from the sitting room. "That wasn't very nice."

Making a movement as if to dust her sister's nose, Beth reached out and tweaked one of her dark brown braids instead. "I guess you're right, but it's true."

"Will and I are going to look at some land in Stoneboro, Beth." Polly grabbed their winter coats. "We'll be back after awhile."

Twila was by Polly's side in a flash. "Can I come too?"

"Maybe next time. Just Will and I for now."

The corners of Twila's mouth drooped. "Why are you looking at land? You aren't going to move are you?" She looked first at Polly, then at Will.

They exchanged a glance. Then Polly shrugged. "Nothing is definite yet." Before her sister could ask any more questions, Polly grabbed Will's hand, opened the door and pulled him through it behind her.

♠

Garrett jumped to his feet when footsteps sounded in the hall of the jail. Was he hoping to make a quick exit if Mr. Burns turned mean?

Instead he found himself stretching to shake the hand of the man in the black-and-white striped, one-piece uniform. The minute his hand touched Mr. Burns,' his heart melted. All the animosity, bitterness, and anger he'd nursed for years drained from him as though someone had pulled a plug in a bathtub.

"Mr. Burns, it's good to see you." Garrett shook the large hand he held.

The big man stared at him. "They told me you was coming to visit me today. I didn't believe 'em. Why should you want to visit me after I kidnapped the woman you love?"

The guard who'd been leaving the room, turned back. "You didn't tell us that."

"To be honest, it never occurred to me to tell you. I'm a pastor and when my friend, Reverend Caldwell, moved to Akron, he asked me to visit Mr. Burns."

Nodding, the guard smiled. "If Reverend Caldwell asked you to visit, you must be all right."

It didn't seem like the right time to say that Reverend Caldwell had more faith in Garrett than he'd had in himself, so he just nodded.

The guard plunked down in a chair in the hall, and George continued to stare at Garrett. "I still don't understand why you'd agree to visit me, even if Reverend Caldwell asked you."

Garrett bit his lip and dropped into one of the chairs, gesturing for George to do the same. The truth seemed like the best strategy. "I didn't want to come. I was still angry even when I walked in this door, but the minute I shook your hand, all the bad feelings disappeared."

"But why did you come if you didn't want to?" Burns' brow crinkled.

"Partly because Reverend Caldwell asked me to come. Mainly because I knew God wanted me to come."

Mr. Burns' mouth dropped. "God wanted you to come? I doubt that. God doesn't care about me."

"I'm sure Reverend Caldwell told you no matter what we've done, God loves us. He cares about you, George, and so do I. Are you still going to the chapel services?

"We don't have a chaplain for the prison right now, so there ain't no services. But I've still been reading that Bible Caldwell gave me." Burns cleared his throat. "It gets pretty boring in here."

"I imagine it does. Is there anything you've been reading you have questions about?" Garrett opened his Bible. "If I don't know the answers, I can try to find out. I'm still kind of new at this."

"Caldwell used to tell me a Scripture that said God forgives our sins if we ask Him. I lost the paper I wrote it on. Do you know where that one is?"

Garrett smiled. "That's one of my favorites too." He flipped toward the back of the Bible and read. "If we confess our sins, He is faithful and just to forgive us our sins, and to cleanse us from all unrighteousness."

"Could you write down the address? That's what Caldwell used to call it."

"Sure." Garrett pulled some paper from his Bible and copied the words of 1 John 1:9 with the reference, and then handed it to George.

He took it, folded it into fourths and stuck it in his pocket. "Do you think you could do something for me?"

"I will if I can."

Mr. Burns ducked his head. "D'you think…" He hesitated. "Nah, I can't ask you to do that."

"What is it, George?"

"Do you think Savannah could ever find it in her heart to forgive me?"

"Believe it or not," Garrett rubbed his nose, "she already has."

Burns' eyes widened. "Without me even asking?"

"Savannah is an amazing woman. She said she forgave you long ago."

Moisture that might have been tears gleamed in George's eyes as he whispered, "Now if only I could forgive myself."

Chapter 16

Polly kept her eyes on the road as Will drove down Walnut Street into Stoneboro. How could she be excited when her pride was still hurt? *Help me forgive him, Lord. He didn't mean to pick his mother over me.*

They turned on to Franklin Street, and Will pulled Nellie, his faithful Model T, off to the side of the road and jumped out. He had Polly's door open in a flash and reached for her hand as though she were a princess. How could you stay mad at a man like that?

"This corner lot is what Clyde is selling." His eyes sparkled.

Polly stepped out beside him. "Where are the boundaries?"

"Let's walk and I'll show you." He tucked her hand in the crook of his arm. "Our house would be here on the north side of East Walnut Street, so let's head up that direction. There's fifty feet facing Walnut."

"Is that big enough for a house?"

"Plenty big enough. The lot is 50 x 120 so there's plenty of room in the back. Maybe we'll want to add on later to make room for our family."

She swallowed and took a deep breath. "I was thinking maybe a bungalow would be big enough. No use building something bigger than we need."

Will shrugged. "Maybe you're right, Lass. The smaller it

is the sooner it'll be ready for us to move in." He stopped. "The property line would be somewhere around here. We'd own 120 feet back to the alley."

They turned left and walked toward the alley between Walnut and Orchard Street, then fifty feet back toward Franklin. Polly could picture a small bungalow fitting into this space. At least they wouldn't be on Chestnut Street.

"Can we afford to do this, Will? How much is Clyde asking for the lot?"

"$500, Lass. And yes, we can afford it. I've been savin' me money for a long time."

She certainly hadn't married Will for his money, although she'd heard train brakemen were fairly well-paid because of the danger of their job. Quieting her heart, she directed her attention toward their Heavenly Father. *Is this your plan for us, Lord?*

Let the peace of God rule in your heart... She recognized the Scripture from Colossians as peace flowed through her. This must be the place God had prepared for them.

♠

With a light heart, Garrett followed the guard through the door into the outer area of the jail. The officer stepped from behind the counter.

"Reverend Young, could I talk to you for a minute?"

"Of course. Just call me Garrett." He shook the man's hand.

The man hesitated. "How about Pastor Garrett?" He smiled. "I'm Officer Ron Swartz. Maybe George told you, the jail has been without a chaplain since Reverend Caldwell left. I was wondering... Well, I was hoping maybe you'd agree to fill out papers to apply for that position."

Garrett bit his lip. "I should tell you, I'm not a pastor through a regular denomination. I'm a circuit riding preacher hired by an alliance of pastors in Mercer County."

"If you have an alliance of pastors who vouch for you, it shouldn't be a problem." Officer Ron tugged on his moustache.

"I'm not a religious person myself, but I've seen a change in the men since Reverend Caldwell doesn't visit—and not for the better."

Nodding, Garrett took a deep breath. "What are the duties of the chaplain?"

"Reverend Caldwell preached once a month and held a Bible study every week when he didn't preach. He also gave spiritual counsel to the prisoners at their request."

Garrett stared at the floor for a few moments, then looked at Officer Ron. "Let me pray about it and talk to my wife, if you don't mind."

"That's fine. Let me give you the papers you'd need to fill out in case your answer is yes."

A few minutes later, Garrett walked out of the jail toward his car, cranked the engine and jumped in. *Is this something you want me to do, Father? It feels right but I don't want to run ahead of you.*

Putting that decision aside for the moment, he couldn't stop smiling as he relived his visit with Mr. Burns. Savannah would be in awe of what God had done. He'd heard the saying, *God is never late but He's seldom early.* That certainly applied to God not changing his heart toward Burns until the moment he took his hand.

Were you testing my faith, Father? Did you want me to go to the jail by faith because that's what you asked me to do, even though I didn't feel like I'd forgiven? I believe Jim was right. I think George Burns is very close to making a commitment to you. Wash away his self-condemnation and assure him of your forgiveness.

He had almost reached Mr. Black's store when he sensed a nudge from the Holy Spirit to pull into the store's parking lot. *Are you sure about this, Lord? Things were never the same between us after he tried to get Savannah to meet him at the hotel.*

The urge to stop grew stronger, so Garrett made a quick turn into the lot and turned off the engine. With a prayer on his lips, he got out of his automobile and headed for the front door. He'd always entered from the back while employed there. The bell jangled as he went in.

The store appeared to be empty at first glance, so Garrett walked around a bit, looking at the merchandise. No clerk in sight. Mr. Black must be in his office. Perhaps he hadn't heard the bell since the door was almost closed.

Garrett advanced toward the office until Mr. Black's desk came into view through the slightly open door. His former boss sat, unmoving, head down on folded arms.

Chapter 17

Bob hung up his coat, then washed up and changed his clothes. He'd spent most of his Saturday at the mine, not leaving much of the day to accomplish his goal.

He went downstairs and smiled at Beth, playing a game of jacks with Twila and Elsie on the sitting room floor. "Where are Florence and Will?"

Beth paused and rattled her jacks in one hand as she responded. "They went to look at a lot in Stoneboro."

"I asked her why they were looking for land. She just said there was nothing definite." Twila scowled at Bob. "Do you know why she and Will are looking for land?"

Bob stared at the jacks scattered over the linoleum floor. He hadn't meant for them to find out this way. "I didn't want to tell the family until I'm sure what Will and Florence plan to do…" He looked up at his girls, then paused and took a few steps toward the door. "We'll have a family meeting soon."

"Father," Twila and Elsie wailed with one voice.

"It isn't fair to keep us hanging like this." Elsie's lower lip protruded, blue eyes flashing.

A few backfires from a car stopping in front of the house interrupted the discussion. Bob turned and sprinted to the living room window. "Will and Florence are back. I'll talk to them first upstairs, then we can have our meeting."

"But Father—"

"No arguing, Twila." Father walked out and closed the

door, ending the discussion.

He was waiting by the front door when Florence and Will entered the house.

"Hello, Father." Florence smiled and started toward the kitchen. "I'd better get supper started."

"Supper can wait." Bob motioned toward the stairway. "Let's go upstairs and talk."

Florence raised an eyebrow at Will, then followed Bob with Will close behind. "What's this about?"

"The girls said you looked at a lot in Stoneboro." Bob glanced back at them. "Have you figured out what you plan to do when Lydia and I get married?"

Someone must have opened the door he'd closed downstairs because an anguished voice echoed below. "Why didn't you tell us you and Lydia were getting married?"

"Twila, why are you eavesdropping?" He seldom shouted at the girls but his nerves were on edge lately. "Go back into the sitting room and shut the door."

"You don't have to shout." Florence passed him on the stairs. She was protective of her girls. He followed her.

"Last time we talked you weren't even sure Mrs. Wilds would marry you. Now all of a sudden, you act like it's a sure thing." She stared at him. "No wonder the girls are upset. They knew nothing about it."

Bob walked into the room off the hall and dropped heavily into the loveseat. Florence and Will followed him, then Will went around to get a stool from their bedroom and Florence closed the door. Seeming to understand that Florence wouldn't want to sit beside Bob, Will dropped down beside him while Florence perched on the stool facing them.

Emotions ran high. Arguments often ended badly. Bob took a deep, calming breath. "Are you planning to buy a lot and build a house?"

Florence and Will exchanged a glance. "Aye, that we are, sir."

"If you marry and move in with Lydia, we'll buy land

and have a house built." Florence swallowed as though her throat was sore. "Meanwhile, we'll stay here until George and Beth graduate. Hopefully, our house will be finished before Lydia wants to sell or rent her house."

Bob expelled a sigh of relief. "All right. That sounds like a good plan. Elsie and Twila can decide what they want to do."

"Father, are you sure Lydia is willing to help raise the girls? Didn't she tell you a long time ago she couldn't live here because your house was full of children?"

Bob jumped up. "The house isn't 'full of children' any more. It would be just Elsie and Twila and they're not little girls." He started toward the door, breathing heavily.

"Wait." Apparently, Florence wasn't finished. "You said you weren't sure Lydia was going to marry you. What happened?"

"That was just a lover's spat. She was over it the next day."

♠

Garrett knocked gently. "Mr. Black, are you all right?"

The man lifted his head. As he did, the smell of alcohol wafted to Garrett's nostrils. He pushed the office door open a little wider and stepped inside. "Mr. Black, is something wrong?"

A groan escaped the man's lips. "What are you doing here, Young?" The words slurred together. "Didja come here to gloat?"

"What?" Garrett edged toward the desk. "I don't know what you're talking about. Why would I be here to gloat?"

"Oh c'mon. Don't tell me you jest happened to stop by." Mr. Black glared at him.

Garrett rubbed his forehead. Had he gone down a rabbit hole? He hadn't a clue what his former boss was talking about.

Coffee. He needed coffee to sober up Mr. Black. He sniffed. The aroma of coffee seemed to float from a table in the corner. Maybe Mr. Black had invested in one of those new Drip-O-Lators. He took a few quick steps in that direction. This must be it. Grabbing a none-too-clean mug, Garrett picked up the interesting contraption and poured some coffee. It smelled strong enough to curl your hair, but maybe that's just what the doctor ordered.

When he reached Mr. Black's side, the man swatted the mug from his hand. Coffee ran down the side of the desk and splashed onto the floor and Garrett's shoe. "Not coffee. I need more whiskey. Just ran out."

"The last thing you need is more whiskey. Besides it's illegal." He looked for something to clean up the coffee mess but found nothing.

All the fight seemed to leave Mr. Black. "S'been my downfall."

Garrett sighed and dropped into a chair beside the man's desk. "What's been your downfall?"

"Doing illegal things, that's what."

"Which of the illegal things you've done has caught up with you?"

"You 'member the picture I took of S'vannah?" Mr. Black tapped the dark green blotter that covered the top of his desk. "The one you found under here?"

With a quick nod, Garrett gritted his teeth. What a dark day that had been.

"Should have thrown it away. Never did. My wife found it."

Chapter 18

Polly jumped down from the stool she'd perched on during their discussion with Father "I'd better go start supper." She avoided Father's eyes and headed for the door.

"Let's have our family meeting first. Twila and Elsie will hound me mercilessly until we do."

Will stood. "Do ya want me at the family meetin', sir?"

"Of course. You're part of the family now." Father glanced at Polly standing in the doorway. "Is your brother in his room?"

"I'll check."

She rapped on the door across the hall, opened it and stuck her head in at an abrupt, "Come."

Speaking to her brother in an undertone probably didn't keep them from hearing his snort at the news she conveyed. Polly closed the door and looked at her father. "He'll be down in a few minutes. Give him a little time."

When she and Will reached the bottom of the stairs, she opened the sitting room door and spoke to Beth, Twila and Elsie. "We're going to have a family meeting in a little while." They stared at her, wide-eyed. "Try to stay calm. Everything will be okay." Who did she think she was kidding? She didn't even believe her own words.

♠

Garrett stared at Mr. Black as bile rose in him. *Has this man been lusting after my wife all these years? Would God forgive me if I punch him in the nose?*

He swallowed, unclenched his fists and bit back the snide remark on his lips. This wasn't about him. What would a pastor say? "What did your wife do when she found the picture of Savannah?"

"Threw me out. Says she wants a d'vorce. I've been shleeping here in the back room."

So that's why the man's clothes were so rumpled. What to do? If only he hadn't come. An inner prompting told him he couldn't leave Mr. Black here, and for sure, he couldn't take him home—not fair to Savannah. Maybe his parents could put the man up for a few days in the spare bedroom that used to be his.

"Come on, Mr. Black. I'm taking you with me."

He didn't budge. "S'not time to close."

Garrett snorted. "Just how do you think you'll wait on customers the shape you're in? Of course, if anyone from the prohibition board stops in, then you'd have a place to stay."

"Whaddya mean?"

"Jail, Mr. Black. I mean jail. Is that what you want?'

"Course not. Just leave me alone."

How can I help him if he doesn't want to be helped, Lord?

"All right, have it your way. But if any of your customers find you in this condition, they won't be back." Garrett started for the door.

"Jus'a minute." Mr. Black stood, and shuffled some papers on his desk. "Where were you gonna take me?"

Garrett turned back. "To my parents' house. My mother is a saint. She'll know what to do with you."

"Do you think she'd give me s'hing to eat?" Mr. Black rubbed his stomach.

"Something to eat for sure, but no alcohol." Garrett shifted from one foot to the other. "So what's it going to be?"

"I'll go with you." He rummaged around in the papers on his desk. "Let's put a sign on the door. *Closed—family emergency.*"

"A bit of a stretch to call being drunk a family emergency." Garrett raised an eyebrow.

"Wouldn't be drunk 'cept for my wife leaving."

"I guess." Garrett found the pathetic man's coat and helped him put it on. Then he made a sign and grabbed the tape. "Let's go." He grasped Mr. Black's arm and headed for the front door, muttering under his breath, "I can't believe I'm doing this."

♠

After what seemed like a very long time, the family was all seated around the table in their regular spots. Polly tried to memorize each face in this moment before everything changed. Father, at the head of the table, George, to Father's right, Beth beside George, patting his arm— she'd make a great nurse. Twila, Elsie and Polly to Father's left with Will at the foot of the table.

Father cleared his throat. "I haven't been trying to hide anything from you. I just wanted to know what options you'd have before we talked."

Her blond, blue-eyed brother snorted as he had upstairs. "Options? You're the only one who has real options. The rest of us just have to make the best of whatever you've decided to do. You're going to marry Lydia Wilds, aren't you?"

Father sighed. "Yes, I am. Your mother has been gone almost ten years. I think she would want me to be happy."

"If you want to be happy, the last thing you should do is marry Mrs. Wilds." George's tone was pleading. "I mean it, Father, I don't think—"

"That's enough." Father's tone brooked no interference. "You're entitled to your opinion, but I won't let it rule my life. Now if you all will just listen…"

Polly glanced around the table. Twila's eyes were wide and Elsie's jaw jutted as it did when she suspected someone was going to try to make her do something she didn't want to do. Beth, the peacemaker, was chewing her lower lip. Will reached for Polly's hand and held it. Then there was George, lips compressed in a straight line.

"Lydia and I will marry soon. We'll live in her house while Florence and Will continue to live here until after graduation when their house is finished. Then Lydia will either rent or sell her house, and we'll move in here."

Bob looked around the table. "I imagine Beth and George will want to remain with Will and Florence. Twila and Elsie, you may live with Lydia and me or continue to live here, which ever you want."

Silence reigned. No one said a word. A tear trickled down Twila's cheek. Father glanced at her. "Lydia and I would be happy to have you live with us. She has plenty of room. Or if you decide to stay here, you can visit us as often as you want."

Twila swiped at her tears. "It's just that… we won't be a family anymore."

Chapter 19

Garrett peered through the windshield at the falling snow. The car swerved as he hit a slippery spot and he slowed down. He'd be late for dinner. No way to tell Savannah. Since he'd never visited the jail before, perhaps she had no preconceived idea of when he'd return.

He glanced at Mr. Black, snoring beside him. His former boss drunk? His lip curled— just as his automobile skidded toward the ditch. *I'm sorry, Lord. I just forgave Mr. Burns. I don't want to start a new grudge toward Mr. Black. Help me extend to this man the same grace you extended to me.*

If only there was some way to warn his parents of what he was about to do. Perhaps he shouldn't have put them in this position. Too late now. He squinted, the large snowflakes making it impossible to see more than a few feet in front of him. *Keep us safe, Lord.*

There, on the outskirts of Sandy Lake at last. Breathing a sigh of relief, he pulled up to the first stop sign.

Mr. Black jerked awake and stared out the window. "Where in the blazes are we?"

"Sandy Lake. I told you I was bringing you here."

Shaking his head vehemently, Mr. Black swore. "I vowed I'd never come back here after S'vannah and Will'yum…" He stopped.

Savannah had told him about Mr. Black's efforts to entice her to a rendezvous at a hotel in Sandy Lake after she'd left her old life. Her friend, William Sider, had come to her rescue. "That was a long time ago. Besides, no one knows except William Sider, Savannah and me. You'd better pray my father is in a good mood. He's not as understanding as Ma."

Mr. Black groaned and threw his head against the back of the seat, which was none too soft. "Just take me home."

"Home? I thought your wife threw you out."

"I mean to the store."

"There's no way I'm taking you back to Mercer. Here we are." Garrett pulled into the driveway of his parents' home. A cheery light shone through the kitchen window.

Managing to get Mr. Black out of the car without accident, Garrett half-dragged the reluctant man to the house and up the steps.

His mother had already caught a glimpse of them and had the door open. Her eyes were wide, her jaw slack. "What's this, Son? Mr. Black, is that you?"

Mr. Black grunted and stumbled past her, just as Garrett's father came into the kitchen.

His jaw dropped. "What have we here, Son?"

"I think we need some coffee if you have any." Garrett clamped his lips together.

"Of course, let me take your coats." Ma bustled around taking coats and pouring cups of coffee. "Harold, do you want a cup?"

"Thanks, Mildred. Looks like I might need one." Pa dropped into a chair, keeping his gaze on Mr. Black.

Garrett got his former employer into a chair, then sat beside him. "Mr. Black has a bit of a dilemma." He told his parents Mr. Black's story, omitting the part about the picture. "He's been staying at the store and I thought perhaps you could put him up in my room for a few days until he finds a suitable place."

Garrett glanced at Ma, then at Pa. He couldn't tell what message they were sending each other.

His father took a few swallows of coffee, walked over to

the wood stove, and cleared his throat. "You can stay for a few days but there'll be no drinking. You spend your time either attempting to reconcile with your wife or finding a room or an apartment near your store. If you come in drunk, our agreement is over."

"We also ask that you attend church with us tomorrow, Mr. Black." Ma smiled. "Did you know Reverend Caldwell is preaching, Garrett?"

Garrett couldn't have contained his smile if he'd tried. "I'm preaching at the Presbyterian Church in Sandy Lake tomorrow, so maybe Jim and I could meet with Mr. Black later in the afternoon. I'll call him."

"There's no way I'm going to church with you. You can't..."

"It's part of the agreement, Mr. Black." Pa took a few steps in the man's direction. "You're not in a position to say no. Seems like someone in your situation might realize he needs help from the Almighty."

Ma's expression showed her approval. "Drink your coffee and then I'll show you to your room. I bet it'll feel good to be sleeping in a real bed."

♠

Garrett bounded up the steps into the Methodist church he'd attended growing up and the one he still looked on as his church home.

Jim opened the door as Garrett reached the top of the stairs. "Come in. How've you been?" They exchanged a hearty handshake. "Mr. Black is downstairs waiting for us."

"Thanks so much for doing this on such short notice."

"Always my pleasure to help a friend." Jim headed for the basement steps, then stopped. "So this is your former employer, right?"

"Right. The Holy Spirit prompted me to stop on my way back from seeing Mr. Burns." Garrett lowered his voice. "I found Mr. Black at his store in pretty bad shape. I hope you can help him."

Jim smiled. "I think God's already at work." He started down the stairs. "You said your visit with Burns went well?"

"Very well. I'll tell you more later."

They walked into the adult Sunday school classroom. Garrett stopped and blinked, barely recognizing the man waiting for them. Gone was the down and out character he'd dealt with yesterday. Mr. Black's eyes were clear and his shoulders back. "What…what happened to you?"

"I guess you could say I had an encounter with God."

Chapter 20

Garrett stared at Mr. Black seated in the uncomfortable folding chair at the sturdy table. The corners of his former employer's mouth actually turned up. Was this for real or just a show the man was putting on?

"What did you preach about today, Jim?"

"Don't give the credit to me. Only God can change hearts." Jim dropped into a chair on the other side of Mr. Black.

"I know but…" Garrett put his Bible on the table and sat facing Jim and Mr. Black.

"The Scripture God put on my heart all week was Isaiah 61. I wasn't sure why."

Garrett turned to Isaiah, flipped the pages to chapter 61 and read. *The Spirit of the Lord God is upon me, to preach good tidings unto the meek; He hath sent me to bind up the brokenhearted…*

A stifled sound drew Garrett's attention. Mr. Black's eyes glistened with unshed tears. After a brief pause, Garrett continued. *… to proclaim liberty to the captives and the opening of the prison to them that are bound…*

He glanced at Mr. Black again as a tear slid down his cheek. This man never cried.

"I didn't want to go to church with your parents today, Garrett." Mr. Black blinked away more unshed tears. "My head was pounding and my stomach churning, but your mother wouldn't accept any excuses. She said I needed to be in God's house today because I'd given my word.

Garrett covered his mouth to hide a smile. Ma was a formidable opponent when she set her mind to something.

"When Reverend Caldwell read the Scripture, it seemed like God spoke directly to me. Then he reached the part about binding up the brokenhearted, and it released a flood. I didn't know I had so many tears stored up until the dam broke." Mr. Black wiped his face and cleared his throat.

"I've made a mess of my life. I've put the blame on my wife when I'm at fault. God took off my blinders so I could see myself as I am."

This sounded real but still… "I remember the day God did that for me." Garrett stared at the table. "It's painful, but the only way to healing and change."

Mr. Black nodded. "I practically ran to the altar when the Reverend asked if anyone wanted to receive Jesus and the forgiveness of their sins. When he prayed with me, the doors of my prison opened and the chains that have held me in bondage fell off. I'm free, Garrett. I'm free."

Despite his misgivings, Garrett reached to shake his hand and said the right words. "You're a new creature in Christ. We're brothers in God's family."

A smile brighter than any Garrett had ever seen him wear covered the man's face. "If we're brothers, you've got to call me Devon. I would have asked you to do that years ago except for my stubborn pride."

"Devon it is." Garrett glanced at Jim who had remained silent during this exchange. A tear sparkled on his friend's cheek. Apparently, Jim believed in Mr. Bl—Devon's transformation.

"It never ceases to amaze me the lengths God will go to in order to bring one wayward sheep into the fold." After a moment of silence, Jim began to sing softly.

> *There were ninety and nine that safely lay*
> *In the shelter of the fold;*
> *But one was out on the hills away,*
> *Far off from the gates of gold.*

> *Away on the mountains wild and bare;*
> *Away from the tender Shepherd's care.*

How had he missed the fact that Jim had a beautiful, melodious voice?

"And all heaven rejoices when one lost sheep comes into the fold as Devon did this morning." Jim paused. "They're rejoicing just as we are."

Devon smiled, but his smile dimmed a moment later. "I know God has forgiven me, but I don't know if my wife ever will."

Jim steepled his long, slender fingers on the table. "Our sins have consequences and those consequences don't automatically leave when we receive Christ."

"Why don't you tell Pastor Jim what you told me yesterday?" Garrett gestured at Jim. Maybe if his friend knew the whole story, he'd see through Devon's act, if that's what it was.

Devon's gaze dropped. "I'm so ashamed. If only I could turn back the hands of time."

"You aren't the first and you won't be the last to wish that. But God can redeem our past if we'll let Him." Kindness shone in Jim's eyes. "I'd like to hear what happened."

After clearing his throat several times, Devon unburdened his heart. He told how his wife discovered his unfaithfulness and her actions afterward. "I haven't seen her in over a week. Been staying at my store."

Jim nodded slowly. No indication he thought Devon was faking.

"I suggest you write her a letter, rather than just showing up at her door. Tell her how sorry you are and ask if you could arrange a time to talk."

"Should I tell her about my…my… what should I call it?"

"You mean your conversion? If you think it would mean something to her, tell her."

Devon rubbed his forehead. "How can I expect my wife

to forgive me when I've been such a nincompoop?"

♠

Devon Black dropped into a chair at the oak kitchen table in the Young's kitchen. He opened the lined tablet Garrett had loaned him before he left. He bowed his head and prayed for wisdom. Who would have ever thought he'd pray?

When he opened his eyes, Mrs. Young stood beside him. "May I ask who you're writing to?"

"To my wife. Please pray for me."

Mrs. Young held up one finger and went to her small oak desk that matched the table. Pulling out a box of fine stationary, she handed it to him. "One needs special stationary for a special letter."

He thanked her, slipped out a piece of the blue and gold-edged paper, then rummaged for a pen in his pocket. Mrs. Young patted his arm and went back to the living room.

Dear Delores... That's creative, he scoffed at himself and nibbled on the top of his pen. His insides quaked at the importance of this correspondence.

How can I ever tell you how sorry I am for hurting you? Even though I don't deserve your forgiveness, if you could ever find it in your heart to forgive me, I would spend the rest of my life being the best husband God could ever make me to be. If I had gone to church with you from the beginning like you wanted, perhaps this break up would never have happened. I went today, and I don't think I'll ever be the same. Garrett says I'm a new creature in Christ. Would you give this "new creature" a chance to be the kind of husband you deserve? All my love, Devon.

Chapter 21

Polly kissed Will lightly on the cheek before rolling out of bed. Time to get breakfast for the family. He didn't have return to work until tomorrow, so she'd talked him into sleeping in this morning.

She went into the sitting room, lit the lamp on the small table, and put on the green work dress she'd laid out the night before. Always tempted to dress up when Will was home, she had opted for the practical today. It was such a luxury to have Will at home. She gathered her Bible, journal, and Chartreuse to take downstairs.

In the hall, she tapped on the girls' door, tiptoed down the steps, and put her quiet time items on the table beside Mother's chair. Oatmeal with raisins and brown sugar would be a treat on this chilly morning.

She rubbed her hands together and hustled into the kitchen. Father had added wood to the cook stove before he left for work, so the fire blazed. In a matter of minutes, she'd filled a pan with water, oatmeal, raisins and a pinch of salt and set it on the stove. The water should boil soon.

After pulling white bowls from the cupboard, she scooped up silverware with her other hand and went to set the table. She never asked the girls to do this job on a school morning. Who would get their breakfast in a few weeks? With a quick shake of her head, she went to stir the oatmeal. Not a question she could answer.

When Twila stumbled into the kitchen, rubbing her eyes, Polly hugged her. "You don't look very wide awake. Didn't you sleep well last night?"

Twila shrugged. "So-so, I guess. My mind keeps going round and round."

Polly gazed at her youngest sister while continuing to stir. She didn't need to ask why her mind was spinning. The decision looming ahead was too heavy for the shoulders of an eleven year old.

"Did you and Will decide if you'll buy the land in Stoneboro?" Elsie's question startled her.

"I didn't hear you come in." Polly smiled and pulled Elsie in for a hug before returning to her stirring. "Maybe we'll decide today."

"Why don't you buy Mrs. Wilds' house when she and Father move in here? Then you'd be right down the street." Twila's tone was plaintive.

"It's hard to explain, Little One." Polly hadn't called Twila by her pet name in a long while. "But you can visit us in Stoneboro as often as you like."

"Do you want me to set out milk and more brown sugar, Pol?" Beth had become her right arm in the kitchen since Maggie married and had two children.

"Yes, please. The oatmeal is almost ready." She gazed at her pretty teen-age sister. "Are you okay with living here with Will and me when Father marries?"

"Of course. I'll miss him but not too much will change. He spends most of his time at Mrs. Wilds' house anyway." Beth put some brown sugar in a bowl and pulled the milk bottle from the ice box.

Her tall brother clattered into the kitchen. "Need me to carry anything?"

It was unusual for him to offer. Did he also sense the changes coming? Polly patted George's arm. "I think we've got it. Let's go eat."

When they'd all plopped into their usual places and

bowed their heads, Polly prayed over their food. "And help us remember, Father, that we'll always be a family no matter where we live."

♠

Savannah smoothed a brush through her long, satin fine hair, then gathered it into a French twist, securing it with black hair pins. She allowed a few strands to curl around her face. One glance in the mirror and she cringed. Why did her reflection remind her of Mrs. Greely's fierce glare yesterday? An even better question, why did the woman hate her so?

Would their presence at Reverend Greely's church yesterday stir up more gossip? Two stories in the past five months had reached her ears. One implied she dyed her hair, the other that she'd cut her hair, but used a ratt to hide what she'd done. Both stories came through her office mate under the guise of concern that Savannah should know what was being said.

She sighed. With her past, the stories could be much worse. Her cheeks flushed crimson as possible story lines occurred to her. What if Mr. Black told someone about his past involvement with her while he stayed with Garrett's parents? Nausea rose in her throat. Garrett said Mr. Black was a new creature in Christ, but… Savannah's lips trembled and her chin quivered.

Sitting on the edge of the bed, she buckled the shoes she wore to the office, gulping down saliva that pooled on her tongue. Since Garrett had an early appointment this morning, she wouldn't bother with breakfast. He never allowed her to get up early to cook for him.

She grabbed her handbag and ran down the steps to the insurance office. Dorothy greeted her, early as usual. For all her flaws, Dorothy was punctual. Of course, if she had been late, she might have missed the opportunity to be the first to pass along the most recent gossip.

Savannah smoothed her rose-colored dress and opened the office door. "Good morning, Dorothy." She smiled at the short dumpy woman who sometimes made her blood boil.

Dorothy had given her many chances to perfect the art of forgiveness.

Dorothy surveyed Savannah in silence for a moment. "I don't know how one person can cause so much trouble."

Frowning, Savannah stared back. "What do you mean?"

"Word is that Mrs. Greely plans to have Garrett fired so your presence won't tempt the good men of the alliance of churches."

Chapter 22

When the door closed behind her brother and sisters, Polly dropped into Mother's chair and tilted her head. The stillness settled around her as she quieted her heart. She picked up Chartreuse and opened her journal.

Father, my heart is full this morning. I love Will so much and my relationship with him comes above all others except for my relationship with you. Still, often I find myself on the verge of tears when I think of our lives changing. Father will probably leave and I don't know what Twila and Elsie will do. I've been a mother to them for so long.

A tear fell and pooled on the green ink. She blew on it gently, trying unsuccessfully to keep it from smearing. She sighed.

Help me not to make a mess of things, Father. Don't let me make the same mistake as Sarah Davis did, holding too tightly to her children. The girls need to make the decision that's best for them. Even if they stay here now, graduation is only about three months away.

Polly's heart clenched and another tear dropped. *Stop it. Crying won't change anything.*

Footsteps on the stairs. Will was awake. She swiped the tears from her face, and blew again on the green smudges, then set her journal on the table as Will entered the living room.

He came and knelt in front of her. Despite of her efforts to hide her tears, he spotted them. "Ah, Lass, you've been cryin'." He leaned in and kissed away her tears. "Is it the girls again, or somethin' I did?"

"Not just the girls and nothing you did. Almost ten years ago, we lost Mother. Now we may be losing Father, too." Polly sniffed. "It's so silly. I'm a married woman. Most married women no longer live with their families anyway."

"Ah, Lass, yours hasn't been an ordinary family. You've been the mother for almost ten years. It's a big change that's comin.' No wonder your heart is breakin.' "

Polly dropped her head and allowed the sobs she'd repressed to come. Will drew her close and continued to kiss away her tears.

♠

Polly sat across from Will as he devoured the eggs she'd scrambled. He ate Irish-style with great gusto, knife in his right hand and fork, tines down, in the left. She sometimes had to nudge her younger sisters to keep them from watching him, spellbound, instead of eating.

"What's on your mind, Lass?" He glanced at her. "Or are ya that fascinated with me eatin'?" The twinkle in his eyes always appeared when he teased.

"Ya are downright fascinatin,' ya know." Polly giggled.

"Thank ya, kindly, then, Miss." He grinned broadly at her imitation of his accent and gave a mock, half bow.

"All kidding aside, are we going to decide about the land today, Will, or is there some other property you want to see first?"

"Only if you're not happy with Clyde Truxell's land." Will peered at her as though trying to read her mind.

"I like it." Polly tapped her fingers on the table as he took a bite of homemade bread. "Far enough from your family that it won't be like living in a fishbowl."

His eyebrows went up and his knife and fork stopped in mid-motion. "A fishbowl?"

She sighed. "Fish have very little privacy when they live in a fishbowl, you know. Nothing against your family, but life might have been like that if we'd lived on Chestnut Street surrounded by your family."

Will set his silverware on either side of his plate. His voice was deceptively quiet. "Are ya sayin' me family is nosy?"

"No, no, Will. You're taking this all wrong. I shouldn't have said anything. I like the lot on Walnut Street." Why had she opened her mouth?

He blew out a breath, then picked up his knife and fork. When he spoke it was more to himself than to Polly. "I was willin' to live in the same house with your family, but you're not willin' to live on the same street with mine…"

"Will…" Polly wailed, but could find no words to undo the damage. She left her chair and squatted on the floor beside him, leaning her cheek against his arm. "I'm sorry. I didn't mean to hurt your feelings. I shouldn't have been so outspoken. Mother always said I didn't know how to beat around the bush."

A smile tugged at the corners of Will's mouth as he took another bite of eggs. "I wish I could have known your mother, Lass. Everyone speaks so highly of her."

"She was one of a kind." Polly went back to her chair. "I could do the things she did but I could never be who she was."

"Don't sell yourself short, Lass. You've been an amazin' mother to your brothers and sisters. Your mam would be so proud of you."

"I hope so." After a pause, Polly glanced at Will out of the corner of her eye. "I know you want me to get to know your family better. But every time I try, it seems like your mother shuts me out."

"Are ya sure it isn't the other way round?" Will took his last bite of eggs. "Ya aren't ever over eager to visit my Mam."

It was true—but which had come first, being shut out or not wanting to visit? A matter of opinion maybe. Polly sighed and tapped her fingers on the table again. This discussion was going nowhere. "How do we go about finishing the transaction on Mr. Truxell's land?"

"I'm surprised you're in such a hurry, sad as ya were this

morning about the changes."

"I guess I'm sad and excited at the same time. But mostly I want to be sure we have a place to go when Father and Mrs. Wild's are ready to move in here." Polly stood and picked up Will's plate and silverware.

"Aye. Now I'm understandin' your haste. I'll call to find out if Clyde can meet us at the lot in an hour. That'll give us time to take another look at the land, before we settle the deal."

Will pulled a scrap of paper from his pocket and headed for the telephone while Polly carried his dishes to the kitchen. She added some hot water to the dishpan where she'd washed the children's breakfast dishes. By the time Will joined her, the kitchen sparkled.

"Clyde says an hour will be just about right." Will went to the living room to grab their coats and she followed. "Better bundle up so ya don't get cold walkin' around the lot."

Polly pulled her yellow scarf out of one coat sleeve and a knitted green hat out of the other. "I'm well prepared." She put on her beige coat, then wrapped her scarf around her throat and jammed her hat on her head.

Will kissed the tip of her nose. "That should do, Lass." He put on his own coonskin hat and gloves. "Where are your gloves?"

She dug around in her pockets but her hands came out empty. "Twila probably borrowed them. That child can't keep track of her gloves. I'll put my hands in my pockets. I'll be fine."

After a few false cranks that showed Nellie's distaste for being asked to provide transportation on this cold morning, they were on their way. What a blessing that Will's hometown was so close to hers. Maybe that was why competition between the two towns was so fierce.

Will broke the silence, his breath forming little clouds in the frigid air. "The Walnut Street area is still bein' developed, ya know. I heard W. B. Slater will soon be erectin' his residence on this street, too."

"I heard that too. What if the builders are too busy

building his house to work on ours?" Polly scraped a peek hole in the frost on her window.

"I don't know. I've never had a house built before. We'll ask Mr. Truxell who he recommends to do our construction and hope for the best." He shot Polly a sideways glance. "We can always live with me mam for a little while if we need to."

Chapter 23

When they reached their destination in Stoneboro, Will took Polly's hand. She twisted in her seat and gazed at the vacant lot. "So what do ya think, Lass? Can ya picture a little bungalow nestlin' on this spot?"

She turned back toward him, her green eyes dreamy. "A little brown bungalow with red tulips and yellow daffodils blooming in the front yard and some fruit trees in the back."

"Sounds like a warm, comfortable love nest for you 'n me. And when the young'ens come along, we'll add on."

The sparkle vanished from her eyes. She withdrew her hand and scooted over to open her door. "Let's scout out the lot again and see who our neighbors will be."

Will sprinted around the car in time to take her hand as she stepped out. "Lass..." He hesitated, then planted both feet, put his hands on her shoulders, and turned her to face him. "Is it me imagination, or are ya not over-anxious to have wee ones?"

She stared at the third copper button on his black woolen coat, avoiding his eyes. "I…I guess you could say I'm not over-anxious seeing as I've mostly raised one family all ready."

Taking two steps back, Will dropped his hands and turned away. His shoulders sagged. Polly followed, reaching for his hand. "I'm sorry, Will. If God gives us children, I'll love them. But I couldn't lie when you asked me."

Will continued up the side of the lot bordered by Franklin Street, his long legs setting a pace that had Polly almost running.

When he reached the end of Clyde's property, he stopped and allowed her to catch up. His throat rasped when he spoke. "Why is it I'm just now learnin' how you feel 'bout this?"

Polly bowed her head. "At first, I couldn't bring myself to tell you I didn't want any children. Specially since…" Her voice trailed away.

"Specially since I'm Catholic?" Was this Catholic Protestant thing never going away?

Her cheeks flushed. "Will, please don't tell your mother." Not only her voice but her eyes pleaded with him.

If he'd abided by his mother's wishes, chances were he wouldn't be in this situation. A good Catholic girl surely wouldn't express misgivin's about having children. He hunched his shoulders against the cold and disappointment, then shrugged away the thought. He'd been all through this before. He didn't want a *good Catholic girl.* It was Polly he loved.

He gazed into her tear-filled green eyes and sighed. "You are the most unselfish person I've ever met, Lass. I don't know anyone else who has spent the last ten years raisin' their brothers and sisters. No wonder you're not enthusiastic about startin' over again. If I'd have been thinkin' of anyone but meself, I'd have figured that out."

She sniffled and blinked away tears. "When you were so willing to live with my family, allowing me to keep my promise to my mother, I told myself I'd be willing to have children—and I am." She sniffled again and blew her nose hard. "I'm just not over eager."

He thrust his hand into the pocket of his blue jeans, pulled out a clean handkerchief, and wiped her eyes. "It will be all right, Lass. You'll see. We both have nieces and nephews besides your younger sisters to love if God honors your desire not to raise more children."

A few backfires alerted them that Clyde Truxell had arrived. He pulled off Franklin Street near where they stood. Polly turned away and took a few deep breaths as Clyde jumped from his well-used Chevrolet 490 pickup.

"Been waiting long?" The tall, broad-shouldered farmer, wearing a pine green winter coat that had seen better days, covered the distance between them. He reached to shake Will's hand. His roughened, chapped skin indicated he was no stranger to hard work.

"Not long. Wanted to get the lay of the land, so to speak, before closin' the deal."

"Of course, of course. Are you looking to build a house?" Clyde gestured at the lot.

Will gripped Polly's hand. "That we are, sir. You haven't changed your mind 'bout sellin,' have ya?"

"No, indeed." Clyde eyed their clasped hands indulgently. "Newly-weds, are you?"

"Less than three months, sir. We've been livin' with Polly's family."

"Ah, well, you'll be wanting a place of your own then. Most young folk do." He eyed Polly appraisingly. "Bob Dye's daughter, aren't you?"

She cleared her throat, caught off guard at the turn the conversation had taken. "Umm, yes. Yes, I am. You know my father?"

Clyde gave a brief nod. "I'm from Jackson Center. The Dyes are well-known there."

Polly smiled. "My family moved from there ten years ago." Recognition lit her eyes. "You own a farm over there don't you?"

"I do. I have no need for this property and would be happy to see it put to good use. Have you made a decision? Should I have my lawyer draw up the papers?"

Will glanced at Polly, who smiled and nodded. "We'd like that, sir. Let us know when they're ready."

♠

The Dye family settled round the table at dinner, serving themselves generous portions of beef stew Polly had cooked. Will cleared his throat and glanced at her. "Shall we be tellin' the family our news?"

Father peered at him from the head of the table. "You have news?"

"We do." Polly's stomach churned and her appetite for the fragrant beef stew dwindled.

"We talked to Clyde Truxell today about the lot." Will directed his announcement to Father but every eye was on him.

Father nodded. "He's a good man."

"It's very highly he thinks of you, sir."

"So what did you decide?" George just wanted the facts.

"We've decided to buy. He's havin' his lawyer draw up papers he is."

A snuffle beside her drew Polly's attention. Twila blinked rapidly. "Does this mean you'll be moving out, Polly?"

Before she could answer, Father beamed at Twila, as though telling her she'd won the lottery. "It means you'll be getting a new stepmother, my dear. I'll be marrying Lydia Wilds."

Twila dropped her spoon, screeched back her chair and ran from the room.

Chapter 24

Savannah put away her stenographer's pad and pen, and then gathered her handbag and scarlet coat. The first work day of another week finished. So far no evidence that Mrs. Greely had made good on her threat to have Garrett fired. Surely the woman's husband wouldn't encourage her less-than-Christ-like behavior.

The outer door of the office opened and closed. Maybe Garrett had returned earlier than expected. She hurried to meet him, then halted abruptly. Mr. Black, in a well-cut winter coat, stood talking to Dorothy. Her heart thudded against her ribs and her palms began to sweat. She hadn't met him face-to-face since… Her cheeks heated. Mr. Black stopped in mid-sentence and a blush crept up his neck when their eyes met.

Dorothy peered at Savannah, then back at Mr. Black. "You two know each other?"

They both spoke at once, then Garrett's former employer held up his hand. "Garrett used to work for me. I was looking for him."

"I'm expecting him any time." Savannah licked dry lips. What to do with the man? If she invited him to her office or to their apartment, who knew what juicy story Dorothy would invent. "Would you like to wait for Garrett in his office?"

"Thank you, I can do that." Mr. Black came around the front counter and followed her. He spoke as soon as they were out of Dorothy's sight. "Savannah, I wanted to apolo—"

Savannah put a finger to her lips and gave her head a slight shake. Dorothy could hear a pin drop in a thunderstorm. She opened the door to the office Garrett shared with the other agents. It was empty.

Stepping aside for him to enter, she motioned Mr. Black to come in. "You can wait here."

"Savannah," Mr. Black began again.

Again, she shook her head and spoke in a voice as light as a breath. "We can't talk here."

"Go ahead, Mr. Black."

She gasped. Dorothy had followed them. "I'd be interested to hear what you have to say to *Mrs.* Young. I imagine it would interest Garrett, too. No wonder Mrs. Greely has *concerns.*"

"Mr. Black is probably here to see me." Garrett's voice from behind Dorothy had an edge of steel. "Have you forgotten I'm a pastor and sometimes people seek spiritual counsel?"

Dorothy backed up a few steps with the speed of a turtle. Garrett stepped around her, then turned in her direction. "Oh and Dorothy, if I hear any embroidered stories about this incident, I'll have a talk with my father."

The woman's pale blue eyes narrowed to slits. "Nepotism."

Garrett went into the office with Savannah and Mr. Black and shut the door.

He sank into a chair, closed his eyes, and then opened them and shook his head. "She's the town crier. Probably not a good idea to come here, Mr. Bla—Devon." He motioned for his wife and former employer to sit down. They each pulled a chair from the conference table in the center of the room.

"I'm so sorry. I didn't know Savannah worked here. I was as surprised to see her as she was to see me." Mr. Black looked from Savannah to Garrett.

Garrett cleared his throat. "What can I do for you?"

"I stopped to ask for prayer. I'm going to talk to my wife tonight. Please pray she'll forgive me and give us another chance." He rubbed the back of his neck. "And while I'm here, I also wanted to ask Savannah to forgive me. I'm so sorry for…for…"

Savannah gulped. *Please don't say it.* "I owe you an apology as well. The life-style I chose—well, it took a long time to acknowledge how much damage I did. But God has forgiven us, so I hope we can forgive each other and ourselves. Sometimes that's the hardest part."

Garrett hesitated, then reached a hand to each of them and bowed his head. *Heavenly Father, thank you that you are the author of mercy and compassion. Thank you that you forgive us again and again when we are truly sorry."* He cleared his throat. *"Please make the circle of forgiveness complete between Savannah, Devon and me, as well as between Devon and his wife. Only you can pick up the broken pieces and mend broken hearts. Amen.*

♠

"Are ya excited, Lass?" Will took Polly's hand and gently kissed her lips, then pulled her out of the car.

"I think so. Just worried about my younger sisters." She glanced at the car parked in front of Will's mother's house. "Looks like Mr. Truxell got here ahead of us."

"Meetin' him here to sign the papers seemed like the most sensible arrangement."

Polly had agreed to stay for dinner. When Mam opened the door as they headed up the sidewalk, Will's stomach clenched. His steps slowed. Would he regret asking her?

"Step lively, now. Don't be dawdling. Mr. Truxell be waitin' for ya."

"All right. Sorry he got here first." Will bent to kiss his mother's cheek. Polly did the same.

"Hello, Mrs. Reiser. Nice to see you."

"It's nice ya had time to come with Will tonight. I guess ya didn't have much choice since ya both need to sign these papers."

Neither he nor Polly responded to this. Mam always

implied that Polly didn't want to come. He sighed, threw their coats over a chair, and greeted Clyde who had come into the living room. "Thanks for meetin' us here, Clyde. Do ya have the papers ready for us to sign?"

"Indeed I do, Will. May we sit at the kitchen table, Mrs. Reiser?"

When she agreed. They moved to the kitchen, and he handed Polly and Will each a pen. "Your mother can be your witness to the signatures, if that's all right with everyone." Mam took the silver pen he extended and sat across from her son.

After a few minutes of explanations, silence reigned except for the scratching of pens. Will counted out five crisp one hundred dollar bills. His mother's eyes widened, but she said nothing.

Clyde stood and folded the money into his denim pants pocket. "If you like, I can take care of getting this registered at the Courthouse."

"Thank you, Clyde. Much appreciated." Will stood too as Mr. Truxell thanked Mam and Polly, then shook Will's hand. Will walked with him to the door.

"Can I help you get supper on the table, Mrs. Reiser?" Polly stood and cleared her throat.

"No, no. Don't trouble yourself. Will can give me a hand." She motioned Will to her side as he returned to the kitchen, then gazed at Polly. "You're lookin' a bit peeked. I'm thinkin' maybe you're in the family way."

Polly's face paled as she turned and left the room.

Chapter 25

The aroma of fried chicken wafted down the steps when Garrett opened the door to their apartment, shifting the bouquet of flowers to his left hand. A smile wreathed his face as he sniffed. Savannah definitely had a knack for creating tasty meals. He ran up the stairs and held out the bouquet to his lovely wife, so feminine with a frilly pink apron tied over her "office clothes," as she called them.

Her eyebrows went up. "What are these for?"

"Do I need a reason to buy flowers for my wife?" He kissed her on both cheeks, then on her lips.

The corners of her mouth lifted as a warm smile blossomed on her face. "I guess not. Thank you, Garrett." She glanced at the bouquet, then at the sizzling chicken.

"I'll put these in a vase for you." He put the flowers on the counter and dug around in the white kitchen cupboard until he produced a tall, cut-glass vase.

"Thanks, Love. They say flowers will last longer if you cut off the bottom of the stems." Savannah raised an eyebrow at him.

"Oh they do, do they?" He moved to kiss her ticklish spot at the base of her throat. She lowered her chin as she giggled and backed away. "I've always wondered who *they* are, always so well informed."

Garrett rummaged in the large junk drawer for the scissors Savannah kept for cutting flowers. "You never told me how you feel about me applying for the prison chaplain position." He snipped the ends from a few stems into the wastebasket. "It would mean four visits to the jail every month if I understood Mr. Swartz correctly."

Savannah continued turning the fragrant chicken. "Is this something you want to do or feel led to do?"

He couldn't read her expression. "I want to know how you feel about it first."

She grinned at him and shook her head.

Savannah wouldn't give him a clue. He sighed. "It's not something I ever thought I'd want to do, but after spending time with Mr. Burns… Well, I'm finding it's satisfying to relate to someone who's truly sorry and wants to change." He finished snipping, stuck the flowers in the water-filled vase, then went to stand beside her.

"Many people come to church but have no desire to change. They're in the pew every Sunday because it's expected, not from any desire to grow spiritually. At least that's how it appears to me."

"You believe Mr. Burns is truly sorry, don't you?"

"I do. He wanted me to ask if you'd forgive him, but I said you already had."

Savannah nodded. "You mentioned that." Then she peered at him, forehead wrinkled. "What about Mr. Black? Do you believe his sorrow is genuine?"

Garrett hesitated. "I've had my doubts about Mr. Black. Maybe afraid he was putting on an act. What do you think?"

"I don't think he's that good an actor." Savannah took his hand. "Do you remember when Mr. Burns made accusations about me, what a hard time you had trusting me?"

He sighed and squeezed her hand. "I wanted everyone to believe I'd changed but I didn't extend that same mercy to you. God keeps reminding me of that." Garrett clapped his hand to his forehead. "I can't believe I forgot to tell you. Pa said things went well when Devon talked to his wife. She isn't ready for him to move back in yet, but she's willing for them to have counseling with her minister." He took the vase and set it in the center of the dining room table.

"God's at work changing all of us, isn't He?" His wife smiled in his direction. "Sounds like a yes on being the prison chaplain?"

He bit his lip and tapped his fingers together. "I guess so."

"Fill out the application and take it with you when you visit Mr. Burns next Saturday." Savannah grabbed a platter and transferred chicken from the skillet. "Will Mr. Black have to return to living in his store?" She handed the platter of chicken to Garrett and went back for the potatoes and green beans.

"Pa will let him stay with them while they get counseling." Garrett filled a pitcher with water and poured it into their glasses.

"Your parents are amazing, Garrett." Savannah gazed at her husband. "When no one else wanted anything to do with me, your mother treated me like a daughter. And your father gave me a job."

Garrett nodded. "Pa still doesn't profess to be a Christian, but he goes to church with Ma every Sunday. I think he's come a long way."

♠

On Friday evening after the supper dishes were done, Polly curled up on the loveseat in Mother's sitting room. The next few days stretched ahead of her with Will away all weekend on a longer run than usual. At least she wouldn't have to make any excuses about not going with him to see his mother. She yawned and closed her eyes. Maybe she'd go to bed early.

The cushion of the loveseat bounced as Twila plopped down beside her. Opening one eye, Polly smiled. "Did you need something?"

"Can I talk to you?" Her sister's dark brown eyes were solemn.

"Of course." Polly sat up and gazed at Twila. "What would you like to talk about?"

"About Papa marrying Mrs. Wilds. Do you think he'll be mad at me if I stay here when they get married?"

"I don't think so. He said it was your decision." Polly smoothed the wrinkles from her sister's forehead. "Is that what you want to do?"

"I think so. If I move to Mrs. Wilds' house, I'll have to move back here in a few months." Twila threw her hands in the air. "It doesn't make sense."

Elsie appeared in the doorway. "What doesn't make sense?"

Twila repeated her reasoning. Elsie nodded. "That's what I've been thinking, too. Anyway, I'm not sure about Mrs. Wilds, she can't even remember my name."

"Just that one time, she called you Evie." Polly tugged Elsie down between Twila and her on the loveseat. "You shouldn't hold that against her."

What a hypocrite, telling Elsie not to hold things against Mrs. Wilds when she herself could hardly stand to be in the same room with her. Polly closed her eyes.

"What's wrong, Polly." Elsie tugged on her arm.

Polly shook her head. "Nothing. Nothing at all. You'll eventually live here with Papa and Mrs. Wilds, so you want to get off to a good start."

Easy to say that to the girls but probably a little late for Polly.

Chapter 26

Bob turned away from the sitting room door and tiptoed back up the stairs. He hadn't meant to eavesdrop, but he couldn't help overhearing Twila and Elsie's conversation with Polly. He'd come down to ask Polly a question, but it could wait.

He finished washing up and patted on a little Pinaud-Clubman aftershave. The fragrance reminded him of his father, who used it in his younger days. Lydia usually sniffed his cheek when he wore it. How would she react when she learned that the girls would stay with Polly until George and Beth graduated? He never knew what to expect.

Staring into his mirror, he found himself talking to Margaret. *Am I doing the right thing, Margaret? Can I justify not having the girls with me? On the other hand, would it be right to take them away from the person who's been a mother to them?*

He ducked his head. Lydia wouldn't be pleased that he'd been talking to Margaret. No question about that. Occasionally, he still slipped up and referred to her as "my wife." Surely after he married Lydia, he would break that habit. Picking up a comb from the heavy, dark mahogany dresser, Bob slicked his hair in place, then grabbed his newsboy hat, and ran down the stairs. Lydia liked him to wear a hat.

Poking his head into the room where Polly, Twila and Elsie sat, he gave a brief wave. "Going to see Lydia to discuss wedding plans. Don't wait up."

He slipped on his coat and hat and stepped outside.

♠

Bob walked up to Lydia's door, reached for the knob, then shook his head. No matter what Lydia said, he couldn't just walk in. He tapped lightly. What would it be like when they married? Not having to knock?

The door opened and Lydia stood bathed in the light from the gas lamp sitting on the hall table, looking quite angelic in her pale blue dress. She reached for his hand and pulled him inside. "I told you not to knock, now that we're practically married." Her voice, low and intimate, sent shivers up his spine.

When he bent to kiss her lips, she stood on tiptoe and wound her arms around his neck, deepening their kiss. His heart hammered in his chest. At last she stepped back. "What took you so long? Seems like I've been waiting forever." Her lower lip protruded in an adorable pout.

"I thought you'd prefer me clean, rather than covered with coal dust." He fingered the soft fabric of her dress. "I'd hate to soil your pretty frock."

"You're right, of course." She wrinkled her nose. "I suppose seeing you covered in coal dust is something I must get used to when we're married." Grabbing his hand, she drew him into the dimly lit living room. "Speaking of getting married, we need to make plans."

Bob looked around. "We'll probably need a little more light if we want to write things down." He sat on the settee and Lydia snuggled up beside him.

"Let's talk first, then we can write things down later if we need to." She leaned her head on his shoulder. "When can we get married?"

"When do you want to get married?"

She smiled. "Tomorrow."

Bob choked and coughed, unprepared for her answer. "Tomorrow? We have to get a marriage license first."

She sat up straight and frowned. "Of course. How long does that take?"

"Three days, I believe." He peered at her. "So I'm assuming you don't want a big wedding?"

"I've been married twice and you once. Why waste the money on a lot of frills?"

"Okay." Lydia's practicality took him by surprise. "I don't know if our minister will perform a marriage ceremony without counseling for a situation such as ours."

Lydia pulled away. "What do you mean 'a situation such as ours?'"

"People who've had a previous troubled marriage."

"That doesn't seem fair. He knows nothing about me or my second marriage." She stood and stomped her foot. "Let's just get married at the courthouse."

Bob pulled her back down beside him. "I'm sure I can find another Presbyterian minister who'll marry us."

With a long-suffering sigh, Lydia nodded. "All right. I'll leave it to you to find a minister. Or maybe my mother's minister, Reverend Frampton, would perform the ceremony."

"I'd rather stay with someone from the Presbyterian Church." After fumbling in his pocket, Bob drew out a small tablet and made a note. "Who do you want to invite to our wedding? I have a list of my side of the family." He flipped a few pages in his tablet.

Lydia jumped up and paced in front of him. "If we invite one person, soon the numbers will mushroom and there'll be hundreds. Maybe the minister who marries us can ask his wife and the organist to be our witnesses."

Bob slumped and dropped his head against the back of the settee. "You mean not invite anyone? Not even your mother and my father?" This wasn't turning out at all as he'd expected.

Lydia stopped pacing and glared at him. "Oh all right, if you insist." She plopped down beside him again.

"I'm not insisting, just wondering why you don't want to invite at least our..." Bob's voice faded as thunder clouds descended on Lydia's face. Better just let her have her way. Polly and George would most likely appreciate avoiding the wedding. "All right, if that's what you want. I guess that'll keep things simple."

All smiles now, Lydia sprang to her feet and stood in front of him. "How about next Friday? Can you have a minister by then?"

"I'll make some phone calls tomorrow." Bob shifted in his seat, his tone flat.

"What's the problem? Do you think it'll be too hard to find a minister by next Friday?" Lydia withdrew to a dark blue wingchair, the corners of her mouth turning downward.

"No, it's just..." Bob hesitated "Won't folks wonder about this hurry-up wedding?"

Lydia huffed. "It's not anyone else's business, is it? At least they won't think I'm in the family way."

Bob couldn't repress a chuckle at the very idea. Despite his misgivings about how fast things were moving, he ignored them. This was what he wanted, wasn't it? He'd wanted to marry Lydia ever since he'd helped with surveying her property after the death of her estranged husband. Besides, He couldn't take a chance on her former fiancé changing his mind.

Is this God's plan?

He scratched his head. How could he possibly know?

It's only by learning to be guided by the Holy Spirit and not following our own desires and schemes. Margaret's words to Florence when she'd asked how she could know God's will.

He sighed. Even if it wasn't God's desire for him to marry Lydia, he'd walked way too far down this path to turn back now.

Chapter 27

Bob knotted his narrow, dark blue tie for the fourth time. Where had the week gone? He'd intended to spend some extra time with his family before his wedding day, but too many other things had crept in. Other than telling them he and Lydia were getting married today and that they weren't inviting anyone to the wedding, there hadn't been a lot of communication.

He gazed at his face in the mirror which did nothing to encourage him. Instead of the joy he'd expected to experience on this day, a huge void threatened to engulf him. What had made him think someone with that mug could hold the interest of a woman like Lydia? He scrubbed his hand over his eyes. After today, they'd be married. Surely she wouldn't leave him after he put a wedding ring on her finger.

She left Rufus Wilds.

He closed his eyes. That was different. Lydia said Rufus was depressed.

You might be depressed, too, after living with her a few years. There's still time to change your mind.

Bob opened his eyes and shook his head. He was a man of his word. He'd promised Lydia they would marry today at the Presbyterian Church in Mercer. Dr. Duncan, his wife and the organist would be waiting for them.

He glanced around the sparsely furnished room at the top of the steps. This had been his room since Will and Florence moved in. Most of his clothes were already at Lydia's house.

When they moved back in a few months, they'd use the bedroom he and Margaret had shared.

Up until now, he'd blocked that from his mind. Would memories of his wife haunt him? Margaret, not his wife, he had to stop calling her that.

He started down the stairs. How would Lydia feel? Too late for those concerns now. The plans were made.

He stepped into the living room to find Twila and Elsie playing jacks, Beth and Florence seated on the davenport. George was working at the garage today so he'd said good-bye to him last night. Will wouldn't be home until later.

"Come give your papa a hug." He spoke to the room at large.

They glanced at him. No one smiled but at least they weren't crying.

Twila came first. Her deep brown eyes shone almost black. "When will we see you again?"

"After our wedding trip." Bob hugged her tight. "Florence knows where to reach me."

Elsie stepped forward. She sniffed and folded her arms across her chest. "Why aren't we invited to your wedding?"

A teenager now, Elsie still had a keen sense of what was fair. "Lydia and I didn't want a big wedding. It seemed simpler not to invite anyone than to only invite select people. It wouldn't be right."

Elsie's huffed and gave him a half-hearted hug, jacks and a ball still grasped in one hand.

Beth and Florence had lingered by the davenport, but Beth, with her usual generosity, motioned Florence to go first.

Florence bit her lip but remained silent as she hugged him.

He raised an eyebrow at his eldest daughter. "Did you have something to say?"

She sighed. "Nothing I haven't said before." She stepped back. "I hope you and Lydia will be very happy." Her tone was flat.

Beth squeezed her sister's arm, then took her place. "You should have pleasant weather for your wedding, Papa. The paper says it'll be warmer today than yesterday." Her warm blue eyes held no judgment and her hug seemed sincere.

Bob held her tight a minute longer, then released her. "It looks like a grand day for a wedding." He swallowed. "I love you all." Those words never came easily.

As his girls chorused their replies, he grabbed his dark blue suit coat, opened the door, and left before he changed his mind.

♠

Lydia paced back and forth across the bathroom at the First Presbyterian Church of Mercer. What had she been thinking, not inviting any of her family to her wedding? Her mother was especially disappointed, her married children surprised. Still, she couldn't invite them without inviting Bob's children. Her stomach twisted. They might have refused to come. She couldn't risk the humiliation.

Conversation had been minimal when her son, Delbert, brought her to the church early so she wouldn't have to ride with the groom. When she pressed him for answers, she got the impression he was less than satisfied with his job in New Castle. What if he moved to another state as her daughter had done? How could she bear separation from both her children? Was it too late to change her mind about marrying Bob?

If she didn't get married, she would need to take in laundry again unless she sold the wristwatch Byron had given her or the small house she owned on Lacock. Her funds from her widow's settlement were running low.

She shook her head. How could she move away and leave her elderly mother behind? She sighed and glanced at her Cartier diamond-encrusted wristwatch. Almost time. After one last look in the mirror, she pulled a lipstick from her handbag, added a touch more color and left the restroom.

The wedding march, though muffled, could be heard even before Lydia opened the door to the large sanctuary. How ridiculous for the two of them to get married in this cavernous place, but Bob was adamant that the ceremony be held in a church. He stood beside the minister in his Sunday-best suit with a crisp, white shirt. Surprising that Polly would have ironed it for him for this occasion.

As Lydia approached the altar, Bob's eyes held an unsettled look. What did he see in hers?

Chapter 28

Garrett gathered up his Bible and the chaplain application papers, stepped out of the car and glanced at the forbidding structure that housed prisoners. Maybe when leaves sprouted on the trees that surrounded the building, it wouldn't look so dismal.

A lot had happened since he'd visited Mr. Burns. Had it only been three weeks? It probably seemed much longer to those who sat idly in a jail cell. The black and white stripped uniform Burns had worn flashed through his mind. Probably intended to be an embarrassment to the prisoners. He glanced at his own casual flannel shirt and denim pants. What had Jim worn when he went to the jail? He shrugged. Must not have been worth mentioning.

Thank you for helping me forgive this man, Lord. I'm actually looking forward to talking to him instead of dreading it as I did last time.

He whistled a lively tune. A spring in his step took him across the parking area and up the weathered wooden steps in no time. When Garrett pushed the heavy door open and entered, Ron Swartz looked up, then smiled and stood as Garrett walked to the reception desk. Had the room smelled this musty last time?

"Good morning, Pastor Garrett. Nice to see you." Ron came from behind the desk and extended his hand.

Garrett shook it and returned his smile. "Good to see you, too. How's Mr. Burns doing?"

"He's been a bit better since your visit. Not as hostile and resentful." Ron gave Garrett a searching look that took in the papers he held. "Any decision on applying for the chaplain position? We could sure use you."

Garrett held out the papers. "I'm applying for the position."

A smile spread across Officer Ron's face as he took the application. "That's wonderful news. I think Burns will be pleased. I know I am."

He pressed a buzzer, opened the door, and pointed at a guard further down the hall. "Detrick there will escort you to Burns' cell."

The tall, husky guard in a dark green uniform motioned for him to come. He indicated the room Garrett and George had occupied three weeks earlier. "Have a seat. We'll be with you in a few minutes."

Garrett plopped his Bible on the table and sank into the rickety folding chair. He glanced around at the off-white, bare walls. Couldn't say much for the décor. Heavy footfalls announced Mr. Burns' approach, and Garrett stood to greet him.

A smile. Burns was actually smiling with his Bible in his hand. "Pastor Garrett, you came."

"I said I'd be back." Garrett pumped Burns' huge, thick-knuckled hand.

"I know but… Well, I wouldn't be here if I didn't have to be, so how can I expect someone else to come?" He dropped into the chair that matched Garrett's but was dwarfed by his bulk.

"I'm happy to be here, George. If Jesus says one lost sheep is worth searching for, I can certainly come to see you in jail."

George tilted his head. "Jesus said that?"

"He did. He told a story about it when the religious leaders grumbled because Jesus ate with sinners."

Another smile filled George's face. "Is it in here?" He plunked his Bible on the table.

Garrett pulled it toward him and flipped to the book of Luke, then to chapter fifteen. "Here it is. This chapter is about the lost sheep, the lost coin, and the lost son. Jesus shows that God cares about those who've lost their way."

After rummaging in his pocket, George pulled out a pencil and the paper Garrett had written on last time. He peered at the chapter heading and wrote, Luke 15 on his paper. "Tell me again what was lost."

George scrawled the words as Garrett repeated what he'd said. He tapped the tip of his pencil on the table. "Reverend Caldwell said Jesus came to seek and save the lost. That's in the Bible, too, isn't it?"

After turning a few pages, Garrett showed him the verse in chapter nineteen of Luke. "There it is. Same book of the Bible. In fact, I've heard it said this verse is the theme of the entire book of Luke. God wants the lost found."

Staring into space, George chewed on the eraser of his pencil. Then he looked at Garrett. "Is that why you're here?"

"It is, George. Jesus already paid for your sins when He died on the cross, and God sent Reverend Caldwell and me to tell you, your debt has been paid. All you have to do is accept the free gift Jesus offers you. He'll cleanse you of all your sins and give you a new beginning."

A tear slid down Burns' stubbly cheek and he closed his eyes. "That night I barged into Savannah's room at the boarding house to…to take what I wanted, she told me God had given her a new beginning and that He'd give me one too. If only I'd listened to her."

"It's not too late, George. God will meet you right here, right now, to give you a new, pure heart if that's what you want."

George put his head on the cold, metal table, shoulders heaving, and sobbed out loud. The guard seated outside stuck his head in the doorway with a raised eyebrow. Garrett shook his head and motioned him back. Burns didn't need an audience.

At last the big man sat up and pulled a huge, red handkerchief from his pocket. He mopped his eyes, then blew his nose with loud trumpet blasts. "It is what I want, Reverend Young. It's what I've wanted for a long time but I didn't think I deserved to be forgiven."

Garrett smiled. "Just call me Pastor Garrett. Let's pray. You can thank Jesus for paying your debt and ask Him to give you a new heart."

Burns clambered out of his chair and dropped to his knees. "This is how Granny always liked for me to pray. He folded his hands on the chair. *Dear Jesus, thank you for paying the debt for my sins. I don't deserve it, but I sure do appreciate it. Would you wash me on the inside and give me a new, clean heart? And could you give me that new beginning Savannah told me about? Pastor Garrett says it's not too late, but I'm sorry I waited so long. Amen.*

Chapter 29

*What can wash away my sin? Nothing but the blood of
Jesus.*
*What can make me whole again? Nothing but the blood
of Jesus.*
Garrett sang at the top of his lungs as he cranked the car
and jumped in. He wasn't a great singer, but he couldn't keep
from belting out the old familiar hymn as he headed for home.
*Thank you, Lord. Thank you, thank you, thank you. The angels in
heaven are rejoicing!*

*They rejoiced the day Devon Black came into the
Kingdom too.*

He groaned. *I'm sorry, Lord. I'm sorry my flesh doesn't
want to believe that man's transformation is real. Maybe
because it happened so fast. Maybe because I didn't see it
happen.*

As if by it's own volition, Garrett's car made a right turn
at the stop sign, then a left turn onto Diamond Street and into the
parking lot of Devon's store. He groaned. Not again. He didn't
want to go in.

Make a friendly visit.

Okay, Lord.

Nausea rose in his gut and he clutched his belly. *Father, I
want to obey you, but I have so many bad memories of this place.
The scene with Mr. Black two weeks ago brought it all back—the
picture of Savannah, the relationship he had with her, the*

discovery he'd been lusting after her all this time. It's just too much to ask...

♠

Polly couldn't stop looking at the clock. When Will walked in around one o'clock, even her kiss was half-hearted.

"How was your day, Darlin'?" Will peered at her.

"Fine."

He tried again. "Did ja have a tryin' mornin'?"

His words seemed to be coming from a long way off. She gave a slight shake of her head but had no words to respond. Usually she was like a water faucet turned on full force, talking continuously for the first hour or so after he came home. Today, they sat in silence on the davenport. The girls had retreated to the sitting room.

After Polly's fourth look at the wristwatch she seldom wore, Will glanced at her. "Why are ya watchin' the clock? Are ya expectin' someone?"

She shrugged. "Not really. Time has crept by since Father left, but by now I can assume he and Mrs. Wilds..." Polly gulped. "What do I call her now? I can't keep calling her Mrs. Wilds, and I can't imagine calling her Mrs. Dye, and certainly not mother."

"How about Lydia? Could ya call her Lydia?"

Polly gave a nod that barely tipped her head. "I guess. Anyway, Father and Lydia are probably married now, unless one of them got cold feet."

He peered at her. "Is that what you're hopin' for?"

A tear slid down Polly's cheek. "I can't lie to you but telling the truth would sound terrible."

He drew her close. "It'll be all right, Lass. You'll see."

She leaned her head on his chest, not bothering to wipe her tears. "That's what you always say. This time I'm not so sure."

Springing to his feet, Will pulled Polly up. "Come on. Let's get us some paper and a pencil. We can be sketchin' out our bungalow. It shouldn't be too long until work commences."

Polly hesitated, head bowed.

"Go on, Lass. It'll make you feel better, I promise."

With a mighty effort, she headed to the sitting room where Mother had always kept paper and pencils. There were even some extra long pieces of paper that would be excellent for sketching.

Twila looked up from the book she'd been buried in for the past hour. Unusual for her to read for this long a time. Perhaps her own way of blocking out reality. "What are you doing, Polly?"

Polly's mouth was open to give an explanation. She closed it. It wouldn't comfort Twila to know Will planned to make sketches of their bungalow. She swallowed. "Will needs some paper." She hurried from the room, leaving Twila to draw her own conclusions.

♠

Garrett stumbled up the stairs that led to their apartment. He had mixed feelings about talking to Savannah. Why did life always have to be such a mixture of joy and sorrow?

"Hello, my Darling." Savannah's voice preceded her as she met him at the top of the steps. "You missed lunch. Can I make you a sandwich?"

He shook his head. "I'm not hungry. But thanks for offering." After kissing his wife, he hung his jacket on the wooden coat rack.

She peered at him. "Didn't your visit with Mr. Burns go well? You look discouraged."

Taking his time, Garrett walked to the table, pulled out a chair and dropped into it. "Mr. Burns was converted today."

A frown puckered Savannah's brow as she sat down across from him. "Isn't that a good thing?"

"It's a wonderful thing." He took a deep breath and tried to push the corners of his lips into a smile.

Savannah reached across the table to take his hand. "Why aren't you happy?"

"Because God asked me to visit Devon Black on the way

home—I refused." He groaned and hung his head. "The thought of going back into his store after what happened last time made me sick to my stomach. I can't let it go."

His wife squeezed his hand. In a voice soft as a whisper, she asked, "Have you forgiven him?"

He stared at her, shaking his head. "I think I know what the problem is. When God asked me to forgive Mr. Burns, it was hard, but years and years had gone by since the kidnapping. He'd paid for his crime." He let go of Savannah's hand, pushed back his chair, and stood.

Pacing back and forth to the window, he chewed his lower lip. "Devon went on living his life, lusting after you all these years. Somehow it seems like God let him off the hook too soon."

Chapter 30

Polly chopped vegetables and scooped them into the simmering beef broth. Beth had been right about one thing, not much had changed after Father and Lydia married two and a half months ago. If anything, they saw him more now. He stopped in on his way home from the mines every work day to be sure all was well.

The question was, what was happening in the house down the street? He said little about his life with Lydia. When pressed, he said she visited her mother often. She was seriously ill and lived with Lydia's brother north of Sandy Lake. Polly's fears that her stepmother would interfere with their household hadn't materialized. Had all her suspicions about Lydia been wrong? Why did she feel like she was waiting for the other shoe to drop?

Polly blew a strand of hair out of her eyes, then brushed it aside with the back of her hand. How had Sarah kept herself from dwelling on her fears? Perhaps by meditating on things that were true and of good report instead of suspicions.

A pleasant flutter swept through her. It was true that at the beginning of April, Will had broken ground on their lot. By the middle of the month, he'd signed a contract with J. Edward Sullivan to build their bungalow, and by the end of April the cellar was dug, ready for the foundation of pressed tile. Polly often rode the train to Stoneboro to watch the developments. Excited, yet dreading being parted from her family.

As if on cue, the door crashed open and the loud voices

of her younger sisters and brother broke the stillness.

"Polly, where are you?" Beth seldom shouted.

She swallowed a lump in her throat and trotted to the kitchen doorway. "In the kitchen, Beth."

"I need a snack." George's voice rumbled as he pushed past her.

"Oatmeal cookies in the cookie jar. Did you need me, Beth?"

"I have to read my essay on the class motto for our Class Night Exercises on Thursday evening. Would you listen to me practice?" Beth slid by her to grab a few cookies.

"Of course, after supper.. I'm making beef stew. Will should be home soon."

"Can you believe baccalaureate is Sunday night and commencement exercises a week from tonight?" Beth nibbled her cookie.

Polly nodded, then walked back to the sink and reached for a potato. "And then in July, off to nurse's training."

"When are Father and Lydia moving into this house?" Beth raised an eyebrow. "I thought they were coming after graduation."

Putting a finger to her lips, Polly shrugged. Their bungalow wasn't ready and she'd prefer that no one bring up the subject of moving. "No one has mentioned it. Maybe because Lydia's mother is so ill."

Her brother had loitered in the kitchen doorway, eating his four cookies in giant bites. "I hope they don't move until I start my job in Sharon. I should be ready to move before Beth leaves."

Twila wriggled past him and squeezed around Beth to reach the cookie jar. "I'm hoping Papa and Lydia decide to stay where they are. "

Polly's eyes widened. "You and Elsie can't live here by yourselves."

"Why can't you and Will just stay here?" Her little sister, who was fast catching up to her in height, tilted her head, dark eyes pleading.

Will appeared beside George. "Who would live in our house?"

"I didn't even hear you come in." Polly dropped her potato and met Will halfway across the kitchen for a hug and kiss.

"You all were makin' too much noise." He sniffed. "Somethin' sure smells tasty."

"I'm making stew. One of your favorites." Polly returned to finish peeling and chopping the potatoes.

Will moved to the stove and gave a few stirs with the wooden spoon. "Have your father's plans chang…" Catching the miniscule shake of Polly's head, he stopped. "Umm… Where's everyone gettin' those cookies?" He headed for the cookie jar.

Twila stared at Polly. "You didn't answer my question. Why can't you and Will just stay here?"

♠

On Thursday evening, Bob arrived just in time to accompany the family to the Class Night Exercises.

"Where's Lydia?" Elsie peeked out the window, as though expecting to find Lydia loitering by Father's car.

"Visiting her mother. Dr. Cooley says it's Bright's disease. He won't say exactly but I don't think Janet has long to live. Lydia is taking it pretty hard. She's been staying at her brother's house."

"Do you think you should be with her?" Without exception, Beth put the needs of others before her own.

"That's so considerate of you." Bob patted her arm. "You and George will only graduate once so I need to be with you tonight and Friday night. I want to be there to hear your essay and I know your brother will shine as the class donor."

George wrinkled his nose and shrugged. "You really think Lydia would have come with you if her mother wasn't sick?"

Chapter 31

Bob stood behind his wife as she put the finishing touches on her hair. He gazed at their reflection in the large mirror over her dresser. What was she thinking behind those inscrutable, storm-cloud gray eyes? Would he ever be able to read her thoughts as he'd often read Margaret's?

He sighed and pulled a comb from his pocket, slicked his hair back, then straightened his dark blue bowtie. Lydia's bright blue taffeta dress might be a touch fancy for graduation, but at least she was going with him. "You look lovely, as always." He patted her shoulder.

She leaned close to the mirror and applied some lipstick of a brighter pink than Bob preferred. Margaret would never have—

"I don't know why you want me to go with you tonight. I could spend the time with Kathleen."

Lydia's married daughter, Kathleen, had come home for the Alumni Banquet following graduation. Maybe he shouldn't have insisted Lydia come with him.

"George doesn't like me anyway."

How could he disagree with her? "George just needs some time to adjust. He'll come around. It might help if you come to commencement."

Something close to a snort came from Lydia's lady-like, pink lips. "Why should I want to be where I'm not wanted?"

Bob stepped away from the mirror. "Beth will be happy to see you, and I'd like you to become friends with Twila and Elsie. It's important you get off to a good start with them."

Lydia turned away from the looking glass, then swiveled back for one more look. "It's hard to concentrate on anything else when I'm so worried about my mother. I want to spend every minute of the time she has left with her."

He scolded himself inwardly for being insensitive and put his arm around Lydia. "I'm so sorry about your mother. I know this has been hard for you. You can spend the rest of the weekend with her and Kathleen."

When he leaned down to kiss her, she drew back. "Careful, you'll smear my lipstick."

♠

Polly peered out the window as Father's car pulled up beside the house and a horn honked. Her father, who had always been a stickler on punctuality, didn't always adhere to those standards since he married Lydia.

"Come on everyone, it's time to go. Father and Lydia are waiting."

Will joined her from the sitting-room and feet thundered down the stairs as her four siblings poured into the room. George and Beth both carried the standard gray caps and gowns.

"You mean she really came?" George peered out the window. "I don't believe it."

"Don't start anything." Polly gave her brother a dark look. "Let's not spoil this special evening."

George scowled but said nothing.

Will reached for Polly's hand. "Ready?"

"Ready." She smiled at her husband, blessed by his easy-going nature that remained unruffled regardless of the emotional turbulence.

Will opened the door just as her father stepped out of his car.

"Some of you can go with us." Father motioned to them. "Let's get started before the rain begins."

"Twila and Elsie, why don't you go with Father?" Polly glanced back at the two youngest Dyes as they followed her through the door.

Elsie frowned and shook her head. "I want to go with you and Will."

"I'll go with them." Beth grabbed Twila's hand. "Come on, let's not be late."

Twila hesitated. "Why do I have to—"

Father opened his mouth, storm clouds forming on his face as ominous as those in the sky. "Twila, don't argue. It's time to go."

Polly breathed a sigh of relief as Twila obeyed. How much of the discussion had Lydia overheard? "I'll let you sit up front, George, since your legs are longer." Polly ran down the porch steps and squeezed into the backseat, followed by Elsie whose lower lip pooched out.

"I've never gotten to sit in the front seat with Will. It isn't fair."

"Elsie!" Polly's tone was uncharacteristically sharp. Why did everything have to be an argument? "Life isn't fair. You might as well learn that now. George's legs are longer than yours. No discussion."

Elsie folded her arms across her chest and harrumphed.

As thunder boomed and torrents of rain began, Polly closed her eyes and took deep breaths to calm herself. At least her annoyance with all the arguing had banished any sentimental thoughts that might have produced tears.

♠

After making sure George and Beth dried off and had everything they needed, Polly rejoined Will and headed for the gymnasium where chairs had been set up. After scanning the crowd, Polly spotted her father. Maggie and her family, as well as Ben and his girlfriend, had joined Father, Lydia and the girls. "There they are." She grabbed Will's hand. "Let's go before they dim the lights and we lose them."

They made quick work of reaching the correct row. Lydia

sat on her father's left, next to the empty chairs they'd saved for her and Will. Not giving herself time to dwell on this less than ideal arrangement, she turned right and hurried to sit beside Lydia just as the lights dimmed.

Tears welled up in her eyes as the solemn music of Pomp and Circumstance filled the auditorium. She craned her neck to see past Lydia as the processional began. If the twenty-one graduates walked in alphabetical order, Beth and George would be near the beginning. There they were.

Polly managed her emotions quite well throughout the rest of the ceremony until Beth marched across the platform to get her diploma. As she shook the hand of Harry Means, President of the school board, a sob rose in Polly's throat. *Mother, if only you could be here.* Lydia's head whipped around. Had she said those words aloud?

Chapter 32

Bob basked in the rare treat of having all his children except Robert in the same place. Robert hadn't been able to make the trip from Akron. Two more of their children were fulfilling Margaret's dream of completing their education. All was right with the world. Even as he reveled in this blessing, Lydia stiffened beside him.

He glanced at her. Difficult to read her expression in the dim light, but he sensed trouble in her ramrod posture. Polly, on the other side of his wife, had one hand clamped over her mouth. That couldn't be good. What had she said? His eldest daughter's impulsive tongue and Lydia's super-sensitivity weren't a good combination.

Turning back to the stage, he sighed. Distracted by the drama playing out beside him, he'd missed seeing George get his diploma. *Oh, Margaret, I miss you.* He thought getting married would ease his loneliness and the void he'd experienced since his wife had died ten years ago. If anything, it had caused him to miss her more. Being married to Lydia made him realize what a treasure Margaret had been.

As soon as the last amen was said and the lights came on, Lydia turned to him. "I want you to take me home."

"But we're having a celebration at my house afterward. Ben and Maggie will be there, too."

"I'm sure you can celebrate just fine without me." Lydia's nose, tilted high in the air, marred her attractive features.

It never helped to try to find out why she was upset but Bob couldn't resist. "Are you sick, Lydia?"

She huffed and turned her back, her answer muffled.

"I couldn't hear you. What did you say?"

Facing him, she spat the words as though ridding herself of a bad taste. "I said, 'I'm sick of your family.'"

Bob rubbed his forehead. So much for his plans to introduce Lydia to his son, Ben, who operated a butcher shop and a garage in Conneautville. Bob hadn't even met Ben's girl friend yet. What a great first impression this would make.

♠

Polly slid out of the back seat of Will's car, thankful the rain had stopped. Despite her determination not to give in to Elsie's pouting, she had allowed her to ride home in the front seat with Will. Polly sprinted up the steps with her husband close behind. They needed to finish preparing for the celebration.

"Slow down, Lass. I'll help set out the refreshments. No one will go hungry while they wait."

She chuckled and slowed her pace, smoothing her hand over her hair and the pale green dress she'd chosen to wear tonight. "I guess you're right. It took longer to greet the graduates than I expected. Maybe we've kept everyone waiting." Opening the front door, she glanced behind Will at the row of cars parked beside Broad Street. "I don't see Father's car anywhere."

Twila pulled the door open further from the inside. "He left Beth and me off and took Lydia home, said she wasn't feeling well."

Polly's hand went to her mouth as she stopped in the doorway and glanced back at Will. "Oh no, she must have heard what I said."

He guided her gently into the living room and spoke in an undertone. "We'll talk about it later, Lass. We've a houseful of people to consider."

As though awakening from a bad dream, Polly's gaze roved over the folks seated around the living room and the dining room table. Her mouth formed an O before she forced a smile. "Sorry to be slow getting here. Thank you for coming. We'll have the refreshments out in a minute."

Ben and his pretty fiancé joined them in the kitchen. "What can we do to help?"

Her oldest brother was as sweet as ever. Polly tied on a frilly dark green apron, and handed her brother the large chocolate cake with maple syrup icing she'd spent most of the day making. "You and Delores can carry the cake into the living room."

"Will, here's a stack of cake plates and forks you can take in. I'll start water for coffee."

"What can I do?" Twila's luminous brown eyes begged to help.

"You can carry in the sugar and cream. Thank you for asking." She gave Twila a quick hug.

Maggie stuck her head into the kitchen just then, her chubby eighteen-month-old daughter chewing her fist. "I'd offer to help but I think Leah and I would do more harm than good."

"Thanks. Everything's under control." Polly tickled Leah under her double chin and kissed her round cheek. Leah giggled. "Does Paul have Eugene?"

"Yes, we were in Mother's… ah, in the sitting room, trying to stay out of the way." Maggie hitched Leah up higher on her hip. "Do you still have that problem?"

"Calling it Mother's sitting room? I do things worse than that." Polly told Maggie what had popped out of her mouth at commencement.

"But there's nothing wrong with you wishing Mother could be at Beth and George's graduation." Maggie patted Polly's cheek.

"I thought things were getting better between Lydia and me but I guess the truth is, we've just stayed out of each other's way."

Chapter 33

A knock on the outer door drew Polly from the kitchen before Maggie could respond to her sister's observation about her relationship with Lydia. As Polly reached for the knob, the door flew open. Her best friend in the world stood in the doorway. With a cry of welcome, Polly threw herself on Savannah.

Savannah returned her hug, followed by a look that said, *Is everything all right?*

Mouthing a quick, "I'll tell you later," Polly pulled Garrett into the house. "Thank you for coming. I'm so glad to see you."

After handing their coats to Twila who had come for hugs, Savannah and Garrett followed Polly to the kitchen. "What can we do to help?"

Polly motioned to the large pot of coffee. "Garrett, you can take this to the living room table." She stacked two piles of cups and saucers on a tray and gave them to Savannah. "And you can take this."

After taking off her apron, Polly followed her friends. Father entered the house as she came into the living room. She gave him a despairing glance. Could he read her apology? He shed his coat into Twila's waiting arms, and then squeezed Polly's shoulder. His smiling eyes indicated he didn't blame her for Lydia's absence.

Breathing a sigh of relief, she turned and picked up the

knife to cut the cake.

♠

When the door closed behind the last guests, other than Savannah and Garrett whom Polly counted as family, she flopped onto the loveseat in the sitting room. Will had offered to help the girls wash the dishes and she didn't refuse.

Savannah followed Polly and dropped down beside her as Garrett pulled a chair closer to them and sat.

"It was a grand party, my friend." Savannah squeezed Polly's hand. "What had you so frantic when we first arrived?"

Polly pushed a tendril of hair behind her ear and sat up straight. "Tonight was the first time I'd been around Lydia since she and Father got married." She shared what happened at graduation. "She wouldn't come to the party."

"Are you sure that's the reason?" Savannah searched Polly's face.

"Pretty sure."

Father stuck his head in the doorway. "Is this a private party or can I join you?"

Polly motioned to him. "Come on in but maybe we should close the door. Sometimes Elsie and Twila have the ears of spies."

Father did as she asked, then drew up another chair. "Did something happen at commencement that I missed? I'm not blaming you, Florence. I'd just like to know."

Polly repeated her story. "It's all my fault, Father. I didn't mean to upset Lydia. The words just popped out of my mouth."

He shrugged. "What you were feeling was natural. I missed your mother too. She's the mother of my children, and I was sad that she couldn't see them graduate." He paused. "I think Margaret would have said Lydia reacts that way because of insecurity."

"We all miss our counselor, don't we?" Polly smiled at her father.

"We do. But even knowing what the problem might be doesn't help me fix it." Father threw up his hands.

Polly shook her head. "Me either, but enough about us. How's your mother, Garrett? I haven't made it to Bible study for a while."

"She's the same as always." Garrett's eyes turned warm whenever he spoke of his mother. "Maybe she could advise you about Lydia. Pa always said she could be a counselor."

"Thanks for the suggestion. I might ask her." Polly turned to Savannah. "What about Mrs. Greely? Is she still causing trouble?"

Garrett cleared his throat, drawing a glance from Savannah. "I'm sorry, Garrett. We need to tell somebody what's going on. Polly and her father won't say a word to anyone."

Polly's spine straightened, eyes blazing. "What now?"

After Savannah filled her in on the latest rumor from Dorothy, Polly shook her head. "How long ago did this happen?"

Savannah raised an eyebrow and met Garrett's eyes. "Maybe three months?"

"And nothing from Reverend Greely?"

"Nothing, thank God." Garrett blew out his breath and crossed his legs.

Polly hadn't finished. "Was Dorothy angry at you when she told you this?"

"I don't think so. I had just arrived at work. A week later she was mad at us." Savannah's forehead wrinkled. "Why do you ask?"

"Just wondering…" Polly pursed her lips. "Do you think Dorothy could be lying?"

Garrett looked at Savannah and shrugged. "She has an uncanny way of ferreting out what happens in Sandy Lake almost before it happens, so I tend to believe her. I guess time will tell."

Father cleared his throat. "I'm not the counselor Margaret was, but maybe you should talk to Reverend Greely instead of continually worrying about it."

"It would be nice to have one less thing preying on my mind." Garrett passed a hand over his eyes. "Although the thought of confronting the issue with Reverend Greely scares me."

Laying a hand on Garrett's shoulder, Father swiveled in his direction. "What else is weighing you down, young man?"

Garrett swallowed and smiled at his wife. "I guess we might as well air all our dirty laundry. God wants me to befriend Devon Black, my former boss, but I have yet to obey."

Chapter 34

A week after the graduation celebration, Bob walked down the steps toward his car. He had stopped in to see his children on his way home from work as was his practice. Not that he liked visiting while covered with coal dust. He stared at his grimy hands as he turned the crank.

He usually stopped to visit his children after work so he wouldn't have to leave Lydia to visit them after he cleaned up. It didn't matter now since she was staying at her brother's. How much longer would this go on?

He got into the car, berating himself for his lack of patience. Lydia's mother was dying. What sort of person was he that he would begrudge her these days with her mother? He drove down the road, turned into their driveway. His eyes widened at the light in the kitchen window. Could it be that Lydia had come home to cook dinner for him?

The fragrance of roast beef reached his nostrils when he entered the house. Lydia appeared in the kitchen doorway. "Are you glad to see me?" She raised an eyebrow flirtatiously.

Bob swallowed his surprise and hustled over to kiss her. "Let me get cleaned up. I'll be right back."

Maybe washing away the day's accumulation of coal dust would shut out the cynical voices expressing doubt about how long this good mood would last. He stripped and scrubbed vigorously. Lydia hated any lingering coal dust or odors from the mine.

Satisfied that he was clean, he returned to the kitchen and hugged his wife. "I've missed you. How's your mother doing?"

"She's better today. I believe the danger is past." Lydia went back to cutting the beef.

"What does the Doc say?" When Dr. Cooley talked to the family last week, Bob hadn't gotten the impression there was any chance of Janet getting well.

"Oh, you know how doctors are. They never want a person to get their hopes up, so they try to prepare you for the worst." Lydia handed him a Noritake China plate. "But I know she's better."

His wife's optimism set off warning bells. Somewhere he'd read or heard that patients sometimes rallied briefly when the end was near. "Are you going back to your brother's house tonight?"

Lydia shook her head. "It won't be necessary for me to be there at night anymore. Wouldn't you rather I stay here with you?" She reached around him to get her own plate, pressing herself against him in the process.

"Of course, but maybe we could visit your mother together this evening." He had a bad feeling this could be their last chance.

Lydia drew back and scowled. "I just got home. We can visit her tomorrow night."

♠

Regardless of how tired he was, Bob could not find a comfortable resting place. Lydia had been asleep for hours. What was wrong with him? As he turned over for the tenth time, the jangling of the telephone broke the stillness. It was Lydia's ring, three long shrill blasts. He rolled out of bed and headed for the stairs, Lydia stumbling along behind him.

When they reached the downstairs hall, Bob picked up the receiver. "Hello?"

Lydia's brother, James, replied, "Bob? It's Mother. She passed away a few minutes ago. I knew Lydia would want to know."

Before Bob could respond, Lydia grabbed his arm. "Who is it?"

"Just a minute, James." He put his hand over the receiver. "I'm so sorry, Lydia. Your mother…your mother, passed away."

Lydia wailed aloud. "No, no. It can't be. She was better." She grabbed the receiver. "Are you sure, James? Did Dr. Cooley say she's gone?"

Two seconds later, his wife tossed the receiver in the direction of the telephone and flew up the stairs. She called to Bob over her shoulder. "Dr. Cooley hasn't arrived yet. We need to hurry. Maybe James is mistaken."

He took the stairs two at a time, then slowed his pace. What would he do if he caught her? Reasoning with her had never worked. Why would this time be any different?

In their bedroom, Lydia flung clothes around, discarding everything she selected. He yanked a blue cotton shirt from a hook, a pair of socks and pants from a bureau drawer and dressed as fast as he could. His example seemed to spur Lydia to action as she began putting on some of the items she'd discarded.

In minutes, they dashed down the stairs, threw on their jackets, and left the house. Lydia grabbed a comb from her handbag and took a stab at fixing her hair while Bob cranked the car. It roared to life, shattering the stillness of the night.

He ran around to open Lydia's car door, and soon, they were off. Although the trip took only ten minutes, it seemed much longer. He made no attempt at conversation. What could he say?

Before the car came to a complete stop in front of James' house, Lydia jumped out and rushed to the house, sobbing noisily. Her brother met her, stopping her pell-mell rush with a hug. She wrestled to get free. "I have to talk to Mother."

James didn't release her but soothed her with gentle words. "It's too late. Mother is gone."

"I don't believe it." Lydia's sobs grew wilder as she escaped her brother's grip. She ran to her mother's downstair's bedroom, James and Bob close behind her.

Lydia knelt beside the bed, where her mother lay very still, and grabbed the hands folded on top of the coverlet. "Mother, speak to me. Mother, please." When there was no response, she collapsed to the floor, wailing. "I didn't even get to say good bye."

Chapter 35

When Doc Cooley's Model T pulled up in front of James' house, Lydia sprang to her feet and dashed into the bathroom. Bob's jaw dropped. By the time the doctor collected his bag, approached the house and knocked, she reappeared, having completely regained her composure.

She joined her brother at the door to greet Dr. Cooley. "We're so sorry to get you out in the middle of the night."

Lydia's appearance of self-control squashed Bob's hopes of obtaining a sedative from the doctor. Her ability to make lightning mood changes never ceased to amaze him.

When the doctor completed his examination, confirming Janet's death, Bob slipped his arm around Lydia. "I'm so sorry." She moved away without responding, and his arm slid to his side.

Dr. Cooley removed a death certificate from his bag, and Lydia immediately cleared a spot on the dresser for him to use as a desk. After filling it out and blowing on the ink, the doctor handed it to James. "Please accept my sympathy." He turned to include Lydia. "I know how much your mother will be missed."

"Thank you, doctor." A single tear trickled down Lydia's cheek. Bob extended a clean handkerchief toward her, but she swiped the tear with her fingers. With a baleful glance in Bob's direction, she added, "I didn't get to say good bye."

"Your mother knew you loved her and you'll see her again one day." Dr. Cooley's eyes were kind.

Lydia nodded and squeezed the doctor's hand. "Thank you again for coming."

When James and Dr. Cooley left the room, Lydia pulled a chair closer to her mother's bed and sat down.

Bob squatted beside her. "Can I get you anything, Lydia? A glass of water?"

She shook her head. "I think it would be best if you go home. James and I will have things we need to talk about. He can bring me home later."

A long sigh escaped Bob's lips as he left the house. Did Lydia's chilliness suggest he was somehow to blame for her absence when her mother died? He drove slowly to Sandy Lake, then pulled off in front of his house on Broad Street.

Would Florence be up yet? Maybe not on a Saturday. He couldn't face going back to Lydia's empty house, so he let himself in. Silence surrounded him. With a sigh, he sank down in Margaret's chair. He closed his eyes and leaned his head against the back of the chair, allowing the peace of the household to permeate his troubled soul.

"Father, are you all right?"

Florence's voice startled Bob. He sat up and rubbed his eyes. "I'm all right but Lydia…"

He paused. "Lydia's mother passed away during the night."

"I'm so sorry. I'm sure it's hard even though she expected it."

"Lydia thought her mother had taken a turn for the better yesterday, so she was very disappointed." He paused. "I think she blames me that she wasn't there when Janet died."

Florence sighed and bit her lip, as though restraining herself from speaking. "You look so tired, Father. Why don't you lie down in your room. It might do you good."

"Thank you, Florence. I think I'll do that."

♠

On Tuesday, Bob headed north of Sandy Lake. The funeral would be held at James' house at one o'clock. It would be a small family affair.

Except for a trip home to pick up clothes, Lydia had stayed at her brother's house since Saturday. She evaded his repeated efforts to talk to her, commissioning her brother to relay information about the service. In her absence, Bob spent most of his time with his children, taking comfort from their delight in having him there.

He sighed. Which Lydia would he encounter today? Married just over three months and already it seemed like a lifetime.

Lydia's four sisters had arrived, and she met him at the door with her happily married façade firmly in place. She planted a kiss on his lips and tucked her hand in the crook of his arm as she escorted him to meet her sister from Versailles.

"Ida, this is my wonderful husband, Bob."

"Oh, you mean the one who didn't invite us to the wedding?" Ida made a pretense of making a joke.

"Now, Ida, you know he had a good reason."

I had a good reason? It was her idea not to invite our families. Bob swallowed the bitterness that threatened to choke him. "It's nice to meet you, Ida." Did Lydia's sisters see through her brittle veneer? Or did it only ring false to him?

He walked to the open casket with his wife to pay their respects. Staring at Janet's face before finding a seat with her family, he felt nothing. Numbness had set in. It was his only defense against living with someone whose moods were as changeable as the weather in April. How could he allow himself to have feelings for her that would, in the next moment, be shot down?

Reverend Frampton from the Methodist Episcopal Church conducted the informal service. He shared words of praise for Janet Dodds as an honest, industrious woman, and a devoted wife and mother. Bob hadn't known her well and found himself pondering whether the words were true or if this was another case of a person being elevated to sainthood after they died.

What a dreadful thing to think at someone's funeral. Margaret would have chastised him for such unworthy thoughts. His disillusionment with Lydia was coloring his view of the world.

Chapter 36

"Aunt Flo invited me to go to Conneaut Lake after church Sunday with some of their family and friends." Beth's cheeks were flushed and her blue eyes bright.

Polly smiled as she continued to peel apples. This might be the last outing Beth would have with her favorite aunt's family. "That's nice. I hope you'll have good weather."

"Me too. Auntie said we'll stop at the Dye cottage on the way home for a rest and refreshments."

"Why didn't Aunt Flo invite me?" Elsie never missed an opportunity to feel slighted.

"Her daughters are nearer Beth's age than yours, so Beth was the obvious choice." How easily Elsie's pretty mouth turned into a pout. "This might be her last chance before she leaves for nurses' training."

Elsie stared into space, then turned her gaze on Polly. "Is Will coming home for supper?"

Polly breathed a sigh of relief. "He'll be here soon. Why don't you and Beth set the table?"

"What about Twi—"

"It's probably my turn." Beth cut in before Elsie could whine about another injustice. "Come on. You take the plates and I'll take the tumblers, see who gets done first."

Polly would miss the peacemaker when she went to

Pittsburgh for nurses' training. Pittsburgh was only a couple hours away, but too far for Beth to come home easily. And even when she did, things would be different with Will and Polly in their own home.

What if you're not yet? Polly's heart thudded as it always did when she pictured living here with Father and Lydia. Lydia who had just lost her mother.

A twinge of sympathy surprised Polly. It was hard to lose one's mother no matter how young or old a person might be. Father said Lydia had been very depressed since her mother's funeral.

Maybe she should take this pie to Lydia and Father when it was finished. A smile crept to her lips. If her family discovered the pie wasn't for them, howls of protest would ensue. But if her mother knew, she would be pleased.

The fragrance of the apple dumplings baking for supper reminded her to check on them. Heat rolled out as she opened the oven door and pricked a dumpling with a sharp fork. Perfect. Her mouth watered. The dumplings should keep her family from being too disappointed. Tomato soup and apple dumplings. It was an unusual meal but it was nice to have something different for a change.

A few backfires alerted her that Will had arrived. She hurried to greet him. Almost seven months since they'd said "I do," and her heart still beat a happy rhythm when he came home. The summer months provided welcome relief from fretting about his dangerous job in the winter.

"Hello, Lass." Will seldom walked if he could run and he took the steps two at a time. His eyes lit as they always did when he caught his first glimpse of her. She swung the screen door wide, unable to wait to be in his arms. Her feet left the floor as he lifted her in a giant hug.

Elsie darted into the living room. "Will, you're here." Even as grown up as Elsie pretended to be at almost fourteen, Will's arrival always brought a response.

"I am, Lassie." Will set Polly down, patted Elsie's

shoulder and sniffed. "Somethin' smells grand. Someone's been makin' somethin' tasty."

"Apple dumplings." Polly headed back to the kitchen. "Does your mam make apple dumplings?"

"Aye, that she does." Will smacked his lips. "Delicious, they are, but no better'n yours, I'll wager."

He followed her into the kitchen where she removed the dumplings from the oven and set them on a wire rack to cool.

"What else are ya makin'?" He nodded toward the peeled apples waiting in cold water.

"A pie to take to Lydia and Father. He says she's very depressed."

A smile covered Will's face. "That's good of ya, Lass. Are ya feelin' more kindly toward her of late?"

Polly shrugged. "I know what it's like to lose one's mother."

He nodded. "That ya do."

She gave the pot of tomato soup a few stirs with a wooden spoon. Almost done. Turning to Will, she licked her lips. Time to ask him the question he kept avoiding. "Will, have you asked Mr. Sullivan when our house will be ready?"

He bit his lip, the remnants of his smile fading. "I did, Lass, but ya won't like the answer."

"What did he say?" Polly held the spoon in midair.

"He said it won't be ready until some time in the fall."

"But Will…"

"The men are workin' as fast as they can, Lass. Some of his crew are buildin' Mr. Slater's house."

Polly said nothing but her shoulders drooped as she gave the soup one more stir and transferred the kettle to a red-checkered potholder.

Will put his hands on her shoulders and turned her toward him. "Why don't you ask your da if they can wait to move until our house is finished? No mention has been made of a moving date anyway, what with Lydia's mother passin' an all."

"I'm afraid if I bring it up, Lydia will decide she wants to

move right away just out of spite."
"What was it you told me your mam always used to say? Love always believes the best?"

Chapter 37

"Where are you going with that apple pie?" George bounded to his feet when Polly came through the living room, headed toward the door.

"I'm taking it down the street. Maybe it will help cheer Lydia up." Polly smiled at her tall, handsome brother who would be leaving so soon.

"How about using it to cheer me up?" He grinned and tugged on a fly-away strand of her hair, then pretended to wipe a tear from his eye.

She elbowed him as best she could without dropping the pie. "I don't think you need any cheering up. What are you so happy about, by the way?"

"Just excited about starting my new job. Moving to Sharon." He dropped back into Mother's gray chair.

"Do you know when you'll begin work?"

"Wednesday, July sixth. The boarding house has furnished rooms, so I won't need to take much." He stretched his long legs. "Father will drive me over the day before."

"You said you'll be working for the Allen A Company. Have they told you what you'll be doing?"

"The Company is opening branch offices all over the Country. I'll travel around in the northeastern United States as a representative."

"Mother would be so proud of you." Polly leaned down and patted George's arm. "Allen A is a well-known company."

Will sauntered in from the kitchen where he'd been cleaning up after supper as he often did. "Dishes are done. Do you want me company to take the pie?"

Polly glanced at him. "No, I guess not. I won't be gone long." She stood on tiptoe and kissed his cheek.

As she stepped out on the porch, Polly drew in a long breath of fresh air. The fragrance of wild honeysuckle would soon fill the air.

Now that school was out, her times alone were few. It was always an adjustment. She loved her husband and her family but sometimes she just wanted to be by herself.

She was in no hurry and meandered at a snail's pace, clutching her pie. What sort of reception would she get from Lydia? Her stomach clenched. *Don't think about it. Just go.* Should she bring up the subject of a moving date? Her stomach clenched again, and her footsteps slowed even more. Why hadn't she brought Will along for backup? Why had she come at all?

Turning back, she looked longingly at the place they'd called home for more than ten years. If she went back, she'd have to explain why she still had the pie. Forcing herself to face forward, she headed for Lydia's house, feet dragging, heart pounding. A light glowed in the window.

Polly walked up to the door and reached for the knob, then paused. Her father lived here but she could never go in without knocking. She rapped twice.

The door swung open and Lydia stood before her, hair uncombed, clothed in a wrinkled housecoat. Polly gasped, then quickly covered her mouth. No words came from her lips.

"Polly." Lydia opened the screen door. "Did you need to speak to your father?"

"Actually," Polly took a tentative step forward, "I wanted to talk to you."

Lydia's brows rose but she motioned for Polly to come in. Father, who had gotten to his feet in the living room, sat back down.

Polly held out the pie. "I wanted to give you this and say

how sorry I am about your mother." She swallowed and licked her dry lips. "I remember how sad I was when my mother died."

Her stepmother took the pie, her face puzzled. "Thank you, Polly. I'm surprised that you..." Her voice trailed off. "Well, I know you weren't too happy about your father marrying me so..." She was having trouble finishing a sentence.

"I'm sorry we haven't gotten off to a very good start." Polly touched Lydia's arm. "Maybe we could begin again."

Lydia nodded and spoke to Father, who was fiddling with a radio. "Bob, why don't you come have a piece of the pie Polly brought us."

A smile broke out across Father's face as he stood and walked with them to the dining room. "That sounds wonderful. Thanks, Florence."

"You two have a seat at the table and I'll get a knife and some plates." Lydia set the pie on the table. "Would you like some tea, Polly?"

"If it's not too much trouble."

Father sat at the head of the table and Polly sat at his right. As Lydia went to the kitchen, he patted Polly's hand and lowered his voice. "Thank you. She's been so depressed, I didn't know what to do."

Polly responded, keeping her voice low. "Mother would say the Holy Spirit prompted me to do it. I was scared to dea..." Polly's voice faded as Lydia returned.

"Here's a knife and the plates, Polly. Maybe you can start cutting while we wait for the water to heat." Lydia sank down on Father's left.

"Of course." Polly cut the pie in half, then cut three generous slices.

"I've never been much good at making pies." Lydia wrinkled her nose. "How did you learn?"

"My—" She stopped and glanced at Lydia.

"Your mother taught you, didn't she?" Lydia pulled in a deep breath. "I have to get used to you all talking about Margaret. She was good at so many things."

"I'm sure you have a lot of talents, too." Polly smiled across the table.

Father squeezed Lydia's hand. "She's good at lots of things."

Lydia shrugged, not looking convinced, then got to her feet to answer the whistle of the tea kettle.

Polly hurried to change the subject. "So it looks like everything is set for Beth and George, both leaving the same day."

"I'll take Beth to the train station in Stoneboro where she'll board a train to Pittsburgh, and then take George to Sharon." Father shook his head. "I can't believe they're leaving so soon. Maybe we could have a farewell fourth of July picnic for them."

As Lydia entered, carrying a tray with three cups of tea, Polly nodded. "That's a great idea."

When Lydia handed her a cup of tea, she blew on it, then took a small sip. "Some time ago, you said you wanted to move to our house after George and Beth graduated so Lydia could sell or rent her house." She cleared her throat. "But the house Will and I are building won't be ready until fall. Would you mind waiting to move until our house is finished?"

Lydia stared at her, her gaze turning icy. "So that's what all this was about? Pretending to care about me and bringing us pie so we'd wait to move until you're ready?"

Chapter 38

Garrett took one last bite of fried chicken and laid down his fork. "Delicious as usual, my dear." He leaned across the small vase filled with fragrant roses to kiss Savannah's cheek.

She smiled and gathered the plates and silverware. "I'm glad you enjoyed it, Love. How are you feeling about talking to Reverend Greely this evening?"

Garrett's face sobered as he got to his feet to help clear the table. "Scared. Maybe by tomorrow I'll be back to being an insurance agent full time."

"Are you serious?" Savannah glanced over her shoulder as she carried the dishes to the sink.

He shrugged. "I guess I just want to be prepared in case things don't go well. Maybe better to expect the worst."

"Polly, your mother and I will be praying for you." Savannah began rinsing plates.

Garrett squeezed her shoulder. "I know you will. Do you want me to take you to Bible study?"

"It's a beautiful evening so I'd rather walk. You can stop in later to give me a ride home."

♠

Polly and Savannah arrived at Mildred Young's at the same time. They hugged and walked up the porch steps together, admiring the lovely row of gladiolus under the kitchen window.

Before they could knock, Mildred appeared in the doorway, beaming, dressed in a checkered-blue housedress.

"Come in, come in. You are a sight for sore eyes, Polly. How I've missed you."

The warmth of Mildred's love settled over Polly as Garrett's mother hugged them, and they found their usual places around the table. Why couldn't her stepmother be like this woman?

Mildred bustled around pouring iced tea in tall amber-colored glasses. When they were all settled, she smiled at the younger women. "Is there anything special you'd like to talk or pray about this evening?"

Savannah and Polly looked at each other. "You go first, Polly. Fill Mother in on the latest in your stepmother saga."

Polly gave a deep sigh. "I'm sorry. Seems like last time I was here, we talked about my stepmother problems. You'd think we'd have figured things out by now."

"Don't apologize." Mildred clasped Polly's hand. "Just tell us what's happening that has upset you."

"All right." Polly straightened her posture and told Savannah and Mildred about her attempt to comfort Lydia with a pie and the subsequent misunderstanding. She leaned her elbows on the table and clasped her hands under her chin. "I give up. No matter how I try, Lydia always takes things the wrong way. It seems like she looks for things to get mad about."

Mildred's eyes were thoughtful. "Seems that way, doesn't it?"

"Father thinks Mother would say Lydia acts this way because she's insecure. Maybe so, but that doesn't solve the problem." Polly fixed Mildred with an imploring look.

The pleasant lady picked up her worn Bible. "I thought we'd look at two related Scriptures this evening. They might be relevant to your situation." She flipped open her Bible as Savannah and Polly opened theirs. "Let's look at Luke 6:32-36. Polly, would you read that?"

When Polly finished reading, she raised her eyes to meet Mildred's gaze. "So Jesus was saying if I only love people who love me, even sinners do that. But He wants me to love my enemies and do good to them, expecting nothing in return." She paused. "Did I get that right?"

"I believe you got it exactly right. Savannah, would you read the other verse, please. Romans 12:21."

Savannah nodded. "Be not overcome of evil but overcome evil with good." She looked up. "So don't let evil win. Keep doing good things instead."

Polly sighed. "So just giving a pie to Lydia one time isn't enough? Is that what you're saying?"

"Is that what you think Jesus is saying?" Mildred raised an eyebrow.

"I guess. But it seems like no matter what we do, Lydia isn't happy."

"No one can *make* someone else happy. Being happy is something we have to choose for ourselves. We don't do good things for our enemies to make them happy. We do it because it's what Jesus told us to do." Mildred tapped the worn pages of her Bible.

"Polly isn't the only one who has an enemy." Savannah glanced at her mother-in-law.

"Mrs. Greely?"

"Yes. Garrett made an appointment to talk to Reverend Greely about the situation tonight. I promised him we'd pray for him."

♠

Garrett pulled into the parking lot at the Jackson Center United Presbyterian Church just as Reverend Greely stepped out of his car. *Father…* It was the only prayer he could pray.

Reverend Greely waited for him and they walked to the church together. "It's good to see you, Garrett. I'm always glad for an opportunity to meet with you."

He doesn't sound angry. With a sideways glance at the older man, Garrett responded with a smile. "Thanks, Reverend Greely."

When they were seated in the classroom where Garrett had met with Reverend Caldwell for years, Reverend Greely bowed his head. "Let's have a word of prayer before we talk."

Father, I've sensed that something is troubling my friend. Give us wisdom as we talk and reveal yourself to us. Amen.

Garrett straightened as the head of the alliance of pastors lifted his head. "Tell me what's bothering you, Garrett. I'll do whatever I can to help."

He squirmed and stared at the table. Why had he thought this was a good idea? Maybe he'd stir up trouble by telling Reverend Greely about the rumor he'd heard. He cleared his throat.

"If something is troubling you, then it's worth sharing."

It almost seemed like Reverend Greely had read his mind. Garrett swallowed and met his gaze. "The truth is…I was told that you planned to fire me so that," Garrett's face reddened, "my wife wouldn't be a temptation to the men of the alliance of churches."

Reverend Greely's countenance darkened. "Who told you that?"

"The woman Savannah works with said it was your wife's plan."

The pastor seemed to grow three inches as he drew himself up in his chair. "My wife is not the head of this organization, I am." He leaned across the table. "Let me assure you, if I have a problem with you or your wife, you will be the first to know."

Chapter 39

Polly hummed as she peeled hardboiled eggs. A day of preparing devilled eggs, potato salad and egg salad for their picnic on Monday lay before her. Ben and Dorothy, Robert and his family, and of course, Maggie and hers would all come to bid farewell to George and Beth at the 4th of July picnic. It would be wonderful to have everyone together.

Almost everyone. She stopped humming. It remained to be seen whether or not Lydia would attend.

More than a week had passed since Polly's attempt to overcome evil with good. The note she'd sent apologizing for the misunderstanding had received no response.

She shrugged. Mildred said one couldn't control how people responded to one's efforts to make amends.

A knock on the front door interrupted her thoughts. Beth and George were upstairs finishing their packing but Will and the younger girls were playing a game in the sitting room. Maybe one of them would open the door.

Will stuck his head into the kitchen. "Lydia is here."

Polly didn't move. "What does she want?"

He shrugged. "She asked to talk to you."

Glancing down at her worn brown work dress, she wiped the sweat from her brow and blew several strands of hair out of her eyes. The hot, humid weather of late didn't do her hair any favors. She must look a sight.

"You look fine, Lass. Better come see what she's

a'needin.'"

With a sigh, Polly followed him into the living room where Lydia waited beside the door, wearing a crisply ironed frock, every hair in place. She certainly looked better than she had the last time Polly had seen her. Pasting a smile on her lips, Polly approached her. "Hello, Lydia. What can I do for you?"

Lydia shifted from one foot to the other. "Can I talk to you?" She glanced at Will. "Alone?"

With a quick nod, he went back to the sitting room while Polly motioned Lydia to follow her to the dining room. Polly hesitated before sitting down. Was this a social visit? "Please sit down. Can I get you a glass of cold mint tea?"

"No, no. Nothing for me, thanks." Lydia sank down on one of the oak dining room chairs across from Polly. "I wanted to thank you for your note. I'm… I'm…" Her voice dropped to almost a whisper. "I'm sorry I was so unkind to you. I'm not myself since Mother died."

Polly's eyebrows rose. Lydia had been difficult long before her mother passed away.

"I hope you can forgive me. There's no reason your father and I can't wait to move until your house is finished." Her voice dropped even lower. "I'm not really up to moving yet anyway."

Surprise stole Polly's breath. This was the last thing she'd expected. "Thank you, Lydia. Thank you. That's so kind of you. It would be such a help."

Lydia nodded, not quite meeting her eyes. What had brought about this sudden change of heart? Polly shook off the thought. "I hope you'll come to the picnic on Monday. Everyone in the family will be there."

"I'll come." Lydia hesitated. "I'd offer to bring something but it might not be up to your standards."

"Oh, everyone will bring something to share. Each family will bring sandwiches and one other dish. I'm making devilled eggs, potato salad and egg salad sandwiches." Polly smiled. "We'll set up tables and chairs outside and blankets on the ground for the children to sit on. It'll be fun."

Lydia chewed her lip and then stood. "Okay. I'll think of something." She started for the door.

Polly scrambled to her feet and followed. "Thank you for stopping, Lydia. I'll see you Monday."

Long after Lydia had disappeared, Polly stared after her, scratching her head.

♠

The 4th of July dawned hot and humid as many days had been throughout the month of June. In fact the newspaper had deemed it the strangest June in 35 years, with uncomfortably hot days and a prolonged drought. Only the rains of the last few days of June had saved a critical situation for the crops.

Polly yawned and glanced at the clock. Sleep had been scarce with the temperatures soaring close to 100 degrees and humidity so high it felt a dozen degrees warmer. She kissed Will's cheek, already warm before he was out of bed. She hoped he would sleep a bit longer while she got an early start on finishing picnic preparations.

She donned her thinnest cotton dress, added a flowered, pastel apron, and headed for the stairs, pausing to gaze fondly at the sleeping faces of George and Beth as she passed their open doors. Tonight would be their last night, at least for awhile, to sleep in this house where they'd spent half their lives.

The changes she'd known were coming had arrived. In a few months Polly would spend her last night in this house. Emotions she hadn't expected crashed over her like waves in the ocean. She always sensed her mother's presence in this house. Leaving would be almost like losing her all over again.

Chapter 40

The rest of the family began to arrive after breakfast dishes were done. Laughter and loud voices filled the house to overflowing. Polly soon made friends with Robert's son, Edward, and carried him around as she supervised the setting up of tables in the shaded area of the side yard. Everyone helped and Will often carried out instructions almost before they were out of her mouth.

As usual, she included Garrett and Savannah. They fit in like members of the family. Ever since Savannah lived with the Dyes after the boarding house burned, the bond between the two families was very strong.

When they arrived, Garrett clapped Will on the back as the two greeted each other while Savannah and Polly hugged. "Hey, I'll be going to the jail in Mercer every Sunday evening to hold a chapel service or a Bible study. If we can get you approved, would you want to go with me?"

"Sounds right interestin.' I might just take ya up on that." Will tapped his foot. "Mam might not be opposed to somethin' like that."

Polly smiled. "Maybe we can change our Monday evening Bible study to Sunday evening, then we could have our girls' night out while you boys have yours."

A huge smile almost split Will's face. "Then you could go with me to Mam's for dinner on Monday evenings. She'd be so pleased."

Polly's smile dimmed. "We'll have to check with Mildred first. Maybe Sunday evening isn't a good night for her."

The smile slid from Will's face. "Don't forget we need to go and join in me family's picnic some time this afternoon."

"Why didn't you tell me your family was having a picnic?" Polly's brows drew together. "This is the first time my family has been together for ages. And tomorrow George and Beth are leaving." Humidity had nothing to do with the heat that crept up Polly's neck.

Sensing the tension between Will and Polly, Garrett and Savannah moved on to greet Twila and Elsie in the sitting room.

"I'm sorry, Lass. I did tell ya. More than once. But I don't think ya ever heard."

Before Polly could answer, her father's car pulled up in front of the house. He and Lydia were the last to arrive. Had Father needed to convince his wife to keep her promise? A stabbing pain in Polly's temple warned of a headache to follow.

"I didn't know if she'd come." Her whisper was more to herself than to Will. Did he see the irony of it? Lydia wasn't thrilled about coming to their house and Polly wasn't excited about going to Will's family picnic. She pushed the discouraging thoughts aside and held the door open as Father and Lydia came up the steps.

"Ummm. That looks good." Polly smiled at Lydia, eying the luscious slices of watermelon heaped on a plate.

"Your father picked it. Hard to ruin watermelon."

Father patted Lydia's shoulder as they entered the house. "Don't be so hard on yourself. You're a good cook."

"I'll never be able to live up to Margaret's reputation." Lydia's lips turned down at the corners.

"Nobody's comparin' ya to Margaret." Will beamed at Lydia. "We just want ya to be yourself."

That sounded good but in this case, Polly wasn't sure it was true. Did they really want Lydia to be herself? Probably not the self they'd seen thus far. She pasted a smile on her face and reached for the tray. "Would you like me to take that? Father will want to introduce you to the rest of the family."

"All right. Better keep it covered so flies don't land on it. I'm always worried about malaria."

Malaria in Pennsylvania? Polly bit her lip just as Twila and Elsie entered the living room.

"Oh, here's Evie and Twila." Lydia's smile didn't quite reach her eyes.

"Elsie. My name is Elsie." There was no smile in Elsie's eyes and the look she gave her stepmother didn't bode well for their relationship.

Father drew Lydia's hand through the crook of his arm. "Let's go outside so you can meet the rest of the family."

Polly hurried ahead of them to the food table. The crisp, green and yellow checkered cloth she'd chosen covered it perfectly. A vase of daisies in the middle of the table contributed to the beauty. She didn't often take time for the small touches Mother had done so well. She eyed the tray of watermelon and her mouth watered. A clean tea towel spread over it would keep off the flies. Her lips quirked. She wouldn't want anyone to get malaria.

By the time Polly had arranged the table and Father had finished the introductions, Robert's wife had roped Lydia into a deep conversation. Mary hadn't been overly friendly with anyone else. The intent expressions on their faces created an uneasy sensation in her belly.

Stop borrowing trouble. Mother always used to say she had an overactive imagination. But what if she was right? What if Mary and Lydia were a bad combination?

Chapter 41

Polly lay in bed at Will's insistence that she stay there until a more civilized hour than his usual time to get up. In the quiet of the room, she could process all that happened the day before. So much love and laughter in spite of her misgivings about Lydia and Mary.

There had been a few rough spots like when George remarked sarcastically he was glad Lydia could attend their graduation party, or when Robert and his wife exchanged a few barbs, each blaming the other for their financial woes. Then there had been the moment Polly had discovered that Will expected her to attend the Reiser picnic while hosting her own.

Polly sighed. Had Will really told her about his family's picnic more than once? He never lied to her, so it must be true. Her heart still stung at the remarks Mrs. Reiser had made because they hadn't stayed for the entire picnic. "I guess we'll always come in second to Polly's family."

Will had tried to explain about the out-of-town family members and George and Beth leaving the next day. His words seemed to fall on deaf ears as far as his mother was concerned. It was hard to tell how the rest of the family felt about Polly. There seemed to be an unspoken rule to follow Mam's lead.

It was no use lying here with thoughts chasing around in her head. She sat up and reached for her journal and Chartreuse. Uncapping her fountain pen, she wrote, *July 5, 1921. Father, please help me in my relationship with Will's mother. I don't want to be like Lydia and cause trouble in the family I married into.*

She paused and stared at the sheet in front of her. *Since I can't get along with either my stepmother or my mother-in-law, maybe I'm to blame. Am I the problem? Mildred said if I only love those who love me, it's no credit to me. Neither of them seem to love me or even like me much.*

I don't think I'm very good at loving people who don't love me. Please show me how.

She capped her pen, replaced her journal and Chartreuse on the bedside table, and got out of bed. Time to fix breakfast for George and Beth one last time before they ventured out into the world. Mother would be so proud of them.

♠

Bob cranked his car and made the short drive up to his house. He hadn't invited Lydia to go along to the train station in Stoneboro or to Sharon. He doubted she wanted to go. Also, George had shown at the picnic yesterday that he hadn't completely accepted her—no use asking for trouble on George's last day.

He got out of his car and found Beth waiting at the door, packed suitcase beside her. She would make a wonderful nurse, no doubt about it. Was it really possible she was old enough to leave home?

Florence stood beside Beth and called the rest of the family. "Come on everyone. Time to say our goodbyes. No crying allowed."

George's footsteps pounded down the stairs. "Look at who's talking," he scoffed. "If anyone cries, it'll be you."

Florence didn't argue, just touched his cheek fondly. "You're not as hardhearted as you'd like us to think, little brother."

"Little brother? I'm bigger than you are." George pulled himself to his full height and looked down at the top of her head.

"Reminds me of the days you and Robert had contests to see who could look the tallest." Florence shook her head. "That was a long time ago."

One by one, Beth went around the circle giving hugs and whispering loving words. By the time it was her turn, Florence was blinking hard to clear her eyes of tears. "I'm going to miss you so much. But I won't complain about you leaving. You'll make a grand nurse—fulfilling the dream you've carried for so long."

Reaching to give Florence a long hug, Beth whispered in her ear, "Thank you just isn't enough, Polly. You've worked so hard to raise this family and I'm ever so grateful."

They both wiped tears as they separated.

Father picked up Beth's bag. "All right, here we come, World." His blue eyes twinkled. "I'll be back to pick you up, George, after the train leaves for Pittsburgh."

♠

When Bob returned, he didn't find George waiting by the door. No surprise there, so he spoke in a tone that could be heard all over the house. "Ready, George?"

On cue, all his remaining children gathered at the front door, waiting for another round of good-byes. Although George was seldom early, he was almost never late, and he put in an appearance just minutes after his sisters joined Bob.

"Do we have to do this again?" George raised an eyebrow. "Sharon isn't that far away. I can get home now and then."

Bob winked at Florence. "Maybe he's afraid he'll shed a tear or two if we give hugs."

"No, I'm not. Come on, let's get this over with." In spite of his disclaimers, George gave Twila, Elsie, and Florence adequate hugs.

"We'll miss you, little brother." Florence patted George's shoulder affectionately. "Try to stay out of trouble."

"You don't have to worry about me." George picked up his suitcase and opened the door. He hesitated, then glanced at Florence. "I'm not far away if you need me." The words were barely out of his mouth when he sprinted across the front porch.

Bob smiled at his eldest daughter. "He's growing up but a little embarrassed to show it."

The drive to Sharon was over all too quickly with light conversation and companionable silences. All too soon, he delivered George into the boarding house.

Glancing around the small room his son would call home, Bob turned to him. "Is there anything else you need before I go?"

"Not a thing. I've been saving my money from working at the garage, so I'm set until my first payday."

Aware that George no longer had to look up to make eye contact, Bob swallowed a lump in his throat and gave him a hearty slap on the back before he headed toward the stairs. He was going to miss his last remaining son. George's little sisters might deny it but they would miss him too.

Life was changing. Ben had shared the news that he'd be getting married later this year, though no date had been set.

Our family is growing up, Margaret. How I wish you were here to see the fine young men and women they've become.

An ache began in his chest as it always did when he thought of his wife. How he missed her. Her passing had been the biggest change, one from which he might never recover.

Chapter 42

Savannah sat on the loveseat in the living room, breathing in the fresh-washed air from the open window. The showers this afternoon hadn't lowered the above-normal temperatures much but the humidity had fallen. The fan Father Young had bought them also helped cool the air in the apartment.

Garrett was preparing his lesson for Bible study at the jail tonight. Will would accompany him for the first time. She knelt by the window, staring unseeingly down the street. Where had this restlessness come from?

Was it because Garrett had plans for the evening that didn't include her? Polly had hedged when Savannah asked if they should talk to her mother-in-law about changing their Bible study to Sunday evenings. Maybe because it would rob Polly of an excuse for not accompanying Will to his mother's house for dinner on Mondays.

Flopping down on a wing chair, she picked up Sarah's diary that she'd borrowed again from Polly. Maybe rereading it would be the spark she needed to ignite her relationship with the Lord. Stale and lifeless were the only adjectives that seemed to fit her spiritual condition these days.

Opening the small book at random, she glanced down at the page before her. *Only God could get me through the loss of a child.* She stared at the page, as tears trickled down her cheeks. In her case, she'd never had a child to lose. Which was more difficult—losing a child or never having a child?

Dr. Cooley's words echoed in her ears. "It appears too much damage has been done for Savannah ever to conceive."

As though someone had pulled back a curtain, the reason for her restlessness became apparent. She would be thirty years old this year and still her arms remained empty. They had talked of adopting now and then, but when Garrett began preaching, in addition to his day job, the idea had receded.

Would she ever hold a baby in her arms? One who would grow up to call her Mama? Or was she destined to go through life childless? Sarah might say *Only God could get me through the heartbreak of childlessness*, but did Savannah believe that was true?

A knock on the apartment door drew Savannah back to the present. Unusual for them to get unannounced company on Sunday afternoon. She sprinted across the living area and started down the stairs, calling, "Who's there?"

"Will Reiser. No hurry."

"Come on in." As Savannah reached for the knob, the door swung open.

Will's pleasant, smiling face and tall, lean frame appeared. He wore a pale blue, short-sleeved shirt and denim pants. "Savannah. It's nice to see ya."

"Nice to see you, too, Will. I thought Garrett planned to pick you up."

"He did, but I was thinkin' to save him a trip." Will followed her up the stairs.

"I'll tell Garrett you're here. He's in the study."

"I'm early. I can wait outside if you're busy."

Savannah laughed. "You won't wait outside in this heat. Come enjoy our new fan."

Just as she motioned for Will to sit down, Garrett came out.

"I thought I heard voices. How are you, Will?" Garrett and Will met halfway across the room with a hearty handshake.

"It's better than good that I am." Will's brown eyes sparkled. "Thank you for invitin' me to go with ya tonight."

"Does your mam know you're going?" Garrett had teased Will more than once for his concern about upsetting his mother by going to a Bible study.

"Nay. I haven't told her yet. No need worryin' her needlessly." He punched Garrett's arm. "It's lovin' it, ya are, to torment me about that."

"You know me well, old man." In spite of Will being only a few years older than Garrett, Garrett liked to rub it in at every opportunity. "Let's get on the road. I wouldn't mind being a few minutes early to introduce you to everyone."

♠

Garrett cranked his car and they were off. Conversation flowed easily even though it was the first time he and Will had been together without their wives. Will was the closest thing to a brother Garrett had.

"Mrs. Greely causin' ya any more trouble since ya met with the Reverend?"

"Not lately. We haven't been to their church in a while. That always seems to stir the pot." Garrett blew out a breath. "Maybe I shouldn't say yes when they ask me to preach there."

"Are ya allowed to say no if any of the alliance of churches ask?"

"If I have a good reason."

Will nodded and was silent a moment. "Have ya done anythin' about befriendin' your former employer?"

Garrett's head jerked up. "How did you know about that?"

"Polly said ya mentioned it after the graduation party."

A groan was Garrett's only answer and silence reigned. Then he glanced at Will. "How much do you know about my relationship with Devon Black?"

"I'm not knowin' much. Polly said he's a new believer and he stayed with your parents for awhile when his marriage broke up."

This evening wasn't going the way Garrett thought it would. Shouldn't he be the one helping Will grow spiritually?

Drumming the steering wheel for a few minutes, he looked at Will again. "I might as well tell you the whole thing."

By the time they got to the jail, Garrett had bared his soul—telling Will about Savannah's involvement with Devon, about the picture he'd seen on Devon's desk, and about his former boss's miraculous conversion. "Ma says Devon and his wife have reconciled and he's back home. I don't know how he's doing spiritually. I know the Lord wants me to befriend him but I can't bring myself to go back to his store. Too many memories."

Garrett turned off the car and looked into Will's compassionate brown eyes. "Maybe that was more than you wanted to know about my past."

"Not a'tall, my friend. Not a'tall." Will slapped Garrett's shoulder. "Why don't ya invite Devon to come along to Sunday evenings at the prison? Ya could obey the Lord without havin' to go back into the bad memories at the store."

"You're a genius, Will. Why didn't I think of that?"

"I'm glad I could help ya with your problem. Now maybe you can help me with mine."

"If I can. What is it, brother?"

"Tomorrow is the Reiser Labor Day picnic. How can I help Polly and mam get along?"

Chapter 43

Polly stared at the overcast skies when Will joined her at the empty breakfast table the next morning. Father had invited Twila and Elsie to spend the day with him and Lydia prior to going to Aunt Flo's Labor Day picnic.

Disappointment clogged her throat and made it difficult for Polly to swallow her bite of cereal and respond to Will's greeting. How she'd love to join them, but today would be about making amends for having missed Will telling her about the Reiser 4th of July picnic. It was the least she could do. Her attitude about having to leave her family picnic to attend his had left a lot to be desired. Today she wouldn't even mention the gathering at Aunt Flo's.

She sighed. She couldn't imagine herself going with Will to Mam's house every Monday evening until they'd developed a better relationship.

"You're awful quiet, Lass." Will touched her cheek. "Somethin' troublin' you?"

Pasting a smile on her face, she shook her head. "Not really. Still debating what to take to the picnic." To be honest, Lydia's hesitancy about bringing something to the Dye picnic became more understandable as she fretted about whether her offering would be up to Mam Reiser's standards.

"I'm sure whatever ya take will be fine." Will bit into the bread Polly had toasted, then layered with butter and strawberry jam.

"But I haven't learned how to cook any Irish picnic foods."

"My family likes American picnic foods too." Will finished his cereal and took another bite of toast.

"Maybe I'll cut up the rest of the watermelon in the icebox and take that. Hard to go wrong with watermelon." Her lips quirked, hearing the echo of Lydia's words at the Dye picnic. "Does your family like watermelon?"

"That they do. Me thinks it'll be a hit."

Polly gathered their dishes and stood. Will sprang to his feet and reached around the dishes between them to put his hands on her shoulders. "Slow down, Lass. It's not often we have the house to ourselves. You scooted out of bed so fast this mornin,' I missed gettin' a kiss."

"I'm sorry, Love." Polly emptied her arms and put them around her husband. He pulled her in tighter, then kissed her upturned lips until she was breathless.

"Promise me somethin,' Lass."

"Anything."

"Promise me you'll love me always no matter how me mam rubs ya the wrong way."

"Oh Will, I'm sorry your mam and I can't seem to get along. I've been praying about it." Polly pressed her cheek against his. "I'm asking the Lord to help me love her even though she doesn't seem to love me."

♠

The Reiser picnic wouldn't start until mid-afternoon, so Will and Polly enjoyed a leisurely morning together.

Will allowed himself to smile and bask in the knowledge that before too many weeks passed, they'd move into their bungalow in Stoneboro. Mr. Sullivan had made good progress on their new home.

"Want to stop and see our house on the way to the picnic?" Will picked up the tray of watermelon.

"Oh yes, let's do that." Polly clapped twice, her eyes gleaming.

Will prayed silently as they headed for the car. *Lord, please prepare me mam's heart and Polly's for livin' in the same town. I don't know what I'll do if movin' to Stoneboro makes things worse.*

He parked in the shade in their new driveway, and Polly leaped out, not waiting for him to open her door. She raced to the front porch, then paused for Will to catch up. "Where are the workmen?"

"It's a holiday, Lass. You can't expect them to work on a holiday."

Polly bit her lip. "I guess."

Now that the house was taking shape, his wife had trouble controlling her impatience. They walked hand in hand from room to room, noting the progress since their last visit.

"It won't be long now." Will pulled her close and kissed her. "Nice not to have to worry about offendin' the workmen." He rested his cheek on her hair.

All too soon, Polly pulled away and squinted at her watch. "We'd better hurry. We don't want to be late."

The worry in her voice tugged at his emotions. He had to admit Polly couldn't seem to do anything right in Mam's eyes. No wonder she didn't like going there and was on edge every minute. *God please...*

"All right, come along then." He kissed the tip of her nose and headed for the front door.

On the short trip to Chestnut Street a few blocks away, Polly's tension was evident in her straight spine and folded arms. They pulled in front of the house just as his youngest nieces arrived from across the street. Dorabell, Frances, and Ruthie yanked open his car door.

Without waiting for him to get out of the car, Dorabell reached for his hand. "Uncle Will, we've missed ya."

Ruthie jumped up and down. "When are you gonna move to Stoneboro?"

"As soon as our house is finished. Then you'll be able to visit Aunt Polly and me."

Will stepped out of the car as his mother opened the front door. Polly got out too, balancing the tray of watermelon as she elbowed her door shut.

"Watermelon, ya brought watermelon." Frances beamed at the luscious fruit.

Mam sniffed. "I guess it would be too much to expect ya to actually cook or bake something for our picnic."

Chapter 44

Will clenched his jaw as Polly handed the tray to Mam and turned away, but not before a tear slipped down her cheek. This had to end. Instead of the usual embrace for his mother, he locked eyes with her. "We need to talk."

"Now what have I done?" Her chin lifted as it always did when she was offended.

Will was not to be sidetracked. Thanks to Polly's desire not to upset Mam by being late, they were the first adults to arrive. "Let's go inside." He opened the screen door and stepped back to let Mam enter. Polly had joined his nieces in a game of hopscotch on the new sidewalk in front of the house.

Following his mother, he prayed all the way to the kitchen. *Oh God, give me the right words. Don't let me make things worse.*

When Mam faced him, he gently took the tray and set it on the table. "Polly tries so hard to please ya, Mam. Why do ya find fault with everythin' she does?"

His mother pressed her lips together and stared at the floor, refusing to meet his eyes. She said nothing.

After a few seconds of silence, Will tilted her chin. "When are ya goin' to forgive Polly for bein' Protestant, Mam?"

Mam's jaw dropped. His own breath caught. He hadn't known what he was going to say until the words were out of his mouth.

"That's the problem, isn't it? Ya can't forgive her for not bein' Catholic."

Mam slumped heavily into a chair, her shoulders heaving. "I would na' care about her religion if she had na' married you. What if she tries to convert ya?"

Will squatted beside her. "So that's the problem. You're frightened that I'll leave the church?"

Mam wiped her eyes on her rust brown apron. "I could na' bear it if ya were to do that."

"I'm not trying to convert Will, Mam."

Will swiveled his head. When had Polly come in? He scooted back, making room for her.

"I promise you, that was never my intention." Polly crouched beside him. "Will and I don't always agree, but we respect each other's beliefs."

The front door slammed. "Anybody home?" The rest of the family was arriving.

Mam wiped her eyes again. "We're in the kitchen."

Their private time was over. There was no way of telling if they'd made things better or worse. He squeezed Polly's shoulder and eased into the living room as his brothers' wives, Nelly and Dora, carried in platters of food.

♠

Polly held her breath until, Nelly, who hadn't missed a thing, asked no questions. Polly's shoulders sank with relief.

Dora was right behind Nelly. "Shall we have the men set up tables outside for food, Mam?"

"That would be good." Mam got to her feet. "We won't all fit in here. I think the rain's goin' to hold off."

"I'll go tell Will." Polly jumped at the opportunity to get out of the kitchen. Would she ever fit in instead of standing awkwardly with nothing to do?

After passing the message along to Will and his brothers, she hesitated. Should she go to the kitchen where she was a fifth wheel or return to the hopscotch game? Remembering her commitment to love those who didn't love her, she stuck her head in the kitchen doorway. "Mam…" The word tasted foreign to her tongue but she persevered, louder the second time. "Mam, is there something you'd like me to do?"

Mam bit her lip. "Maybe you and the children can carry the plates and utensils to the tables when they're set up."

Polly nodded. She'd been given work even children could—no, she wouldn't let this bother her. "All right. I'll get the girls."

The hopscotch game was still in session, and Frances, not quite four, wasn't faring too well. Hopping on one foot was a challenge.

Putting out her hand, Polly smiled. "Want to come help me carry things to the tables in the yard, Frances? Dorabell and Ruthie, you can come, too, if you want."

Dorabell, two years older than six-year-old Ruthie, was intent on winning the competition. "Can we finish the game first?"

Polly smiled. "Sure, Frances and I can manage. Right, Frances?"

The little girl in her blue playsuit ran to Polly, her chubby legs churning. "I can help."

After assisting Frances with washing her hands, Polly put silverware in a basket to make it easier for her to carry. As she stood to collect a pile of plates, she noticed perhaps the first look of approval she'd ever received from Will's mother. Warmth flooded her cheeks. What had she done to garner such a look? Perhaps showing kindness to Mam's granddaughter?

When they'd finished the job, Polly joined Nelly and Dora in carrying out food. She included little Frances as much as possible, letting her tote anything small—a hot pad, salt and pepper shakers. Meanwhile Mam put the finishing touches on a few of the foods still on the stove. Tantalizing aromas wafted to Polly's nostrils.

"Whatever you're making smells wonderful, Mam." The screen door slammed behind Polly as she made one more trip to the kitchen.

"I hope…" Will's mother stopped, swallowed and began again. "Thank you, Polly. I hope you'll find it tasty. I know our food might be strange to you."

"You'll have to teach me to make some of Will's favorite dishes."

For a minute, an emotion flickered in Mam's eyes that Polly couldn't identify. The warmth she'd sensed earlier was gone and the walls were back in place.

Chapter 45

Will whistled as he clocked out early and headed for the parking lot. He loved surprising his beloved wife but was seldom able to pull it off. This time everything was in place.

Today was the last evening of the Stoneboro Fair. A year ago, he had proposed on an aeroplane ride the last day of the Fair. No aeroplane rides this year but there would be fireworks and Nicky's Atlantic City Steel Pier Orchestra performing with a soloist in the grandstand. Polly hadn't mentioned wanting to go but it didn't take a mind reader to figure it out. A perfect way to celebrate the anniversary of their engagement.

He cranked his car and got on his way to Sandy Lake. He'd told Polly they needed to move a few things to their new home tonight, so she'd keep the evening free. The big move would happen two days later on Saturday.

All the way home, he whistled and sang Bing Cosby and Rosemary Clooney's *Ain't We Got Fun.* He couldn't wait to see Polly's face.

♠

Polly hummed as she sliced her freshly baked bread. Twila and Elsie had gone to the Fair with Blanche and Billy Davis. She had the house to herself.

Today she'd done some packing and couldn't wait to start moving things into their little brown bungalow. Father said he and Lydia were also packing. He seemed eager to have Twila and Elsie with him again. Determined to keep a positive attitude,

Polly hadn't allowed herself to dwell on how much she would miss the girls. They could come visit often and life would be good.

Bread stashed in the bread box, Polly picked up the broom to sweep the kitchen. Lydia had been as good as her word and hadn't pushed Polly to move before she was ready. They'd seen little of each other since the 4th of July party, and a peaceful atmosphere prevailed. Her father's demeanor seemed best described as a forced cheerfulness when he came to visit.

What would happen when her father and Lydia added Twila and Elsie to what already seemed an uneasy mix? *Stop it, Polly*. She'd promised herself not to focus on those things. *Be anxious in nothing, be anxious in nothing...* One of mother's favorite verses, and now also a favorite of hers.

A car pulled off in front of the house. Who could it be? Will shouldn't be home for several hours. Had Blanche brought the girls home early?

She headed for the front door, broom in hand, as Will ran up the porch steps. "Will, what are you doing here? Aren't you supposed to be working?"

He opened the screen door and swept her off her feet, broom and all, guiding her in a little jig, her feet resting on his. "Do you know what today is?"

Polly stepped back and her brows drew together. "You mean what holiday?"

"Well, not exactly, although it's so important, perhaps it will be declared a holiday." He chuckled.

Lower lip pulled between her teeth, Polly peered at the colorful Mercer County State Bank calendar on the living room wall. September 29. Nothing to indicate a special day.

"Ah, Lassie, you've forgotten so soon? 'Tis the one-year-anniversary of our engagement, the day ya made me the happiest man alive."

"You are undoubtedly the most romantic man alive, that's for sure." Polly moved back into Will's arms and snuggled there. "That's why you're home early?"

"Indeed it is." Will smoothed strands of her fly-away hair that often came loose when she swept. "There are no aeroplanes this year but lots of other fun to be had at the Fair. You'll love the fireworks and the orchestra and soloist come all the way from Atlantic City."

"Just being there with you will be the best treat of all." Polly stood on tiptoe to press her cheek against his.

He turned his head to find her lips, pulling her so close that her heart thudded against his chest. Giving her one more gentle kiss, he smiled into her eyes. "Ya always look good to me, but I'm thinkin' ya might want to change your clothes."

She glanced down at her faded green work dress and giggled. "I'd say so."

Will clasped her hand. "I'd better go with ya in case ya need any help." He nuzzled her neck. "We have plenty of time before the main festivities begin at the Fair."

♠

The night was every bit as magical as Will had anticipated with perfect weather, despite showers expected later. They found a parking space behind the grandstand where the Stoneboro Fair Association had cut down trees to provide needed space for the ever-increasing number of cars each year.

Polly's face glowed as she clung to his arm. They walked around observing other improvements the Fair Association had made. The old dining and merchants' buildings and all the check rooms had been torn down and replaced by one huge hall made of vitrified tile. In the basement of that new building were the check rooms, as well as an immense dining room, touted to be "one of the most sanitary and modern in the country." On the main floor was an exhibition hall over twenty feet high.

The farmers' exhibition hall had also been demolished and replaced by a T-Shaped building capable of housing two hundred cattle. The judging arena in the center could seat three thousand people.

"Do you suppose this is the most modern facility of any Fair in the world?" Polly turned her head from side to side, taking in the amazing arena. Her voice was almost lost amid the mooing of cows brought in from surrounding farms.

"Maybe so." Will guided her outside so he wouldn't have to shout. "I believe their motto is 'The Oldest and Best.'" Clasping her hand more tightly, Will steered Polly away from the festivities.

"Where are we going?"

He smiled into her eyes. "You'll see soon enough."

At first she glanced in all directions as he led her to an open field. Then a sparkle came into her eyes. Will bent his head to catch her soft words. "The field where the aeroplane rides were given."

"Aye, where you agreed to be my wife." He lifted her left hand and kissed the engagement ring he'd placed on her finger. "Are ya still happy with your decision, Lass? Even with the struggles with me mam?"

Polly lifted her face to his. "For better, for worse, for richer, for poorer, in sickness and in health, to love and to cherish…till death do us part."

When the last phrase slid from her lips, a shudder shook him, as though an icy hand had slid over his body. Her fingers slipped from his as he lost his grip on them.

He shook his head and took a deep breath. "Mam would probably say someone walked over me grave."

Chapter 46

The alarm clock jangled and Polly automatically quieted it. Why had they set the alarm for such an early hour? Surely it must be the middle of the night. Swallowing an enormous yawn, she reached for Will, as had become her habit, and breathed a sigh of contentment when she clasped his arm.

The emptiness when he slipped out quietly on his early days never failed to jar her, no matter how she tried to prepare herself the night before. This is what life would be like without Will. What was it he had said at the Fair? Someone had walked over his grave? She shuddered.

Usually she only wrestled with the dangers of Will's job during the winter months but this fall her fears had begun early.

"Mornin,' Lass." Will turned and slid his arms around her. "Movin' day, here at last."

Polly sat bolt upright, Will's arms still keeping her close. "That's why we set the alarm early, so we can move out and Father and Lydia can move in." She leaned over to kiss Will's cheek. "We'd better get up."

Will didn't release her, but turned his head so his lips found hers. "Tonight, Lass, tonight, we'll be in our own house."

"Tonight." A sensation, part excitement, part dread, gripped Polly. The little brown bungalow called her name, while the reality of leaving behind her girlhood home and her younger sisters could no longer be avoided.

She kissed Will once more, then swung her legs over the

edge of the bed.

♠

As Polly sliced bread for toast, tears stung her eyes. Her last morning to prepare breakfast for Twila and Elsie. They usually fended for themselves on Saturday morning but today was different. She and Will had already taken a few loads of clothing and bedclothes to Stoneboro, and the girls should be up soon.

She fried bacon, scrambled eggs and made toast, while Will and Uncle Jim hauled a load of furniture to Stoneboro in her uncle's wagon. Father had given them the sitting room loveseat and a few other items to make room for some of Lydia's belongings. Uncle Jim would help Father and Lydia bring their things after Will and Polly were finished.

Running footsteps pounded down the stairs as Polly carried food to the dining room.

Twila clomped in. "Polly, why didn't you wake us? We wanted to help you move. Your bedroom is almost empty." Her mouth drooped.

Elsie looked none too happy as she followed her sister into the room.

"You wouldn't have wanted to get up that early. We were up by five o'clock." Polly set a bowl of eggs on the table.

"Why did you start so early?" Elsie plopped into her chair.

"Because Father and Lydia want to move in today, so we need to move out to make room for them." Her heart twinged as she memorized their faces.

Stop it. You're only moving to Stoneboro. It's not like you can't see them every day if you want.

The outer door opened and Will and Uncle Jim entered with a flurry of cool air and talk.

"You sleepy heads finally out of bed?" Will loved to tease the girls and even Elsie received it with good grace.

Her sisters would miss Will, no doubt about it. He would miss them too. Polly sighed.

"Get washed up. Breakfast is ready." She went to the kitchen for the bacon and toast.

When everyone was seated with heads bowed, Polly swallowed the lump in her throat and then swallowed again before she could squeeze out the words of a prayer. "Thank you for our food, Heavenly Father, which you so generously provided. Help us all adjust to a new normal as Will and I move to Stoneboro and Father and Lydia move in here." She cleared her throat. "Amen."

A few backfires alerted them to a car's arrival before Lydia and Father entered the house. Polly stood to greet them, offering breakfast, determined to extend love. "There's plenty. Let's all eat together."

Father glanced at Lydia, then nodded. "That sounds good. We didn't take time to eat this morning."

Polly bustled to the kitchen, and grabbed plates, cups, and silverware. Putting the place settings in front of the newcomers, she concentrated on being friendly, refusing her bent toward trying to read Lydia's mind. Uncle Jim, Will and Father kept the conversation going and breakfast was soon over.

She enlisted Elsie and Twila's help to clean up and as usual, Will joined them. After the dishes were done and she had wiped the table for the third time, it became evident even to Polly that she was finding reasons to avoid the inevitable. She met Will's eyes and nodded. It was time to go.

Although Polly had always guided the farewells as each of the Dyes spread their wings to leave the nest, now that it was her turn, she had no words. Father joined her and Will at the front door and pulled them both into a hug. "We'll miss having you here. Thank you, Polly, for all you've done to make this house a home. I don't know what I'd have done without you."

A tear slid down Polly's cheek and a lump rose in her throat. She nodded and turned to Twila whose eyes glistened. "I don't know why you and Will have to leave. Lydia and Papa could sleep in his room." Her voice was hoarse, her words low.

Polly pulled her close. "It's time, Twila." She cleared her

throat. "I won't be far away."

Elsie had Will in a strangle-hold as though her life depended on not letting him go. His easy-going nature had a calming effect on her abrasive one. Polly gently pried Elsie's fingers apart so he could step away as Polly stepped closer. Tears ran down Elsie's cheeks.

"You can come visit us often, Elsie." Polly's emotions were under control as she rose to the occasion.

"I don't want to visit you. I want to live with you. You have room for Twila and me. Why can't we live at your house?"

Involuntarily, Polly's eyes rose to Lydia's face. Her stepmother's lips formed a rigid line as their eyes met.

Chapter 47

Garrett and Will pulled out of the parking lot behind Savannah and Garrett's apartment and headed for Mercer. It had been a huge blessing having Will with him for the past several weeks at the jail. Adding Devon tonight might be another matter.

He shelved that negative attitude and glanced at Will. "Polly still not ready to change the meeting night for their Bible study to Sundays?"

Will shook his head. "She says she doesn't want to give up her excuse for not goin' to Mam's for dinner on Monday evenin' until she and my mother are getting along better."

"Things still not good between them?"

"I had a talk with Mam at our Labor Day picnic. Polly said Mam acted a little kinder until Polly said she wanted to learn how to make my favorite dishes."

Garrett scowled. "My ma was happy to teach Savannah how to cook."

"Aye, but your ma still cooks for your da. Mam cooked for me for years after my father was gone. I didn't leave home until I was thirty-three." Will cleared his throat. "This might sound silly, but I think losin' me was sorta like losin' me da all over again."

"You may very well be right. And losing you to a non-Catholic didn't help."

Will sighed. "Mam admitted she was afraid Polly would try to convert me, so that's been part of the problem."

The drive to Mercer flew as he and Will continued their conversation. Garrett pulled into the driveway of Devon's home just a few blocks from his clothing store. He was so relieved he didn't need to go to the store.

As Garrett waited on Devon's front porch, his heart pounded. This needed to stop, he'd chosen to forgive the man and trust that his conversion was real.

"Jesus," Garrett whispered. "Jesus." As soon as he said His name, the Holy Spirit took him back in time. He stood in a small room at the jail awaiting the arrival of George Burns, another man he'd been unable to forgive. The moment George appeared and Garrett stretched out his hand, all anger, bitterness and animosity had drained away.

A load lifted from Garrett's chest. *Thank you, Lord.*

When Devon opened the door and stepped out, Garrett reached for his hand and shook it. "So glad you could join us today." To his astonishment, he found that he meant it.

♠

Savannah paced to the window and back several times, then collapsed onto the loveseat. This Sunday evening restlessness was becoming a weekly occurrence which she had not yet discussed with Garrett. Guilt plagued her. She should be able to handle him being away one evening a week. How could she let her weakness interfere with his ministry at the jail?

In addition, Polly had moved to Stoneboro yesterday and even though it was only two miles away, Savannah's sense of isolation increased. She couldn't walk to Stoneboro at this hour and the last train to Stoneboro had already left. Neither could she casually drop in at the Dyes now that Bob and Lydia lived there. No telling whether or not she would be welcome.

For the first time in years, Savannah allowed herself to think about her family in Georgia, the mother who had rejected her and the father who had never cared enough to override anything her mother decreed. Tears crept down her cheeks. She swiped them away but couldn't stop sobbing.

Father, I can't blame you for the loss of my family. I'm reaping the consequences of the bad choices I made years ago. I'm so sad and alone, but I know you've forgiven me even if they haven't.

She bolted upright. *Why am I sitting here crying and feeling sorry for myself when you've given me a family who love me? Garrett's parents have totally accepted me. I'm not limited to only going there on Monday evenings.*

Grabbing a light jacket, she ran down the stairs and out the door.

♠

When Garrett returned from the jail and walked into the apartment, he sensed its emptiness. Where was Savannah? Unlikely she'd have gone to visit Polly in Stoneboro. Even less likely she'd have gone to see Dorothy.

As he hesitated at the top of the stairs, tires crunched on gravel as a car pulled up outside their building, followed by Savannah's voice thanking someone and bidding them good night.

The door opened, and his voice came out harsher than he'd meant it to be. "Savannah, where have you been? I was worried about you."

She started up the stairs. "I'm sorry. I should have left a note. I went to visit your parents."

Garrett leaned down and kissed her cheek before she reached the top of the stairs.

"How was your evening? Did you pick up Mr. Black?" Savannah's cheeks still flushed when she mentioned Mr. Black, and she refused to call him by his first name.

Garrett drew her to the loveseat and settled beside her. "I did. I didn't want to. But while I waited for him on his porch, God reminded me of how He enabled me to forgive George Burns when I shook his hand."

"I remember." Savannah's eyes lit.

"So I greeted him with a handshake, and God did it again."

"Praise God." Savannah's shoulders sagged and she blew out a breath. "I don't know why God required this of you, but I'm glad He helped you forgive."

Garrett nodded. "Me too."

They sat in silence for a few minutes before Garrett spoke again. "Were you lonely tonight?"

"Restless, and I suppose lonely." Savannah shrugged. "Your mother says I need to tell you how I'm feeling…" Her voice trailed away.

He pulled back to better see her face. "How *are* you feeling?"

"After Dr. Cooley said I probably couldn't conceive, we talked about adopting. Then God called you to be an itinerant pastor and then chaplain at the jail, and your life became so busy." Savannah hesitated. "It seemed—selfish of me to bring up my longing for a child."

"Oh, my Love, I'm afraid I'm the one who's been selfish." Garrett drew her close again. "I should have been more sensitive to how you're feeling."

Savannah pulled away and picked at a loose thread on the hem of her deep blue skirt. "There's something else though. I'm afraid adoption agencies won't consider us as perspective parents when they find out about my past."

Chapter 48

Mildred Young put the tea kettle on to make hot water for tea. Savannah and Polly should be arriving soon for Bible study. Savannah would use her newly acquired driving skills to pick up Polly in Stoneboro since Will was away.

Her forehead puckered as she rehearsed details of Savannah's visit the previous evening. She could identify with her daughter-in-law's longing for a child because of the long years they'd waited for God to bless their home with a little one. She didn't admit to her daughter-in-law that she also longed for a grandchild.

Brakes squealing sent her bustling to open the door. Savannah hadn't quite perfected the art of making a smooth stop. Mildred's relationship with these young women was a huge gift since she'd never had a daughter. She hugged each of them as they entered her kitchen.

"Thank you for last night." Savannah spoke in a low voice, pressing her cheek to Mildred's.

"You're welcome, dear one." She patted Savannah's shoulder. "Did you talk to Garrett?"

Savannah nodded and headed for the table where Mildred teacups and sugar cookies waiting. "We can talk about it this evening. I don't have any secrets from Polly." She squeezed her friend's arm as she sat next to her.

A smile lit Polly's face. "You'd better not. What are we going to talk about?"

Mildred poured tea into their cups, then sat on the other side of Savannah who was sharing their conversation of the previous evening with Polly.

♠

As always, guilt nagged at Polly as Savannah shared her longing for a child. Although she would trust God's grace to be sufficient if He gave her and Will a child, she had no desire to go back to those days of interrupted sleep, diapers, and nonstop care that she'd experienced with Twila when her mother died. In truth, she'd already spent ten years raising a family. Not that Will's mother would approve of such thinking.

Shoving aside her guilt, she met Savannah's eyes. "So are you going to apply to an adoption agency? You and Garrett would be wonderful parents."

Savannah dropped her head and sighed, her voice muffled by the hand she raised to cover her mouth. "They'd find out about my past. How could we expect to be approved when that information became known?"

Silence followed Savannah's statement. Polly glanced at Mildred. Would she have a solution?

Mildred picked up her Bible. "When I face hopeless situations, I go to God's Word for a promise to claim." She flipped to the book of Psalms, then turned to the thirty-seventh chapter. Skimming down the page, she stopped at the fourth verse. *"Delight thyself in the Lord and He will give thee the desires of thy heart."*

"What does it mean to delight myself in the Lord?" Savannah's violet-blue eyes probed her mother-in-law's kind face.

"It means to make God your greatest treasure, to love Him above everything and everyone else. When we do that, our desires begin to line up with His and He can give us what we desire."

Polly drew a deep breath. "I need a promise to claim for my relationship with Will's mam. I know I should have gone to dinner with her tonight since Will is away, but to be honest, I'm afraid of her. She doesn't like me."

Mildred flipped to the book of Proverbs, wrinkled her forehead, then turned to the sixteen chapter, the seventh verse. *"When a man's ways please the Lord, He makes even his enemies to be at peace with him."* She smiled. "That's true for women too."

"How do I know if my ways please the Lord?" Polly chewed her lip.

"You ask Him and be willing to listen to what He has to say."

♠

The next day Polly walked through the quiet, empty house, trying to recapture the excitement of having their very own home. What was wrong with her?

Last week her enthusiasm had run high as she and Will arranged and then rearranged the furniture from her father and from the Sears and Roebuck catalogue. She'd been like a little girl playing house, experimenting with their combination gas, wood, and coal stove, reveling in their electric lights, and trying out their new mattress with Will. Her cheeks warmed. It had been like a second honeymoon.

While Will was at work, she'd kept busy sewing ruffled yellow curtains for the kitchen, spring green drapes with sprigs of yellow flowers for the living room, and restful pale blue curtains for the bedroom. She had finished unpacking yesterday after Will left on an extended three-day run.

The house was sparkling and, with no one to mess it up, there was nothing to do. The unnatural quiet was wearing on her nerves. Somehow this stillness was different from the quiet in the Dye household. There she had known Twila and Elsie would be home from school at the same time each school day.

Polly bit her lip. She missed her sisters. Will's family lived in this town, but she was hesitant to connect with them until her relationship with Will's mother became more friendly.

When a man's ways please the Lord, He makes even his enemies to be at peace with him. What did God think of her ways?

She stood and went into the bedroom to retrieve her journal and Chartreuse. Her intentions were good but writing in her journal seemed to come last in her list of priorities.

October 11, 1921 Father, I know you want me to love Will's mother even if she doesn't love me, and I've been trying. Even so, things aren't going well. I want to claim the promise Mildred gave me last night, but first I need to know if my ways please you.

Savannah's question from the night before echoed in her ears. *What does it mean to delight myself in the Lord?* And Mildred's answer, *"It means to make God your greatest treasure, to love Him above everything and everyone else."*

She picked up Chartreuse. *If I'm honest, Lord, Will is my greatest treasure. I love him more than anything or anyone. I don't know how to love someone I can't see more than a flesh and bones' person who treats me like a queen.* She nibbled the tip of her pen.

First, you ask me to love people who don't love me, then you ask me to love you more than I love the person who loves me most. If it's possible, Lord, please show me how.

Chapter 49

The jangling of the telephone in the stillness startled Polly, and Little Women slipped through her fingers as she leaped from the olive green davenport. Was she that desperate for someone to talk to? Only one more day until Will came home.

"Hello?"

Her father's voice came across the line. "Polly, I need to talk to you."

She chuckled. "I'm fine. How are you?"

Father didn't laugh. "I'm sorry to be so abrupt, but I really need to talk to you."

Polly sobered and gripped the telephone. "Okay, go ahead."

"Not on the party line. Can I come to your house?"

"Of course. I'll turn on the porch light and wait for you."

Polly hurried to the kitchen. Electricity had come to Sandy Lake and Stoneboro in time for Will to have their home wired when it was being built. She never tired of the miracle of having light at the flip of a switch.

This would be Father's first visit since their house was truly finished. Would he be impressed or would he be too worried to notice? If Polly were a betting woman, she'd bet this crisis had to do with Elsie or Lydia or both. She sighed. They were both difficult. Together, they might prove to be a catastrophe.

She set the tea kettle on the stove. Father might need a cup of strong tea.

The speed with which he arrived told Polly he hadn't wasted any time getting here. When she opened the door to welcome him, his face was drawn and pale. "Come in, Papa." The childhood name slipped from her lips, unnoticed by her father.

"Florence, I'm sorry to barge in on you like this." He sat on a kitchen chair without waiting to be asked or taking off his jacket.

"You're always welcome, Father. You know that. Would you like a cup of tea?" Polly turned toward the stove. Ordinarily he would have been interested in their new-fangled stove. Not tonight.

"No, no. Nothing for me."

Polly turned off the stove and sat in a chair across from him. "What happened, Father, to get you so upset?"

"Well, it's Elsie and Lydia." He swallowed. "Elsie makes no secret of the fact that she doesn't like Lydia and doesn't want to live with us."

"I'm sorry." Polly scrubbed her hands over her face. "I'm afraid I didn't do a very good job of teaching Elsie to be courteous."

Father waved away her comment. "If anyone's at fault, it's me. I probably should have taken a firmer hand when she was small."

"Elsie was so young when Mother passed away." Polly sighed. "It's hard to say how much she was affected by her death while unable to communicate her feelings."

"Maybe her harsh attitude is just her way of protecting herself from more hurt." Father stood and began pacing. "But Lydia is so sensitive and takes it all personally."

Polly stood and turned the stove back on. Father needed a cup of tea whether he realized it or not. Her gaze followed him as he paced. "What can I do to help?"

"I should never have married Lydia." The words burst from Father's lips. "But it's too late now. I don't know what to do."

Gazing into space, Polly was silent for a moment. "I have an idea. What if Elsie and Twila come here every day after school? You could pick them up after work. That way Lydia wouldn't be there alone with them." The teakettle whistled and Polly turned off the gas. "They could also stay with me when Will is away on extended runs and every other weekend."

"But that isn't fair to you, Florence. You and Will are still newly-weds who need your privacy."

"To be honest, I've been lonely and bored this week." Polly poured tea into two tea cups and handed one to Father. "I'd be happy for the company."

He blew on it and then took several long gulps. "All right, if you're sure, I'll talk to Lydia and the girls. If this doesn't work, I don't know what I'll do."

♠

After her father left, Polly took over the pacing while she prayed. *Heavenly Father, please give my father wisdom. This is so difficult. I don't understand why you allowed him to marry Lydia. Surely you knew it wasn't a good idea.*

An old proverb her mother used to quote tugged at her subconscious. "God gave us each a 'chooser' and we have to learn to use it." Perhaps she couldn't blame God for Father's choice. She picked up Little Women, then put it down. No use trying to read. Instead, she picked up the telephone and dialed Savannah's number. When her friend answered, she asked for prayers about her father's situation.

"I haven't been over since you're unpacked. Are you in the mood for company?"

"Absolutely. I'll put the tea kettle on."

♠

Savannah oohed and ahed as Polly took her on a guided tour of the cozy bungalow. "This is so nice, Polly. You must be so happy here."

"Actually, to be honest, I've been lonely since Will left."

Her friend gazed at her, a speculative look in her eye. "Maybe you'll change your mind about wanting a family."

Polly shook her head. "Being involved with my sisters is about all the family I need, unless God has other ideas. Speaking of families, what have you and Garrett decided to do about adoption?"

Savannah turned away. "I'm not ready to share my history with a caseworker yet, so for now, we're just going to pray."

Part 2

Chapter 50
April 14, 1922

Polly curled up in the cozy rocker, waiting for Twila and Elsie to come home from school. Life had settled into a pleasant routine since the girls had started coming to the little brown bungalow on an arranged schedule. She loved the rhythm of time alone with Will, time alone with her sisters, and time as a family.

Although there were ups and downs at the Dye residence on Broad Street, Father testified that an uneasy peace reigned most of the time.

Easter Sunday would be the true test. Everyone except Robert's family in Akron would come after church to celebrate Easter with Father and Lydia. He said it was Lydia's idea. Polly stilled the rocking chair and wrinkled her brow. She had a bad feeling about Sunday. Despite Polly's efforts to befriend Lydia since asking the Lord if her "ways" pleased Him, Lydia apparently hadn't connected with anyone except Robert's wife. Father said they exchanged occasional letters whose contents she never divulged.

Starting the chair rocking again, she tapped her fingers on the wooden arm. Why couldn't Lydia just leave well enough alone? Did she think if they all came for dinner, they'd magically become one big happy family? She began counting on her fingers. Maggie and Paul and their two children would come, of course, from just a few streets away. Ben would bring his lovely bride, Dorothy, from Conneautville, and Father planned to pick up George in Sharon and Beth from the train station in Stoneboro.

That made eight, plus Father, Lydia, Twila and Elsie and, of course, her and Will. Fourteen in all. Where would they all sit? But that wasn't her concern. For the first time, she would be a guest in her mother's house.

She planted her feet, stopping the rocker again. Was that the problem? Did her uneasiness stem from the fact that for the first time, Lydia would entertain the family in Mother's house? *Let it go, Polly. Let it go.*

Footsteps on the porch told her the girls had arrived. Twila, nearly always a few steps ahead of Elsie, came in first. She would be a teenager in a few months—so tall for her age and in the awkward, gangly stage.

Twila sniffed. "What's for dinner?"

Elsie pushed past her and huffed. "Don't you ever think of anything but food?" Almost two years older than her sister, Elsie was already every inch a lady, blonde hair beautifully styled.

"Sometimes." Twila's eyes were riveted on Polly, waiting for an answer.

"Meat loaf, boiled potatoes, corn, and applesauce. But we won't eat until Will gets home." Sometimes the girls ate with Will and Polly, sometimes with Father and Lydia, but they always ate here on the Friday night of their weekends in Stoneboro.

Twila plopped on the floor and leaned her head against Polly's knee, while Elsie sank down on the davenport and smoothed her teal green dress around her.

"Oh..." Twila lifted her head and sat up straight. "Did you know Lydia sold her little house at the corner of Mill and Lacock in Sandy Lake?"

Polly's jaw dropped and she glanced at Elsie for confirmation. "I didn't know she owned a house besides the one on Broad Street."

Elsie nodded. "She'd been renting it out since she moved into Rufus Wilds' house after he passed away. Father said she didn't want to spend the money to make the repairs the little house needed."

"I see. What about the house she and Father lived in?" Polly pleated the folds of her gingham cotton housedress.

"It's still empty, right?" Twila raised an eyebrow at Elsie.

"Far as I know." Elsie pulled a metal compact out of her pocket and checked her nose for shininess. Since the Supreme Court had ratified the women's right to vote in February, Elsie paid less and less attention to her father's concerns about makeup. "I'm hoping Lydia will decide to move back to her own house."

"Elsie!" Her sister's snide remark yanked Polly from her concentration on her compact. "What a thing to say."

Elsie snapped the makeup case shut and squinted her eyes at Polly. "Since I had no opportunity to vote on whether or not Father married Lydia, why should I pretend to be happy about it?"

If they survived Sunday without a major blowup, it would be a miracle.

♠

Polly basked in the joy of being surrounded by her family in church Sunday morning. In no hurry for Easter dinner, she dawdled as long as possible after the service, stopping to say hello to folks at every pew. Will, always popular with his ready smile, didn't complain. Most folks seemed to have forgotten he was Catholic.

Will's mother hadn't forgotten Polly was Presbyterian, of that she was sure, although their relationship was more congenial than it had once been. She and Savannah had switched their Bible study to Sunday evenings last month, and Polly had been accompanying Will to Monday evening dinners at Mam's house. Mam had even offered to teach Polly to make Shepherd's Pie if she wanted to come early this week.

She shook Reverend Lawrence's hand and headed for the car. *Are you pleased with my ways, Lord? I want so much to please you, so you can make even my enemies to be at peace with me. I want to live at peace with Lydia and Mam.*

The trip home was short, and before Polly was ready, they pulled into a parking space in front of Father's house. No more stalling. When Will opened the front door, a strong odor assaulted her nostrils—she couldn't call it a fragrance. She sniffed carefully as she stepped into the living room. Saurkraut. Lydia had made sauerkraut and pork for Easter dinner. Why hadn't Father warned her that every single one of his children hated sauerkraut?

"What is it, Lass?" Will's gaze honed in on her face.

Polly shuddered and spoke in a low voice. "We all *hate* sauerkraut."

Will's forehead crinkled. "But surely just for one day—"

"What is that awful smell?" George and Elsie entered the house together and spoke in unison as Lydia looked up from the beautifully set table.

The warmth in her blue eyes turned to ice as she whirled and ran out of the dining room.

Chapter 51

As Savannah and Garrett walked down the steps from the Deer Creek Church after the Easter service, a flash of red caught Savannah's eye. She twisted her head around. "Did you see that?"

Garrett turned his head in the same direction. "See what?"

Savannah frowned. "Something red, and it's not the first time. A few weeks ago when you preached here, I caught a glimpse of something when we left the building."

At the bottom of the stairs, Garrett paused and bit his lip. "Now that you mention it, the last few times we've been here, I've had a sense that someone moved things around in the basement."

"Like what?"

"Two chairs in one of the Sunday School rooms had been pulled away from the table to face each other. Some cushions kept in one of the pews for the elderly ladies were placed on the chairs like… Well, like someone had been sleeping there." Garrett raised an eyebrow, as though testing whether she believed him.

"That's odd. How could anyone get into the church?" Savannah turned and stared at the door behind them. "Isn't it kept locked?"

"I don't have a key, so I assume someone else comes back to lock it." Garrett gazed at the door, too. "But maybe not.

Some are of the opinion we have no right to lock God's house, that its doors should always be open."

"Really? That's an interesting idea." Savannah turned toward the car.

Garrett didn't move. "Tell you what. How about we walk to the car and you get into the driver's seat. I'll go stand behind one of the trees at the edge of the parking lot. You can drive away, and I'll watch to see if anyone shows up."

"All right." Savannah shrugged. "Where shall I go? And how long shall I wait before I come back?"

"There's a dirt lane about a mile down the road. Turn around there, and wait for about ten minutes." A grin took over Garrett's lips. "I have a hunch we might catch ourselves a tramp."

Alarm widened Savannah's eyes. "Are you sure you'll be safe? What if it's a dangerous person?"

"I'll stay out of sight until I see what we're dealing with."

♠

As Savannah drove away, Garrett positioned himself behind a tree that gave him a view of the two front doors of the church. It was an unusual arrangement with one door going into the basement and the other going into the vestibule. He stood quietly, scanning the front of the church and the woods on the other side.

Their car was barely out of sight when a miniature figure in a red, tattered jacket emerged from the woods and headed up the church steps. Surprise stole Garrett's breath. He was prepared for a tramp seeking shelter, but a child?

The red-haired boy looked in all directions. When Garrett stepped out from behind the tree, he dashed back down the stairs and headed for the woods.

Garrett charged after him. "Hold on. Hold on. I want to talk to you. I won't hurt you."

The boy obviously was taking no chances and he had lightning speed. But his short legs were no match for Garrett's long ones. When Garrett grabbed for his jacket, he tried to wriggle out of it, but didn't succeed.

Seeing that he couldn't escape, he burst into tears. "I won't go back. I won't! I won't! I won't!"

"There now. No one said anything about going back, did they?" Garrett grasped one of the boy's hands, trying to judge his age. "Come on. Let's have a talk, shall we?"

Maybe six years old, small for his age and much too thin.

As they perched on the church steps, Garrett kept a gentle hold on the child's hand lest he try to escape. "Now then, what's your name?"

The boy pressed his lips together in a stubborn line, then opened them long enough to speak. "If I tell ya, you'll try to make me go back."

Garrett drew a slow breath. "All right, I'll just call you Ronnie. How's that?"

Ronnie's lips twitched into something close to a smile, and he nodded.

"Why don't you tell me why you're living in the church?" Garrett peered at the boy. "That's what you're doing, isn't it?"

Just then Savannah drove back into the parking lot. At the first glimpse of the car, Ronnie leapt to his feet and might have gotten away if not for Garrett's tight grasp on his hand.

"That's my wife, Savannah. You don't need to be afraid. She loves children."

"I ain't a child." The young boy stretched as tall as possible.

A smile tugged at Garrett's lips. "Okay, she loves people of all ages. All right?"

Ronnie nodded as Savannah got out and hurried over to them, her eyes wide.

"Savannah, I'd like you to meet my new friend, Ronnie. He was about to tell me why he's living at the church, weren't you, Ronnie?"

Gritting his teeth, Ronnie stared back at them. "Because I ain't gonna steal for them no more. I don't care how much they beat me or refuse to give me food. I learned in Sunday School Jesus don't like stealing."

Garrett could barely maintain his calm demeanor and Savannah's jaw dropped. "You mean someone is forcing you to steal for them?" Her voice squeaked at the end.

Ronnie nodded. "They told me I could quit when I turned six 'cause I might get in big trouble since I'm not a little kid anymore." He straightened his spine again. "But they lied. I shoulda known I couldn't trust 'em."

"Where do your parents live?" Garrett turned to look up the road.

"Not my parents." When Garrett raised an eyebrow, he added, "My aunt and uncle, sorta."

"So where do your aunt and uncle live?"

Wrinkling his forehead and pressing his lips together again, Ronnie shook his head."I ain't gonna tell ya. If I tell ya, ya might try to make me go back."

Chapter 52

Garrett locked eyes with Savannah over the red-haired boy's head. What to do? If they left him here, he might find shelter somewhere else where they'd never find him. "What about your grandparents? Where do they live?"

"They died. That's what started all the trouble."

Another dead end. He telegraphed a mental SOS to Savannah. He was all out of ideas. No officials to contact out here in the sticks.

Savannah dropped down on the step on the other side of Ronnie. "Did you know today is Easter Sunday?"

He nodded, his expression softening. "My teacher said Easter Sunday is good news, and we should tell everyone Jesus is alive."

Easter dinner. Surely no one would fault them for not leaving this child here alone. Garrett stood, pulling Ronnie up with him. "Here's what I think. No one should be alone on this special day. Would you like to have Easter dinner with us? My ma always cooks enough for an army."

Ronnie's eyes lit, then dimmed. "I don't got no fancy clothes to wear for a special dinner, and I ain't had a bath fer some time."

"Ma and Pa don't care about those things." Garrett patted the boy's head. "They'll be ever so happy to have an extra person to help eat Ma's cooking."

"Are ya sure?" Ronnie glanced at Savannah, as if to

verify Garrett's words.

"We're sure." Savannah stood, then stooped to his level. "They made me welcome when no one else cared what happened to me."

"But you have nice clothes and you smell good." Ronnie reached as if to touch the skirt of Savannah's lisle, navy blue dress, then yanked his hand back.

"I might have been clean on the outside, but my heart was dirty. I did lots of bad things, and not because someone made me do them." Savannah smoothed back a lock of Ronnie's curly hair that hung in his eyes. "Garrett's mother and father loved me anyway."

Ronnie looked back and forth from Savannah to Garrett. "You'll bring me back here then, after dinner?"

Garrett hesitated. "Do you really like living at the church?"

"It's better'n living with my aunt and uncle." Ronnie set his jaw.

"I'm sure we can do better than that." Garrett knelt beside him. "We'll have to talk to the sher… to the people who make decisions about children who are being mistreated."

"Why can't I just come live with you?" Ronnie's lower lip trembled.

Garrett locked eyes again with his wife. "We have to talk to the right people so we don't get in trouble with the law." He grabbed Ronnie's hand. "Come on, I'm hungry. Let's get something to eat."

♠

The smell of ham wafted to Garrett's nostrils as soon as Ma opened the door and encased them in a warm hug. "Happy Easter. I hope you're hung— Well, who do we have here?"

Ronnie slid behind Garrett as Ma smiled at him. "This is Ronnie, well, that's what we call him. We brought him to help eat the good Easter dinner we knew you were fixing."

"We're so happy to have you, Ronnie. I hate throwing food away." Ma's eyes twinkled.

"Oh no, ma'am." The words burst out of him. He rubbed his stomach. "Don't be throwin' nothin' away."

Pa joined them and held out his hand to Ronnie. "Welcome to our home, young man. We're happy to have you. Garrett didn't tell us he was bringing a guest."

"I ain't really a guest in these old clothes." Ronnie glanced down at his worn jacket. "But I'll be happy to help ya eat all that delicious food." He eyed the table, laden with well-filled bowls and platters, and the desserts on the kitchen counter.

"Whee, that's a relief." Pa ruffled Ronnie's hair. "Let's go get washed up for dinner."

When they left the room, Ma raised an eyebrow at Garrett. "Where did you find that delightful child?"

In as few words as possible, Garrett filled her in. "I need to talk to the sheriff about him, see if he knows of a missing child."

"We have room to keep him here if the sheriff needs a temporary place." Ma gestured toward the door to the stairway. "I'd be happy to have him."

Garrett's soul warmed. Ma's heart was as big as all outdoors. She'd never known a stranger. "We haven't had a chance to talk yet, but if we move the boxes out of our storage room and get a bed, we could fix a place for him." Garrett's eyes questioned his wife.

"You mean the room I'd hoped to use for a nursery some day?" She nodded. "How long were you thinking to keep him?"

Before Garrett could answer, Pa and Ronnie returned and Ma set another plate and silverware on the table between Pa and Garrett. She smiled at Ronnie. "I thought you'd like to sit here with the other men."

Ronnie nodded and slid into the chair at his place, beaming. "Let's eat," he boomed, his shyness forgotten. He bowed his head while the others sat down. Someone had taught him to pray before eating.

Ma thanked God for their welcome guest. Her amen was barely said before the boy leaned forward, staring longingly at the platter of ham in front of him. "Help yourself to the ham, Ronnie. Take all you want."

He took two large pieces, then started to put one back. "I'm sorry. I shouldn't take seconds before everyone has firsts."

"It's okay." Garrett put the second piece back on his plate. "There's plenty for everyone to have all they want." When Ronnie speared the meat and began taking bites from it, Garrett reached for his knife. "Let me cut that for you. It'll be so much easier to eat."

Ronnie was so busy shoveling food into his mouth that Garrett served him from the heaping platters and bowls instead of passing them to him.

Ma glowed as he smacked his lips and moaned after each bite. How long had it been since the boy had a decent meal?

A loud knock interrupted the festive occasion. When Pa opened the door, a gruff, grating voice filled the room and Ronnie disappeared under the table. "We heard tell our boy, Samuel, was seen riding in your car. He's been missin' for over a week." The man's voice took on a syrupy sweetness. "We been so worried 'bout him."

Chapter 53

Polly stood frozen, unable to come up with a single plan to rescue this Easter dinner from disaster. Where was Father? His muffled voice reached Polly's ears before he entered the dining room. Apparently he'd been in the kitchen, lending Lydia a hand.

Galvanized into action, Polly darted to his side. "I'm so sorry, Father. Why didn't you tell her…" She stopped. Placing blame wouldn't change the situation.

He lifted his hands in a helpless gesture. "Lydia didn't want any advice or help in planning. She wanted this dinner to be hers from start to finish. I didn't even know what she made until I smelled it cooking when we got home from church."

Subdued sobs came from the kitchen as Maggie and her family arrived. After one glimpse of Polly and Father's faces, Maggie handed Leah to her husband and joined them in the dining room. "What's wrong? What happened?"

Polly quickly filled her in on the unfortunate situation.

"Paul likes sauerkraut and so does Father, maybe Ben's wife too. And Beth will eat anything to make Lydia happy. The rest of us can eat pork and the other dishes Lydia prepared." Maggie grabbed Polly's arm. "Let's go apologize."

Thankful for back up, Polly accompanied her sister to the kitchen where Lydia stood with her back turned, looking out the window. They approached her, one on each side.

"We're so sorry Elsie and George hurt your feelings." Polly touched Lydia's arm. "I know how hard you worked on this dinner."

Maggie nodded. "None of us liked sauerkraut growing up, and Mother never forced us to eat—"

Lydia spun and glared at Maggie. "So this is all my fault for making something your saintly mother never made you eat?" She stomped her foot. "It's just like Mary says, nothing we do is ever good enough."

Polly's mouth dropped. "I don't understand. We've never criticized Robert's wife."

"So it's only me you criticize?" Lydia spat out the words. Before either Polly or Maggie could respond, she ripped off her apron and threw it on the counter as Father entered the kitchen. "I'm calling my son in New Castle to come get me. I won't stay where I'm not wanted."

Father, standing behind Lydia, rolled his eyes. "Lydia, please calm down. No one said you're not wanted."

"Some things don't have to be said." She headed for the telephone, but Father stepped in front of her.

"If you're determined to go to your son's house, I'll take you. No need to interrupt his dinner."

♠

Garrett pushed his chair back with a loud screech and glared at the overweight, bearded man on their doorstep. "I'm calling the sheriff. You'll have to answer some questions."

The man, dressed in a shapeless brown jacket and well-worn coveralls, scowled. "You got no right to keep my boy from me." He stepped across the threshold.

Garrett shoved the man out of the way. "Call the sheriff, Pa." He stepped outside, and slammed the door behind him. "I don't know who you are, but someone needs to teach you some manners. You can't show up unannounced and force your way into people's houses."

"All I want is for you to give me what belongs to me." The man took a menacing step toward Garrett.

"Children aren't to be treated like pieces of property." Garrett stood nose to nose with the uncouth character.

"You don't know nothin' about it." The man stepped back and made a run for the door as Garrett stuck out his foot. Samuel's uncle crashed to the floor, cursing and swearing as he fell.

The sheriff pulled up in front of the house and leaped out of his dark green Model T. "What are you doing here, Jake? I seem to recall we had some trouble last time you were in town."

"You got no right to keep me out of Sandy Lake." Jake stumbled to his feet and rubbed his hip.

"What's going on, Garrett?" Sheriff Dickson turned to Garrett as his father opened the door.

"This man tried to force his way into our house. Could you get rid of him so I could talk to you alone?"

"You ain't puttin' me in no jail cell." Jake lowered his head and rammed Sheriff Dickson out of his way.

"I wouldn't…be…trying to…make a get away." Despite being winded, the sheriff had managed to get a firm grip on Jake's arm. He pulled handcuffs from his pocket, clicked them into place, and gestured for Jake to get into the sheriff's vehicle. "I'll take care of him and return soon."

♠

Garrett reentered the kitchen where Samuel still crouched under the table, a lock of hair hanging in his eyes. "You can come out now, Sam. Your uncle's on his way to jail."

The small boy crept out, shoulders hunched, head down. "Is the sheriff gonna put me in jail for stealin'?"

"They don't put children in jail." Garrett sat down and drew Sam toward him. "I'll explain your situation to Sheriff Dickson."

Sam raised his head, gazing into Garrett's eyes. "Will he let me stay with you?"

Was Savannah as drawn to this child as he was? Or would she resent Sam using the room she'd meant to use for a nursery? After a quick glance at her with a raised eyebrow, Garrett drew a deep breath and pulled the little boy close. "I hope so, Sammy. I hope so."

Chapter 54

Savannah's pulse sped up as Garrett enveloped Sammy in a giant hug. His eyes meeting hers had told her he knew they needed to talk. Was this how the Lord would fulfill her desire for a child? Her heart twinged. *But I wanted a baby, Lord.* Guilt overwhelmed her. How could she put her longing for a baby ahead of this child's need?

Garrett set the boy on his knee. "I have to see what the sheriff says. Most important thing is to keep you safe."

The corners of Sammy's mouth drooped. "But I wanna stay with you."

Sheriff Dickson knocked on the door, and Mother Young held out her hand to Sammy. "Let's go look for some of Garrett's old toys. I'm sure there are a few up in his room."

He took her hand, blue eyes sparkling.

♠

Garrett strode to the door as his mother and Sam left the room. "Come in and sit down, Sheriff Dickson." Garrett waved him to a seat at the table. "Did you lock him up?"

"I did. Attacking me was a good enough reason." The sheriff sat down and stretched his long legs. "What started all this?"

Garrett and Savannah filled him in, starting with their discovery that Sam had been hiding out at the church.

The sheriff sighed and shook his head. "I'm afraid the situation that put Samuel in Jake's home hasn't been thoroughly investigated. Looks like the boy ended up in a bad place."

"What situation is that?" Garrett's father raised a puzzled eyebrow.

"Some years back, Samuel's mother and father disappeared. No one seemed to know where they went or why. Deer Creek isn't in my jurisdiction, but I heard they were newcomers. No one was aware of any next of kin to notify.

Sheriff Dickson cleared his throat. "I didn't even know Samuel existed until I heard Jake and his wife had taken him in. Not an ideal situation but not much I could do about it."

Garrett straightened and raised his voice several notches. "Are you saying there's nothing you can do about this?"

"Not at all, now that we have reason to believe the boy's being misused." The sheriff glanced from Garrett to his father. "You folks willing to get involved?"

They both nodded and Garrett added, "Absolutely. What can we do?"

"Could you provide the boy a place to stay until this is settled?"

"I believe Garrett and Savannah want to fix a room for him." Pa waved a hand at them. "But we'll be happy to take him in while they get ready."

"That's good of you. I'll talk to law enforcement in Cochranton." Sheriff Dickson pulled a notebook from his pocket. "Maybe we can find some stores that have had things go missing. If people will press charges, we shouldn't have any trouble keeping the boy away from Jake since he's not a legal guardian."

"Surely you wouldn't let him go back there even if people won't press charges." Red splotches crept up Garrett's neck.

Sheriff Dickson bit his lip. "Final decision probably won't be up to me."

As the door closed behind the sheriff, Ma and Sam returned to the room, the boy carrying a green metal tractor and hay bailer. "Look what we found." Sam's eyes glowed, and he turned to Garrett. "Was this yours?"

"Indeed it was." Garrett stroked the tractor fondly. "Would you like to have it?"

"You'd give it to me?"

Garrett grinned. "I'm a little old to be playing with tractors, so I'd like you to have it." He stood. "Savannah and I should go fix up a room for you."

"Can't I go with ya?" Sam took a few steps closer to Garrett.

"Maybe you could help me with the dishes while Savannah and Garrett get things ready." Ma ruffled Sam's hair. "I sure could use your help."

He set the toys on the floor, squared his shoulders and scooped Garrett's plate from the table. "Why, sure. I could do that."

♠

"Where will we get a bed for Sammy?" Savannah climbed the stairs to their apartment, Garrett close behind her.

"Maybe my cousin, Irv, has a single bed he's storing in his shed. I'll call and ask him."

"Wait." Savannah reached the top of the stairs and turned to Garrett. "What will Sammy do while we're at work? I don't think we should leave him here alone."

"He could stay with Ma. She'd be happy to have him."

Savannah nodded. "All right."

"You don't sound happy." Garrett tilted Savannah's chin so he could see her eyes. "Is this all moving too fast for you?"

"It's just that…" Savannah stared at the floor. "I thought we'd start out with a baby, not a five year old."

Chapter 55

"I'm going to walk up to your mam's house so she can teach me to make Shepherd's Pie." Polly kissed Will's cheek as he came in the door on Monday evening.

"You're goin' without me? I could get washed up and come along now." Will searched her face with tender eyes.

"Some day I have to get over my fear of your mam." Polly pressed her cheek against his. "Might as well be today."

"Okay, if you're sure." Will's kiss demonstrated his gratitude for her effort to be friends with his mam. "Were Elsie and Twila here today? No school on Easter Monday, right?"

"No school but they stayed at home. Lydia hasn't come back from New Castle yet."

Will frowned. "When's she coming back?"

Polly shrugged. "Who knows? I haven't talked to Father since he took her there yesterday. I'd better go—Mam will be waiting for me."

She kissed him again and headed for Chestnut Street, breathing in the air, crisp with a touch of spring. *Please, Lord, let things go well tonight with Will's mam. It seems like since I married Will and Father married Lydia, we have one crisis after another with my mother-in-law and my stepmother. I don't know how much more we can take.*

Mam was waiting when she knocked on the front door near the Stoneboro Fair entrance. "Come in, Polly."

The corners of Mam's mouth turned up in something close to a smile. On an impulse, Polly kissed her cheek. "Did you have a nice Easter?" Immediately, she bit her tongue. Had she just started a fuss because she and Will hadn't come here for Easter dinner?

But Mam smiled and nodded. "George and Dora invited me to eat with them. Dora is such a good cook." She bustled into the kitchen with Polly following.

Would Mam ever say that about her? Polly swallowed. She had to stop being so sensitive, taking compliments about others as put downs about her. "What did you have?"

"Dora made lamb roast with herbs." Mam smacked her lips. "Will said your da's wife was cookin' for the Dye family. What did she serve?"

"She made…" Polly hesitated. "She made sauerkraut and pork."

Mam had cracked the icebox door, but turned to stare at Polly. "Sauerkraut and pork? Is that a, well, a traditional Easter dinner or just something your family really likes?"

Polly choked and coughed. "It's a traditional New Year's Day dinner, and definitely not something my family likes."

"Oh." The word was laden with meaning.

Mam and Polly stared at each other and then burst out laughing. It was the first time she'd smiled since Lydia's outburst.

"So how did that work out, then?" Mam's shoulders still heaved as she tried to contain her mirth.

"Just about as you'd expect." Polly laughed until tears ran down her cheeks, her tensions draining away.

Mam nodded. "Sounds as if you'n me aren't the only ones ta have our moments."

♠

Savannah smoothed the colorful quilt on the bed donated by Irv, fluffed the feather pillow and propped up the sock monkey Garrett's mother had made. Would Sam like his room? They had worked late into the night clearing out boxes while

Sam slept at his parents' house in Garrett's old room. Garrett had just gone to pick him up.

Mixed feelings churned in her belly. Part of her was afraid to love Sammy, only to lose him in a few days, weeks, months, or even years. What was to stop his parents from waltzing into town when he was ten years old, demanding him back? And he was five. Not the baby she'd dreamed of.

She dropped down beside the bed on her knees. *Father, I thought it was enough to accept that I'd never give birth to a baby. Are you asking me now to give up the dream of raising someone else's baby?*

Although she had no guarantee that she would ever be approved to adopt a child because of her past, giving up the dream seemed too much to ask. She walked into the bedroom she and Garrett shared. Sarah's diary lay on her bedside table. Picking it up, she opened it at random.

If I turn against God, to whom will I go for the comfort and strength I need to get through the days ahead?

Even after losing five children, Sarah had never turned against God. Her own losses appeared small compared to those experienced by the woman whose diary she held. She couldn't imagine losing five precious children. God was offering her the opportunity to be a mother to this one small boy, at least for a little while.

Resolutely, she put down the diary, walked back into Sammy's room and knelt beside the bed. Placing her hands, palms up, on the bedspread, she closed her eyes. *I surrender my desire for a baby to you, Father. Thank you for placing Sammy in our path. Help me love him as though he were my own for whatever period of time you choose.*

Chapter 56

A little over a week had passed since Polly's sisters had come to her house after school. Lydia still hadn't returned. Polly, out of sorts with Will away on a long run, had invited Father, Elsie and Twila for dinner. She hated cooking for one, and her sisters' attempts to make meals weren't always palatable.

Pork chops gave off a tantalizing fragrance and the table set for four lifted her spirits. Parsley potatoes, peas and some peaches, canned last summer, completed the menu. Her stomach lurched and churned, and suddenly the food didn't smell as appetizing as it had. Why did her favorite foods make her feel green? Two days in a row? Maybe she'd picked up a virus.

A car pulling up in her driveway drew Polly into the living room. The mercury had climbed to 65 degrees today but was already falling, and Polly shivered as the girls and Father breezed into the living room. "Close the door. You're letting all the warm air out."

Father pushed the door shut. "Thanks for inviting us for dinner. We were getting awful hungry." He grinned at Twila and Elsie.

"Speak for yourself." Elsie tossed her blonde curls. "I'd rather eat our cooking than Lydia's any day."

Removing his jacket and tossing it on the davenport, Father sighed. "Lydia isn't a bad cook."

"I didn't say she was a bad cook. I said I'd rather eat our cooking than hers."

"We shouldn't have to tell you why." Twila squinted at her father, then turned to Polly. "Is dinner ready?"

"It is. Take off your jackets and come to the kitchen."

Her father followed Polly to the stove, sniffing. "Smells good."

"Thank you." She lowered her voice and swallowed her nausea. "Have you talked to Lydia?"

"I've tried." Father shrugged. "The girls are so happy that she's gone, makes me hesitant to push too hard for her to come home."

Polly dished up the food while her sisters filled the glasses on the table. Everyone found chairs and after a brief prayer, they helped themselves to the food.

"Have you heard anymore about the coal strike, Father?" Polly passed a basket of bread.

"It's not good. April first, the United Mine Workers honored the birthday of Johnny Mitchell, their former leader, with parades and speeches. That evening they declared a national coal mining strike. They've settled nothing." Her father shook his head.

"Polly noted the worry lines etched on his forehead. "Do you think it will affect the mines here?"

"Hard to say. No strikers here yet, but all it takes is one powder keg shooting off his mouth."

Father's shoulders sagged and the dark circles under his eyes were bigger than last time she'd seen him. Lydia leaving, unrest in the mining world, and coping with Elsie's attitude, he was aging before Polly's eyes.

♠

Savannah hummed snatches of hymns as she prepared spaghetti for supper—Sammy's favorite. He was building a fort in the living area with wooden blocks Garrett's mother had found in their attic. Garrett would be home soon.

"Getting hungry, Sammy?"

He ran into the kitchen, sniffing as he came. "Hungry enough to eat a cow. Smells so good." He leaned against her for a moment before returning to his fort.

Amazing how quickly they'd adapted to this addition to their family. Sheriff Dickson had spoken to Garrett several times by telephone, but no new developments. Jake had been fined, counseled to stay away from Sammy, and released while the investigation continued.

The telephone rang and Savannah startled as she did every time it rang these days. Would it be someone calling to say they'd found Sammy's parents or close relatives? She swallowed around the lump in her throat and headed for the telephone. No use letting it ring. They'd call back.

"Hello?" Did they notice the tremor in her voice?

"Savannah. Sheriff Dickson. Need to talk to you and Garrett. This evening a good time?"

"Anytime after dinner, unless you'd like to eat with us?"

"Better not. Wife is expecting me. 7:00 work for you folks?"

Savannah nodded. Then forced her vocal chords to function. "Yes, of course. We'll be here."

A click in her ear ended the conversation. Would he have good news? Or would they have to say good-bye to the boy they'd already begun to love?

"Who was that?" Sammy had moved soundlessly to her side.

They still hadn't figured out what he should call them. A few times he'd slipped and called her Ma, but how could she encourage that?

"Sheriff Dickson." She squatted beside him. "He has some news for us."

Sammy's body stilled and his blue eyes darkened. "What kind of news?"

"I don't know yet. He'll come by later." She reached out to the child, but he backed away, eyes never leaving her face.

"What if they make me go back to…you know…"

Savannah rocked back on her heels. "Let's not borrow trouble. Maybe the sheriff has good news."

Gravel crunched on the parking lot out back. Garrett might be home.

Sammy beat her to the top of the stairs. "Garrett won't let them take me away." He stared at her, seeming to will her to agree with him.

The opening of the door and Garrett's entrance saved her from having to answer. "Hello, my Love." She had never been happier to see him.

"Hello." Garrett's warm smile included them both as he bounded up the stairs and engulfed them in a hug. "Wow. I could use this kind of welcome every day." He kissed Savannah's lips, then dropped a kiss on top of Sammy's head.

Savannah clung to him, then spoke quietly. "Sheriff Dickson is coming this evening at seven o'clock. He has news for us."

Chapter 57

Savannah hung up Sheriff Dickson's coat and motioned for him to follow her into the living room. He sat in the wing chair, while Garrett, Savannah and Sam huddled together on the davenport. The sheriff folded and unfolded his hands, looking ill at ease.

"I guess the news I have is that I don't have any news." He shifted in his chair. "I've been working with Sheriff Green in Cochranton, but it seems like any clues grew cold in the year since Samuel's parents disappeared."

Garrett nodded. "What about evidence of Jake using Sam to steal?"

"There were business owners who admitted to theft but were reluctant to place blame." The sheriff shook his head.

"So where does that leave us?" Garrett stiffened his spine. He'd fight for this little boy if need be.

"I'm guessing it'll have to go before the judge." He sighed. "Jake doesn't have any legal claim to the boy but…"

"I won't go back. I won't. I won't." Sam shrank closer to Garrett.

"Now, now. Don't take on so, young man. No one said anything about sending you back." Sheriff Dickson glanced at Garrett. "I guess the question is, are you willing to take care of the boy until a hearing can be scheduled?"

"Of course we are. I told you we'd keep him forever if we could."

"All right, then. Sheriff Green will set up a hearing at the courthouse. I'll let you know when we have a date. You can testify on the boy's behalf. Your parents too."

After the sheriff left, Garrett turned to Sam. "Let's go for a drive." The boy seemed to open up more while riding in the car.

When they were underway, he glanced at Sam who was gazing at him.

"Where we goin'?"

"Nowhere in particular. I just wanted to have a talk. Did you know Jake and Ida before your parents disappeared?"

Sam nodded. "They came to visit a lot. I never liked 'em." His lower lip trembled. "Maybe I'm just a 'fraidy cat, but I didn't trust them."

Garrett squeezed his shoulder. "Maybe your gut was telling you something."

Sam screwed up his face. "Huh?"

"Just means sometimes deep inside we know someone isn't trustworthy, even though we don't know why. Did they ever say or do anything that made you uncomfortable?"

"My pa inher—inherited, is that the right word?" At Garrett's nod, Sam continued. "Pa got some money when his parents died. His brothers and sisters was mad at him, said it wasn't fair. That's why we left town, to get away from them."

"What town did you leave?"

Sam shook his head. "I ain't tellin' cause I don't want to go back there neither."

Garrett sighed. "All right. What did Jake and Ida do that made you uncomfortable?"

"I was gettin' to that. For some reason, my pa told 'em about the money. After that, they was always askin' questions about it and coming around if my pa and ma weren't at home. I think they mighta figgered out where the money was."

Sam rubbed his hands over his face, and a tear trickled down his cheek. "Then one day, Ma and Pa went into town and never come back." Tears were coursing down his cheeks at a rapid pace. "That night Jake and Ida come and got me. They told the sheriff my ma and pa had gone off and left me, but they'd give me a place to stay. I had no say about nothin.' And my folks is still missin'."

Garrett pulled off beside the road and drew Sam close. When his sobs quieted, Garrett gave him a clean handkerchief from his pocket. "Did you tell the sheriff about the money?"

"No one ever asked me. Jake and Ida said my ma and pa probably left because of my red hair and because they didn't want to share their money with me. They said it'd be best if I didn't tell nobody about it."

After a few mighty blows in the handkerchief, Sam looked at Garrett. "They said I had to steal to earn my keep since they was taking care of me."

Pulling the little boy close again, Garrett leaned his head against Sam's. "We'll get this straightened out.. I smell a rat."

"A rat?" Sam's lip curled.

"That means I think someone did something bad. We just have to prove it." Garrett got out, cranked the car, and started the engine. "By God's grace, we will."

♠

Will bounded up the porch steps, the fragrance of pork chops greeting him as he opened the front door. "Smells good in here."

Polly came from the kitchen to welcome him, less enthusiastically than usual. She turned her cheek to his kiss.

"What's wrong, Lass?"

"I don't know. I haven't been feeling quite right. My stomach…" She covered her mouth with her hand. "It's worse when I cook."

"Sounds like…" Should he say it?

"Sounds like what?"

"Mam said she loved cookin' except when she was in the family way. Said the smell of food cookin' always made her sick."

Polly walked back into the kitchen to the colorful

calendar on the wall.

Will followed. "What are ya doin'?"

"I'm counting the weeks since my last monthly."

Chapter 58

Without a word, Elsie and Twila burst through the doorway, clomped into the house and flopped down on the davenport.

Polly put down the sock she was darning and stared at them. "This is a surprise. I wasn't expecting you."

"Didn't Father tell you Lydia came home last night?" Elsie glared at Polly as though it were somehow her fault.

"Not a word." Polly pasted a smile on her face and refused to be offended. "Maybe he hoped you girls and Lydia would get along better after a break from each other."

Elsie snorted. Twila shook her head and sighed. "We just try to stay out of her way. Coming here after school helps. Maybe we could eat here tonight." A lock of dark brown hair fell over Twila's hopeful eyes. She pushed it behind her ear.

Polly had toyed with the idea of feeding Will a sandwich instead of risking another bout of nausea. Her stomach had settled a bit more today, but her monthly hadn't come yet.

Aware of Twila's imploring eyes still fixed on her, Polly gave herself a mental shake. "We're just having sandwiches—"

"Sandwiches are good. Please let us stay." Elsie joined forces with her sister.

"Well..." Polly hesitated. "Perhaps it would be good for Father and Lydia to have some time to themselves. If you're sure you don't mind sandwiches."

♠

Garrett left work early and headed for his parents' house. An idea had pursued him relentlessly and refused to give him any rest since he and Sam had talked. It seemed a little too convenient that Jake and Ida had shown up at Sam's house the same day his parents hadn't come back.

As usual, Ma spotted him before he could open the door. She seemed to have a sixth sense that told her he was coming. "Garrett, you finished work early." She stood on tiptoe to kiss his cheek as Sam latched on to his arm.

"Sam and I are going to take a little ride." He swung Sam high above his head as the little boy whooped and hollered.

When Sam caught his breath, he grabbed Garrett's hand. "Where are we goin' this time, or are we just takin' a ride?"

"I'll tell you later. Thanks for watching Sam, Ma."

"You know I love having him. Almost like having a…" She stopped. "Better not get the cart before the horse."

Garrett kissed Ma's cheek and lifted Sam so he could do the same. "No harm in hoping."

As they backed out of the driveway, Garrett glanced at Sam. "If we drove out to the Deer Creek Church, could you show me your house and Jake and Ida's?"

"Why?" A worried frown puckered Sam's face.

"I'm not taking you there to stay. I'd just like to get a feel for where you lived if you can find it."

Sam's face cleared. "Sure. I'm good at d'rections. My pa said I done took after him." Sam's brows drew together. "If'n I had a boy who took after me, I wouldn't go off and leave him. Would you?"

"No, I wouldn't, especially if it was as fine a boy as you." Garrett patted Sam's head. "But maybe your pa didn't take off. Maybe something happened that kept him from coming back."

Sam nibbled his lower lip. "Like what?"

Garrett glanced at the boy's small frame, then back to the country road where they'd just passed the church. He slowed his speed. "Was your pa a big man?"

"Nah. Bigger'n me, of course, but not big."

"So maybe somebody bigger than him wouldn't let him come back."

Sam's small body stilled. "Like maybe they tied 'im up or hurt 'im real bad?"

"I'm not sure, but it's possible something happened." Garrett took Sam's hand.

Blue eyes thoughtful, Sam nodded, then pointed out the window. "There's the house where me'n Pa 'n Ma lived. Jake and Ida live just over the next hill."

Garrett pulled into the driveway and got out to look around. Sam joined him. The house had a deserted air, with tall grass and a broken window.

"What are ya lookin' fer?" Sam peered at him as Garrett headed toward the back of the house.

"I won't know until I see it." It was unlikely he'd tell Sam if he noticed anything suspicious. He started down a path into the woods. He'd have to come back alone…

Garrett stopped. To his left was a steep embankment that would be a perfect place to get rid of a… He wouldn't allow himself to say the words, even to himself. "I guess that's far enough for today." He grabbed Sam's hand and drew him back toward the house.

The boy dug in his heels and refused to go any further. "Are ya thinkin' somebody did Pa and Ma in on account of the money?"

No doubt about it, Sam was quick. "I don't know, Sam. Did your pa tell anyone but Jake about the inheritance?"

"Not that I know of. I don't think Pa would a told Jake if he hadn't pestered him with questions about why we moved here. Finally, Pa told him, maybe so he'd quit askin.'"

Garrett nodded. "We'll head back to Sandy Lake, and I'll have a talk with the sheriff. We won't tell anyone about this but Savannah, and my pa and ma."

Chapter 59

Savannah and Polly hugged on the porch steps of the house where Garrett's folks lived. Will and Garrett had dropped them off and were headed to pick up Devon on their way to the prison for Bible study.

"What a week it's been." Savannah waved to the men. "I'm sorry I didn't have time to call you."

"I ran into Dorothy when I came to Sandy Lake to get some supplies on Friday. She gave me some details." Polly winked at Savannah. "But I want to hear it from you."

"I'd rather not even know what she told you, although it's likely some of it's true."

Mother Young opened the door and drew them inside with her usual cheery smile.

Polly glanced around the kitchen. "Where's Sammy?"

"So obviously, Dorothy told you about him." Savannah dropped into a chair.

"Of course." Polly grinned.

"Harold went to stay with him at Savannah and Garrett's apartment so we can speak freely without upsetting him." Mother bustled around pouring hot tea and setting out a plate of sugar cookies.

"Good idea." Polly clasped her hands on the table. "So tell me everything. I'm all ears."

"Did Dorothy tell you Sammy had been living at the Deer Creek church and we took him home with us on Easter Sunday?" Savannah raised an eyebrow.

"She did. But don't worry about what she told me. Just tell me your story."

Savannah went on to tell Polly about Jake and Ida and Garrett's suspicions. "After Sammy showed Garrett where he lived with his parents, Garrett called the sheriffs in Sandy Lake and in Cochranton."

Polly shook her head. "My goodness. We haven't had this much excitement since George Burns kidnapped you ten years ago."

Savannah shuddered. "Don't remind me. Where was I? Oh, so Garrett took the two sheriffs to Sammy's house and showed them the steep embankment." She closed her eyes for a moment. "I don't know if Garrett will ever get over what he saw next."

Sliding to the edge of her seat, Polly drew a long breath. "So Jake Dresher did away with Sammy's parents and dumped them over that embankment like Dorothy said?"

"They haven't proved it yet, of course, but it looks that way. Jake is being held on suspicion of murder and locked up. They took him to Mercer." Savannah's eyes widened. "Poor Sammy."

"Dorothy wasn't real clear on the details." Polly frowned. "Why did Jake do it? What did he have against Sammy's parents?"

"He had nothing against them. He just wanted the money Sammy's father inherited." Savannah stared at the table. "It's like the Bible says, money is the root of all evil."

"Not quite." Mother Young tapped the table. "It's the *love of money* that is the root of all evil, not the money itself."

"Ah." Savannah hesitated. "Actually, I was guilty of the same sin. I loved money and the things it could buy so much that I adopted a sinful lifestyle to get them. I hope one day Jake will be as sorry for his sin as I am."

Polly took Savannah's hand between both of hers and Mother rubbed her other arm. "You know God has forgiven you, don't you?"

"I do. The hardest thing has been forgiving myself."

After a moment of silence, Polly let go of Savannah's hand. "So what will happen to Sammy now?"

"He finally told us his last name and where he came from so the sheriff could contact his relatives. It's unlikely they'll want him, now that the money is gone." Savannah glanced at Mother.

"How awful to be unwanted." Polly's lips trembled.

Savannah smiled. "That's not exactly true. *We* want him."

Polly's face lit. "You mean you'll adopt him if his aunts and uncles reject him?"

"I think the authorities will allow it because of our involvement from the start."

"That's wonderful, Savannah, but I'm glad I'm not the one in your situation." She paused. "You know how I feel about having children and starting all over again." She bit her lip and lowered her voice. "Last week, I thought I might be in the family way."

Savannah stilled as Polly blew out a sigh of relief. "But I'm not. My monthly was just late and I must have had a touch of the flu."

Catching a glimpse of Savannah's stricken face, Polly clapped her hand over her mouth. "Oh, Savannah, I'm so sorry. I shouldn't have said that. I didn't think."

♠

Bob ambled down Broad Street with no particular destination. He had invited Lydia to walk with him, as he and Margaret used to do, but she declined. Memories of his wife… his first wife, were everywhere.

What a failure he'd made of this second marriage. Instead of replacing his memories of Margaret by bringing Lydia into this house, he found himself continually comparing the two. It wasn't fair to Lydia, of course. He couldn't expect her to love his daughters the way their mother had. Was it also too much to expect her to love *him* the way Margaret had loved him?

He groaned. The loneliness he'd hoped to escape had only grown stronger. Perhaps expecting the void to be filled had made him all the more aware of it. If only Lydia had married Byron Chesterfield, Bob would have avoided the trap he'd fallen into. No, there was no use blaming anyone else. He had entered this marriage of his own free will. As his mother used to say, he'd made his bed, now he'd have to lie in it.

Chapter 60

Savannah tore the month of May from the calendar above her small desk in the corner of their bedroom. What an eventful month it had been. She walked down the hall and stood gazing at Sammy's room, her heart thudding a happy rhythm at the good news they had received in today's mail.

None of Sammy's family members had stepped up to claim him and no one, not even Mrs. Greely, had come forward to say anything against her during the investigation. The last obstacle that could have prevented them from adopting Sammy had been removed. They were having a celebration dinner to tell Sammy this evening.

Love coursed through her veins as it did whenever Sammy came to mind. Never having given birth to a child, she had nothing with which to compare her feelings for him, but surely no one could love him more.

And yet... Much as she loved Sammy, her heart still yearned for an infant. Like an ache from an ailing tooth that twinged at unexpected times. No matter how she attempted to repress it, overcome by guilt that having Sammy hadn't eliminated her longing, it wouldn't go away.

What was it Mother Young had said? *Delight thyself in the Lord and He will give thee the desires of thy heart.*

Help me delight myself in you, Father. Help me long for a closer relationship with you more than I long for a baby.

Footsteps on the stairs drew her from her prayer, and she

ran to meet the two people she loved more than anyone else on earth.

"Mama, what smells so good?" Sammy flung his coat toward the rack at the top of the stairs. In spite of their concerns about the adoption process not being complete, Sammy began calling them Mama and Papa. They didn't correct him.

"It's your favorite—spaghetti and meatballs." She gathered him in her arms.

"We're celebrating tonight." Garrett tousled Sammy's red hair affectionately.

"Celebratin'? What are we celebratin'?" Sammy's blue eyes sparkled.

Garrett pulled them close. "Shall we tell him, Mama?"

"No reason to wait. Let's sit down." Savannah took Sammy's hand and led him to the davenport, Garrett close behind.

Garrett sat down and set Sammy on his knee, facing them. "Sam, do you remember when you asked if the sheriff would let you stay with us?"

Sammy nodded, his blue eyes wide. "I told him that's what I wanted."

"I know you did." Garrett squeezed his shoulder. "Today we got a letter telling us we can adopt you."

With a whoop that almost shattered Savannah's eardrums, Sammy jumped off Garrett's lap and began leaping around the living room, whooping and hollering.

"I was going to ask if you knew what that meant." Garrett grinned.

"Course I know." Sammy puffed out his chest. "It means I can be your boy for real and forever."

"It does, indeed. When the judge signs all the papers, your name will be Samuel Garrett Young if that's okay with you." Garrett squeezed her fingers. They had agreed to use Garrett as Sammy's middle name.

Sammy stared at them, a tear trickling down his cheek. "You mean you're gonna share your name with me?"

Garrett nodded. "I can't think of anyone I'd rather have share my name."

♠

Polly turned and rubbed her nose against Will's when he came to stand behind her at the stove. "Hungry? Supper is almost ready."

Will bit his lip and sighed. "Not really. But I can always eat."

Wrinkling her forehead, Polly gazed at him. "Is something bothering you? You've not been yourself lately."

"I'm all right." Will walked out of the kitchen.

"No," Polly muttered under her breath, "you're not all right." It was so rare for Will to be moody. If either of them had ups and downs, it was usually her. Since she discovered she wasn't in the family way, she'd been almost giddy with relief.

Dishing up the Irish stew and homemade bread, she set them on the table with the vase of mountain laurel. "Come and get it, Love."

Still without his usual smile, her husband sat at the table. Polly plopped down across from him and took his hand. "Do you want to say the blessing or shall I do it?"

"You go ahead."

"Thank you for the many blessings you've poured out on us, Father, and especially thank you for this food. Bless our families and our town. Amen."

When Polly scooped a big spoonful of stew into Will's bowl, he frowned. "I don't know if I can eat that much."

"You can't eat a regular helping of Irish stew? You must be sick. Mam said you've always loved Irish Stew. Or don't you like the way I make it?"

Will waved his hand. "It's fine. I'll do my best to finish it."

They ate in silence and he helped her clear the table and wash the dishes as usual.

Finally, he spoke. "Were your sisters here earlier?"

"Yes. They left with Father a few minutes before you got

home. Why?"

"No reason. I been missin' them, is all."

"They'll be here this weekend. Maybe we can play some games." Polly emptied the dish pan of soapy water. "It's a beautiful evening. Let's take a walk."

Will nodded and followed her outdoors. As they headed for the lake, Polly grabbed his hand. "It's obvious something is bothering you. You might as well tell me what it is."

"Ya know I don't like to talk about my feelin's. I'll likely get over it." He didn't meet her eyes.

She stepped in front of him and reached for his other hand. "Did I do something to upset you? Sometimes I don't think before I speak. I'm sorry if I hurt your feelings."

At last his dark brown eyes met hers before his gaze slipped away. "I know how ya feel about having young'uns…but well, did ya have to be so happy that ya weren't in the family way?"

"Oh, Will. I'm so sorry." Polly stood on tiptoe and pressed her cheek against his. "I know how much you love children. Seems like when it comes to this subject, I don't think of anyone but myself." She tilted his chin toward her, trying to meet his eyes. "Can you forgive me?"

He shrugged. "Even though you've already raised a family, it's hard for me to understand anyone not wantin' a baby. Me mam loves babies more'n anythin.'"

Polly swallowed around the giant lump in her throat. "I guess there's something wrong with me. Savannah wants a baby so bad, and I hurt her too by my attitude."

She dropped Will's hands and walked toward the lake. He caught up in two long strides. "I'm sorry, Lass. It isn't your fault the Lord hasn't given us a baby. I guess it isn't your fault He hasn't given ya a desire for a baby, either. I shouldn't hold ya accountable for things only God can do."

He grasped her hand and pulled her toward him. "I have lots of nieces and nephews who'd be happy to spend time with me. I don't need to be feelin' sorry for myself."

"Maybe it is my fault, Will." Polly stared toward the lake. "Maybe I wished so hard not to have a baby that it came true. Maybe you should have married Susie O'Toole."

Chapter 61

"Hurry up girls. We still have to pick up Florence before we go to Pittsburgh. We don't want to miss seeing Beth get her nurse's certification." Bob had taken the day off from the mines for this special occasion. Had a year really passed since Beth started nursing school?

Lydia told him last night she had too much to do to attend. He shrugged. How she could possibly be that busy with all the chores he'd assigned to Elsie and Twila was beyond him. To be honest, he was mostly relieved she wasn't going. The peace that existed between his wife and daughters was too fragile. The tension in his shoulders eased. Lydia staying home might be for the best.

Twila hurtled into the living room with Elsie close behind at a more sedate pace. His youngest daughter was still trying to put a blue bow in her hair while Elsie's hair was perfectly combed. He suppressed a smile at the difference in them.

"Ready?" He opened the front door. "Let's go."

A few minutes later, with Florence beside him, they were on their way to the Shadyside School of Nursing. From playing nurse as a child with her brothers and sisters, to accepting a degree today. Beth had achieved her dream. Bob couldn't wipe the smile from his face. What a help she had been during Margaret's last days, running up and down the stairs.

How he longed for Margaret to be here on Beth's special day. Actually he longed for her to be here every day. He shook his head. *Stop dwelling on things that make you sad.*

He glanced at his eldest daughter. "How's Will doing?"

"He's fine. We've been spending lots of time with his nieces and nephews. He so loves children." Florence paused. "He asked me last night whether you got everything straightened out with Alton Vogan?"

"Our insurance companies are working on it. The driver I hired for the Venice Coal Company truck shouldn't have stopped so suddenly, but Alton wouldn't have messed up his beautiful touring car if he hadn't been following too close."

Florence sighed. "Always something isn't there? I hope he doesn't sue you like the Collins's did."

That was a cheerful thought. Silence settled over them, broken only by the occasional argument from the back seat. Bob glanced at Florence. Her thirty-first birthday was coming soon. So many years she'd given to help raise her brothers and sisters, and still willing to help when he needed her. Was she happy? "A penny for your thoughts."

She shrugged. "I'm especially missing Mother today. These milestones are always difficult without her."

Bob nodded. "For me too. I don't think I'll ever get over missing her."

"Marrying Lydia didn't help, did it?" Florence stole a glance at him.

"Not really." Bob rubbed his jaw. "I should have known no one could ever take your mother's place."

Florence shifted uneasily on the lightly-padded seat. "I don't think I'd ever remarry if Will—" Her voice cracked. "If something were to happen to Will."

"You've never been comfortable with his job, have you?"

She shook her head. "A brakeman has one of the most dangerous jobs in the world."

Another glance in Florence's direction showed her hands tightly clenched in her lap.

♠

Bob carried Beth's last piece of luggage down the steep

stairs of the boarding house. Although eventually, she might get a hospital job that would require her to leave Sandy Lake, it would be good to have her home for now.

Perhaps her presence would smooth the rough edges of Twila and Elsie's relationship with Lydia. Beth was a born peacemaker and could get along with anyone. Even the woman who ran the boarding house, who he'd been told was impossible, shed a few tears when Beth said good bye.

With his car full of females, Beth now seated between Elsie and Twila, Bob cranked the engine and headed for home. Beth kept them laughing with tales of the more humorous escapades of her nurse's training. According to her, she went through quite a hefty supply of perfume. She used it to saturate her handkerchiefs, then kept them tucked up her sleeve in case of bedpan duty or bathing a homeless person.

"I shouldn't laugh." Beth sobered. "The homeless are plentiful in big cities. Some are unwilling to work, while others are down on their luck, struggling to get back on their feet. Regardless, the hospital staff must treat each person with dignity and kindness."

"It takes a special type of person to be a nurse." Florence's voice was pensive. "I cleaned up a lot of messes for my younger brothers and sisters, but to clean up after a stranger…" Her voice trailed away. "I don't think I could do it."

Beth leaned forward. "If you had your choice of any career, what would you do, Polly?" She was great at asking questions no one had ever asked.

"Hmmm…" Florence turned to look at Beth. "Maybe run a boarding house, where people had to clean up their own messes. Or, better still, run a hotel. Maybe I wouldn't have to cook for folks at a hotel, and I could hire other people to clean up after them."

Bob smiled as he pulled up in front of their house. "Maybe one day you'll find out if you enjoy that sort of work."

Everyone piled out of the car and helped Beth carry her bundles and luggage into the house. Would Lydia greet Beth at the door? When they entered the house, the living room was empty. Apparently not. The small rocking chair Lydia had brought with her was missing, as were various other knick knacks and wall hangings that belonged to her.

"What's wrong, Father?" Beth was always attentive to people around her.

"I think Lydia is…gone."

"Maybe she went to visit a neighbor." Florence joined them.

"No, I mean, I think she's really gone. Her chair, the painting she did in high school, the purple afghan…" As Bob's gaze roamed around the room, he hesitated, then walked to the table. "Here's an envelope on the table with my name on it."

He picked it up and sank into Margaret's chair. Running his finger under the flap, he drew out a single piece of paper.

Bob, I'm sorry to end things this way, but I thought it would be easier than doing it in person. I told you a long time ago, I couldn't be a mother to your children. I was right. I also can't take Margaret's place. I've decided to go to Cleveland to live with my daughter and her husband. They have room for me. Maybe eventually my son and his wife will come too. I don't want a divorce but I think it's best if we go our separate ways. Lydia.

Part 3

Chapter 62
November 17, 1923

Bob sat with his head in his hands as the newspaper clipping Robert had handed him fell to the floor. Ever since Lydia left, his son had been more willing to open up about his marital problems, even coming home to share the latest news. Although the charges his son was bringing against Mary in his divorce suit were no surprise, seeing them in print sickened Bob.

From his seat on the davenport, Robert met Bob's gaze as he lifted his head. "So Mary has already moved to California?"

"She left a few weeks ago." His son's expressionless tone matched the bleak look in his eyes.

"What about Edward?"

Robert shrugged. "He went with Mary. You know it's almost impossible to take a child from his mother."

Bob sighed. What would become of his grandson? Without question he and his son had made poor choices, he in his second marriage, Robert in his first. He picked up the clipping and smoothed it between his fingers.

"Are you and Lydia getting a divorce?" Robert's question was blunt.

After a firm shake of his head, Bob met Robert's direct gaze. "I took your Uncle Peter with me to Cleveland last December so I could talk to her about a possible reconciliation."

"Why would you do that?" Robert's brow furrowed.

"Because I've always believed marriage is forever. But seeing Lydia face to face brought back enough painful memories to know reconciliation wasn't possible even if she were willing. Which she wasn't." Bob paused. "Anyway, right or wrong, I won't put myself or Lydia through the public humiliation of a divorce."

Robert's head jerked up, but Bob hurried to add, "Her offenses were few compared to the ones you've suffered."

His son didn't respond. What more could Bob say? Oh where was Margaret when he needed her?

"Are you hungry?" Sometimes food helped solve problems, or at least made a person feel better.

When Robert nodded, Bob got up and walked into the empty kitchen. Ever since Lydia left, the refrigerator was empty and dishes multiplied in the sink quicker than rabbits. He opened the icebox, scanned the empty shelves and closed it again. At fourteen and sixteen, his two youngest were old enough to take on the household tasks, but he grew weary of the constant battle. They'd struggled since Beth took a job last April at the Barberton Citizen's hospital in Ohio.

Today, like most days, he'd arrived home from work to no dinner and dishes from the previous day still in the sink.

Walking back to the living room, his stomach growled. "Twila and Elsie left a note saying they went to visit a friend after school. I suspect they'll impose on her for a dinner invitation." He slumped into Margaret's chair. "I should hire a housekeeper but I don't know of anyone I'd want to bring into the house on a daily basis."

"Maybe Polly could help."

"That's not fair to her. She has her own house to clean and meals to cook." Bob straightened his shoulders and stood. "Let's go to Aunt Adda's restaurant. They always have something good. Shall we walk or drive?"

"Let's walk." Robert got to his feet. "I sat all the way from Akron."

They grabbed light coats and took off at a brisk pace.

"Did you know George came from Wisconsin for a Remembrance Day visit last weekend?" Bob glanced at Robert.

"From Wisconsin? Why was he in Wisconsin?"

"Didn't I tell you his company transferred him to Kenosha a few months back? He's doing well." Bob chuckled. "He said he came to visit me but I don't think it was a coincidence that Isabel Gilmore came home from Allegheny College the same weekend."

A thoughtful expression settled on Robert's face. "Perhaps wedding bells are in the offing?"

"Isabel has a couple more years of college, so probably not just yet." A chilly wind swirled around him, and Bob hitched his coat higher. "Beth might soon have plans with the young man she met in Barberton."

"Beth has a young man? I can't keep up with the news from home."

"I'm sorry, Robert. Something else I'm not good at is passing along news."

"What do you think of Beth's young man?" Robert's tone was skeptical. His experience with Mary had apparently made him cautious.

"Elmer seems like a fine young man, and I trust Beth's judgment…" Bob bit his lip. "More than I trust my own…"

♠

Savannah snuggled Sammy close. He allowed it on occasion, in spite of his protests about not being a child. His hair was damp from his Saturday night bath, and the apple fragrance of the homemade soap Mother Young provided clung to him.

Garrett stepped into the living room and beamed at them as he always did when he found Sammy in her arms. It was no secret that she still longed for a baby even though her heart overflowed with love for Sammy.

"How's your sermon for Jackson Center tomorrow?"

"It's coming along fine. Are you worried about seeing…" Garrett hesitated. "Mrs. Reely-Gay?" He sat beside them on the davenport.

Savannah giggled at his Pig Latin. "Actually, she hasn't been rude for a while, and last month, she was downright nice." Savannah raised an eyebrow. "I'm almost afraid to hope she's started to like me."

"What's not to like?" Garrett grinned. "Right, Sam?" He put both arms around them, pulling them close, and rubbing his cheek on Sammy's hair.

Sammy giggled and wriggled out of Savannah's arms onto Garrett's lap. "Right, Papa. Who's Mrs. Reely-Gay? And why doesn't she like Mama?"

Savannah swallowed hard but kept her tone light. "Nothing for you to worry about, Sweetie!" The look she exchanged with Garrett raised the question *How long until he starts asking questions we'll have to answer?*

He gave a quick shake of his head and mouthed his usual answer. *Don't borrow trouble.*

Easy for him to say. Although their adoption of Sammy had gone through with no one dredging up her past, people hadn't forgotten. Someday, someone would take it upon themselves to make Sammy aware of his adoptive mother's colorful history.

Chapter 63

On Sunday morning, Savannah settled herself and Sammy in the third row behind Mrs. Greely where Garrett preferred them to sit. In the past, she had refused to make a spectacle of herself by sitting near the front, but recently, she had given in. Garrett, seated on the platform, caught her eye and smiled.

When the organ prelude ended, he stood and took his place behind the pulpit, his bronze gold hair gleaming in the sun. *How handsome he looked.* It was hard to concentrate on anything else until a loud sniff from Mrs. Greely caught her attention. As Savannah turned her gaze that way, a tear dripped off the woman's chin. Why was she crying? During the singing of the first hymn and scripture reading, Mrs. Greely swiped at her cheeks repeatedly.

Garrett captured Savannah's attention as he began his message. "Today I've chosen to talk about the similarities between the Pharisees and the elder brother in the parable of the prodigal son. It seems that both the Pharisees and the elder brother loved to focus on the sins of others, while believing themselves to be sinless. Neither seemed to place any value on loving and restoring sinners, only on condemning them."

A louder sniff from Mrs. Greely. The woman had removed her glasses and was wiping her eyes with a large white handkerchief. What on earth?

"The Pharisees were far more interested in keeping the

rules than in having a close relationship with God and the same seemed to be true of the elder brother and his relationship with his father. Although he had served his father and obeyed him for many years, there's no indication of a close relationship."

Savannah became so distracted by the scene playing out in front of her that she missed a great deal of Garrett's sermon, until the change in his tone told her he was getting ready to close.

"I suspect that, if we're honest, there are many of us who would make excellent Pharisees and elder brothers. We pride ourselves on keeping all the rules and condemning those who don't, while having no love for sinners nor the God who came to save them." Garrett paused and looked over the congregation.

"Today I'm specifically inviting repentant Pharisees and elder brothers to come and pray. If you fit into that category, the altar is open."

♠

The words were barely out of Garrett's mouth when Mrs. Greely stood and stumbled toward the altar. Then strains of *Softly and Tenderly Jesus is Calling* filled the sanctuary, muffling her sobs as she sank to her knees.

As a pastor, he'd become a master at hiding his emotions but it was all he could do to keep his jaw from dropping. Mrs. Greely at an altar of prayer? He wouldn't have believed it if he hadn't seen it. Pride was a stalwart adversary. He should know, battling it often himself.

Sending up a prayer for wisdom, he knelt in front of Mrs. Greely on the opposite side of the altar rail. Her face was completely buried in her handkerchief. He placed his hand gently on her heaving shoulders.

At last she lowered her soaked hanky and raised her head. "Pastor Young, I don't know if you can ever forgive me..." His eyebrows went up but before he could answer, she continued, "for the way I've treated Savannah. I was so self-righteous and unforgiving. Now I'm afraid I'm reaping what I've sown."

"I don't understand—"

Once again she cut him off. "Our fourteen-year-old

granddaughter is…is in the family way. This will ruin her life and her reputation—and ours. I don't know what we're going to do."

If only he could trade places with anyone else at that moment, anyone who might know what to say to Mrs. Greely. He cleared his throat. "What do your granddaughter's parents want to do?"

"They want to send her to a distant relative until after the baby is born. If we can find someone to adopt the child, perhaps no one will ever know." Mrs. Greely raised her tear-dimmed eyes to his. "I was wondering… I mean do you think perhaps…"

Mrs. Greely gripped his hand. "I know I have no right to expect any favors from you and your wife. But because of her past, I thought she might find it in her heart to be merciful to my Amanda and her baby. And seeing as how you haven't had a baby of your own…"

Garrett put up a hand to stop her. "I think this conversation needs to take place first between you and my wife." He didn't tell her of his wife's longing for a baby. That secret wasn't his to tell.

"After I dismiss the congregation, I'll ask Savannah. If she's willing, you can talk to her in the little room off the platform while Sam and I greet folks at the door."

Mrs. Greely nodded and drew a long shuddering breath as she got to her feet.

♠

Savannah had remained in her seat along with the rest of the congregation while Garrett knelt with Mrs. Greely. She shushed Sammy when he whispered, "Why is that woman crying, Mama? Why is she talking to Papa?" She had no answers to his questions.

After giving the benediction, Garrett stooped beside Sammy. "Would you excuse Mama and me for a few minutes? Then you and I will go back and shake hands with people, okay?"

Sammy straightened his spine and beamed at his father.

"Okay, I'll go and get started with the hand shaking." He marched up the aisle, as Garrett returned to Savannah.

"Mrs. Greely has something to say to you, my Love, and a request to make." Garrett clasped her shoulder, gazing into her eyes. "I said if you're willing, she could speak to you in the front room." He nodded toward the door beside the platform.

Savannah hesitated, her heart racing. What in the world did Mrs. Greely want? And what request did she have?

Picturing Mrs. Greely's tears throughout the service and her heaving shoulders at the altar, Savannah couldn't refuse. Obviously, the woman was very troubled. "All right. I'll go. Pray for me."

Garrett nodded to Mrs. Greely and gestured toward the slightly open door. He pressed a kiss on Savannah's cheek before she followed the woman into the small room where the choir robes hung. A hint of Ben Gay assaulted her nostrils.

Savannah caught her breath and forced herself to meet Mrs. Greely's eyes. "What did you want to talk to me about?"

Mrs. Greely cleared her throat. "I...I owe you an apology. I had no right to judge you or spread rumors about you. Can you forgive me?"

"I can forgive you but..." Savannah bit her lower lip. "Why did you hate me so?"

"Because I was a Pharisee, an elder brother, just like Garrett said today. I thought you were getting off too easy for what you'd done, and I didn't trust you.

Savannah nodded. "So what changed your mind?"

Mrs. Greely's shoulders slumped. She repeated her story about her granddaughter. "When the 'sinner' was my fourteen-year-old granddaughter being in the family way, everything changed. I knew what I'd done was wrong. I didn't want her—or me—to be treated the way I'd treated you."

"I see." Savannah nodded. "Garrett said you also had a request."

Clasping and unclasping her hands, Mrs. Greely stared at the floor. "No, it's too much to ask after the way I treated you.

Your willingness to forgive me ought to be enough."

Savannah frowned. "Please, let me make that decision."

Mrs. Greely shifted from one foot to the other and cleared her throat again. "My granddaughter is too young to be a mother. Because of your past, I thought you and your husband might be willing to overlook how the baby was conceived and adopt it as your own." She met Savannah's gaze, fresh tears rolling down her cheeks.

A strangled sob rose from Savannah's throat. She clasped Mrs. Greely's hands. "Who would have thought anything good could come from my past? I've longed for a baby more than anything, and it's only because of my past that you're giving us this opportunity."

Chapter 64

Garrett ran down the stairs, hand-cranked the engine and jumped into the car. He had missed dinner again with last minute preparations for his message tonight. He tore out of the parking lot to head for Stoneboro.

How long could he keep up this pace? Although he loved every minute he spent with Sam, life had become more complicated since his arrival. Too often his choices seemed to be either a poorly prepared message or time missed with Sam. But what could he change? His income with the alliance of pastors wasn't enough for him to quit selling life insurance, especially since Savannah would probably need to leave her job if a new baby joined the family.

He pulled into Will and Polly's driveway, honked lightly, then waited for his long-legged friend to appear. Polly planned to transport herself and Savannah to his mother's house for Bible study. She'd passed her driver's test last week.

Just as he reached to tap the horn again, Will opened the door and loped down the stairs. A gust of chilly wind rushed in as Will opened the passenger door. Winter was coming… never a welcome season for his friend. Will said every year Polly struggled with depression as inclement weather approached.

"Evenin,' my friend." The warmth in Will's brown eyes always brought a smile to Garrett's face. As Will blossomed spiritually, their friendship deepened and he gave thanks to God.

"How are you, Will?" Garrett backed his car out of the

driveway and headed for Mercer.

"I'm good now that I've decided to stop feelin' sorry for meself because Polly isn't expectin'." Will's lips curved into a grin. "Such good times we're havin' with my nieces and nephews. How about you?"

"I'm good too. I'm glad you're having fun with your nieces and nephews. By the way, speaking of expecting, I think you're looking at an expectant father."

Will raised an eyebrow. "Expectant father? I thought Doc Cooley said—"

Garrett chuckled. "He said he didn't think Savannah could conceive, but God moves in mysterious ways His wonders to perform." He told Will what happened in church that morning. "I'm still pinching myself to make sure it's real."

He glanced at Will in time to see the corners of his mouth droop. "What's wrong? Do you think this isn't a good idea? Maybe you're right. What if Mrs. Greely doesn't think we're raising her grandchild right?"

"No, no. I wasn't thinkin' anythin' like that. I'm ashamed ta say I'm just bein' selfish." Will cleared his throat. "I guess I'm wonderin' about God givin' you and Savannah a second child when much as I've longed for one…"

"I'm sorry, Will. It doesn't seem fair does it?" How could he be so inconsiderate. He shouldn't have made such a fuss over this new baby. "I guess there's no guarantee Mrs. Greely or her granddaughter won't change their minds."

Will gulped a big mouthful of air and straightened his shoulders. "I believe I'm just bein' tested to see if I'm serious about overcomin' self-pity. I promised the Lord to be grateful for what I have instead of focusin' on what I don't."

Garrett stared at his friend. "Sometimes you put me to shame with your maturity, Will. I forget who's the preacher."

"If I'm growin' spiritually it's thanks to your messages and Bible studies. I'm so glad you invited me to go with ya to the jail. Seems strange to say but it's one of the highlights of my week."

Warmth rose in Garrett. Nothing gave him more satisfaction than knowing he'd helped someone grow closer to Jesus. "Mine too. Devon is growing in his faith, and I have strong hopes for their marriage."

"Who would have thought going to the jail could give us so much joy?" Will beamed at him. "I always thought people were exaggeratin' when they said they couldn't wait to see Jesus face to face, but now I know it's true."

Garrett stole a peek at Will's glowing face just before it sobered.

"That reminds me, I've been meanin' to talk to ya about somethin'."

"What's troubling you?"

"Somethin' I read in me railroad journal the other day. The author quoted Henry Cabot Lodge sayin,' 'Those who work on the railroad suffer as if they were fighting a war.'" Will scowled. "Those who go to war, know well they may not come home."

He paused and stared out the window. "If somethin' were to happen to me, I'd want to be sure Polly was taken care of."

"Is Polly worried about finances if you were in an accident?"

"She's never mentioned money." Will gave a long sigh. "But it sure enough worries me. I'd like to provide somethin' more than what New York Central would give her, maybe a monthly income for awhile. Would your insurance company have anythin' like that?"

Garrett swallowed, his heart growing heavy. Usually a possible sale lifted his spirits but not this one. "Sounds like an annuity is what you're looking for. What would NYC provide?"

"$800 is the maximum death benefit."

This was his business, this is what he did. But this time it felt so personal. "I'll put together a proposal for you to look at."

♠

Polly backed out of the driveway, creeping onto Walnut Street. Backing the car didn't come easily to her but it was necessary. Deciding to get a driver's license had been a spur-of-the-moment decision and she wasn't ready to make trips much longer than to Sandy Lake and back, especially with winter coming on.

She shuddered. Why did winter have to come at all? It had never been her favorite season, but with Will's safety to consider it was a thousand times worse. Ice and snow made his job so much more dangerous.

Forcing herself to smile, she chose not to allow her fears to ruin the evening with her friends. Savannah and Sammy were waiting outside their apartment door when Polly pulled up behind the building. Savannah, always beautiful, had a radiance about her that caught Polly's attention.

As Savannah settled herself in the front with Sammy in the back, Polly gazed at her friend's face. "What are you so happy about?"

"Does it show?" Savannah's smile broadened even more. "Garrett and I got some very good news today. Sammy is going to have a baby brother or sister." She turned to pat Sammy's head affectionately.

Polly's jaw dropped. "How can that be?"

After Savannah told her story, Polly squeezed her hand. "I knew God would hear your prayer. Sort of like Hannah in the temple praying for a child. When is the baby due?"

"Sometime in April near as they can tell."

Polly turned and looked at Sammy. "What do you think about the new brother or sister, Sammy?"

He shrugged. "I dunno. It might take some gettin' used to. Specially if he fusses and cries all the time." The smile slid from his face. "I reckon if Mama and Papa was good enough to take me in, I gotta be willin' to make room for one more."

Chapter 65

The next few weeks flew by with lots of food at Thanksgiving and a flurry of gift buying as the Christmas shopping began. Polly and Will bought small gifts for all their nieces and nephews. She couldn't wipe the smile from her face as they picked out presents appropriate for each age. They also bought gifts for each other, for Polly's younger sisters, and for Will's mam and Polly's father.

The Friday before Christmas vacation began, Polly attended a sacred concert at the Sandy Lake High School. With Will at work, Father unavoidably detained at the mine, and Maggie's children sick, Polly was the only representative from the Dye family. Elsie had the voice of an angel as she sang *O Holy Night* with Allison Wright, and *The World's Redeemer King* with a ladies' quartette.

When the entire school rose to sing *Joy to the World*, the words and music washed over Polly, taking with it the fears that often assaulted her as winter set in.

Joy to the world! The Lord has come!
Let earth receive her King.
Let every heart prepare Him room…

She refused to picture Will running on the roofs of snow-covered train cars, allowing the words of joy to replace those pictures, preparing room in her heart for Jesus.

♠

The last Saturday before Christmas, Polly invited Will's

youngest nieces, Frances, Ruthie and Dorabell to bake Christmas cookies. With Mam's help she'd found a recipe for Irish holiday biscuits for Santa, in addition to the sugar cookie recipe Mother had always baked for the family for the holidays.

Polly and Will had picked out cookie cutters at Simcox's general store for the occasion: a Christmas tree, bell, Santa Claus, and reindeer. She dug them out as the outer door opened and the girls and Will barged in. Light snow falling added to the holiday spirit. Polly actually enjoyed the snow since Will had no trips until Monday.

Frances, now a big girl of five, ran to Polly and threw her wet, snowy arms around her. Will had walked to his brother's house and borrowed Mam's buggy to bring the girls back. They loved riding in the snow.

Stooping beside Will's youngest niece, Polly unbuttoned her coat. "Let's get you out of your wet things."

The older girls took off their coats and also came for hugs.

"Thanks for having us, Aunt Polly." As the eldest, Dorabell always tried to do her duty, thanking Polly and Will for whatever treat or fun times they provided.

"You're welcome, of course." Polly smiled at the girls' eager, shining faces. "Dorabell, why don't you help Will with the cookies for Santa. Frances, Ruthie and I can mix up the Dye family sugar cookie recipe."

"Let's have some Christmas music to bake by." Will brought out his prized portable Victrola and record collection including some Irish Christmas carols.

Soon the smell of molasses for the Irish Christmas cookies mixed with the smells of sugar and cinnamon from the sugar cookie recipe, against the background of Christmas music. Polly rolled out the dough and let the younger girls choose the shapes they wanted to use.

As the cookies baked in Polly's new-fangled oven, as Father called it, the fragrance in the kitchen became almost too tempting to resist. Polly spread the freshly baked sugar cookies on clean dish towels while Frances and Ruthie stood by eyeing the cookies.

"Do you have any sprinkles, Polly?" Frances licked her lips. "We like sprinkles."

"Don't beg, Frances." Dorabell frowned at her younger sister. "You know Mam said not to beg for things."

"It's all right, Dorabell. Thanks for reminding me, Frances." Polly whisked to her Hoosier-style cupboard, advertised to be the best servant in one's kitchen, and opened one of the upper doors on the right. Standing on tiptoe, she produced a brightly colored tin container. "Here we are."

Frances cheered and reached for the tin. "May I sprinkle some on the sugar cookies we haven't baked yet?"

"Of course." Polly pulled a chair from the table for Frances to kneel on. "I should have done this sooner. Ruthie, after Frances sprinkles these cookies, you can use this spatula to put them on the cookie sheets."

Polly moved to the other side of the Hoosier cupboard where Will and Dorabell were hard at work mixing the Irish cookies. "How's it going over here?"

"I almost forgot you have to melt the shortenin' and margarine before you add other ingredients." Will wiped his brow. "Good thing Dora read the recipe card."

"When we're finished mixing all the ingredients, we have to make one-inch balls and roll them in sugar." Dorabell grinned. "This will take all day, but I don't mind. I love baking."

"Maybe after I roll out another batch of sugar cookies, you'd like to take a turn using the cookie cutters while Frances and Ruthie roll some balls of dough in sugar." Polly wiped a smudge of molasses from Dorabell's cheek.

"Oh, I'd like that. Thanks, Aunt Polly."

Polly couldn't take her eyes off Will, his cheeks flushed and flour sprinkled on his shirt, having the time of his life. He was so good with the girls. Was being involved in his nieces' and nephews' lives enough for him?

Ever since Savannah shared her news about the baby

Mrs. Greely wanted them to adopt, Polly had wrestled with the question of whether or not she and Will should consider adoption. So far other than one false alarm, there was no evidence of nature taking its course. What did God want them to do? What was His plan?

Chapter 66

Christmas Eve dawned snowy and cold and Polly snuggled closer to Will, reveling in the opportunity to stay in bed a bit longer since he had a few days off over the holidays. He rolled over to face her, perhaps sensing she was awake. As she nuzzled her nose into his neck, he flinched.

"I'd better add more coal to the furnace, your nose is cold, Lass."

"Oh, don't get up yet. I'll soon be warm now that I'm in your arms." Polly never ceased to be amazed at the warmth that emanated from Will when he pulled her against him.

He chuckled. "You talked me into it. It's twisted around your little finger I am. But then you'd already be knowin' that, wouldn't ya?"

Polly raised up on one elbow and smiled into the bottomless depths of his brown eyes. She traced his jawbone to the corner of his mouth before leaning in to kiss his lips. "I don't know who is twisted around whose finger, Love."

"Perhaps 'tis six of one, half dozen of the other." He gently attempted to draw her back to his level.

She resisted for a moment. If only she could peer into the depth of his soul. "Are you happy, Will? Truly happy?"

"Aye, I couldn't be happier, Love. You made me the happiest man on earth the day you said you'd marry me. How could I be askin' for anything more?"

Blowing out a happy breath, Polly dove back into his arms.

♠

Christmas plans came together easily since Polly's family had been celebrating on Christmas Eve since her sister Maggie married, while Will's family's main celebration was mid-afternoon on Christmas Day. Later today Polly and Will had invited her family to come to their house for dinner and exchanging gifts. Tomorrow they would go to his mother's house around three o'clock to open gifts and eat.

They'd made plans to cut a fresh Christmas tree this morning and decorate it with popcorn and cranberries Will's nieces and nephews had helped to string.

Polly buttoned her coat and tied a green muffler around her neck, covering her nose and mouth. She smiled at Will bundled up in a warm wool coat and winter stocking cap. "Ready?"

"I'm ready."

She could barely see his eyes but knew they were twinkling in anticipation. After a short drive to Uncle Jim's woods, she and Will piled out of the car and trudged through the snow, looking for the perfect tree.

"Here it is, Lass." Will motioned for her to come closer to the most spindly, anemic tree Polly had ever seen.

"No, that's ugly, Will."

"Shhh… Its feelin's will be hurt. It's not that bad."

Every tree Polly found, Will contended that his pick had more character.

After a fair amount of debate, Will conceded that Polly had found one superior to his. He swung the axe with ringing blows until the tall, shapely blue spruce crashed to the ground, spreading the scent of pine all around. Together they dragged it back to the car and tied it to the roof with some strong bailer twine Will had begged from one of his farmer friends.

The day passed in a pleasant blur as they decorated and prepared food. The smell of turkey roasting had them salivating.

When evening came, the little brown bungalow rang with fun and laughter as the Dye's streamed into the house, putting packages under the tree and food on the well-laden table. Maggie set her candied yams on the kitchen counter, her children's favorite. The fragrance of spices filled the house as Dorothy and Ben arrived with their homemade pumpkin pies. George asked for a can opener to open the can of cranberry sauce he'd brought from Kenosha.

When everyone had arrived and gathered round except Beth, who was scheduled to work, and Robert, who planned to visit his son in California, Polly smiled at her father. "As the patriarch of the Dye family, would you like to ask the blessing?"

He nodded, even as he added, "How I miss your mother's prayers at times like these."

♠

Polly stood beside Mam, helping to serve the spiced beef and other tasty dishes Mam and other family members had prepared. Some had gathered here the night before to carry out some of their Christmas Eve traditions, including eating Oyster Stew, but not a word of complaint passed Mam's lips that Will and Polly hadn't come.

Impulsively, Polly leaned over to kiss Mam's wrinkled cheek.

Mam paused and smiled, her eyes warm with Christmas spirit. "Thank you for helpin', Polly."

"I'm just thanking the Lord that we buried the hatchet." Polly would never have dared to say that when she and Mam were feuding.

"Will was right. I had to forgive ya for not being Catholic. And I had to trust ya not to convert my son." Mam bit her lip. "I wish I had done it sooner."

"My mother would have said, 'No use crying over spilt milk.' Let's enjoy the good times." Polly smiled into Mam's blue eyes.

"You still miss your mam don't ya, Polly? Such a long time you've had to fill the gap for her. You've been a great help to your da."

"Thank you, Mam. I'm so grateful that now I have you. Merry Christmas, Mam."

♠

Savannah and Sammy snuggled on the davenport, her son clutching his teddy bear, one of his favorite gifts. To be honest, none of the gifts Savannah received today could compare with what God had already given her, a husband and a beautiful son, and the promise of a baby to come. She had done nothing to deserve such blessings.

Garrett entered the room with a Christmas cookie in one hand and his new Kodak camera in the other. He had been snapping random pictures ever since they returned from their Christmas dinner and gift exchange at his parents.

When he caught sight of Savannah and Sammy, he set down his cookie and squatted in front of the davenport, peering through the viewfinder, tilting the camera at various angles.

"Garrett, I'm so happy it almost scares me." Savannah tried to maintain her smile for the camera.

"Why would it scare you?" He snapped one more picture and then paused, a puzzled frown on his face.

"I don't deserve this joy. My mother used to say people would eventually figure out I was worthless. I keep thinking—" She gestured around her, "it's all too good to be true."

Chapter 67

"Is my policy ready yet?" Will asked the question before Garrett closed the car door, his friend's woodsy-scented aftershave already hanging in the air. More than two months since Will had asked Garrett to prepare a life insurance policy for him on a previous trip to the jail.

"To be honest, I'm having a hard time with this." Garrett sighed. "Have you told Polly what you're doing?"

Will shook his head. "I'm afraid it'll convince her somethin' bad is goin' to happen. I'd rather keep it between me and you. Why are ya havin' a hard time doing this? Are ya makin' too much money?" He chuckled.

"I guess I'm like Polly." Garrett's tone was solemn in spite of Will's attempt at humor. "I'm afraid if I finish writing it, something bad will happen." Garrett leaned forward. If only he could see Will's eyes but the early darkness of January made it impossible.

"Once I make up me mind to do something, I want it done as soon as possible." Will's tone now matched Garrett's. "I won't rest easy until it's finished."

The finality in Will's tone made clear the time for stalling was past. "I'll bring the forms along next Sunday. I can ask you the questions while you drive."

No matter how difficult, he needed to finish writing this

annuity. How awful would it be if something bad happened and Garrett hadn't finished the policy?

♠

Savannah hung up the telephone and wiped away a tear. Sammy, who had been playing with his miniature cowboys and Indians under the dining room table, stopped and stared at her. "What'sa matter, Mama?" His baby blue eyes peered into hers. "Why are ya cryin'?"

That child didn't miss a thing. Before she could answer, Garrett returned from the service at the jail wearing the same sober face she'd seen earlier. He'd been quiet recently and spent a lot of time in his study.

Savannah went to the davenport and motioned for Garrett and Sammy to join her. "They're happy tears, Sweetie. Mrs. Greely's granddaughter, Amanda, saw the doctor today and he says everything is going well. The baby should be born in about two months." Her questioning gaze settled on Garrett. "But I think your papa seems sad. Did something go wrong at the jail? Are you having second thoughts about the baby?"

"Oh no, no, nothing like that. The service went well and I'm happy about the baby."

"You haven't *looked* happy for a month. What's bothering you?" Savannah reached for his hand.

Garrett took a deep breath. "I'm probably making too much of this."

"Of what?" The furrows on Savannah's brow deepened.

In a few sentences, he told her about Will's request for him to design a policy to provide for Polly in case something should happen to Will. "I can't get it out of my mind. I'm wondering if—well, if the Holy Spirit is prompting him to do this. Polly always had a bad feeling about his job. "

Savannah covered her mouth, her pupils dilated, then she removed her hand. "Did you do what he asked?"

Garrett nodded. "I put it off as long as I could, but he kept asking if it was ready. I started working on it two weeks ago. Will signed it tonight."

♠

Will entered the house, removed his coat, and flopped on the couch. Silence surrounded him. Savannah hadn't brought Polly home yet from Bible study. He studied his copy of the policy Garrett had given him. So many words he didn't understand but he trusted his friend. Where should he put the paperwork? Polly mustn't find it.

He searched the house for a likely hiding place. Finally, his beige and black rucksack caught his eye, stashed in the corner of their bedroom. He used it to take toiletries and a change of clothing when he was gone overnight or longer. Folding the papers into fourths, he tucked them into the bottom of his bag. He always packed it himself, and there was no reason for Polly to open it. Peace flooded his soul.

A motor running in the driveway prompted him to toss the bag in the corner and return to the living room where he met Polly at the door. He pulled her into his arms and held her close, his cheek cushioned by her thick red hair, his heart filled with an ocean of love.

When he let her go, she gazed at him, her eyes pools of green. "That was quite a welcome."

"It's that kind of a welcome I should give ya every time ya come home." Will leaned in to kiss her lips.

She smiled. "It's not often you get to welcome me home. Usually I'm the one welcoming you. How was the service at the jail?"

Will's mind had been so consumed with the paperwork Garrett had for him, he'd barely heard his friend's message. "The service is always good, that it is. How was Bible study?"

"It's always good too." Polly sprinted to the kitchen, putting on water to make Will a cup of tea. "Sammy stayed with us this evening. He's such a sweet boy."

Will pulled out a chair at the dining room table and slid into it, not taking his eyes from his wife. She seldom mentioned Savannah's son. "Aye, he does seem to be that. Savannah and Garrett appear to be right taken with him."

Polly brought him a small plate of holiday biscuits, a cup of fragrant peppermint tea, and then sat across from him. "Will, I want you to be honest with me."

"I always aim to be honest, Lass." The papers in the bottom of his rucksack jabbed his conscience but he pushed it aside.

"Are you sure you don't want to adopt a child since I, since we, don't seem to be starting a family?" She gazed into his eyes.

"I thought we'd put that to rest, Love. If the good Lord sees fit to bless us with children, we'll welcome them. But I know you've already had quite a spell of child-rearin'." Will leaned across the table to kiss her cheek. "I appreciate that you're willin' to adopt but I'm content with the life we have."

Polly nodded, seeming to accept his answer.

"Besides…" He hesitated, then fell silent.

"Besides what?" A question mark formed in her green eyes.

"Never mind."

"What are you not telling me?" Polly peered at him with wrinkled brow.

He sighed. "I don't want to worry you, Lass." As Polly took a threatening step toward him, he stepped back. "All right. Did ya hear what Henry Cabot Lodge said about men who work on the railroad?"

"No." Polly's brows puckered at the change of subject. "Why?"

"He said, 'Those who work on the railroad suffer as if they were fighting a war.'

Understanding dawned in Polly's eyes. "And you're thinking perhaps those with such dangerous jobs as that aren't the best people to adopt children who've already lost one set of parents."

Chapter 68

Garrett hung up the telephone and stared at Savannah as he bit his lip.

"Who was that?" Savannah shifted in her seat on the davenport to have a better view of her husband. "Is something wrong?"

He dropped into the blue wing chair. "It was Derek Green, the head of the Governing Board at the Methodist Episcopal Church in Sandy Lake."

Savannah tilted her head. "What did he want?"

"The Board wants to meet with me after I preach there on Sunday morning. I don't know why." He leaned his head against the back of the chair. "I hope there isn't a complaint against me."

"It's more likely they have a complaint against me." Savannah sighed.

"Don't say that. It's been years since anyone except—" he glanced at Sam, "you-know-who has complained about you, and look at how God changed her heart." Garrett stood and joined his wife on the davenport, circling around their son playing near her feet. He put his arm around Savannah.

"This is the first time I've been asked to preach there in a long while. I thought it was because they have Jonathan Williams now, the seminary student who'll be replacing Reverend Desmond soon. Now I'm not so sure."

Savannah rested her head on his shoulder. "At least we should soon know. Day after tomorrow." Patting his knee, she sat up. "Change of subject. We need to decide where to have the nursery when our new baby comes."

"I assumed the baby would share Sam's room. It's quite large."

Sam lifted his head, a plastic horse falling from his hand in mid-air. He glanced from Garrett to Savannah.

"I'm concerned the baby's crying would wake Sam." She grinned at Garrett and winked at Sam. "Babies *do* sometimes cry at night, you know."

"I thought Sam would take care of the baby at night." Now it was Garrett's turn to wink at Sam.

Sam blinked, then sat up, his spine straight as a ramrod. "I could probably do that."

Savannah chuckled. "Thank you, Sammy, but I think Papa's teasing you. It wouldn't be fair to expect you to get up with the baby."

Blowing out his breath, Sam relaxed and leaned back on his hands, then straightened again. "You won't put the baby in your room, will you?" A worried frown wrinkled his forehead.

Garrett leaned down and ruffled Sam's hair. "Mama and I will figure something out, buddy. Not to worry."

♠

Garrett kissed Savannah's cheek after they'd shaken hands with folks at the close of the service on Sunday morning. She hadn't argued about greeting people here as she used to do and appeared comfortable in her role as a pastor's wife.

Sam had gone home with Grandpa and Grandma Young. Savannah would join them while he met with the Board. His stomach gurgled, queasy with the uncertainty of today's meeting.

Derek shook his hand and motioned to follow him. When they arrived at the pastor's office, Reverend Desmond and other members of the Council were already seated. Where was Jonathan Williams, who'd been assisting Reverend Desmond in serving the congregation for several years?

Dropping into one of the empty chairs, Garrett, took a few slow, deep breaths, while Derek sat beside their Pastor and cleared his throat. "A number of years ago, Reverend Caldwell spoke to you, Garrett, about our pastor retiring and inquired about your interest in eventually taking his place."

Garrett nodded, glancing around the circle of men, many leaders in the community. No open scowls. His stomach settled.

"At the time, you declined, and later, we hired Jonathan Williams, who has been serving alongside Reverend Desmond while completing seminary."

"Yes. I assume Jonathan will be graduating soon?" Garrett glanced at Reverend Desmond. He was fairly certain the older pastor had intended to retire long before now.

Derek, who had been rocking his chair gently from four legs to two, hesitated and coughed. "He'll be graduating in April, which coincides with our Pastor's retirement." He crashed down, none too gently, to four legs again. "However, he's accepted a call from a church in eastern Pennsylvania where his wife's family lives."

Raising an eyebrow, Garrett glanced around the circle again, focusing on Reverend Desmond. What a disappointment this must be for him.

"We've not told many folks, respecting Reverend Desmond's wishes, but Dr. Cooley has made it clear our pastor's retirement needs to take place in April as planned." Derek blew out a strong breath, and tilted his chair against the pastor's desk. "Because of your service with the alliance of pastors, we feel you'd be qualified to step into his position at that time. Would you have any interest in doing that?"

Garrett let out a breath he hadn't realized he'd been holding. How would Savannah feel about this? Her misgivings about her acceptance in the role of a pastor's wife had been the main reason for his previous refusal.

He steepled his fingers, resting his chin on them, while doing his best to hide his interest. He needed to talk to Savannah. As their family grew, his longing to settle into a church home, rather than preaching in a different church almost every Sunday, had grown. If he were honest, he was also weary of the hectic pace of serving with the alliance of pastors and the jail, as well as working many hours as an agent. Was this God's answer to the longing he'd never voiced even to Savannah?

Chapter 69

Garrett sniffed as he ran up the steps to his parents' house. Roast beef and potatoes. Ummm. The meal, always a favorite of his, had also won the hearts of his wife and Sam.

"How did things go with the church board?" Savannah leaned in for a kiss when Garrett sat down beside her at the table. They had no secrets from his parents, so he shared everything that had been said. "I told Derek we needed to think and pray. He gave us two weeks to give them an answer."

Savannah tapped her finger on her lips, a thoughtful frown puckering her forehead.

Garrett peered at her. "What do you think, or do you need time?"

"A better question is, what do *you* think? It will mean some major changes in your life. Is that what you want?" She touched his arm.

Dropping the shield he'd kept in place for weeks, he nodded. "To be honest, yes. I'm weary of driving to different places almost every Sunday, to the jail Sunday night, working all week, and studying in the evenings. I'd like more time to enjoy my family, especially with another baby on the way."

"You never complain, but you're so busy. Your family would like more time to enjoy you, too." Savannah's eyes sparkled.

Pa eyed Garrett as he loaded his plate. "Should I assume if you take this position, your days of being an insurance agent are over?"

Garrett chewed rapidly. "I'd like to keep a few of my more personal accounts like Will Reiser, but yes, I'd want to mostly retire from the agency. Maybe share the chaplaincy at the Mercer jail with some other pastors so I could cut back to once a month."

"It sounds like a wise move, son." His mother was nodding, an approving smile on her lips.

"Before," Garrett paused and gazed at his wife, "you had concerns…" He glanced at Sam. "About being a pastor's wife at this church. Do you feel differently now?"

Savannah drew a long breath. "I'm not as concerned as I used to be—although it still makes me a little nervous. But I'm looking forward to being home more when the new baby comes, and it would be wonderful if you'd be there too."

Garrett set down his fork and clasped her fingers. "Another advantage, having an office at the church frees up the space I use at our apartment for a nursery."

A huge smile split Sam's face. "God works out everything, doesn't He? This way everyone can have their own room."

"Well, not quite everyone." Garrett grinned. "I still want to share Mama's room."

"Speaking of you being home when the baby comes, Savannah, I'm thinking of hiring two people part time to take your place." Pa buttered a piece of bread. "Do you think Polly might be interested in working mornings?"

"I'll ask her, Father." Savannah smiled at her father-in-law. "Do you have someone in mind for Garrett's position?"

"As a matter of fact, I do. Garrett's cousin, Irv, has been hankering to try his hand at selling insurance. Just ready to do something different, I guess. Quite a change from selling fertilizer, but I'm willing to let him give it a try."

"What do you think about all this, Sammy?" Ma smiled at her first grandchild. "Papa changing jobs, Mama staying home more, a new baby coming?"

Sammy screwed up his face as he often did when he was thinking. "Papa changing jobs is a new one, but I'm getting used to the idea of a new baby. And having Mama home will be nice."

"I bet you'll still want to spend time with Grandma sometimes though, won't you?" Savannah ruffled Sam's hair.

"Can I, Grandma? I'd miss you if I didn't see you most every day." He turned woebegone eyes on Ma.

"Of course you can. I'd miss you too. We've gotten to be good buddies, haven't we?" Sam leaned his head on Ma's shoulder for a moment.

Garrett's heart swelled at the goodness of God. A beautiful wife, a growing family, and God changing Savannah's heart and opening a door for him to pastor a church. What more could he ask? He would miss seeing the men at the jail every week, but it would be good for them to connect with other pastors too.

"Is this really what you want, son?" Pa's tone was more open than Garrett might have expected to the possible change in his job. In the past, he'd been quite resistant to the idea.

"It is, Pa. I like selling insurance and I appreciate all the confidence you've shown in me over the years. But selling insurance isn't my heart's desire."

Pa nodded. "You're good at selling insurance. I always said you could sell snow to an Eskimo. But you're a good preacher too, and if that's what the Lord's calling you to do, I won't stand in your way."

Garrett caught Ma's eye as her eyebrow raised a trifle. Not the reaction she'd expected from his father either. "That means a lot to me, Pa. If I can please both my heavenly Father and my earthly one, I'm a happy man."

It was, as Savannah had said recently, too good to be true. Was all this happiness too good to last?

Chapter 70

"You'll be leaving early on a longer run tomorrow, won't you?" Polly passed the moist platter of meatloaf to Will.

Will nodded, his mouth full of meatloaf and scalloped potatoes. He swallowed. "That I will, Lass, but I'll be home in time for Valentine's Day." He took another piece of meatloaf and leaned over the table to kiss her.

Polly usually dreaded these longer runs but she had plans for Mam to teach her to make more of Will's favorite dishes for Valentine's Day dinner. "I'll be counting on it." She smiled into his eyes. "I'm going to get up and make breakfast for you tomorrow morning."

Shaking his head, Will chewed and swallowed again. "No, indeed, you're not. I've told ya before, there's no use in ya gettin' up before daybreak. I'm not hungry for more than a piece of bread at that hour."

Cutting up her meatloaf, Polly sighed. It was hard for Will to let her to do anything special for him. She'd kept her plans to make a special dinner a secret so he wouldn't insist it was too much trouble. "All right, at least I'll pack your lunch tonight."

"If that makes ya feel better. Thank you, Lass." The words weren't mechanical. His heartfelt gratitude always warmed her heart. "This meatloaf will be mighty tasty in a sandwich."

They cleaned up the kitchen and the evening sped by all too quickly. Their moments together were extra precious when a separation of several days awaited them. Finally, the warmth of the furnace and Will's early rising caught up with him. He couldn't hide his yawns. Polly set his shoes by the door, one of the few things he allowed her to do for him each evening, tugged him to his feet, and led him to the bedroom.

Soon they'd reached her favorite part of the day, snuggling into bed with Will's arm around her and her head on his shoulder. Even though Will often fell asleep within minutes on work days, the warmth of his body comforted her and helped keep her worrisome thoughts at bay.

Polly deliberately focused on the recipes she and Mam planned to practice making, while purposely shoving out of her mind the words that had haunted her since Will quoted Henry Cabot Lodge. *Those who work on the railroad suffer as if fighting a war.* If only she hadn't pushed him to tell her.

Time for a promise. One of her favorites. *Be anxious for nothing; but in every thing by prayer and supplication with thanksgiving let your requests be made known unto God. And the peace of God, which passeth all understanding, shall keep your hearts and minds through Christ Jesus.*

She needed God's peace to keep her heart and mind.

♠

Tuesday and Wednesday passed pleasantly enough as Polly learned to make creamy potato and leek soup loaded with bacon, Steak and Guinness pie, and Barley's Irish cream cheesecake. Frances didn't attend school yet so she came to help off and on. Dorabell and Ruthie rushed over each day after school. Mam hummed and sang Irish choruses as they worked. Were their days of being in competition for Will's affections gone forever?

Mam invited her to stay for dinner to help eat the food they'd prepared and Polly was happy to oblige. She was in no hurry to return to the empty house, although she could have eaten with Twila, Elsie, and her father. Her father made no secret of the fact her cooking would be welcome anytime. He couldn't bring himself to hire a housekeeper. Rumor had it that coal wasn't as plentiful in their area as it had been in the past. Perhaps that was the reason for his reluctance.

At last she had no more excuses not to return home. She kissed Mam good bye and walked the short distance to their house through light snow. A good tired seeped through her body as she got into her flannel nightgown. *I shouldn't have any trouble falling asleep tonight* After climbing into bed, she picked up Sarah's diary lying on her bedside table. Her eyelids drooped and after flipping through several pages, she closed it.

Despite all her evil forebodings, her life had been relatively problem free since Lydia's departure. *That wasn't nice, Polly.* She reached for her Bible. As always, she had less urgency to study God's Word when adversity didn't rear its ugly head. She read a few verses with no understanding before closing the Bible. Forcing her eyelids open, she made a feeble attempt to pray before giving up and turning out the light.

Polly wore her heaviest nightgown, as she always did when Will was away, but still curled up in a ball to generate warmth. She drifted off to sleep, a smile tugging at her lips. *Will would be so surprised at the dinner she'd prepare tomorrow.*

♠

Disoriented and bleary-eyed, Polly shot up in bed at the loud banging on her door. She glanced at the clock. Five o'clock. Who would be at her door at that hour? Her insides twisted. *Something had happened to Will.*

No, no. She pushed away the frightening thought. Maybe Will had come home early to surprise her and forgotten his key. That must be it.

Polly swung her feet to the chilly floor and grabbed a warm robe from the bottom of the bed. Knotting the belt around her waist in case it wasn't Will, she ran to the door, turned on the porch light and peered out. The man looked familiar. After a moment of hesitation, she opened the door. The agent from the Stoneboro Station of the New York Central Railroad stood on her porch. Her mind went blank as her pulse galloped. She bit her lower lip so hard she drew blood.

Chapter 71

The man on her front porch spoke, but the roaring in Polly's ears prevented her from hearing. "Wh—What did you say?"

He reached out, grasping her trembling hand. "I'm so sorry, Mrs. Reiser. There's been an accident."

Polly's head had already begun to shake from side to side of its own volition. "No, no."

The man squeezed her hand harder. "I just got word from the Eclipse Station agent. Your husband has been…" he paused and licked his lips.

She wanted to pull her hand from his and cover her ears, but his grip was too tight.

Adamantly, he began again. "Your husband has been seriously injured."

Sobs began deep in her throat and tears poured down her cheeks. Between sobs, she choked out, "But it didn't snow very much. He's so sure footed. What happened?"

Swallowing hard, Mr...Breese. Yes, that was his name. Mr. Breese shook his head. "Will couldn't tell them what happened except he was crushed between two cars in the Eclipse Oil Refinery yard. He's been transferred to the Franklin Hospital in crit—"

Mr. Breese's face blurred and his words faded as Polly's world went black.

♠

When things around her began to take shape, Polly's name penetrated her consciousness.

"Mrs. Reiser, Mrs. Reiser." A cool, wet cloth slid across her face.

She lay on the couch with a pillow under her head. Mr. Breese knelt beside her. "Is there someone I can call to take care of you? I'm not much of a nurse."

Polly took a deep breath and pushed herself to a sitting position. "I need to get to the hospital." She rubbed her throbbing head. "If only I could think…My father, I need to call my father. And Will's mother needs to be told. Father will take us to the hospital." She gingerly swung her bare feet to the floor, and after a short pause, she stood.

Mr. Breese grasped her hand and escorted her to the telephone. She managed to dial the correct number after the second attempt and told Father what happened between ragged breaths. He was coming.

"Will's mother doesn't have a telephone." She clutched her head for a moment. "Could you go tell her while I get dressed? Do you know where she lives?"

A brief nod from Mr.Breese. "Are you sure you'll be all right?"

"Don't worry about me. Just be very gentle with Will's Mam." Polly's tears started again. "Don't frighten her."

A raised eyebrow let Polly know Mr. Breese wanted instructions how to accomplish that in light of the circumstances. But she waved him toward the door. "Just say Will is hurt and is in the hospital."

As soon as the door closed, Polly stumbled blindly toward the bedroom, blocking every thought that attempted to paralyze her limbs. Somehow she found clothes and dressed herself with shaking fingers, putting her dress on backwards on the first try. She shrugged into her cable-knit sweater as the front door opened. Her father must have flown across the familiar road from Sandy Lake to Stoneboro.

She dashed to the door and flung herself at him. "Oh,

Papa, didn't I warn Will over and over about the danger of his job? Didn't I worry and fret every winter about the risks of being a brakeman?"

Her father gently moved her back into the house, following close behind her. "You did, Florence. Of course you did. But railroading is the work he loves. You wouldn't want him to give up doing what he loves."

"But he loves me too. Shouldn't that make a difference?"

"I'm sorry, Polly." He touched her shoulder. "I don't know what to say."

Was it the first time he had ever called her by her nickname? He was trying so hard to comfort her. Tears rolled down her cheeks and sobs choked her.

"Here, let me help you." Father drew her toward him. "Your sweater is on inside out." One sleeve at a time, he removed her sweater and turned it right side out as a vehicle skidded into the driveway.

Polly yanked open the front door. "Maybe that's Will now, coming to tell us it's all a mistake." Her shoulders slumped as the car's passengers became visible in the porch light. "It's Mr. Breese, the station agent, bringing Mam."

Her father lifted her coat from the hook by the door. "Come, Lass, let's get Will's Mam and be on our way."

Polly's sobs started afresh at her father's use of Will's favorite name for her.

He helped her put on her coat, whispering all the while, "Sh, sh, let's not upset Mrs. Reiser."

Mam's questions bombarded her as soon as they stepped out the door. "What happened, Polly? What kind of an accident? How badly is Will hurt?"

Polly drew a deep breath. Maybe she'd been wrong to have Mr. Breese withhold information from Will's mother. She nodded at him as he helped Mam up the driveway, mouthing the words, "Tell her everything."

♠

Silence reigned in Father's car, except for sniffs and an

occasional sob as they covered the seemingly endless miles to Franklin. "How much farther, Father?"

"About five miles. We're more than halfway."

Polly leaned forward to check on Mam seated beside her father. Her head and shoulders were erect but her hand, clutching a handkerchief, rested on her chest. Even after Mr. Breese had given Mam all the information, the first half of the trip had been a steady stream of questions, to which Polly had no answers.

As though sensing Polly's scrutiny, Mam turned to meet her eyes. "Will promised he'd be home for Valentine's Day."

♠

"Happy Valentine's Day, My Love." Savannah sat up to kiss her husband, already sitting up staring into space. When he didn't respond, she added, "Is something wrong?"

He gave himself a shake which was more like a shiver. "I'm sorry. Happy Valentine's Day." He paused. "I've been awake since four o'clock, and I can't seem to shake this...this darkness."

"I'm sorry, Love." Savannah patted his arm and attempted a light touch. "Turning on the light might help."

Garrett didn't laugh. "Something's wrong. I feel it in my bones." He got dressed in record time and headed for the kitchen.

What could Savannah say? She joined him a few minutes later, the gloom surrounding him almost palpable. Even Sammy's antics, balancing his cereal bowl on his head and hopping on one foot, didn't draw a smile. Unable to lighten Garrett's mood, she made short work of breakfast and headed for the office while Garrett took Sammy to his mother's.

Dorothy waited for her there, as she always did if she had gossip or bad news. "Did you hear what happened?"

Savannah cringed. Never even a *good morning* to precede whatever news Dorothy itched to tell. "I don't think so."

"My Uncle Jerry said the station agent in Stoneboro told him Will Reiser was injured at the Eclipse Oil Refinery yard soon after four o'clock this morning."

Chapter 72

Keeping a tight grip on Mam's left arm and Father's right, Polly marched into the hospital. Strong antiseptic odors, probably used by the night cleaning crew, opened her sinuses. She cleared her throat and the woman behind the front desk looked up. Polly opened her mouth. At first only a croak came out. She coughed and tried again. "Could you tell me where we can find William Reiser? He was brought in earlier this morning."

The woman's sympathetic brown eyes lowered as she turned a page in her notebook and ran her finger down the lines. "I remember the name. Ah, here it is. Mr. Reiser is in Room 214." She frowned as she read her notes. "Have you talked to his doctor?"

"We received a message through the station agent in Stoneboro." Polly dropped her father's arm and clenched and unclenched her fingers. "He's the only person we've spoken to."

"Why don't you have a seat in the waiting area by the window." Mrs. Snyder, as her nametag identified her, gestured to her right. "I'll try to locate his doctor." Her sturdy white shoes squeaked as she left her desk.

Why was it necessary to speak to Will's doctor first? If only Dr. Cooley could have been here, what a comfort that would have been, but railroad companies hired their own doctors because of all the accidents.

Even as Polly's legs followed Mrs. Snyder's instructions,

she chafed at the delay. She sat facing the room to get the first glimpse of the doctor, with Father and Mam on either side of her. What if the doctor had left the hospital, and they were forced to wait until he returned?

But only a few minutes passed before the squeak of Mrs. Snyder's shoes and a heavier tread coming down the stairs became audible. Polly leaped to her feet and strode across the waiting area, meeting them as they emerged from the hall.

"Mrs. Reiser, this is Dr. Jobson." Mrs. Snyder nodded at the tall, clean-shaven man in a white jacket.

Was that pity in his blue eyes?

"Dr. Jobson can give you an update on your husband's condition."

The man glanced toward the waiting area. "Are other members of your family here?"

Polly nodded. "My father and Will's mother."

"Let's join them so you won't have to repeat what I tell you." Dr. Jobson gestured for her to precede him.

It was the sensible approach but Polly gritted her teeth, impatience reaching fever pitch at the delay. She introduced Dr. Jobson to Father and Mam. Her father stood to shake Dr. Jobson's hand but Polly could restrain herself no longer.

"Please Dr. Jobson…"

He sat down beside her in the chair Father had vacated as Father joined Mam on the sofa. "I know you're eager to hear my report, but I'm afraid I don't have good news." He swallowed and licked his lips.

Polly balled her hands into fists and willed herself not to pass out. She had never passed out before this morning. Mam's heavy breathing filled the silence. *Just tell us and get it over with…*

"Mr. Reiser's left leg and arm were broken and crushed in the accident. Although he is conscious from time to time and may recognize you, the accident has taken a terrible toll. He's in a state of shock." The doctor glanced at Mam and back at Polly. "Are you okay, Mrs. Reiser?"

He was looking at her, so Polly nodded. What else could she do? "Can you fix his arm and leg?"

Dr. Jobson closed his eyes, then opened them. "Amputation would be indicated if there was any chance of recovery. However..." He reached to take her hand. "We've known since he arrived at the hospital that he cannot survive due to the effects of extreme shock on his organs."

Polly yanked her hand from his and covered her face. "No," she wailed. "No, there has to be hope. There has to be. I won't give up."

♠

After a session alone in the women's lavatory, splashing cold water on her face and taking deep breaths, Polly rejoined Father and Mam waiting to visit Will. In spite of Mam's legion of questions earlier, she received the doctor's report dry-eyed, saying only that Father Craig should be called to give the last rites. Mrs. Snyder had agreed to call him.

"I'm sorry." Polly's voice cracked, and she wiped away another tear. She slipped her hand through Mam's arm. "How can you be so brave?"

Mam shook her head. "Job said, 'The Lord giveth and the Lord taketh away. Blessed be the name of the Lord.'" She smoothed Polly's hand as the three of them walked up the stairs. "We're told not to grieve as the world grieves because we have the promise of life beyond the grave."

They hesitated outside the door to Room 214, which was partially closed. Father pushed it open and stepped back for Polly and Mam to enter.

Polly's most precious earthly treasure lay in the hospital bed with a sheet and blanket pulled up to his neck, his eyes closed. His injuries were hidden under the bedclothes and, except for his pallor, Polly could almost convince herself he was okay. As she stepped closer, Will's eyes flickered open, unfocused at first. Then pools of sadness and regret emerged as they registered Polly's presence. His words were slurred and slow. "I'm...so... ...sorry...Lass. So...sorry."

"Sh, sh. Don't waste your breath on regrets. Your Mam and my father are here too."

She stepped to the other side of the bed to make room. Will's eyes flitted to each of their faces. "I'm sorry, Mam. Everything happened so fast…"

Mam patted his cheek. "Father Craig will be coming soon, son. Try to hang on."

He nodded, his eyes coming back to rest on Polly. A single tear slid down his cheek as he attempted to lift his left arm under the bedclothes. His face contorted as he writhed in pain.

Polly pointed to her father. "Get a nurse. Quick."

Father whisked out the door before Polly finished speaking. Within minutes he returned with a nurse, a hypodermic needle in her hand. The soul of efficiency, the stout, round-faced woman folded down the sheet and administered the injection in Will's right arm. "He'll sleep now, Lass."

Her words were directed to Polly whose tears began again at the Irish woman's use of that word. She was barely able to choke out her thanks.

"We won't be puttin' anyone else in this room, so why don't you all sit down." The woman's blue eyes were kind. "There are enough chairs for all of you."

When the woman left, Polly moved to the other side of the bed where she could hold Will's limp hand. She stared at their intertwined fingers on the blanket, willing herself not to think a single second ahead of the present one.

♠

Polly avoided staring at the clock as the minutes crept by. Father Craig had come, speaking words of affirmation lost to Will in his drug-induced sleep but comforting to those around the bed, and then slipped out again. No one knew how long this vigil would continue. She declined food when mealtimes came. Polly couldn't imagine putting anything into her mouth. Father and Mam also refused.

There was almost a sense of déjà vu in this waiting. More than ten years ago they'd waited while Dr. Cooley worked feverishly to save Mother's life. That day when she pleaded with God to spare her mother, His only answer had been, *Be still and know that I am God.* Today, despite her earlier protests, there was no pleading, no begging, only a sense of something happening she'd known would take place. It had only been a matter of time.

The blanket covering Will's chest rose and fell rhythmically while Mam and Father sat across from her, all of them caught in a time warp which held them captive. Nothing could be done to hasten or slow the passing of time. In spite of the inevitability of what lay ahead, Polly longed to do something to overcome the sense of powerlessness that shrouded her.

She continued to hold Will's hand as darkness fell outside the walls of the hospital. When his breathing pattern changed with longer pauses in between, she gripped his fingers tighter. "No, Will, please don't leave me." The words came out in sobs.

His eyes flickered open and with his last breath, he whispered, "Don't cry, Lass. One day we'll celebrate Valentine's Day in heaven."

Chapter 73

Polly stood in the St. Columbkille Cemetery waiting for family and friends to gather. She had chosen to drive herself from the Catholic Church, not wanting to make conversation. The only person she wanted to talk to was gone. She had blindly followed Mam's guidance during the funeral mass so foreign to her. Nothing made sense to her numb brain.

She shivered in the cold February temperatures as she was drawn back to happier memories of this graveyard. At the end of May, it would be four years that she and Will had taken the first steps toward reuniting after being kept apart by misunderstandings for a year and a half.

Her surroundings faded and his hand was on her shoulder, his lilting voice in her ear. "Polly?" They'd both come to a Decoration Day ceremony and what a miracle to find him looking into her eyes. How amazing to hear him say how much he'd missed her. If only there were a way to get back the time they'd wasted. She'd give anything to hear his voice one more time.

Cars and buggies began to arrive, breaking the spell, and Polly returned reluctantly to the present, keeping her back to the plain, wooden coffin ready to be lowered into the ground. A tall, broad-shouldered man and his petite, dark-haired wife approached her. Polly searched for their names. They lived in Stoneboro…she should know.

"Mrs. Reiser." The man's voice was deep and resonant.

"Charles and Jane Clarkson. I'm an engineer with the Pennsylvania Railroad, and we just wanted to tell you how sorry we are about Will's death."

That's why Mr. Clarkson looked familiar. Will had known him as a fellow railroad worker. Suddenly all her pent-up anger at the conditions which allowed one out of every thirty-five railway workers to be injured on the job rose up in her. She clenched her fists, resisting an urge to pound the solid chest of the unsuspecting man.

Instead, she gritted her teeth and dredged up a smile she didn't know she had. "Thank you, Mr. Clarkson." Then her lips turned down and words she hadn't intended spewed from her lips. "But sorry won't bring my husband back, will it? Nor all the other railroad men who've left behind widows and children."

Red crept up Mr. Clarkson's neck and he took a step back. His wife reached to take Polly's hands. "No, Mrs. Reiser, but we would bring him back if only we could. Charles' job isn't nearly as dangerous as that of a brakeman, but I still lose sleep at night when he's out."

The heat of shame suffused Polly's chest. Will's accident wasn't this man's fault. He wasn't even a representative of the railroad, just a fellow worker who cared enough to come to Will's burial service. "I'm sorry." She bowed her head. "Can you forgive me? I don't know what came over me. I'm…I'm not myself today."

"Mrs. Reiser…"

Polly raised her head at Mr. Clarkson's gentle tone. "It's not unusual to be angry when accidents happen or to look for someone to blame. I see it all the time among passengers and among the people I work with."

His words cooled the heat of Polly's shame. "But his accident wasn't your fault."

Mr. Clarkson smiled. "When somebody needed someone to blame, my mother used to say, 'I have broad shoulders.' If it helped you to express some of your anger, I can take it."

His wife smiled at him, then beamed at Polly. "You

won't find that kind of attitude often. We'll be praying for you." Mrs. Clarkson hugged her and the two moved on.

Polly drew a deep breath. Undergirded by the kindness of this couple, she turned and stood tall, steeling herself against the agonizing pain of watching Will's coffin being lowered into the ground. Will's family and hers, including Savannah and Garrett, had arrived to surround her for the rest of the service. Even Beth and her fiancé, Elmer, had come from Ohio. What a sad day for his introduction to the family.

As they all gathered around her, Elsie held one hand and Twila the other. Together, they would get through this.

♠

After a funeral dinner at the Catholic Church, tables laden with food as tasteless as sawdust, Polly said her goodbyes. Many offered to accompany her or to take her with them, but she refused them all. They meant well but she wanted to be alone. Garrett walked with her to the car and told her there was something they needed to discuss later. Although this would normally have whetted her curiosity, it didn't even spark a nibble.

As she drove back to their little brown bungalow, the numbness she'd been experiencing off and on since the agent appeared at her door settled over her again. She might as well get used to it. No one could rescue her from what had happened. The only One who could have had not intervened.

Polly tasted, then swallowed down, the growing bitterness that had been rearing its ugly head. She had every reason to be bitter. She could identify with Naomi's words in the Bible after her husband and sons died. "Call me Mara, for the Almighty hath dealt very bitterly with me."

Mother used to say entertaining that emotion was as bad as drinking poison, but Polly wasn't ready to let it go. She pulled into her driveway and climbed out of the car. Reaching into the backseat where she'd thrown her handbag, she noticed Will's rucksack on the floor. Thoughtfully, she picked it up. She'd never looked inside, always assuming Will could pack what he needed better than she could. It was heavy.

Polly carried it into the house and sank down on the davenport, where she'd snuggled with Will on many a winter night. She held the rucksack close. These would have been the last items he'd handled before his accident. Closing her eyes, she smoothed her fingers over the bag his fingers had touched. One by one she removed work shirts and toiletries, handling each item as though it were fashioned of gold.

At the bottom of the bag, she found papers folded into fourths. An odd thing to carry in his rucksack. She smoothed out the sheets and began to read. Tears slid down her cheeks as it dawned on her what Will had done. Even though he hadn't left the job he loved, he had made sure she would be cared for above and beyond the settlement from the railroad that would come eventually.

Garrett's name, signed as the agent from the life insurance company, told her all she needed to know. Will had chosen not to worry her by telling her about the policy, but instead had counted on his best friend to be the administrator. She leaned her head on the back of the davenport and allowed her tears to flow.

Words she'd marked in Sarah's diary tugged at her brain until she went to get the book from her bedside table. *If I turn against God, to whom will I go for the comfort and strength I need to get through the days ahead?* To whom indeed?

Grabbing her own journal where she'd written truths God had given her over the years, she opened to these words. *"If we'll allow it, He'll use the sorrow and suffering in our lives to shape us into the image of Christ. Otherwise, we'll become brittle and easily shattered by tragedies that come."*

Words from a sermon given by Jim Caldwell many years ago. Her friend, Kitt's, words rang in her ears. "I guess I have a choice to make."

Chapter 74

Garrett slumped in his chair, his head resting on his hand. Maybe he should have taken the day off. He was in no condition to work. The past few days were like a bad dream he couldn't awaken from.

Could it be only a week ago he'd been dwelling on all the blessings God had given him, a life almost too good to be true? All the good things still existed, but the shock of losing his best friend had him reeling. He couldn't concentrate on details of policies he needed to finish. Nothing could have prepared him for this, not even Will's request that he write a policy to provide for Polly should something happen to him.

According to Dorothy, Will's accident had happened soon after four o'clock on Valentine's Day, the exact time he had awakened with a premonition something was wrong. Maybe if he'd been more spiritually alert… maybe if he'd prayed the right prayer, the accident could have been avoided.

He took a deep breath and stepped back from the dark precipice of self-blame. *Stop it. Blaming yourself doesn't change anything.*

Taking another swallow of bland coffee Dorothy had brewed that morning, he straightened in his chair when another jab penetrated his brain. Maybe he wasn't ready to pastor a church if he had failed his best friend.

♠

Polly pushed open the door to Young's Insurance office

on Monday morning, clutching the papers she'd found in the bottom of Will's rucksack. She should have called first, but somehow dialing the telephone prompted too many memories of calling her father to tell him about Will's accident.

"Is Garrett here?" Pushing her hand through her scantily combed hair, she directed her question to Dorothy who was not her usual chatty self. No one knew what to say to her since Will's passing. Fine with her. If people didn't speak, she didn't have to answer.

Dorothy stood. "I'll check. I didn't see him leave."

Smoothing the crumpled pages, Polly read again the words on the first sheet. This must be what Garrett wanted to talk to her about.

"Polly." Garrett's tone was ragged. "I didn't know if you'd be up to... Well, I didn't know how you'd be feeling today." He motioned to her. "Come back to my office."

Polly waved at Savannah as they passed her open door. Savannah would give up her job soon when the new baby came. Polly swallowed around a lump in her throat that almost choked her every time a baby came to mind. The one thing Will had wanted. How could she have been so selfish?

Internally, she shook her head. Regrets wouldn't change the past or enable her to cope with the future. She dropped into the dark green cushioned chair Garrett indicated as he went to a file drawer and slipped out a folder.

"I suppose you're wondering why I—"

Polly interrupted with a shake of her head as she held up the four sheets of paper clasped in her hand. "I found this in Will's rucksack, so I figured this is why you wanted to talk to me."

After Garrett tossed the folder on his desk, he perched on the edge of his chair and stared out the window.

"Polly..." He stopped and closed his eyes for a moment before continuing. "I don't know how to tell you how sorry we are about Will's accident." He swallowed audibly. "I guess you know—he was my best friend."

"Don't Garrett." Polly squeezed her eyes shut, then blinked away tears. "I have to stop crying all the time. No matter how much I cry, it won't bring Will back. It won't change anything."

Garrett pulled a clean handkerchief from his pocket and came around his desk to press it into Polly's hand. As she wiped her eyes, he pulled up another chair beside her. "I'm sorry, Polly. I've never had a policy on someone as close to me as Will, never felt so responsible…" He swallowed. "I don't know how to separate business from personal here." He got up and paced around the small office.

As last, he came back and sat down beside Polly, seeming to have regained control. "As your friend, I want to tell you that although crying won't bring Will back, it will help you grieve. Your loss came so suddenly and it may take a long time and many tears for your soul to grasp it completely."

He reached across the desk to pull the folder toward him. "As Will's friend and his insurance agent, I want to say I believe the Holy Spirit prompted him to take out this annuity to provide for the wife he loved so dearly." He opened the folder. "The money from the railroad will finish paying for your house and funeral expenses, and the monthly payments from the annuity will provide an income for you."

"Thank you, Garrett." Polly met Garrett's eyes. "You were Will's best friend, too. He looked forward to Sunday evenings at the jail with you and Devon and grew so much spiritually."

Garrett nodded. "He told me one evening he didn't believe it before when people talked about wanting to see Jesus face to face, but now he did. Of course, he had no idea how soon that desire would be fulfilled."

After a few minutes of silence, Garrett stood to get a pen from his drawer. "I have a few papers for you to sign that will finalize this transaction so monthly payments can begin."

♠

After a hug from Savannah, Polly got into Will's car—

would she ever think of it as hers?—and leaned her head on the steering wheel. Her life stretched endlessly ahead of her with no destination in view.

For many years her purpose had been to fulfill her promise to her mother to help raise her brothers and sisters. After her marriage to Will, she lived to build a life with him. What was left now?

Starting the car, almost without conscious thought, she headed for Broad Street. Her father needed a housekeeper. Neither of her younger sisters seemed cut out to fulfill those tasks. Her mother had told her more than once the best way to find happiness was to do everything in one's power to bring happiness to someone else. Helping her father finish raising her last two siblings would do that for him.

She pulled up in front of the house where she'd lived for so many years and turned off the engine. One thing was certain, she would never remarry. Losing someone she loved once was hard enough. She wouldn't risk it again. Raising her head, she stared through the windshield. And without question, she would never marry a man who worked for the railroad.

Chapter 75

Savannah gathered up her pens and notepad and slipped them into her desk drawer. Thank God this week was behind her. Concern for Garrett and her best friend vied for her attention, making it difficult to concentrate on anything else.

Regardless, by Sunday they needed to decide about Garrett's call to pastor the Methodist Episcopal Church. Not a good time to make such a serious decision. Garrett hadn't been himself all week. Not that she could blame him. Will had been so dear to him. Still, she sensed something deeper lurked beneath the surface.

As she stood, Garrett opened the door and poked his head into her office. "I called Jim Caldwell today. He's doing revival services at the Methodist Church in Jackson Center this weekend, so I'm going to meet him at the inn over there tomorrow at noon."

"That's wonderful. What a good idea." Savannah's nerves eased, the lump in the pit of her stomach loosened. Whatever Garrett's problem, Jim Caldwell would help him.

♠

Garrett pulled into the parking lot, jumped out of his car and pumped his friend's hand. "So you finally joined the twentieth century and bought a car." He eyed the beat-up Model T Ford. "Although I'm not sure that one was made in this century."

Jim grinned and kicked a tire. "You know I've never

been quick to spend money on luxuries. This shouldn't surprise you."

"Not really." Garrett threw an arm around Pastor Jim's shoulders. "Can't tell you how good it is to see you."

"The feeling is mutual. Although I sensed the reason for getting together might be more than just social."

Garrett had forgotten how intuitive Jim had always been. "You're right, of course." He headed for the inn. "Let's find a private table so we can talk."

After they settled in and a waiter took their order, Garrett told Jim about his call to pastor the Methodist Episcopal Church and the incident the morning of Will's death. "Shouldn't a pastor recognize when God is telling him something and respond appropriately? Maybe I'm not ready to pastor a church."

"Don't you think if God had wanted you to do something, He'd have told you what to do?" Pastor Jim tilted his chair back in that familiar way.

"Well…" Garrett bit his lip. "Don't you think God would have expected me to know what to do without being told?"

Pastor Jim shook his head. "God doesn't play games. I believe he was preparing you for the very difficult news you would soon face. And now Satan is trying to use that gift to build doubts about your readiness to do what God has called you to do."

The waiter brought glasses of water and cups of coffee, assuring them their order would be ready soon.

When he left, Garrett gazed into Pastor Jim's kind brown eyes. "So you really believe I'm ready to pastor a church?"

"I think you were ready a few years ago, but you made the wise decision to wait while God prepared your wife to take on the role of a pastor's wife."

As their waiter arrived, the mouth-watering fragrance of beef stew stirred hunger Garrett hadn't experienced since Will's death. It smelled better than any food he'd eaten in two weeks.

♠

Garrett's car door slammed. Would she have her husband

back or would he be the distant stranger who'd lived with them since Will died? Sammy hurried out of his room to greet his father.

She had her answer as soon as the apartment door opened and the notes of a favorite song ascended to her.

Yes, we'll gather at that river, the beautiful, the beautiful river.

Gather with the saints at the river, that flows by the throne of God.

Garrett's smiling face followed the music and Sammy flung himself on his father. "Papa, I've missed you."

Savannah was right behind their son, leaning in to kiss Garrett's rosy cheek. "Me too."

"I've missed you, too." He hugged them both in a giant embrace.

"I was so worried about you." Savannah spoke in a whisper, near Garrett's ear.

"I'm sorry, Love. I needed someone to talk some sense into me." Garrett released them. "I guess we all need that now and then, if we're not too proud to receive it."

"How's Pastor Jim?"

Sammy screwed up his face. "Who is he?"

"Pastor Jim is our very good friend who now lives in Akron, Ohio. Maybe we can go to Jackson Center tomorrow night so you can meet him." Garrett ruffled his son's red hair. "Now how about you go play in your room so your mama and I can talk."

When Sammy's smile slid from his face, Garrett added, "Just for a few minutes, Son. I promise."

Garrett motioned to the loveseat and Savannah moved in that direction as Sammy disappeared into his room. Before her husband could open his mouth, she began. "We need to make a decision."

"We do. What is your vote?"

"If you have peace about it, I'm ready to say yes." She smiled into his blue eyes. "I don't want my fears to keep you from answering God's call."

"If you're sure, I'll call Derek tomorrow."

Savannah nodded but gazed at him, a small frown wrinkling her brow. "You've been so downhearted all week, I thought you might be having doubts about this."

"I've been in the wilderness, that's for sure. But Jim helped me see how the enemy was attacking me." He sighed. "The Scripture warns us that Satan goes around like a roaring lion looking for someone to attack. We can't let down our guard."

Chapter 76

Polly smoothed the skirt of her black rayon dress and stared out the window of Father's car. The three weeks since Will's burial had dragged. Even helping Father with housekeeping and cooking hadn't distracted her. He had volunteered to take her and Will's mother to the annual Memorial Service held by the Fraternal Order of Eagles in Franklin today. Will had been a member, and each year they honored members who had died the previous year.

To break the oppressive silence, she leaned toward the front seat. "Did I tell you Mr. Young asked if I wanted to work at the Young Insurance Agency in the mornings when Savannah quits?"

Mam turned to look at her. "You mentioned it."

"Are you sure you want to work with the town crier?" There was a smile in Father's voice but a serious undertone.

"I'm not looking forward to working with Dorothy, but if Savannah could do it for so many years, surely I can too."

"Why do you call her the town crier?" Mam tilted her head.

Polly leaned back in her seat as Father explained the nickname to Mam. She glanced at her watch. She'd been told to arrive early since the service was well-attended by members and non-members. How much further? The road to Franklin brought back too many memories of their journey here the morning of Will's accident. Polly pushed the thought away, refusing to relive that awful day.

She had both dreaded and looked forward to attending the service today. On one hand, it would be gratifying to see Will honored. On the other, Polly feared it would bring a fresh bout of tears that waited beneath the surface.

At last her father pulled up to the Park Theatre, allowing her and Mam to get out. Despite the earliness of the hour, throngs of people stood outside the building. A familiar figure approached as they waited for Father, and Polly recognized Charles Clarkson and his wife, Jane.

Mr. Clarkson held out his hand to Mam. "I'm sorry we didn't get to speak to you at the burial, Mrs. Reiser, but Jane and I wanted to say how sorry we are about Will's death. We want to honor him today."

Mam smiled at the couple. "Thank you for coming. We're almost neighbors, Polly. They live on Beech Street in Stoneboro."

Father joined them and exchanged greetings with the Clarkson's before they all followed the crowd into the Theatre. Each person was handed a white carnation and copies of the program as they entered. At the rear stood a large American flag and another draped a stand on which appeared a large eagle. More flags covered the speaker's stand and a row of potted ferns lined the front of the stage.

The quiet elegance prompted Polly to tiptoe to her seat. She sat between Father and Mam and opened her program as the Clarkson's seated themselves on Mam's other side. Will's name printed on the program in bold letters took her breath away. How could it be true?

After many songs and hymns, prayers and readings, the presiding officer began the ritual service. "Again we meet to pay tribute of love and remembrance to those of our brotherhood who have been called away by death."

Called away by death. Is that what happened to Will? She closed her eyes as the roll call of the honored dead began. Six had passed away that year, and 57 others had died since the aerie was instituted. The presiding officer began reciting names and following the reading of each name, a muffled bell sounded. *Edward H. Houser... Charles R. Limber...* She straightened in her seat, holding her breath... *William Reiser* Pain stabbed her heart. The muffled bell rang and she collapsed, bent over, her head touching her knees. How was it possible to go on living when one's heart had been mortally wounded?

♠

A knock on the front door awakened Polly from a grief-induced sleep that held her captive since her return from the Memorial service. Her head throbbed and her eyes were almost swollen shut. She sat up and blinked in the complete darkness that enshrouded her, no light visible even through the slits of her eyelids. It must be the middle of the night.

The more details of the afternoon returned, the less she wanted to go back to reality. She flopped back on the bed and buried her head in Will's pillow which she'd taken as her own. Another knock sounded, louder this time. At least she needn't worry that someone was out there to inform her of Will having a terrible accident.

She crawled out of the twisted mess of blankets created by the tossing and turning that defined her sleep since Will was gone. After a futile effort to smooth the wrinkles from the Sunday clothes she hadn't bothered to change, Polly stumbled to the door and turned on the outside light.

Savannah and Mildred Young stood on the porch, collars turned up in the chilly, drizzly weather.

Polly yanked open the door and stepped back so they could enter. "What time is it?" Not a great way to greet friends.

"Well, hello to you too." There was a smile in Savannah's voice until she caught a glimpse of Polly's condition. "I'm so sorry. It looks like we woke you."

"I thought it was the wee hours of the morning." Polly squinted at the wall clock and then turned on a light. "Only seven o'clock." She scrubbed her hands over her face. "Come and sit down."

"Are you sure? When you didn't show up for Bible study, we decided to come to you." Mildred extended a hand to Polly. "But maybe we should go."

In the silence, they gazed at her. Then wordlessly, Mildred removed her wet coat, took Polly in her arms and began to rock her, crooning a lullaby. Although she had shed a boatload of tears already today, more slid down her cheeks and sobs erupted from her lips.

When at last Polly's tears were spent, Mildred guided her into the kitchen where Savanna had busied herself making tea, setting the table and unwrapping egg salad sandwiches they'd brought.

Looking at the table, Polly shook her head. "How did you know I didn't bother to eat today?"

Savannah poured tea in her best friend's cup. "We prayed and asked God what we should do." She squeezed Polly's shoulder. "Then we remembered how the angels fed Elijah when the journey was too much for him. I don't think we qualify as angels…" The corners of her lips turned up. "But maybe we'll do in a pinch."

Polly put down her sandwich and stared into space, her countenance grim. "Where were the angels when Will needed them?"

Chapter 77

Garrett removed the last stack of folders from the metal filing cabinet, deposited them in the box labeled *church,* and set it outside the soon-to-be nursery. This had all happened so fast, his head was spinning. He lifted the cabinet and carried it to their storage room beside the stairs. As he came out, Savannah appeared from the kitchen and Sammy joined her. "What's going on, Papa?"

"Getting ready for the baby." Garrett patted Sam's head and smiled at Savannah, then tilted his head toward the now-empty room. "It's all yours, Love."

"I hope we have time to get it ready before the baby arrives. They can be so unpredictable." She giggled, then sobered. "I can't believe tomorrow will be my last day of work, the end of March. Your father's been so good to me from the very start when I was such a green horn. And now so understanding about my need to retire." A smile tugged at her lips. "Makes me sound old, doesn't it?"

"You aren't old, Mama." Sam tugged on Savannah's skirt. "No gray hair and no double chin."

"He's right, you know." Garrett chuckled and smoothed her silky black hair, pretending to look for hairs of any other color. "It all looks the same. And a double chin?" He chucked her under her lovely chin. "Never."

Garrett placed a kiss on her lips and then dropped to the floor beside the storage room and pulled Sam into his lap. "I'm pretty much retiring from insurance tomorrow too. What do you think of that, Buddy? I'll only have to work one day a week—Sundays." He winked at Savannah.

"Really?" Sam's jaw dropped.

"No, Sammy. Your papa is teasing." Savannah shook her finger at Garrett. "Some folks like to say preachers only work on Sundays. But it's not true. They have sermons to prepare, people to visit, and meetings to attend."

"Just joking, Sam. But I've lined up other pastors to visit the jail so I'll only go one Sunday a month. I'll miss the fellows but my family comes first." He bit his lip. "I won't miss making those lonely Sunday evening drives without Will."

"I know it's been hard for you." Savannah stooped and touched Garrett's cheek. "I hope working for your father will keep Polly from being so lonely too."

"Is she ready to take over your job?" He stood and pulled Sam up beside him.

"I think so. I've been training her. I hope she and Dorothy can get along. Dorothy can be…" She stopped and looked at Sam. "…astynay."

"Astynay? What does that mean?" A puzzled frown puckered Sam's forehead.

"Nothing for you to worry about, Son. Just a condition she has." Garrett smoothed away Sam's frown and picked up the overflowing box. "I'm taking one more load to the church."

♠

Savannah put down her paintbrush and took the one Sammy handed her. The past two weeks had flown, filled with decorating the nursery and last-minute baby preparations. She surveyed the sunshiny yellow room with calico curtains made by Garrett's mother. "What do you think, Sammy?"

"It's really yellow." Sammy bit his lip. "D'ya think the baby will like it?"

"Babies usually sleep a lot at first, so maybe the color isn't too important. Most children like bright, cheerful colors, though." She gathered up the brushes. "Let's go outside and wash these with kerosene. Maybe you and Papa can set up the baby's crib tonight."

The telephone rang, and Savannah hurried to answer. Mrs. Greely's voice responded to her hello. Even after several months of good communication, Savannah's heart still thudded when hearing her voice.

"How are you, Mrs. Greely?"

"Fine, thanks. Just wanted to tell you our granddaughter's doctor says she'll deliver soon unless he misses his guess. Her due date was a week ago on April 7. The social worker will bring the baby to Sandy Lake as soon as the little one's able to travel."

Savannah swallowed, a glob of fear refusing to go down. Was she ready for this? "All right. Thanks for letting us know. We'll be praying for a safe delivery for Amanda and the baby."

"Thank you. And Savannah…" Mrs. Greely's voice trailed away. "Thank you for forgiving me and for helping us." She choked. "We'll never forget it."

"You're welcome. But the gratitude is ours." The lump in Savannah's throat eased. "You're making one of my dreams come true."

After they said goodbye, Sammy lifted puzzled eyes to hers. "Mama, what was your dream?"

♠

Polly glanced up as Dorothy came into her office. If only she had a key for that door. "Did you need something, Dorothy?"

"I'm just making sure you remember to cover your typewriter before you leave. It's almost noon." Dorothy pulled the cover out of Polly's drawer. "Dust can cause problems if it settles on the type bars characters."

Polly sucked in a breath. If Dorothy reminded her of one more thing, she would surely scream. "Isn't Janene coming in this afternoon?"

"Not today. And even if she were, covering your machine before leaving is the right thing to do." Dorothy pressed her lips into a prissy shape.

"All right. I'll be sure to cover it. I always do." Polly

restrained a sigh.

"And Polly—"

Polly stood, startling Dorothy with the suddenness of her move. She spoke through gritted teeth. "Dorothy, you are going to drive me crazy if you don't stop monitoring my every move. Savannah trained me well. Please, let me do my job."

"Well." Dorothy put her nose in the air and whirled toward the door. "I was only trying to be helpful. If you mess up, don't blame me."

Chapter 78

A car backfired as it pulled in behind their building. Savannah's pulse ratcheted up. It was almost noon. She pressed both hands to her cheeks, warm despite the cool, end-of-April weather, then glanced at her pale green skirt and cream-colored blouse. Was this appropriate clothing for the arrival of a new baby?

Garrett put one arm around her and pulled Sammy close with the other. "You look lovely, Dear, as always. You've already passed the test."

She let out a long breath. "I know. Why am I so nervous? Maybe it's fear Miss Stanley will find a reason not to give us the baby."

Winding his arms around her waist, Sammy leaned against her. "You're the best Mama ever. They couldn't find anyone better than you and Papa to raise this baby." The love and confidence in his round blue eyes calmed her frazzled nerves.

She stooped to his level. "Thank you, Sammy. That means a lot to me." She kissed his rosy cheek.

"Garrett, maybe you should see if Miss Stanley needs help carrying Milly's things." They had decided to name the baby Mildred after Garrett's mother, Milly for short.

The door opened as Garrett started down the steps. Savannah strained to catch her first glimpse of Milly.

"Can I give you a hand with anything, Miss Stanley?" He stepped aside so the woman, carrying a baby wrapped in a pink blanket, could pass. He leaned in to take a peek.

"Yes, please. Could you bring in the boxes and bags on the back seat of my car?" Miss Stanley smiled at Savannah and Sammy as she climbed the stairs. "Here's your daughter, Mrs. Young." She handed the baby to Savannah.

Her daughter. Savannah's heart flooded with emotion. She folded back the blanket. The baby she'd longed for.

Miss Stanley patted Sammy's head as he crept closer. "How are you, young man?"

He was so busy peering at Milly he barely noticed. "Look, she has red hair just like me." Sammy reached to touch her head, then drew back with a questioning look at Savannah.

"It's okay. Just be gentle." Love radiated through her as she bent toward her son. He tenderly smoothed the reddish fuzz on Milly's head. Could life get any better than this?

They moved away from the stairs as Garrett came up, his arms loaded with various bulky items. He dropped them unceremoniously and knelt beside Sammy, tracing the curve of Milly's cheek.

"Isn't she beautiful, Papa? Look at her hair." Sammy snuggled against his father.

In her wildest dreams, Savannah couldn't have anticipated the sweetness of this moment.

Miss Stanley cleared her throat. "I'm so sorry to interrupt but I had a bit of an emergency this morning and need to get back to the office.

Garrett stood. "Do you need our signatures on anything?"

"Just a few more." Miss Stanley took a step toward the dining room table. "Could we go over here?"

"Of course." Savannah turned to Sammy. "Would you like to hold your sister while we sign our names?"

"Really? I can hold her?" Sammy's blue eyes sparkled. Savannah smiled at his enthusiasm and got them settled on the wing chair near the table before joining Garrett.

When they'd finished, Miss Stanley glanced from Garrett to Savannah. "Do you have any questions?"

Before they could answer, Sammy piped up, "You sure this is the right baby?" He squinted at Miss Stanley. "I don't want to get 'tached to her if it ain't."

Miss Stanley smiled. "I'm absolutely sure it's the right baby, Sam. Even her hair is the right color." She moved to his side and ruffled his red locks fondly.

"I haven't told you this, Sammy, but I'm the only child in my family who doesn't have red hair." Savannah smoothed his cowlick that always stood straight up.

Sammy's brows lifted. "You have brothers and sisters? Where are they?"

A puff of a sigh escaped Savannah's lips. Why had she mentioned her brothers and sisters? "They live in Georgia."

"Can we go visit them?"

"No, I'm afraid not. Georgia is far away." Her parents' names were on the forms they'd filled out but no one had mentioned contacting them. She glanced at Miss Stanley.

"Maybe someday you can take a vacation and visit your aunts, uncles and grandparents." Miss Stanley's eyes sparkled. "I'm sure they'd love to meet you, Sam."

Savannah bit her tongue, remembering the last letter from her mother. *We have no use for the likes of you.* She shrugged. "It's a long drive."

♠

After Milly finished her bottle and opened her mouth in a big sleepy yawn, Savannah lifted her daughter for a burp. She continued rocking and patting her back gently.

The day had gone well. Milly gave every indication of being a model baby, eating, sleeping and having her diaper changed. Sammy was enamored with her and stole into the nursery often to see if she was awake.

Despite such a good first day, Savannah could barely keep her eyes open. Her arms and legs sagged as if weights were attached. How could caring for one little person take so much energy? A warm bath and an early bedtime would be heavenly. Garrett was getting Sammy ready for bed.

At last the welcome sound of a gentle burp came, and Savannah placed Milly in her crib with a final pat. As she headed for the door, a loud wail erupted from her daughter. Savannah stopped and frowned. Milly had barely whimpered all day. Maybe she was still hungry.

She picked Milly up and tried to reinsert the bottle, which still contained a few ounces of evaporated milk formula. The baby, who had stopped crying the minute Savannah picked her up, turned her head and pinched her lips together. Not hungry. A few snaps opened and fingers slipped into the tiny sleepers Mildred had sewn for Milly indicated a dry diaper.

Her daughter snuggled against Savannah, eyes closed, soft steady breathing. After a few more minutes of cuddling, Savannah placed her back in her crib. Even before she pulled a light blanket over her, the wailing began again. What now?

Garrett poked his head in the open door and raised an eyebrow. She shrugged and shook her head. "I don't know what's wrong. She's not hungry, and she's not wet. Every time I try to put her down, she cries."

He handed her the book he'd been reading to Sammy. "Let me give it a try. You can finish Sammy's story."

Savannah's head drooped. Only the first day, and already she was a failure as a mother.

Chapter 79

Polly knocked lightly on Mam's front door and went in. When had she stopped being looked on as a guest? Warmth spread through her heart and the fragrance of Irish stew and homemade bread floated to meet her. She shed her light jacket and followed her nose to the kitchen.

If anything her relationship with Mam had grown stronger since Will's death. They had in common their sorrow at losing him. She looked forward to eating supper with her once a week, usually on Mondays, but Tuesday this week since Mam had other plans last night.

Mam's cheeks were rosy from the steaming pot of stew as she scooped large servings. "I'm glad to see you, Lass."

A lump rose in Polly's throat as it always did when Mam called her by the name Will had used most. "I'm happy to see you, too." She kissed Mam's cheek.

"How are ya keepin' these days? Are ya doin' all right?"

Polly squirmed under Mam's scrutiny. "I don't know. I have nothing with which to compare how I'm doing, never having lost a husband before. On Wednesday, it'll be three months. Some days are better than others. How are you doing?"

Mam sniffed. "Losin' my husband was hard, for sure, but losin' my youngest son…" She shook her head as her voice trailed away. "That's not s'posed ta happen." Mam wiped her eyes on a dish towel.

Polly placed the bowls on the table, already set for two,

and put her arms around Mam. It wasn't often Will's mother acknowledged the depth of her pain. Some said the Irish suffered so much loss in the old country that it hardened them to it. Maybe, or maybe they'd just become good at hiding their grief.

After they were seated and Will's mother returned thanks, Mam changed the subject. "Did ya hear Charles Clarkson and another railroad man from Hadley were injured in a train wreck last night?"

Stopping with a bite of soup midway to her mouth, Polly dropped her spoon. "What happened?"

"The freight train they were on collided with an engine coming from Franklin." Mam shook her head.

"Were they badly hurt?"

"Jane said cuts and bruises and badly shaken up. They were taken to the hospital in Franklin. The two men on the engine jumped before the collision occurred and escaped with less injuries."

"They *jumped*? Oh my goodness!" Polly closed her eyes. "What caused the accident?"

"I don't know—maybe a misunderstandin' of orders." Mam stared into her bowl. "Jane said if they'd been travelin' at a high speed, it's likely they all would have been killed."

"Well that settles it." Polly pushed away her bowl, her appetite gone

"Settles what?" Mam peered at her.

"I will never marry another railroad man. Henry Cabot Lodge said, 'Those who work on the railroad suffer as if they were fighting a war.' He was right."

♠

Garrett and his father stumbled up the steps hoisting the heavy cradle his parents used for him when he was a baby. "Maybe Milly will like this better than her crib." Garrett huffed and puffed between words.

"I hope so." Savannah peered over the railing and tucked some strands of hair behind her ear.

"You certainly liked it, Son." Pa chuckled. "Rocking in a

chair or the cradle were your favorite things."

Garrett set down his end as they reached the landing. "Two weeks of sleepless nights and busy days are catching up with Mama." He stole a glance at his wife.

Savannah sighed. "You're right. I'm exhausted. Maybe if we put it close to our bed, I can reach out and rock the cradle until Milly falls asleep."

Sammy, who had been playing under the table with his miniature train set, popped out at her words. "You're going to put Milly's cradle in your bedroom?"

"We're going to try." Savannah rubbed her eyes. "She's keeping you and me up at night with her crying. Only Papa, who could sleep through a freight train chugging through our bedroom, is getting any sleep."

Pa nodded vigorously. "Garrett was never a light sleeper."

They were right. Garrett had begged Savannah to wake him so he could give her a break but she insisted it was her job.

"I don't mind losing sleep." Sammy frowned.

"Well, I do." Savannah stifled a yawn. "I *have* to get some rest."

Sammy disappeared under the table as she went back to washing dishes and Garrett and his father entered the nursery. This had to work.

♠

As had become their routine, Garrett helped Sam get ready for bed. He tucked him in and turned to the bookshelf in his room. "What story would you like tonight, Buddy?"

Sam bit his lip, then scooted further under his covers. "I guess I don't need a story."

"No story? What's going on?" Garrett gazed at his son. "You've been awfully quiet this evening."

"Just tired, I guess. G'night." Sam closed his eyes and turned on his side, facing away from his father.

"Well, okay. If you're sure." Garrett stood and started toward the door. "Is Milly's crying getting to you? Is that the problem?"

There was no response. Sam couldn't be asleep already, but at last Garrett gave up and walked away.

As he entered their bedroom, Savannah set down Milly's bottle and prepared to prop her for a burp. Garrett reached for the baby. "You go ahead and get ready for bed, Love. I'll finish here."

Savannah didn't argue. After the obligatory burp, Garrett continued rocking Milly while his exhausted wife took her bath, then handed their daughter to her while he took his turn in the bathroom. The baby was sleeping in Savannah's arms when he returned.

"After I put Milly in the cradle, will you rock her until I get into bed?" Savannah whispered. "Then I'll keep rocking until I'm sure she's sound asleep."

With teamwork, they managed the feat of getting Milly into the rocking bed with no crying. Blessed silence reigned. Eventually, Savannah stopped rocking. They both breathed a sigh of relief when all was still.

"I'm going to open our door so we can hear Sam if he needs us." Garrett slipped out of bed and cracked their door.

A smothered sob broke the stillness. Savannah sat up. "What was that?"

"I think it's our son, but why is he crying?"

Chapter 80

Garrett sprinted into Sam's room and knelt by his bed. "Buddy, what's wrong?"

The sobs stopped and his son stiffened. "I'm sorry, Papa. Did I wake you?"

"We weren't sleeping, but we're worried about you." Garrett leaned closer, squinting into the darkness. "Why are you crying?"

Silence. Than a muffled hiccup. "Are you mad at me, Papa?"

"No, we just want to know what's bothering you." Garrett pulled Sam toward him.

Between ragged breaths, words poured from his son's mouth. "You...and Mama...and Milly are all in your bedroom...together..., and I'm all...alone...again." Sam's shoulders shook.

"Ah, Sammy..." Garrett scooped him up and cradled him in his arms. "We put Milly in our bedroom so Mama can rock the cradle from our bed, but if that makes you sad..." He strode toward the door carrying his son. "It's easily fixed."

Garrett took a few steps into the large room next door and deposited Sam on the bed beside Savannah. "I'll be right back."

After a quick trip to Sam's room to gather his mattress and pillow, he lowered them to the floor close to his side of the bed. He'd transfer Sam onto the mattress after he fell asleep. Heaving a long contented sigh, he crawled in beside Sam, now snuggled in Savannah's arms, and drew them both close. The Garrett and Savannah Young family was complete.

♠

Polly curled up and leaned her head against the back of Mother's gray chair. A pot roast was in the oven and nothing more to do until closer to time for Twila and Elsie to come home from school. She could dust or sweep but the house wasn't dirty enough to inspire her.

She glanced at the Mercer County Bank calendar on the wall. Only a little over a month until Beth's wedding. The family had finally met Elmer when he came home with Beth for Will's funeral—not that Polly had any vivid memory of him. Her state of mind had been so fragile, she could barely picture him.

A shiver crept through her. Glancing at the davenport, an afghan knitted in browns, greens, and yellows caught her attention. Almost certainly one Mother had made. Polly leaned over to grab it, then wrapped it around herself as she dropped back into the chair.

For a moment peace stole over her as she caressed the wool. If only she could sit down and talk to her mother, perhaps life would turn right side up. A haunting memory of the night God had shown her she had substituted a strong faith in her mother for strong faith in Him jarred her from her reverie. She bit her lip. How easily she had fallen back into her long-ago mindset of looking to Mother, instead of to Jesus, for comfort and peace.

Polly stood and grabbed her journal and her Chartreuse from her handbag beside the door. Everything within her had resisted journaling since she'd acknowledged she had a decision to make. The longer she put off choosing to allow God to use her suffering to shape her into the image of Christ, rather than becoming bitter, the more likely she would be to turn back to the one she'd sought comfort from in her younger years. She'd put it off too long.

Bending her head over the dark blue book, she dated her entry. *May 14, 1924.* She stared at the date. Three months had passed since… She rubbed a hand over her eyes, renewed her firm grip on her pen and wrote, *Father*. Then in a rush of green ink, the words poured out. *Why? Why? Why? Why did you take the only man I ever loved? Where were his angels when he needed them? How can I trust you now?*

She stared at the words. What had Savannah said she'd learned from Sarah's diary? *Whenever anything bad happened, Sarah always ran to God instead of blaming Him.* Sarah had said with Job, *The Lord gave and the Lord has taken away, blessed be the name of the Lord.*

Bending over her diary, Polly began to write. *I don't think I can say the words Job and Sarah said, but I want to run to you instead of blaming you for Will's accident. I know Mother can't get me through this and I can't do it alone. Only you can see me through.*

♠

Polly stood beside her precious sister, Beth, in the sitting room, waiting for the recorded organ music to begin. Beth looked lovely in her simple, beaded wedding gown. She and Elmer had chosen to have a small wedding at home out of respect for Polly's loss, and Polly had set aside her dark clothes to be Beth's attendant. She smoothed her hands over the silky, pale green material of her gown. This is what Will would have wanted.

Memories of their special day flooded over her. How quickly the years of their marriage had passed. She closed her eyes, determined to focus on the happy days they'd had together. They squeezed more joy into three years than many folks had in a lifetime. She could never have asked for a better husband.

As the music began, Polly opened the door and walked past Father as he extended his hand to Beth. Elmer and Reverend Lawrence stood in front of the leaded glass window. Elmer's eyes, filled with love, looked beyond Polly to his bride.

Her heart clenched. Had she and Will resembled this starry-eyed couple on their wedding day? What did the years ahead hold for Beth and Elmer? A better question, what did the years ahead hold for her?

Part 4

Chapter 81
April, 1926

Two years later…

Polly tapped her pencil on the desk, waiting for Dorothy to stop lecturing and leave her alone. How many days had she tuned Dorothy out during the past two years, daydreaming about running a hotel as she'd once told Beth she wanted to do? She'd thought of little else since someone told her Central Hotel on Main Street was for sale. Maybe it was a sign.

She pictured herself turning the key and entering the hotel, knowing it belonged to her. Could buying it solve the family's cash flow problem since the coal in the Dye Coal Mines had become less plentiful?

Shaking her head, she focused on Dorothy's monologue. "I found two more mistakes you made yesterday." Dorothy flopped two letters with large red circles on her desk. "You need to be more careful."

Polly bit her lip. "I'll try." Her "mistakes" usually amounted to violating some rule of grammar or punctuation unknown to anyone but Dorothy, but arguing with her office mate accomplished nothing.

Dorothy gazed at her, as though waiting for an answer. Had she missed something? "What is it, Dorothy?"

The woman tapped her foot. "Polly… I just don't think you're happy here."

"You're right about that. Did it ever occur to you…" Polly bit her lip. Suggesting that Polly's unhappiness might be Dorothy's fault wouldn't solve anything. Perhaps it wasn't even true.

Just when Polly had begun to get her emotions under control after losing Will, Mam's heart had started acting up. A few months later, another loss blindsided her. How could anyone expect her to be happy with Will and Mam passing less than two years apart?

Dorothy stared at her. "Did it ever occur to me…?"

Polly chewed on the eraser of her pencil, avoiding Dorothy's eyes. It became increasingly difficult to put up with Dorothy's controlling ways after Mam's death. Maybe she wasn't cut out to be a secretary. Straightening in her chair, she made up her mind. "Dorothy, I'm putting in my two-week notice."

Dorothy's jaw dropped. "What will you do?"

"I'm not sure." There was no way Polly would tell Dorothy about her tentative plans. It would be all over town in a heartbeat.

♠

July 5, 1926

I can't believe I'm doing this, Lord. Polly roamed around the little brown bungalow, memorizing every nook and cranny, occasionally smoothing her hand or fingertip over a door or window. Partially packed boxes created a maze throughout the house. Once she put in her notice at the insurance agency three months ago and contacted the hotel owners, things had moved fast.

Her heart sped up as she visualized the new life she would soon have, then slowed as she grieved the loss of her life with Will. She plopped on the davenport where she and Will had spent so many happy hours.

A car pulled into the driveway and headlights beamed across the living room window. She glanced at the clock. Nine o'clock. Who would be visiting at this hour? She stumbled over a carton of books on her way to the window where her father's silhouette took shape coming up the steps.

Not a surprise. She still hadn't convinced him this was the right decision.

Polly flipped on the porch light and opened the screen door. "Hello, Father." She smiled at her unexpected company. "Is everything all right?"

He nodded. "I could have called but… Can I come in?"

"Of course." She stepped back to let him enter. "Would you like a cup of coffee or tea?"

"This isn't a social call." The corner of his mouth quirked up, despite the seriousness of his countenance.

Polly backed toward the davenport, motioning for Father to sit on the chair facing her. "Are you going to try to talk me out of this decision one more time?"

He sighed. "Florence, I can't let you do this. You've done so much for the family already. I can't let you sell the house you love because the coal in the Dye mines is running low. We'll find a way to get by."

"There's nothing holding me in Stoneboro since Mam—" her voice cracked. "Since Mam passed last fall, I'm lonely here. The money Clyde Vogan gives me for my house will be a good down payment on his hotel, and we can all be together there."

"But that still leaves you with a $6,500 mortgage. That's a lot of money, Florence."

"We've been through this before, Father. Real Estate prices are high, but the Central Hotel has been a good moneymaker for the Vogans. There's no reason it can't be the same for us. We can keep trying to sell your house and you can go on working the mines until the coal runs out. The girls and I will run the hotel." Polly tucked her feet under her as excitement spiraled through her body.

"But—"

"I think I'll call it the *Florence Hotel*. Doesn't that have a nice ring to it?" Before he could answer, she added, "Elsie has a head for numbers. Helping me run the hotel will give her some experience while she decides what to do with her life."

"If she's in the mood to help you, that is." Father rolled his eyes. "You know how stubborn she can be."

Polly lifted her shoulder in a slight shrug. "Twila can help too. It'll be good for her to have some responsibility during her senior year."

"Have you prayed about this, Florence?" Father peered at her, his eyes the deep shade of brown they became when he was very serious. "Really prayed about it? I'm afraid running this hotel will be more work than you ever imagined."

"Of course I've prayed, Father. But the hotel is for sale now. If I wait around, someone else may snap it up. Besides, Dorothy was making my life miserable at the Agency. No matter how much I prayed or sought counsel from Savannah and Garrett's mother, nothing improved. I'm ready for a change."

"All right." Father sighed. "You're an adult. If this is what you want, I won't stand in your way."

♠

Savannah placed a kiss on top of Milly's head, then put her in her crib. Her second birthday had passed, several teeth had erupted, and the endless crying at night was long past. Sometimes her daughter actually cooed to herself before falling asleep or after waking up.

Wiggling her fingers at Milly, Savannah walked around the corner into Sammy's room. They took turns with the children every night. Tonight Garrett had just finished reading their son's story. After a year in first grade, Sam could read some simple stories himself. But bedtime stories were special.

Kneeling beside Sammy's bed as she often did, Savannah held out a hand to each of them as she and Garrett waited to hear their son's prayers.

Dear Jesus. Sammy paused and squeezed their hands tight. *Thank you for Mama, Papa, and Milly. Thank you for food to eat and a bed to sleep in. Thank you for Grandpa and Grandma Young. Please find a Mama and Daddy for the children who don't have one. Amen.*

Savannah's chest squeezed. The last sentence of Sammy's prayers never changed. Many times she'd asked the Lord if she and Garrett should help Him answer that prayer for another orphan. But lately... She smoothed her hand over her belly. No, it couldn't be. Dr. Cooley had said, well, he'd said it was unlikely...

Later, as she and Garrett fell into bed, he pulled her close and stroked her hair. "My favorite time of the day, Mrs. Young. What a favor I've done you. For the rest of your life folks will be calling you *Young*."

Savannah chuckled and snuggled closer. "What a favor, indeed. You will also be forever *Young*." They giggled over their silly joke, then Savannah sobered. "There's something I need to talk to you about."

"Oh, this sounds serious." Garrett drew back and looked into her eyes. "What is it, my Love?"

Savannah's fingers automatically smoothed her nightgown over her abdomen. "You remember when Dr. Cooley said it was unlikely I'd be able to conceive?'

Garrett propped himself on one elbow. "I remember. Why?"

"I haven't had my monthly for some time, and although I'm not nearly as sick as I've heard tell women can be, I've been a bit nauseous lately." Savannah covered her face, then peeked between her fingers. "You don't suppose I could be in the family way, do you?"

Chapter 82

Shifting in her chair for the tenth time, Polly glanced at Mr. and Mrs. Vogan. A rock sat in the pit of her stomach. She had agreed to use their attorney to save costs for both of them and accepted their offer of a ride to his office in Mercer. Why hadn't she asked her father to accompany her? Perhaps this would have been easier if he'd been here.

A door across from her opened, and a tall man with broad shoulders, smoothly parted black hair and a well-fitting gray suit greeted them. "I'm Edward Stranahan. Mr. and Mrs. Vogan, Mrs. Reiser, please come in."

He stepped back, allowing them to enter. A faint aroma of leather hung in the air in a room dominated by a heavy oak table and six chairs with padded leather seats. Mr. Stranahan went to the head of the table and motioned for them to sit—the Vogans on his left and Polly on his right. What had she been thinking coming here alone? She knew nothing about purchasing property.

She gripped her hands in her lap until her knuckles ached. Mr. Stranahan would tell her what to do.

After a few minutes of silence as the attorney shuffled two stacks of papers, leafing through them and nodding, he stretched his lips into a smile. "Everything is in order for the transfer of two pieces of property. The one owned by Mrs. Reiser at the corner of Walnut and Franklin in Stoneboro, and the other owned by Mr. and Mrs. Vogan on Main Street in Sandy Lake."

They all nodded their agreement.

"This is a little out of the ordinary but completely legal, with Mrs. Reiser selling her residence to the Vogans and the Vogans selling their Hotel to Mrs. Reiser. We'll go through the paperwork for each transaction, so you can supply the necessary signatures."

As Mr. Stranahan droned on, Polly stared at the legal forms he'd handed her until her eyes burned. The terms might as well be Latin or Greek. The Vogans could sell her swampland in Florida, and she wouldn't know the difference.

"Mrs. Reiser, did you hear me?"

She jerked her head up to find the attorney staring at her. "I'm sorry. What did you say?" Her cheeks grew warm. Now they'd all know what an idiot she was.

"I asked if you have any questions before you sign the papers for the sale of your house?" Mr. Stranahan's voice was kind. "I'm sure this isn't easy for you."

A tear slipped down Polly's cheek. Nothing had been easy for a very long time. "I'm ready." What else could she do? While the house was dear to her, the painful reminders of Will surrounded her every day. She picked up a pen, signed her name and accepted her check from the Vogans.

They attempted to make eye contact. "We'll take good care of your house, Mrs. Reiser."

Her eyes flooded with more tears as she blindly picked up the other stack of papers. "Can we go over the conditions on the hotel, Mr. Stranahan?" The sooner the better.

♠

With papers signed and stamped, Polly signed her check over to the Vogans and stumbled into the attorney's waiting room. The Vogans had asked for a few minutes to discuss something with Mr. Stranahan, so she took a seat on one of the wooden chairs and closed her eyes. When the outer door opened, she didn't bother to open them.

"Polly Reiser. I didn't expect to see you here."

The deep voice stirred memories and her eyelids popped

up. "Mr. Clarkson. What a surprise."

"Please call me Charles. I had a few legal affairs to attend to."

"I was so sorry to hear about Jane's passing Mr.—Charles." Mam told her about the death of Jane Clarkson a year and a half ago.

He nodded. "It's hard to lose someone we love. I was sorry to hear of your mother-in-law's death in October. Heart trouble, wasn't it?"

"Thank you. Yes, her heart." Polly coughed and looked away.

"Polly—" Charles hesitated. "May I call you Polly?" When she nodded, he continued. "How are you doing? I mean really? Is there anything you need?"

His unexpected kindness nearly undid her. She pressed her lips together to repress a sob but a ragged breath escaped. He straightened, a hint of alarm in his eyes.

Polly pulled a handkerchief from her handbag and blew her nose. "I'm all right. Today is an emotional day. I just sold my house in Stoneboro and bought the Central Hotel in Sandy Lake."

The blue in Charles' eyes became more intense. "No wonder you're on the verge of tears. That's a lot to deal with in one day."

Mr. Stranahan's door opened and the Vogans entered the waiting room. Polly stood. "Charles, this is Clyde and Myra Vogan. We exchanged properties today."

Charles got to his feet and held out his hand to Clyde. "Charles Clarkson. Nice to meet you."

"Nice to meet you, Charles. Are you friends of the Dye family?" Clyde looked from Charles to Polly.

"Actually, I was a fellow railroad worker with Polly's husband, and I also live in Stoneboro." Charles turned to Polly. "So nice to see you. Perhaps I'll have a reason to come to your hotel sometime."

♠

Every day for the past week and a half, Garrett had raised an eyebrow at Savannah when he got home from his office. Every day she shook her head. They had agreed if her monthly visitor hadn't come by noon today, she would make an appointment with Dr. Cooley next week. The morning dragged as he put the finishing touches on his message for tomorrow.

If a new baby was on the way, where would they fit another crib? The Church had offered them the parsonage two years ago, but he couldn't picture his family there. It seemed better suited to a couple without children than to a family. Was it time he and Savannah bought a house?

Closing his Bible and leaving the church, he quoted his favorite admonition to Savannah, "Don't borrow trouble." And then for good measure, a Bible verse: *Sufficient unto the day is the evil thereof.*

God would provide.

He opened the door to their apartment and ran up the steps, calling, "Savannah?" What would her answer be today?

Chapter 83

Polly's brother, George, and his wife, Isabel, who had married a year after Beth, helped Father and Uncle Jim carry the last of her dining room furniture to her uncle's wagon. Polly stood alone on the front porch of the little brown bungalow. When her family climbed into the wagon, she waved and attempted to keep the tremble from her voice. "Thanks for your help."

George jumped from the wagon and covered the ground between them in seconds. "Would you like me to ride with you?" He touched her arm.

"Thanks, but this is something I need to do alone. I'll see you later." She hugged him and stepped back.

Ignoring the tear sliding down her nose, Polly waited until her family was out of sight. Then she went inside to check the locks on doors and windows, willing herself not to cry. The house was just a material thing. Her tears were for Will.

At last having exhausted every excuse to linger, Polly locked the front door to the house that had been her home for five years. She would give the key to the Vogans later today when they gave her the hotel keys. All week they'd worked side by side with her, training her, Elsie and Twila in all the details they needed to learn. When Polly turned out the light each night, facts and figures paraded through her mind relentlessly.

She sighed and opened her car door to head for Sandy Lake. Throbbing headaches often resulted from the effort to keep everything straight. Was Elsie picking up the bookkeeping information they'd given her? Hard to tell. Her sister would never admit she needed help.

Backing down the driveway, Polly paused for one last look at the house. She could come to Stoneboro to see it any time she wanted, but it wouldn't be the same. She wiped a tear from her cheek and backed onto Walnut Street. *Thank you, Lord, for the happy years Will and I had in that house. I pray the next owners will love it like we did.*

For the last few years, she'd been responsible for the care of her house as well as Father's. Would that be enough preparation for the responsibility of taking care of the Florence Hotel?

The question lingered as she drew closer to Sandy Lake. She turned left from Main Street into the alley beside the hotel and then right into her parking spot behind it. Tomorrow would be her first day. She'd have to cook not only for her boarders and guests at the hotel, but also serve Sunday dinner to the public. Her heart pounded. *I can do this.* Myra Vogan had trained her well and surely her sisters would help.

Polly started up the rear-entry steps to the closed-in porch off the kitchen, then hesitated and retraced her steps. A quick detour took her around to the front of the hotel. She crossed Main Street and feasted her eyes on the large stately establishment. It didn't look like a hotel since the original owner had created the hotel by adding an addition to his fine home. The veranda, which extended to run the length of the building, added to the appearance. Overall, she found the white structure trimmed in black appealing. Her heart fluttered. Could it be true that she owned this place? Well, the Vogans still held the mortgage but she'd have that paid off in no time. Wouldn't she?

♠

Savannah's pulse quickened as she responded to Garrett calling her name. "I'm here, fixing some sandwiches." She laid down her knife and hurried to meet him at the top of the stairs.

Sammy raced from his room and joined them. Even Milly

headed in Garrett's direction as fast as her chubby legs could go.

"Coming home never gets old. I love my job but it can't compare to this." Garrett beamed and gathered them all close.

After Sammy and Milly headed back to their toys, Garrett raised an eyebrow at Savannah. "So? What's the word?"

She shook her head. "No visitor yet."

"Nausea?" Garrett peered at her, as though trying to read her mind.

"A little now and then." Savannah shrugged. "But not a lot." She stepped back into the kitchen and picked up her knife. He followed.

"So a telephone call to Dr. Cooley on Monday?"

"I guess so. I'm too young for the change of life. If I'm not…" She lowered her voice. "…pregnant, maybe I'm sick—"

"Don't borrow trouble, my Love." Garrett leaned in to kiss her cheek. "Let's just make an appointment with Doc on Monday. We'll see what he has to say."

"You know me so well. Trusting can be hard."

The telephone rang and Garrett answered as Savannah pulled out three plates and a bowl for Milly.

A long silence followed his hello. She walked to his side with a questioning look. He gave a minimal shake of his head, and then turned his back as though wanting privacy.

Savannah returned to the kitchen, her brows drawn together. She could often discern the identity of the caller by Garrett's manner of speaking, but not today. She cut up some apples and bananas and arranged them on a plate, glancing at her husband occasionally.

As last he replaced the receiver and stood with head bowed. Sprinting to his side, Savannah touched his arm. "What is it? What's wrong?"

Garrett sighed. "I don't want to tell you."

"If something bad has happened, you can't keep it from me." She gripped his arm.

"Come and sit down." He guided her to the davenport.

"That was Mrs. Greely." Garrett cleared his throat.

"Nooooooo…" The cry was out of Savannah's lips before Garrett could continue.

His eyebrows went up. "I haven't even told you what she said."

"I know but—" Savannah swallowed. "I'm sorry. Go ahead." She clenched her hands in her lap.

"Mrs. Greely's daughter and granddaughter are having second thoughts about Milly's adoption."

Savannah's chin dropped to her chest and her shoulders sagged. "We should never have trusted that woman." Then she straightened and lifted her chin. "The adoption is final. They can't take Milly, can they?"

"I don't think so but I'm not a lawyer." Garrett's head drooped. "Mrs. Greely says they thought since we're all Christians, we'd be willing to give her back."

Sparks flew from Savannah's deep violet eyes. "It isn't right for them to ask that of us. We adopted her in good faith at their request."

"Mrs. Greely says since I was working with the alliance of pastors, they thought they'd get to see Milly now and then. Now that I'm at the Methodist Episcopal Church—well, everything has changed."

Chapter 84

Polly jumped out of bed as her alarm clock gave its raucous summons. Darkness surrounded her but it was morning. Leisurely Sunday mornings, lounging until time to attend church, were a thing of the past. No more going to church unless she hired someone to help with the cooking. Neither of her sisters showed interest in cooking, but she would somehow get their help in the kitchen and with the housekeeping.

She ran down the hall to the bathroom and splashed water on her face, her father's words echoing in her ears. *Good luck getting them to help.* Refusing to be discouraged, she brushed his words aside. The hotel would be a family undertaking.

Stopping outside the room Twila and Elsie shared in their family quarters on the third floor, she rapped on the door. No answer. A louder knock brought a similar response. She opened the door. Both girls had their heads buried under their pillows.

"Time to rise and shine." Polly put a bright lilt in her voice. "Our boarders and last night's guests will want their breakfast, and we need to start dinner preparations."

"It's too early." Elsie clung to her pillow as Polly attempted to remove it.

Twila sat up, then flopped back down. "It's still dark."

"I don't have time to argue. I need you in the kitchen in ten minutes." Polly used her most commanding voice. Ten minutes wasn't realistic but maybe it would get the girls moving.

She returned to her bedroom, pulled a beige summer

dress over her head and tied an apron over it. A quick brush to her hair did little to settle the flying strands but it would have to do. Is this what her life would be like from now on? The excitement that carried her through the sale of her home and the purchase of this place dimmed.

You don't have a choice, Polly, you have to do this.

After running down two flights of stairs, she hurried into the kitchen. Thank goodness for the neatly printed menus Mrs. Vogan had given her. She scurried to the closed-in back porch and grabbed ten large roasts from the cooler. It seemed like a lot of beef but the Vogans said many outside guests came when the dining room was open to the public on Sundays. Scurrying back to the kitchen, she put the meat in roasting pans with water and slid them into the ovens.

Next, she took potatoes and carrots from the vegetable bin and began peeling. Footsteps sounded on the stairs and she glanced up. Her father entered the kitchen. Her shoulders drooped. Where were Twila and Elsie?

"Good morning, Florence. What can I do to help?"

Polly frowned. "I wanted the girls to help in the kitchen."

"Maybe they'll be down soon. I heard water running when I passed the bathroom." Father smiled and gestured to the carrots. "I'm good at peeling carrots. Was that your plan for these?"

Polly nodded. "When these vegetables are ready, we'll leave them in water until time to add them to the roasts."

Glancing at the clock, she peeled faster. Next Sunday she would have to get up earlier. Thank God the hotel was only open to the public on Sundays and special occasions. She finished peeling the last potato and the muscles in her neck eased.

Now to start breakfast. Polly opened the enormous, aluminum-lined drawer and pulled out a loaf of homemade bread. Mrs. Vogan had left a good supply of large loaves but she'd have to keep up with baking bread or opt for serving store-bought. That could get expensive.

"How many scoops of coffee do we need for this

percolator?" Father was doing his best to fill in for the still-absent girls.

"Oh dear… I'm sure I wrote that down somewhere." Polly dug through a pile of notes on the small built-in desk in the corner. "I can't find it. How many cups of water do you think it holds?"

Father shook his head. "Maybe ten? I'm not sure."

"Okay, we'll have to guess." Polly shrugged. "Let's say it's ten cups, two tablespoons per cup would be twenty tablespoons. That would be, ummm… uh… four tablespoons in one-fourth cup would make it…" She rubbed her forehead and closed her eyes.

Father frowned. "One and one fourth cups, I believe."

"Close enough." As Polly opened her eyes and began slicing the bread, Twila appeared. "Come slice this bread while I make scrambled eggs, please."

"But I haven't had breakfast yet." Twila's mouth turned down at the corners.

"None of us have had breakfast, but our guests and boarders come first. If we want to eat before our guests, we have to get up earlier." Polly handed her sister the knife and rushed back to the cooler.

She grabbed three cartons of eggs. How many should she use? There were two boarders and three guests from last night, plus four Dyes. So enough for nine. Not so different from the Dye family years ago. But cooking for paying guests wasn't the same as cooking for family.

She pulled a large red bowl from the cupboard and began cracking eggs into it. Would those eating breakfast have large or small appetites? Thirty eggs should be more than enough.

Slow footsteps on the stairs told her Elsie was headed for the kitchen. As soon as she stepped through the doorway, Polly pounced. "Elsie, please grab a couple of large iron skillets from the lower cupboard beside the stove so we can start heating them for these eggs."

Before Elsie could complain, Polly turned to her

youngest sister. "Twila, would you fill that large toaster with bread and get some butter from the cooler?"

Elsie groaned as she dragged the skillets out of the cupboard. "These skillets are too heavy for me to carry."

"Bring them to me one at a time. But hurry, we don't have a lot of time." Polly waited, holding the scrambled egg mixture.

"I don't see why our guests can't go to Aunt Adda's restaurant for breakfast." Elsie always came up with ideas that would decrease her workload. "Why should we have to provide their breakfast?"

"Breakfast is included in the cost of their stay. Mrs. Vogan said that's the way it's always been."

A band of pain began in the back of her neck and her forehead throbbed. She blinked and steeled herself against the increasing discomfort. Breakfast and dinner had to be cooked and served no matter how she felt.

Chapter 85

Garrett straightened Sam's bowtie and smiled into his big blue eyes, tamping down his inner turmoil.

"All right, I'm off to the church to look over my sermon. Can I can count on you to help Mama get Milly to church?" Every Sunday for the past two years, Garrett had asked Sam the same question.

His son stood straight and tall as he did every week. "You can count on me, Papa."

With his usual pat on Sam's slicked-down cowlick, Garrett headed for the nursery where he kissed Savannah and Milly. Not trusting his voice, he gave his wife an extra squeeze before heading for the church.

How would he get through a sermon when his heart was breaking? What good resolution could there be to Mrs. Greely's request? How could they return the little girl who had stolen their hearts? It would turn her world, as well as theirs, upside down.

He slipped into the warm, quiet church, his Bible tucked under his arm. Instead of going to his office, he plodded to the front of the sanctuary, where he fell to his knees. Bending until his forehead rested on the altar rail, he closed his eyes. All the emotion he'd held in surfaced as his shoulders shook and heaved. *Oh, God. Oh, God. Where are you? What are we going to do?*

As he waited, words from the fourteenth chapter of John penetrated his turbulent thoughts. *Let not your heart be troubled, neither let it be afraid.*

"Father, how can I keep my heart from being troubled?" He spoke aloud, overriding his churning emotions.

The heavens were silent as he opened his Bible at random. Words he'd underlined in red leapt out at him. *Be anxious for nothing; but in everything by prayer and supplication with thanksgiving let your requests be made known unto God. And the peace of God, which passeth all understanding, shall keep your hearts and minds through Christ Jesus.*

Let your requests be made known to God. His forehead puckered as he wrestled to put his petition into words. "Father, you know I'm angry at Mrs. Greely. It's no secret to you that I *hate* her for going back on her word."

Salty tears ran into the corner of his mouth as his head dipped to rest on the altar rail again. "But your Word says to be slow to anger because anger doesn't bring about your righteousness, so I'm asking you to take away my hatred and anger."

He pulled out his handkerchief and blew his nose before bowing his head. "You said if any lack wisdom, we can ask and you'll give it to us gladly. So I'm asking for wisdom. Please cause our thoughts to become agreeable with your will concerning this precious child. And I'm thanking you in advance for bringing about a peaceful resolution."

Outward circumstances hadn't changed, but peace flooded his heart as Garrett stood and headed for his office.

♠

Polly stopped beside the table where one of her boarders sat alone. "Mrs. Reagle, can I get you anything? Another cup of tea?"

"Another cup of tea would be wonderful." Mrs. Reagle beamed as Polly smothered a sigh and stole a glance at the clock. Why had she offered?

She whisked to the kitchen and returned with the teapot. "Here we are." She poured deep brown liquid until Mrs. Reagle held up her hand.

"That's plenty. I don't want to make a trip to the necessary during church this morning." When she laughed, her double chin jiggled as did her round belly.

Polly tore her gaze away. "Are you finished except for your tea?"

Mrs. Reagle nodded, prompting another chin jiggle. Polly stacked her plates and silverware and headed to the kitchen.

Did she have time to clean up the smaller dining room before putting the finishing touches on lunch? A bell jingled at the front counter in the lobby. Polly plopped the dishes into the large aluminum sink and dashed to answer the summons.

The overnight guest she had put in room one stood waiting, none too patiently, shifting from one foot to the other. What was his name? "May I help you, sir?"

"I'm ready to check out. The Vogans always had someone at the counter."

Polly's cheeks warmed. "I'm sorry. We're just getting the hang of things." She pulled the guest register toward her, running a finger beside the names. Drat. She had neglected to write down the room numbers when guests checked in.

"What was your name again, sir?"

"James Ebbert. Didn't you write it down?"

"I wrote it down but I didn't enter your room number. I wasn't sure if you were Mr. Ebbert or Mr. Houser. That will be $2."

Mr. Ebbert dug out two crumpled dollar bills. "I hope you're planning to hire a cook. My coffee was too strong and the eggs a trifle burned." He picked up his overnight bag and stomped out.

Polly covered her burning cheeks with trembling hands. Why had she thought she could run a hotel? She scurried from the lobby through the sitting room into the smaller dining room. "Twila, are you almost finished? I need you to stay at the front desk. Our other guests may be checking out soon."

"All right." Twila rose languidly and started in that direction, leaving her breakfast mess on the table.

"Wait. You need to take your dishes to the kitchen first."

"But you were clearing away everyone else's dishes." Twila frowned. "I assumed you'd take care of mine, too."

"Twila, you're not a guest." Polly enunciated each word between gritted teeth.

In spite of being a senior in high school, her youngest sister was her baby, and Polly rarely raised her voice to her. Twila's lips quivered. Polly stretched out a hand. "I'm sorry. There's so much to do. We all have to clean up after ourselves."

She followed her sister to the lobby and went into the larger dining room. Snowy-white tablecloths adorned every table, polished silverware, fresh flowers added luster. Had she missed anything? Guests from the community would begin to arrive in about half an hour… Oh no. She dropped her head in her hands. The potatoes and carrots were still sitting uncooked on the counter. What was she going to do? They would never be ready in time.

Footsteps and a masculine voice broke the silence of the dining room. "Hello Polly. I hope I'm not too early."

Tears rolling down her cheeks, Polly looked into the kind blue eyes of Charles Clarkson.

Chapter 86

Were those tears running down Polly's cheeks? Charles blinked. They turned her lovely green eyes the color of a stormy sea. He leaned toward her. "What's wrong? I can come back later if I'm too early."

Sobs erupted from Polly's lips, her shoulders shook. When she could speak, she said, "My first Sunday dinner for the community will be a disaster."

Charles wrinkled his forehead and sniffed appreciatively. "It smells wonderful. I'm sure it will be fine."

"I forgot to put the vegetables into the roasting pans, so all I have to serve is meat, bread and coleslaw. Oh, and the pies I baked yesterday." Polly wrapped her arms around herself.

"Hmmm…" Charles shifted into problem-solving mode. "You said you have bread?"

Polly nodded, question marks in her eyes.

"How about gravy?" He stepped toward the kitchen.

"Gravy…" She sprinted past Charles. "I forgot to make gravy but that's easily fixed." Her tone of voice had notched up tentatively to hopeful. "What are you thinking?"

"Hot roast beef sandwiches, coleslaw, and dessert. It sounds good to me." Charles was at Polly's heels.

She turned, her cheeks flushed. "We can cut the potatoes smaller, cook them on top of the stove and mash them to serve with the sandwiches as soon as they're ready."

Charles went to the small sink in the corner and washed

his hands. "I'll work on the potatoes while you make the gravy."

Polly hurried to the bottom of the stairs. "Twila and Elsie, get down here right now. We have an emergency." Her voice brooked no objections and her sisters magically appeared.

"Twila, help Mr. Clarkson cut up the potatoes."

Twila stared at Charles, eyes wide, stammering, "But, but…"

Polly grabbed a pan from the cupboard and filled it with water, ignoring her sister's reaction. "Put the potatoes in this pan. Elsie, shred those carrots." Polly pointed. "We'll sprinkle them on top of the coleslaw. It's in the cooler."

Polly was definitely back at the helm. She addressed her father as he joined them. "Could you cut the roast beef into thin slices for hot roast beef sandwiches, please?"

Bob's brows drew together. "I thought we were having roast beef, potatoes, and carrots."

"Change of menu. I'll explain later." She wiped her hands on her apron.

As her father headed for the oven, he stopped and stared. "You've put Charles Clarkson to work?"

"I'm happy to do it, Bob." Charles left his post and shook Bob's hand. "I came for dinner and saw the need for all hands on deck."

"He saved my life, Father." Polly dumped flour in a quart jar and filled it with water. "My menu was ruined because I forgot to put in the potatoes and carrots." Polly screwed on the lid and shook it vigorously. "Charles suggested making sandwiches instead. We have plenty of bread."

Charles stole glances at Polly as he chopped potatoes, his hands in constant motion. He couldn't keep his eyes off her. Tendrils of vibrant red hair escaped her loosely done chignon, curling onto her neck and forehead. Her cheeks were rosy. The heat wave he'd heard forecast had arrived.

Polly's lithe movements as she whisked the flour and broth gave the appearance of youth, but surely not more than ten years separated them. He had come today, hoping for nothing more than a fine meal and perhaps some friendly conversation. But as his gaze followed this lovely woman, his heart yearned for more.

♠

Mid-afternoon on Monday, Savannah kissed Milly and Garrett, closed the apartment door and hurried down the stairs to her appointment with Dr. Cooley. Thank goodness, Garrett's job allowed him to stay with Milly today. Not that she couldn't have asked Garrett's mother to watch her, but that would have required an explanation for this doctor appointment, something she wasn't ready to give.

Savannah jumped into the car her heart racing. Was it possible she might actually be with child? Surely she wasn't imagining these symptoms as she'd heard some women did? How could she bear it if the doctor's findings gave Garrett reason to mistrust her again? Her pulse slowed as forebodings washed over her, what if she had some awful disease, perhaps connected to the dreaded gonorrhea Dr. Cooley had treated them for several years ago?

And overshadowing it all was the overwhelming fear of losing Milly.

Father, help me stay focused on you, no matter what happens. Help me run to you as Sarah did, rather than blaming you. If Dr. Cooley finds something bad, please don't let Garrett react as he did the last time. Help us face this together.

Savannah pulled into the parking space outside the doctor's office and hurried in. Nurse Dayton smiled when she entered the empty waiting room. "Please have a seat, Savannah. The doctor will be with you soon."

Savannah had been here many times since that awful day almost eight years ago. The day they'd received their diagnosis and the accompanying news it was unlikely she could conceive. However, the reason for today's visit brought it all back. She rubbed her eyes and took deep breaths. Garrett had offered to accompany her today, but husbands weren't allowed into the examining room with their wives. To be honest, Savannah wasn't sure which would be worse—to have Garrett with her or to do it alone.

"Savannah, you're next." Nurse Dayton handed a red lollipop to a little boy of three while he and his mother said good bye to the doctor. Motioning to Savannah, she ushered her into the inner office. With a rustling of her taffeta uniform, she squeezed her considerable girth onto the stool at the small desk in the corner, then picked up a pen and smiled at Savannah. "What can we help you with today, Dearie? You don't look sick."

Searching for the right words, Savannah explained her situation, grateful for Nurse Dayton's matter-of-fact manner. "Dr. Cooley said it was unlikely I'd conceive, so perhaps I have some other condition that has interrupted my flow and caused my nausea."

The nurse wrote some words on her chart, tapped the pen against her teeth and then stood. "I'll let the doctor know you're ready." With a swish of skirts, she was gone.

Savannah stared at her fingernails. Never a nail biter, she was sorely tempted. *Oh Jesus, Oh Father, Oh Lord...* She had no other words but simply speaking God's names boosted her courage.

The door opened and Dr. Cooley came in holding her chart. "Hello, Mrs. Young. It's been some time since we've seen you."

"It has, doctor."

He cleared his throat. "Nurse Dayton tells me you haven't had your monthly for a while and are having some nausea."

Savannah nodded. "It's symptoms women often have when they're pregnant, but you said it was unlikely I could conceive."

"Hmmm… Unlikely but not impossible." Dr. Cooley looked at her chart. "When does your nausea occur?"

She wrinkled her forehead. "Usually first thing in the morning."

"How about when you eat greasy foods?"

"I don't think so. I read that sometimes women imagine themselves to have symptoms of pregnancy. Do you think I might be doing that?"

Dr. Cooley smiled and shook his head. "That's rare. There's probably a physical reason for your symptoms." He paused, tapping his foot. "There's a new, non-invasive pregnancy test which is achieving a reputation for accuracy. Since it's easy, let's do that first. If it's negative, we'll do some tests to check your gall bladder and hormones."

He started toward the door. "Nurse Dayton will give you a container to use for a specimen. We'll call you in a few days with the results."

Chapter 87

Ordinarily Garrett loved being alone with either or both his children, but after Savannah left for Dr. Cooley's office, the afternoon dragged. Milly was napping and neither the Methodist Episcopal denominational magazine nor a book on expository preaching held his attention. He welcomed Milly's *Come and get me* cry when it came.

Later, when the apartment door slammed, he dashed from the nursery where he'd finished changing Milly's diaper.

Sam walked up the steps, home from school. "Where's Mama?" Garrett attempted to hide his disappointment that it wasn't Savannah. Even though his son was usually excited to see him, his freckled face showed he was disappointed too.

Garrett punched his shoulder lightly. "What kind of a greeting was that? No, 'Hi Papa' or 'Hi Milly?' "

Sam grinned. "Sorry, Papa. Sorry, Milly. I just worry if Mama isn't here."

When Savannah stopped working, she became Sam's mainstay. His concern at her absence was understandable considering the disappearance of his biological parents. "Mama had a doctor appointment, but I expect her any time."

A cloud settled over Sam's expressive features. "Is she sick?"

"Not exactly." How to explain to a seven-year-old? "She just needed to talk to the doctor."

A frown still wrinkled Sam's forehead but he said no

more.

"How about a snack?" Snacks were a father's answer to everything.

"Okay." Sam's face brightened. "What do we have?"

"How about a peanut butter and jelly sandwich?"

Before Sam could answer, a car pulled up behind the apartment and Garrett headed for the bottom of the stairs with Milly in one arm and Sam close behind. When he opened the door, Savannah was getting out of the car, smiling. Smiling was good. "How did it go?"

"Hello to you, too." Savannah leaned in for a kiss before hugging Sam and scooping Milly into her arms.

Garrett bit his lip. "It's been a long afternoon."

"I was only gone a little while." Savannah glanced at him before starting up the stairs.

"Papa, you said I could have a peanut butter and jelly sandwich." Sammy rarely whined but he was close.

Garrett followed them and reined in his impatience with a sigh. "I did, didn't I? I guess Mama can talk to me while I make your sandwich."

Savannah raised Milly above her head and then lowered her in a whoosh that brought gleeful squeals. "More, more."

"One more, then I need to talk to Papa."

Garrett started on the sandwich while Savannah kept her promise, then set Milly down beside a pile of blocks on the dining room floor.

"Dr. Cooley said it's possible I could be—" Savannah glanced at Sam. "You know—what he thought wasn't likely. So he's doing a test to find out. He'll call us in a few days."

"No other tests?" Should he be relieved or worried?

"Not unless I'm not—you know." Savannah pulled out a handkerchief and wiped the sweat from her brow. "It's hot outside and even hotter in here."

"A heat wave the weatherman said." Garrett handed Sam his sandwich. The boy had been glancing back and forth between his parents.

He took a giant bite and spoke around it. "So you're not going to tell me what the doctor said?"

When they both shook their heads, he took it in stride, then added with an impish grin, "I guess I won't tell you what happened in school today either."

♠

"Twila and Elsie, finish putting away the dishes." Polly gave her sisters last-minute instructions before getting ready for Bible study with Savannah and Mrs. Young.

Dashing through the small dining room, she found Father in the living room. "Can you stay in the sitting room this evening while I'm gone, so you'll have a good view of the lobby?"

He shrugged. "I guess but isn't that why we have a bell on the counter, in case guests arrive or need assistance?"

"That's only for emergencies." Polly started up the stairs. "Besides, we don't always hear the bell if we're back here."

After Mam passed, she and the other two ladies had gone back to meeting on Monday evenings, but they had missed several weeks due to Polly's move. Out of breath from climbing two flights of stairs, she detoured into the bathroom to wash her face before going to her room. After yanking off her food-spattered apron, she brushed a hand over her green work dress. Changing would take too long so this old frock would have to do.

A quick swipe of a comb through her hair finished her toilette, and she headed back downstairs, feet dragging. She paused. Should she stay home and go to bed? A mental picture of herself dissolving into tears in front of Charles yesterday came to mind. She straightened her shoulders. Her Bible study group was the closest thing to church she had, and she'd never needed it more. Too often, she fell asleep while attempting to read her Bible, pray or write in her journal.

The minute she stepped out the front door, oppressive heat pounced as she crossed the veranda. Not that the hotel was cool. Even with several fans blowing, the mugginess dogged her footsteps all day. How did people in the south survive? She headed for Mildred's house, her mind awhirl with menu plans and marketing lists. Who could she ask to buy the groceries? The Vogans had employed several people for various tasks but paying wages to employees frightened her.

Perhaps Charles Clarkson… Where had that thought come from? He'd only helped because she'd cried like a baby. What else could he do? It was unlikely he'd ever attempt to have Sunday dinner here again.

She tapped lightly on Mildred's door, welcoming an interruption to blot out the kind blue eyes that flitted through her mind more often than she wanted to admit.

Chapter 88

Savannah flew to Mildred's door as Polly opened it. Garrett's mother was close behind her. "How are you, Polly? How are things at the hotel?" Savannah hugged her friend and then stepped aside so Mother could do the same.

Polly groaned. "So busy. I need about ten more pair of hands."

"Come sit down, and I'll pour you some iced tea." Mother drew Polly toward the table. "I'm sure this heat doesn't help."

Savannah sat beside Polly as Mother pulled a frosty pitcher from the refrigerator they'd recently purchased. "How did your first Sunday dinner turn out?"

Color crept up Polly's neck. "It would have been a disaster if Charles Clarkson hadn't come to the rescue."

Savannah's eyebrows flew up. "Who is Charles Clarkson?"

"He lives in Stoneboro and works for the railroad. Charles and his wife came to Will's burial and the memorial service in Franklin. He and Will knew each other."

"And how did he happen to come to the rescue on Sunday?" Savannah's forehead crinkled in a puzzled frown.

Polly waved a hand and then fanned herself with it. "It's a long story."

Mother finished pouring tea and dropped into a chair. "We have lots of time—unless you have to be back early?"

"I hope not, barring an emergency. They all have their instructions." She sighed. "I'm such an idiot." With more blushes and self-deprecation, Polly poured out the account of the first Sunday dinner and Charles's role in it.

Mildred took a long swallow of tea, her eyes thoughtful. "His wife passed away a few years ago, didn't she?"

Polly nodded.

Savannah's eyebrows went up again. "Oh, I see."

Setting down her glass with a clatter, Polly's eyes flashed. "Don't be getting any ideas. You know how I feel about men who work for the railroad."

"I'm sorry. I didn't mean anything by it." Savannah suppressed a smile. Regardless of what Polly said, her voice held a certain tone when she spoke Charles's name.

"So how's Milly? Is Sammy doing all right in school." Polly hurried to change the subject.

"Milly's fine, except..." Savannah couldn't suppress the trepidation in her voice. Mother reached for her hand. Garrett had spoken to his parents the day before so they could pray.

Polly straightened. "Except what? What's wrong with Milly?"

"Nothing's wrong with her exactly..." Savannah voice trailed off as she brought her emotions under control so she could tell Polly about Mrs. Greely's request.

"That's awful." Polly snorted. "What an absolutely horrid, unreasonable thing to ask of anyone. I would say I can't believe it but after the things you've told me in the past, I can. What is it they say? A leopard can't change his spots?"

Savannah shook her head. "If that were true, I'd be in trouble. I know God can change a person's heart, but sometimes folks go back to their old ways."

"What will you do?" Polly grabbed Savannah's other hand.

"I don't know. I guess we're supposed to be praying about it. Mrs. Greely thinks since we're Christians, we should just give Milly back."

Polly pinched Savannah's fingers together so hard, she cried out. "I'm sorry, but I'm so angry, I can't see straight. You won't give her back will you?"

"I think Garrett wants to talk to a lawyer."

"Mr. Stranahan in Mercer did the legal work when I bought the hotel, maybe he could help you and Garrett. I'll get his phone number for you tomorrow." Polly let go of Savannah's hand and trailed her fingers up and down her cool glass. "Oh Savannah, I've been so wrapped up in my own little world. I had no idea what was going on in yours. I'm sorry."

Savannah bit her lip, then made a quick decision. She hadn't planned to tell anyone but this seemed like the right time. "That's not all."

"Oh no." Polly stared into her eyes. "What else? Not somebody wanting to take Sammy?"

"No, thank God, not that. This might be a good thing, or it could be bad." Savannah condensed her story of the last few months and her trip to Dr. Cooley's office.

Mother's jaw dropped. "But you and Garrett haven't said a word."

"We hadn't planned to tell anyone until we're sure, but I can't keep it from you and Polly any longer. Even though Dr. Cooley said before it wasn't likely, he says it's possible I'm in the family way. We're waiting for test results."

Polly clapped her hands. "That's so exciting."

Savannah dropped her gaze. "Just pray it isn't something that causes trouble between Garrett and me again."

"My goodness." Mother looked back and forth from Polly to Savannah. "You two have a lot going on." She picked up her Bible. "We won't have any trouble deciding what to pray about tonight, will we? What has the Lord been saying to each of you?"

Savannah clasped her hands in her lap. "God's reminding me that when trouble came to Sarah, she ran to the Lord instead of blaming Him. Some days I remember. Other times, fear takes over."

Mother nodded. "That's understandable. How about you, Polly?"

Polly sighed. "I'm so busy, I probably wouldn't hear God if He spoke with a megaphone. If I had time to think, I'd probably worry that I jumped into buying the hotel too quickly, but it's too late now."

"Hmmm, okay." Mother pursed her lips. "Let's look at Jeremiah 29." As soon as pages stopped turning, Mother asked Polly to read verse eleven.

For I know the thoughts I think towards you, saith the Lord, thoughts of peace, and not of evil to give you an expected end.

Scratching her cheek, Savannah glanced at Mother. "What does that mean?"

"I believe it means God knows the plans He has for you, what He wants to accomplish, and His plans are good, although they may not seem good to us." Mother smiled. "Polly, will you read Romans eight, verse twenty-eight?"

After more page turning, Polly read the verse aloud. *And we know that all things work together for good to them that love God, to them who are the called according to His purpose.*

"So, even if we've run ahead of Him, He can still work things out for good. How many things does that verse say God can work together for good to those who love Him?" Mother's eyes sparkled.

"I know it says 'all.'" Savannah stared at the floor. "But I don't see how God can bring good from Mrs. Greely wanting Milly back."

Chapter 89

Garrett took his last bite of chili and pushed back his chair. "Didn't Dr. Cooley say they'd call us with your test results in a few days?"

With a quick nod, Savannah wiped Milly's face and hands with a warm washcloth. "That's what he said."

"It's been three days. Doesn't a few mean two?" He scowled as he carried his plate and silverware to the sink.

"Listen to you. When did you become an expert on the English language?" Savannah giggled and Milly chuckled agreeably and scrunched up her shoulders as her mother washed under her chin. "I think a few could mean one or two, or two or three."

"Really? I was sure it meant no more than two. I think we should call Dr. Cooley. Maybe they forgot."

Savannah removed the tray from Milly's high chair and handed her to Garrett. "I can do that if you'll entertain your daughter for a few minutes." She closed her eyes.

Garrett took Milly and peered at his wife. "Are you all right?"

"I'm just nervous. What if he says—"

"Let's not speculate, Savannah. No need to borrow trouble." He smiled to soften the effect of his words.

"You're right, of course." Savannah sighed, then crossed the room and cranked Dr. Cooley's number. Garrett followed her and hovered within hearing distance. At the last minute, she handed him the receiver and scooped Milly into her arms.

"What—"

Just then Nurse Dayton's voice reached his ear. "Hello?"

"Oh, hello. This is Garrett Young." Savannah disappeared into the nursery with Milly and closed the door. Taken aback, he lost his voice for a moment. "Uh… I'm calling to check on my wife's test results."

"Oh, Mr. Young, I'm very sorry. We were so busy treating our elderly patients during the heat wave that we overlooked the specimen." The nurse cleared her throat. "Could Savannah come in and provide another one?"

Why hadn't Nurse Dayton called them? Garrett bit his tongue. "When would you like her to come in?"

"Anytime during office hours will be fine."

He managed a gruff response and hung up. Grrrr. More waiting. And why was Savannah hiding in the nursery? She opened the door and peeked out as he crossed the hall.

She pulled Milly close, as though protecting herself behind the child. "What did you find out?"

"Nothing. Why did you give me the phone and hide in here?" He stopped and gentled his voice. He shouldn't take his frustrations out on his wife. "Why are you hiding in the nursery?"

Milly wriggled in her mother's arms and gave a sleepy cry. Savannah crossed the room and sank into the rocking chair with a pink gingham cushion, then began to rock. Her gaze roved around the room, anywhere except at him.

Garrett waited. At times like this, it was best to be silent.

When Savannah finally spoke, her voice was almost a whisper. "Do you remember the day Dr. Cooley told us we had gonorrhea?"

He shuddered as images of that awful day rushed back. "It's one of my worst memories. I wish I could forget—"

"I'm not saying this to make you feel bad, Love. But I'm terrified that I'll get a diagnosis that will cause you to distrust me again." Now it was her turn to shudder. "I'd rather discover I'm dying than go through that."

Garrett strode across the room and dropped to the floor at her feet. "Savannah, I'm so sorry. I wish I could have a do-over of that day. The Bible says if anyone is in Christ, he's a new creation, but there was a resurrection of the old me in Dr. Cooley's office. Can you ever forgive me?"

"I have forgiven you. I understand why someone would have a hard time trusting a person with a past like mine." A tear trickled down Savannah's cheek. "That's why I'm so afraid to find out the results. If I'm not pregnant, maybe the gonorrhea is back."

Standing, Garrett took a now-sleeping Milly from Savannah's arms and placed her in her crib, then drew his wife close. He rocked her gently with his cheek pressed to hers. "I trust you, my Darling. Nurse Dayton says they need another specimen, but whatever it shows, by God's grace we will face it together."

Savannah pulled away and stared at him. "Why do they need another specimen? Does he think something else is wrong?"

"They overlooked your sample during the heat wave, and I suspect they forgot to refrigerate it. He's probably afraid the test wouldn't be valid. You told me it's in experimental stages anyway." As she sighed and leaned her head on his chest, he added, "You can go in anytime during office hours."

She nodded and the lavender shampoo she favored wafted to his nostrils. "Garrett…"

"Yes…"

"I hate to bring this up, but Polly gave me the phone number of the lawyer who helped her when she was buying the hotel."

He groaned. "I admit I keep hoping if I ignore this situation with Milly, it will go away."

"You know it won't unless Mrs. Greely has another change of heart."

Garrett rested his head on her hair. "You're right. I need

to set up an appointment."

Savannah burrowed in closer to him. "Oh Garrett, what will we do if they take her?"

Chapter 90

Charles sucked in a deep breath as he tugged his attention back to the train route he was navigating. He'd been an engineer for many years but the biggest danger was over-confidence. Something unexpected could happen at a moment's notice.

All week, he'd struggled to keep the stormy green eyes and vibrant red hair from stealing his focus. What to do about his increasing desire to see Polly again? He'd never expected to remarry after Jane's death, but the house was so empty, as was his daily existence. Even before the redhead had caught his attention.

There'd be no harm in pursuing a relationship with someone a little younger than me, would there, Father?

Before Jane died, he'd let her do most of the praying. In her absence, he was amazed to find himself talking to God. Even more surprised to be calling him Father as Jane had.

Back when he'd courted Jane, he'd taken a lot of kidding from his railroad buddies for being involved with an "older woman." She was almost ten years his elder, but he hadn't allowed that to stop him.

After wiping the sweat from his forehead, he reached for his thermos. Why was he drinking hot coffee while sweating? At least the temperatures had fallen and the dreaded heat wave was over. He pulled into the station in Franklin and clambered from the engine. The weekend stretched ahead of him, bleak and lonely. Once he had looked forward to his time off. Not anymore.

Maybe he could offer his services to the Dyes on his days off, especially Saturdays and Sundays, probably their busiest days. A non-threatening way to get to know Polly before suggesting a date. He drew in a deep breath. A date. His chest tightened. How did a forty-two-year-old man start dating again?

♠

Polly collapsed in the family living room on Friday evening. Thank goodness their boarders and guests had retired early. Not that they expected her to entertain them—the expectation to socialize even when she was beyond tired was in her. Twila and Elsie had gone bowling while Father sprawled in the deep-blue, wing chair she'd brought from the little brown bungalow.

"Almost done with our first week." Father smiled at her. "How are we doing?"

"You mean financially?" Of course he was talking about money. They fell over each other peeking at Elsie's bookkeeping figures. "I'm not sure. It's hard to tell. I think we'd be okay if we didn't have that mortgage hanging over us." She rubbed her eyes. "I probably should have bargained for a lower price with the former owners, but it's too late now." She seemed to say that a lot.

The telephone rang in the lobby, and she leaped to her feet. It seemed extravagant to have two telephones, so they'd settled on one, even though it meant a lot of running. Polly grabbed the receiver and held it to her ear. "Hello?"

"Hi…" She recognized the pleasant, familiar voice even before he identified himself. "This is Charles Clarkson. I enjoyed giving your family a hand last Sunday and wondered if you could use some help this weekend?"

Heat crept up Polly's neck and not from the temperature. He couldn't know she'd considered asking for his help. "That's so nice of you to offer, but I can't afford to hire anyone."

"Oh, I'm not looking for a second job." He chuckled. "My weekend is free, and it would be a treat to join you folks if you could use another pair of hands."

Polly laughed as he echoed her words to Savannah. "I told my friend last Sunday I needed *ten more* pair of hands."

"Well, I only have one pair but they're yours if you want them."

Hers if she wanted them? She drew deep breaths, settling her thudding heart, and maintained an even tone. "That's so kind of you. I don't know how I can ever repay you."

"None needed or expected."

The same sensation she'd experienced last Sunday rose in her. Gratitude is all it was. She'd been dreading trying to accomplish the long list of waiting tasks in the next two days, and his offer of help lifted her spirits. Nothing more. "Thank you so much, Charles. I appreciate it more than I can say."

"You're welcome. What time should I come tomorrow?"

"How do you feel about going to market?" She cringed as she waited for his answer. Her father hated grocery shopping.

"I'm used to it now."

Of course, since his wife died. "If you wouldn't mind doing the marketing, I can get started on the pies and bread tomorrow morning."

"I can do that." Was there a tinge of disappointment in his voice?

"Are you sure?"

Charles cleared his throat. "I thought you wanted me to go with you to help carry the heavy items, but I don't mind going alone."

His voice implied to the contrary. Maybe she could go with him and do her baking later… Her heart rate picked up.

No, she didn't want to give him the wrong impression. She mustn't forget he was a railroad man.

Chapter 91

Polly spent an unusual amount of time in front of the mirror on Saturday morning. A hotelkeeper should always be careful of her appearance because one never knew when guests would arrive. In the past, she had been lax. Her green dress, crisp and smelling of sunshine, matched her eyes. The image of her apron, as she twirled in front of the mirror, reflected a deeper shade of green with strings tied around her waist in a perky bow. It actually enhanced her appearance.

"Why are you all dressed up?"

Polly spun toward the door, startled by Elsie's voice. It must be late if she was awake. "I need to look like a successful innkeeper."

"While you're baking?" Elsie rolled her eyes.

"We never know when a potential customer will stop in to schedule a party."

Elsie sniffed. "I heard you tell Father that Charles Clarkson offered to help on his weekends off. I bet that's the reason you're dressed to the nines."

Polly glared at her sister. "That's ridiculous. Go get dressed and leave the fantasies to fiction writers." She squeezed past Elsie and ran down the steps to the kitchen.

Oatmeal was on the menu for breakfast, so she mixed it, adding raisins and brown sugar, and put it on the stove before starting her bread dough. Why did everything always take twice as long as expected? If only she didn't have to fix breakfast for guests and boarders, her family could fend for themselves. Maybe she should insist Twila and Elsie prepare breakfast for everyone on weekends. There was no reason they couldn't. Did she want to take on that battle?

♠

Charles stood in front of his closet debating how to dress for a trip to the market. He'd visited the barber shop in Stoneboro yesterday for a fresh haircut, so his thick blond hair responded more obediently than usual. No use kidding himself. The opinion of people at the market didn't matter, only the opinion of the one making the list.

Jane had always been the expert on proper clothing for the occasion. Now he was on his own. He stared at his reflection. Was he being disloyal to her by attempting to get to know Polly better? No. Jane had been a widow when he married her. Surely she wouldn't disapprove.

He pulled a lightweight, pale blue shirt from its hook and a brown pair of trousers from a drawer. Since his ironing skills were nonexistent, he'd hired a neighbor to do that chore. He stared at the clothes he'd picked, then shrugged, and slipped them on. They would have to do.

Polly had said he could come any time but how would it look if he showed up before breakfast? So he'd had a leisurely cup of coffee while he waited. Glancing at his watch, he left the house, got into his roadster and headed for Sandy Lake. Should he enter the hotel by the front or back door since he wasn't a guest? Probably the back. Did that mean it would also be appropriate to park in the back parking area? He opted to do that and rapped lightly on the entry to the screened-in porch.

"Just a minute." Polly appeared drying her hands on a small linen towel. The green of her dress matched her eyes while the cute little apron took more years from her age. Adding to the adorable image was a streak of flour across her nose. She smiled. "Come in, Charles."

"Am I too early? I think I asked you that question last time I was here." He gazed at her smiling face, then chuckled.

"At least, this time it didn't make you cry." He stepped onto the porch. Her laughter was music to his ears—one of the things he loved about her, along with her appealing eyes.

"No crying today and you're not too early. Come in. Have you had breakfast?" Polly headed into the kitchen.

He followed. "I had a cup of coffee. I often don't bother with much breakfast."

"How about some oatmeal?" Polly turned toward the stove. "I should at least provide you with something to eat in exchange for your help."

"I expect nothing in return." He sniffed. "But that oatmeal smells awfully good."

"Do you want to eat in the small dining room?" Polly gestured. "That's where the family and boarders eat."

Charles pulled out a chair at the desk near where Polly appeared to be working. "I'd rather eat here if that's all right with you."

"Suit yourself."

He sat down, and she filled a bowl with oatmeal, adding more brown sugar, raisins and milk, then handed it to him. "How about a cup of coffee?"

"I don't want to interrupt your work." He nodded to the lump of half-kneaded dough.

Her laugh rang out again. "You're saving me so much time I can certainly get you a cup of coffee." She poured one and set it on the desk.

"Thank you, Polly." He could hardly tear his gaze away. She was much more tempting than the oatmeal in his bowl.

♠

Warning bells went off in Polly's ears at the expression in Charles's eyes, an expression that sent tingles up her spine. She would have to watch her step and guard her heart, or the next thing she knew, she would find herself falling in love with him. A mistake she must avoid at all costs.

Her pulse quickened as she turned her attention to the bread dough. With unaccustomed vigor, she rammed her fists into it repeatedly, keeping her eyes on her work. What was wrong with her? She barely knew this man.

Unable to resist the temptation, she glanced at Charles. The sweetness of his smile almost undid her. She hastily returned her gaze to her work.

Remember Polly, no matter how charming and sweet he might be, it doesn't change his occupation.

Chapter 92

Savannah snuggled her daughter close, smelling the sweet essence of clean baby. *Please God, don't let them take Milly. Don't ask us to give her up.*

She clutched Milly even closer to her heart. How she loved this child and Sammy too. If God saw fit to give them a baby by birth, it couldn't possibly be any more precious than the two He'd already given them.

The phone rang and she put her sleeping baby into the crib, then dashed to the telephone. *Maybe it's Dr. Cooley.*

"Hello?"

"Mrs. Young? I have some good news for you." Nurse Dayton's tone was jovial.

Savannah's arms and legs went limp. She almost dropped the receiver.

"Are you there?"

"I'm sorry, Mrs. Dayton. I almost dropped the telephone but I'm here." Savannah plopped down on the floor outside the nursery.

"Dr. Cooley says the pregnancy test is positive. He'll want you to come in for another appointment now that we know what's causing your symptoms."

Her worst nightmare had not come true. Savannah stammered out a thank you and managed to set up another appointment. *Thank you, God. Oh, thank you, thank you.*

She had hardly hung up before the telephone rang again.

Turning back, she grabbed it before it wakened Milly. "Hello."

"Hello…"

Oh no, she'd recognize Mrs. Greely's raspy voice anywhere.

"This is Mrs. Greely."

Resisting the temptation to hang up, Savannah clutched the receiver tighter. Why hadn't they discussed what Savannah should tell her if she called when Garrett wasn't home?

"How are you, Mrs. Greely?"

"I'm fine, but I thought we'd have heard from you folks by now." She paused but Savannah didn't respond. "Have you made a decision?"

Struggling to speak around the lump in her throat, Savannah gave up and coughed before she found her voice. "Not yet. I believe Garrett wants to talk to a lawyer." Would he have wanted her to say that?

"A lawyer?" Mrs. Greely's voice shrilled to a near shriek. "Why would he want to talk to a lawyer? Doesn't he know Christians aren't supposed to sue each other?"

"I didn't say we plan to take you to court. We just want to confirm our rights as Milly's adopted parents."

Mrs. Greely's heavy breathing was the only sound. Then at last she spoke. "I can't believe you'd want to keep a child from its mother."

"Milly's biological mother is a stranger to her, as are you. Garrett and I are the only parents she knows." Savannah paused, forming a question as her brain spun its wheels. "Mrs. Greely, did you change your mind about not wanting anyone to know Milly is Amanda's child?"

The woman sniffed. "Amanda is engaged. Her beau knows about Milly and is willing to adopt her. No one outside the family needs to know the truth."

"Your church and ours, as well as all our friends, would want to know why we gave Milly up." Savannah's voice raised an octave. "We won't lie."

Mrs. Greely's voice matched Savannah's. "It's no one

else's business—"

"Mrs. Greely, my friends think it unconscionable that you would ask us to give up this child whom we have loved and raised as our own for more than two years. I agree. I have nothing else to say to you until Garrett and I see a lawyer. Please don't call us again."

Savannah broke the connection, then let the receiver hang free so no calls could come through. She collapsed on the floor, sobbing, her limbs unable to hold her.

♠

Garrett ran down the steps from the church, stomach growling. What a blessing he could join Savannah and Milly for lunch each day. Sometimes if Milly fell asleep early, he and his wife had a bit of uninterrupted time.

When he opened their apartment door, the unmistakable sound of sobbing greeted him. He took the steps two at a time and found his wife lying on the floor under the telephone, weeping uncontrollably.

He dropped to the floor beside her. "Savannah, Love, whatever is the matter?" He gathered her into his arms.

Savannah's body shook convulsively as she burrowed her face in his shirt, soaking it with tears. "Mrs. Greely…"

It was the only words she spoke, but it was enough. He groaned. "Oh no, what did she say?"

When Savannah regained control, she told Garrett about the conversation. "Is it true that Christians aren't supposed to sue each other?"

"It is true. Between Christians, the Bible says a wise person in the church should be the one to judge. But I didn't plan—"

Savannah sat up so suddenly, she bumped her head on his chin.

"Ouch." Garrett rubbed the sore spot while Savannah rubbed her head.

"I'm sorry, but I was so upset, I forgot to tell you the good news." A smile spread all over her face. "Nurse Dayton called to say we're going to have a baby." Before Garrett could respond, her smile fled. "Oh Garrett, you don't suppose God is giving us another baby because He wants us to give Milly back?"

Chapter 93

Garrett pulled the emergency brake and left the car running while he came around to open the door for Sam. Ma waited on the porch as he lifted Milly from Savannah's arms. "Thanks for watching the children today."

"Of course, you know it's always my pleasure. Take all the time you need with Mr. Stranahan. I'll be praying." Ma pushed a wisp of gray hair behind her ear.

When Garrett re-entered the car, Savannah was wiping her eyes as she'd been doing all week. He kissed her cheek. "Please don't cry, Love. Everything will be okay."

She lifted one shoulder. "I agree that we need to talk to a lawyer, but in the end, it's what God wants us to do that matters." Another tear slid down her cheek.

Garrett released the brake, put the car in reverse and backed onto the road. "You're right, of course. Still, I hope talking to Mr. Stranahan will clarify our thinking."

Silence prevailed in the car for most of the ride to Mercer. The endless treadmill cycle in his brain followed the same path he'd battled all week. Was it selfish of them to keep Milly when God was giving them another baby? Savannah feared it was. On the other hand, how could they hand over their unsuspecting child to complete strangers? How could that be in the child's best interest?

He rubbed one hand over his face while tightening the fingers of his other hand on the steering wheel, his knuckles white with the intensity of his grip. Why was it that circumstances which should have brought unmitigated joy were usually mixed with events that clouded one's perspective? A new life grew in Savannah's womb, a tiny son or daughter, but with the possibility of losing Milly looming, how could they celebrate?

A long sigh escaped his lips. He'd squelched more of them this week than he could count. Savannah glanced at him, then patted his knee. "I'm sorry I haven't done much to lift your spirits." She stretched her lips into a sorry attempt at a smile.

He shook his head as he pulled into a parking space on North Diamond Street. "It's not up to you to cheer me up. I'm sure if not for Ma's prayers, we'd both be deeper in the pits than we are."

Grabbing Savannah's hand, he bowed his head. "Father, I don't even know what to pray. Please make your will clear to us. Use Mr. Stanahan to give us the guidance we need. Amen."

As they stood in front of the lawyer's office, they clasped hands and exchanged a long look before entering. They must remain united.

A few minutes later, the receptionist ushered them into Mr. Stranahan's office. He shook Garrett's hand and gestured toward two chairs as he returned to his seat behind his massive oak desk. "I understand you have some questions concerning your rights now that the biological mother of your adopted daughter has changed her mind."

Garrett nodded. "Yes, we want to know what the law requires under these circumstances."

Mr. Stranahan opened a folder on his desk and ran his finger down a sheet of paper. "I did some research on this case and found everything to be in order. The adoption should stand unless you or the Greely family misled each other in any way or if any other irregularities become evident."

Garrett frowned. "What kind of irregularities?"

Mr. Stranahan shuffled and restacked the papers in the file. "If there were stipulations in the adoption papers that either of you failed to fulfill, that might constitute an irregularity. However, I see nothing like that in the original contract. Also, a breach of contract might be sited if either of you misrepresented yourselves."

Garrett glanced at his wife. Mrs. Greely certainly knew every unsavory fact in Savannah's past. There would have been no basis for saying they'd misrepresented themselves. "So you're saying the Greely family has no legal right to request we return Milly?"

"None that I know of." Mr. Stranahan tapped one long finger on the papers. "Of course, if they decide to bring a case against you, I can't predict what the judge's decision would be. State laws in the field of adoption are relatively new and at times, judges make decisions based more on their personal philosophies than on the laws."

Savannah covered her face with her hands and Garrett groaned. "There's nothing we can do that would guarantee a judge to decide in our favor?"

"Nothing." Mr. Stranahan's concerned expression lightened into a hint of a smile. "I've known folks who tried to bribe the judge, but I don't recommend it."

"No, of course not." Savannah dropped her hands and reached for one of Garrett's. "We wouldn't consider doing anything illegal. My husband is a pastor."

The lawyer shrugged. "It wouldn't be the first time a man of the cloth resorted to an unethical method."

Garrett squared his shoulders. "If we're meant to keep this child, we will trust God to bring that about."

Savannah smoothed her skirts and nodded.

After a long pause, Mr. Stranahan looked from one to the other. "If neither of you have any other questions, we can conclude this session. I'll be happy to represent you in court should the need arise."

They all stood and Mr. Stranahan came from behind his desk to shake Garrett's hand. "I'll have my secretary send you a bill."

On the ride home, Savannah broke the silence. "You don't think the Greelys would take us to court, do you?"

"Not under the circumstances, both Reverend Greely and I being pastors." Garrett drummed his fingers on the steering wheel. "However, Scripture says when Christians have a legal disagreement, they should choose a wise person in the church to settle the dispute. It's difficult to predict what that person's perspective would be. Mrs. Greely is a person of influence."

Chapter 94

Polly's feet dragged as she pushed herself to do the marketing on Saturday morning. Charles was working this weekend so it had fallen on her shoulders again. Even though he'd only helped for two weekends, his absence created an alarming emptiness despite all her efforts to guard her heart.

Her pulse ratcheted up with each item she placed in her basket. She had to pinch pennies. Last night Father had announced the Dye mines would close within three months. What would they do without that source of income? If only Father could sell their house.

Instead of the hotel benefiting the family finances, it seemed to be more of a drain. The hotel mortgage was never far from her mind.

The hot breath of fear on her neck threatened to overwhelm her. What would Sarah Davis have done had she faced a situation like this? As Polly walked aimlessly through the general store, she mentally scanned the pages of Sarah's diary, looking for an answer. But Sarah had never faced a financial crisis, or at least not one she'd recorded. Her husband's business had apparently provided well for the family's needs.

An image of Polly's little brown bungalow rose in her mind and with it a surge of bitterness. Sarah had never sold her beloved home to support her family, never watched her finances dwindling. What if Polly's sacrifice had been in vain? What if she lost not only her home but the hotel? Bile flooded her throat.

How could God let that happen?

If I turn against God, to whom will I go for comfort and strength in the days ahead? While Sarah may not have experienced the same struggles as she, her answer was always the same—running to God, not away from Him when trouble came.

As Polly lifted her chin and gripped her shopping list, another voice echoed in her inner ear. *We evaluate all that happens in light of God's character, rather than evaluating God's character in light of what happens to us.* Her mother's words. How blessed Polly had been to have two godly women from whom to learn.

While God may not prevent bad things from happening, He promises to bring good from them. Her mother's words again. Romans, chapter eight, verse twenty-eight. Another promise to cling to when trouble knocked at the door.

♠

Savannah tossed and turned long after Garrett's breathing told her he was asleep. Every time Mrs. Greely's phone call replayed in her mind, Savannah gritted her teeth and fought the urge to run to Milly's crib to reassure herself that their precious baby was still there.

At last, she climbed out of bed, grabbed a light robe from the bedpost and started toward the nursery. She stumbled over a small body stretched across the doorway.

"Ouch." A muffled yelp came from the barrier.

"Sammy?" Savannah knelt beside her son. "What are you doing?"

He sat up, rubbing his elbow that had collided with her foot. "I'm protecting Milly, making sure Mrs. Greedy doesn't snatch her."

Savannah blew out a puff of air. Sammy had never gotten Mrs. Greely's name right—or had he?

How in the world did he know? They'd been so careful to hide it from him. She pulled Sammy into her arms, snuggling him close. "What a good big brother you are, but no one is trying to kidnap Milly." She steered him toward his bedroom. "I'll tuck you in."

That task finished, Savannah headed for the living room loveseat. No use trying to sleep. What a dreadful loss for Sammy if the Greelys took his sister. She dropped to her knees and buried her face in the padded upholstery, fists clenched at her sides. *Oh God...* Wild plans formed. They could pack up the children and move to a remote area in Canada. No one would ever find them. Garrett's parents would help. Maybe Garrett could find a church to pastor.

Who was she fooling? Her imagination was running wild. She needed God's plan. *Oh, God, what should we do?*

Surrender...

What does that mean, Lord? Give Milly back?

Surrender your will.

Surrender her will. Somehow amid all the turmoil, Self had firmly established itself on the throne of her life—again. A mental image of Abraham placing Isaac on the altar arose. *Oh Lord, help me. I can't do this.* Savannah unclenched her fists, one finger at a time, a guttural groan escaping her lips. *I... surrender... my... will... to... you. I affirm that you are the Lord of my life. All that I am and have are yours.*

As soon as the words left her lips, Savannah felt drawn to her Bible lying on the end table. She turned on a small lamp and opened it at random to Proverbs 31. It was a chapter she avoided because she never measured up to the woman described there. Words she'd written beside verse eight during a message from Reverend Caldwell caught her eye.

Speak up for those who cannot speak for themselves for the rights of all who are destitute. Speak up and judge fairly...

Speak up for those who cannot speak for themselves... Was God asking her to fight for their daughter who could not speak for herself?

Chapter 95

A week later, Savannah hummed snatches of *'Tis So Sweet to Trust in Jesus* as she pulled the hamburgers out of her heavy iron skillet. After Savannah's appointment with Dr. Cooley, Mother Young had jumped at the chance to keep Sammy and Milly through the dinner hour. Savannah had news to discuss with Garrett when he came home from work.

Footsteps on the stairs announced his arrival as she poured tall glasses of iced tea. Lifting her face for his kiss, she set down the pitcher and threw her arms around his neck.

Garrett responded by nibbling on her ear. "That's a welcome I could get used to."

"The children are at your mother's, so it's just you and me."

"Ah…" He tugged her toward the davenport. "Do we have time for an appetizer before dinner?"

Savannah giggled. "Actually, I wanted to talk to you but—"

His kisses stole her breath.

"…it can wait."

Life and concerns about Milly had siphoned romance from them for too long. She relaxed in her husband's arms, all her senses responding to his caresses.

♠

Much later as they ate their cold hamburgers, Savannah cleared her throat.

Garrett grinned around a bite of sandwich. "I forgot you wanted to talk to me. Someone must have distracted me."

A smile flitted over Savannah's lips as she washed down a bite of the hastily made tomato soup with a swallow of iced tea. "I can't imagine what would have distracted you." She nudged his knee with hers.

He kissed her cheek. "How did your appointment go with Doc Cooley? I intended to ask you the minute I got home."

"It went well. Doctor is pleased with the baby's progress and mine."

"When does he think our little stow-away will arrive?" Garrett picked up a stalk of celery.

"He says late January or early February."

"So about six months." He glanced at the small calendar lying on the table and smiled. "Did you put it on the calendar so we won't forget?"

Since Savannah no longer worked in the insurance office, Garrett teased her about her increased attention to detail. Her lips twitched. "I doubt I'll forget." She rubbed her abdomen, even though it barely gave evidence of the addition to their family. "Where will we put everyone?"

Garrett closed his eyes. "I can't think about that yet." He opened his eyes and tilted back his chair. "Was there something else you wanted to talk about?"

She laid down her spoon. "It's about Milly."

Bringing his chair down on all four legs, he groaned.

"Wait until you hear what I have to say." She leaned toward him. "Last Saturday night I couldn't sleep."

"The night you found Sam stretched across Milly's doorway so Mrs. Greedy wouldn't take her?" A hint of a smile touched his lips.

She nodded. "God spoke to me that night. I didn't tell you because I wanted time to pray about it." Taking a deep breath, she told him what she believed God had said. "I think He's telling me He wants us to fight to keep Milly."

"Praise God." He touched her hand. "I never thought God

was asking us to give Milly up because He's giving us another baby, but you were so fearful that He was."

"I had to surrender my will before He released me from that." She told Garrett the process God had taken her through.

"Reminds me of when I had to surrender my will before I could ask you to be my wife."

"That seems so long ago, I had almost forgotten. That was such a difficult time." Her gaze met Garrett's tender one.

"God never promised life would be easy, only that He'd be with us every step of the way." He drew her toward him and kissed her lips.

She pulled away from him at last. "Now who's distracting whom?"

"Isn't our conversation over?" He lifted an eyebrow.

"No, we need to notify Mrs. Greely that we intend to keep Milly before she calls again when you're not home." Savannah stacked her bowl and plate on top of Garrett's and carried them to the sink. "Shall I get a tablet to write her a letter? Or do you want to set up a meeting or tell her over the telephone?"

"A letter is a good idea. We can say what we want without interruption." Garrett brushed a few crumbs from the table while Savannah brought a pen and tablet.

"Do you think Reverend Greely knows what his wife is doing?" She sat down and tore out a sheet of paper.

"Good question." He shook his head. "This might just be his wife's scheme to get her granddaughter what she wants. Do you think we should approach him?"

Savannah picked up the pen and stared at it. "Maybe later. I don't want to waste any time notifying Mrs. Greely of our decision." Leaning over the table, she wrote. *Dear Mrs. Greely...*

Garrett cleared his throat. *After receiving legal counsel...* "No, scratch that."

She started over on a clean sheet and he began again.

Our lawyer informed us that Milly's adoption is in order,

and we are under no legal obligation to return our daughter to her biological mother. In light of this information, we do not believe it would be in the best interests of the child to remove her from the only parents she knows and place her with complete strangers... "Could you read that back to me?"

When Savannah finished, he nodded. "New paragraph." *We trust you will also place the best interests of the child above your own desires and respect our decision.* "Is there anything else we need to say?"

"I don't think so." Savannah reread the letter silently. "Mrs. G won't be happy."

"I don't believe we have any obligation to make her happy. Milly is our primary concern. Just add, *Sincerely yours* and I'll sign it."

Savanna blew out a huge breath and placed the letter in front of her husband. Now there was nothing to do but wait.

Chapter 96

Charles pulled off his engineer's hat and laid it on the arm of the brown wingchair inside the door. Weariness bore down on him as he headed for the bedroom to change clothes. He ran his fingers through his hair and glanced in the mirror beside the door. A few strands of silver mingled with the blond. Is this what getting old alone was going to be like?

He pulled his wallet from his pocket and removed a small calendar. Since Jane's death, he needed a way to keep track of his work schedule. Leaning his head against the back of the chair, he gazed at what was left of this month. Almost the end of August, six weeks since his first trip to Polly's hotel. Although the time he spent there on weekends was a welcome diversion, he longed for more intimate involvement with the owner.

Was it too soon to ask for a date? At times the look in her eyes told him she returned his affection, while at others, he sensed her distancing herself from him. Troubled by the contradiction, he waffled. Would an invitation to go out scare her away?

He picked up the News Herald he'd bought in Franklin. The Stoneboro Fair would be held earlier than usual this year, actually including Labor Day for the first time—September 4, 6-8. The past few years he'd avoided the Fair, not wanting to go alone. He sat up straight. Perhaps attending the Fair would be a good, friendly first date.

Taking a deep breath, he stared at the listing of events.

Would Polly be free to go with him on Labor Day? Although Mondays were often a slow day at the hotel, maybe the holiday would be an exception. He'd ask her tomorrow. Decision made, new energy flowed through him enabling him to search the icebox for something to eat.

♠

Mr. Tillson gave Polly a brief salute as he'd taken to doing when checking out. His brown eyes sparkled. "I'll see you around."

She couldn't restrain a giggle. "Not if I see you first." When had they started this foolish routine? Mr. Tillson had given her the *Not if I see you first* response the first time she'd said, *I'll see you around.* Probably not very dignified behavior on her part.

He saluted once more and walked out the door and across the veranda, her gaze following him. The hotel records showed he'd been a regular for several years since his business with the railroad brought him this way often. His brown eyes didn't increase her pulse like Charles's blue ones did but at least his job as a union worker should be safe.

A cough behind her caught her attention. Charles had arrived to pick up his list for the market and stood watching through the kitchen doorway. Her neck warmed at being caught behaving like a juvenile but his eyes appeared more thoughtful than condemning.

"Good morning, Charles. I'll get the list." He stepped back and she squeezed past him in the doorway. Her pulse picked up as it always did when he was near, and she longed for a reason to linger there.

Giving herself a mental shake, she hurried to her desk, sensing him watching. List in hand, she returned and held it out to him. Instead of taking it, he took her hand, clasping it in his own.

"Polly…" He paused.

She froze, her hand trembling in his. "Yes?"

He stared at their hands. "Would you have time to go to the Fair with me on Labor Day or will it be a busy day here?"

"No…" She hesitated.

"No, you can't go, or no, it won't be a busy day?"

The hope radiating from his eyes penetrated her heart. Polly swallowed, her mouth dry. She should say she couldn't go. She needed to say no. Instead, she found herself smiling into those intense blue eyes. "No, I don't think it will be a busy day after I get breakfast for our guests and boarders. What time do you want to go?"

"How about four o'clock? There are various activities and we can get something to eat. I'll pick you up." He let go of her hand and took the list from her unresisting fingers.

♠

Garrett laid down his pencil and scrubbed his hands over his face. How was he ever going to finish his sermon? Usually his goal was to have the first draft by mid-week allowing a couple of days to polish it before Sunday. Here it was Saturday morning, and the sheet in front of him was only half-filled.

He groaned. How many times had he cautioned Savannah about borrowing trouble, and yet he'd done nothing but worry ever since they'd sent the letter to Mrs. Greely three weeks ago. He'd been prepared for an angry telephone call, a venomous letter, or even an unannounced visit. What he hadn't been prepared for was no response at all. Each day that passed, he waited for the other shoe to drop.

Acid churned in his stomach. He did his best to hide his agitation from Savannah. What else could he do? He was the pastor, the one who should be strong, trusting God.

He rose, stumbled into the sanctuary and fell to his knees at the altar.

Chapter 97

Savannah hurried down the stairs to answer the doorbell. "Mother Young, what a pleasant surprise." Garrett's mother seldom came unannounced.

"Thank you, Savannah." Mother gave her a warm hug and kiss on the cheek. "I've been missing the children. When Garrett told me he had to work on his message today, I thought this might be a good time to kidnap them and give you a break."

"That's so kind of you." Savannah blew a few strands of hair from her forehead. "To be honest, I've been a bit tired. No doubt the children would love to go with you." She peered outside. "Are you walking?"

Mother nodded. "It's such a lovely day and it's good exercise. Perhaps we could use Milly's stroller." She followed Savannah up the steps.

Sammy and Milly were already waiting for Grandma at the top of the stairs. Nothing wrong with their ears. When they heard the plan, Sammy trotted off to get Milly's stroller in the small shed out back. In short order, they strapped Milly in and her brother grabbed the handle to push her. Savannah waved good bye as they headed for Main Street.

She rubbed her back and stretched. *What shall I do with my time?* Perhaps she could surprise Garrett with a brief visit, something she rarely attempted with two children in tow. She smoothed her hair and cradled her hands under the small mound where the baby had begun to make an appearance. "Sweet baby," she breathed, as she turned right on Main Street and walked the short distance to the church.

Knocking lightly on her husband's door, she peeked into the office. His chair was empty. She frowned. Where could he be? She tilted her head and listened. Was that deep groans coming from the sanctuary? Trotting in that direction, a familiar figure with head bowed over the altar railing caught her eye as she stepped inside.

Not wanting to startle Garrett, she tiptoed down the aisle and lowered herself to the floor beside him. "Oh my Love, my Love... What is it?"

He tilted his head in her direction and groaned again. "Savannah, what are you doing here? I didn't want to worry you."

She straightened her spine. "Garrett Young, we are a team. If something is troubling you, I want to know."

Garrett rubbed his eyes and shoved his hand in his pants pocket. Pulling out a handkerchief, he blew his nose vigorously. He took a deep breath, started to say something, then stopped.

"Whatever it is, you can tell me." Savannah touched his face, running her fingers along his jaw.

Words poured from his lips as if from a fire hose. "I can't stand waiting to hear from Mrs. Greely. It's been three weeks. Three weeks, and nothing. Not. one. word. It's driving me crazy."

Savannah studied his face. "Have you surrendered Milly to the Lord?"

He shook his head. "I didn't think I needed to since we decided to keep her."

"No matter what we decided, the outcome is still in God's hands, out of our control." Savannah rubbed her husband's back with a gentle touch. "Surrender to His control is the only way to have peace while we wait. It's the Abraham/Isaac thing."

Garrett blew out a mighty breath. "Okay, I'll do it if it

will bring me peace."

♠

Labor Day dawned cloudy with heavy rain, adding to the precipitation they'd had in previous days. All week Polly had battled the inclination to cancel her date with Charles. Now it was too late. Or perhaps she could use the weather as an excuse?

By the time breakfast was over, the deluge had not let up. As Polly filled the sink with hot water, the raindrops beat against the kitchen windows. The Fairgrounds would be a sea of mud for sure with cars sliding around on the treacherous, steep parking areas.

After her vow not to fall for a railroad man, why had she accepted a date with this one? She scrubbed breakfast dishes while Elsie and Twila dried. Had one of them spoken to her? "What was that?" She glanced from one to the other.

Elsie set the plate she'd been drying on the counter with a thud. "I said, Father tells me you have a date today."

"If I don't decide to cancel. Are you two going to the Fair?" Polly peered at them again.

Twila opened her mouth but before she could answer, Elsie said, "Don't you think it's a little soon to be accepting dates?"

Polly frowned. "What do you mean?"

"Will's only been gone two and a half years. Couldn't you be faithful to him longer than that?"

Throwing her dishcloth into the fast-cooling water, Polly stomped her foot. "It's none of your business how long I wait before accepting dates. It's not considered unfaithful when a widow or widower begins dating."

She stormed up the steps. There would be no canceling this date.

♠

Charles got out of his car and hesitated. It was a bit tricky courting someone who lived in a hotel. It wouldn't do to ring the bell as one would when checking in as a guest, and somehow going to the back door as he did when helping with hotel work didn't seem quite right either. He finally settled on using the front door and finding his way into the family living room to ask someone to let Polly know he was there.

Elsie flounced in from the small dining room and flopped on the davenport. "Don't you think you're a bit old to be dating my sister?" Her gaze, riveted on him, never wavered.

Before he could answer, Polly's voice vibrated down the stairs. "Elsie, that's incredibly rude."

Elsie huffed. "I'm just asking the question most people are probably thinking."

Polly looked at him, misty eyes wavering. "Charles, I'm so sorry. Please forgive my sister who seems to have forgotten any manners she ever had."

"What's going on in here?" Bob Dye came in from the sitting room, a scowl marring his brow.

Elsie jumped up and headed back the way she'd come. "I guess I know when I'm not welcome."

"What is her problem?" Polly shook her head, biting her lip. "She was very rude to Charles."

Father sighed. "I'm sorry, Charles. Elsie was one of Will's biggest fans. I suspect this is her way of exhibiting loyalty." He turned to Polly. "It reminds me a little of your attitude toward Lydia Wilds."

Polly looked ready to do battle with her father. "There is no comparison between Lydia and Charles. She deserved everything she got as we all found out."

Chapter 98

Charles cleared his throat, shifted from one foot to the other and glanced from Polly to her father. Had he stumbled into a hornet's nest? "I'm sorry if I've come at a bad time." A grin tugged at the corners of his mouth. "Should I go out and try again?"

Father chuckled. "No, it probably wouldn't be any better the second time. Sorry to air our dirty laundry in front of you." He sank onto the davenport. "Why don't you and Polly get going. At least the sun is shining. I was at the Fair this morning and narrowly escaped getting stuck. Lots of cars were being pulled out by a team of horses."

With a quick wave to her father, Polly came and tucked her hand in the crook of Charles's arm. "I'm afraid there's no supper prepared, Father, but there are plenty of leftovers from yesterday. All our boarders are going to the Fair."

Scanning the newspaper lying on the arm of the sofa, Father grunted. "No problem. We'll be fine. Have a good time."

Polly sighed as they crossed the veranda. "I'm so embarrassed. You've just seen our family at our worst. Elsie can be difficult but she's not usually this obnoxious."

Charles chuckled. "Well, few of us get to pick our families. Life is often about getting along as best we can with those in our inner circle. Mine is quite small."

"Oh Charles, I'm sorry. Here I am complaining about my family when you'd probably be glad to have one."

Charles held the door for Polly as she climbed into his roadster. "Thank you for coming with me, Polly."

"Thank you for asking."

Polly was smiling and the sun came out as they approached the Fairgrounds. Maybe this day would turn out well after all.

♠

Just as Polly's annoyance at her sister dissipated, they turned onto Chestnut Street and her nerves began to vibrate. If only Charles hadn't chosen this entry to the Fair. She swallowed hard, looking anywhere but at Will's mother's house. Charles turned into the Fairgrounds and with some agile maneuvering, avoided getting stuck. There were hundreds of cars and people everywhere.

Charles found a place to park on a reasonably level area while Polly battled tears. This had been a mistake. Why had she thought coming to the Fair was a good idea, the place where she and Will had their first date, the place where Will proposed?

Not seeming to be aware of the storm raging in Polly, Charles came round and opened her car door. She stared at the sea of mud, avoiding his eyes, and allowed him to take her hand. As they picked their way through the parking area, they sank into the mud up to their ankles. In spite of Charles's firm grip, she twisted her ankle and sobbed aloud.

"Polly, are you hurt? I'm so sorry." Charles swept her up in his arms. "Maybe they have a first aid tent."

"No, no. I'm sure it's nothing serious. I don't need first aid." Another sob escaped Polly's lips.

"But you're crying… I have to do something." Charles wiped a tear from her cheek.

"Just take me to the car. We should never have come." More tears slid down Polly's cheeks.

Charles's bewilderment was evident as he obeyed. After he settled her in the car and slid into the driver's seat, he turned to Polly. "Talk to me, Polly. Tell me what's wrong."

Between sobs Polly explained the significance of the Fair in her relationship with Will. "It's not your fault. I should have known better. Maybe Elsie was right. Maybe it's too soon for me to date."

♠

Charles supported Polly and she leaned on him heavily as they entered the hotel. Her father jumped up in surprise when they came into the sitting room, tears cascading down her cheeks.

"What happened?" Bob looked from one to the other. "What are you two doing home already?"

Charles grasped both Polly's arms and gently lowered her to the loveseat. "Polly twisted her ankle in the slippery mud."

"I'll call Doc Cooley—"

"No." The word exploded from Polly's lips. "I don't need a doctor."

"But you're crying." Bob stooped beside Polly. "You must be in a lot of pain." He glanced at Charles, questions in his eyes.

Charles opened his mouth but Polly shook her head. "It's a long story. My ankle isn't the reason I'm crying. Thanks for bringing me home, Charles."

He stood helplessly gazing at her. Was he being dismissed? How could he leave her like this?

"You'd better go, Charles." A hint of iron entered Bob's tone.

Polly leapt to Charles's defense. "This isn't his fault, Father. I shouldn't have agreed to go with him to a place where I made so many memories with Will."

"Forgive me, Charles." Bob extended his hand. "I jumped to the conclusion you were to blame for Polly's tears."

Charles shook his hand, biting his lip. "I would never purposely do anything to hurt your daughter." He walked toward the door, then hesitated and turned back. "I'm sorry, Polly."

Chapter 99

Garrett jumped into his automobile, turned it around and headed to the jail for his monthly Sunday evening Bible study. Weeks had dragged by since Garrett surrendered Milly to the Lord, and still no communication from Mrs. Greely. Summer had turned into autumn and most of the leaves had fallen from the trees by the time November rolled around.

He scratched his head. What did the woman hope to accomplish by leaving them hanging? Or had she given up on her plan to take Milly? His state of mind had improved since his surrender, but he still spent way too much time dwelling on the puzzling situation.

How he missed his friend, Will, at times like these. Not that Will had been big on giving advice, but he made a great sounding board. He glanced heavenward again. "Why did you take him, God? Why?"

My thoughts are not your thoughts, neither are my ways your ways...

He sighed. That familiar verse didn't answer his question. He spent the remainder of the trip repeatedly re-focusing on the material for the Bible study and drew a sigh of relief when he pulled up in front of Devon's house.

Warmth spread through him as his former employer kissed his wife goodbye and sprinted to the car. The man's growth over the past four years was a source of great joy. Garrett marveled at how God had restored Devon's marriage and brought him to a place of spiritual maturity.

Best of all, God had removed all the hatred from Garrett's heart. The smile on his lips was genuine when Devon opened the car door and climbed in. "How are you, brother?"

Devon punched his arm and smiled back. "I'm better than good. How are you?"

To his own amazement, Garrett found himself pouring out all the worries in his heart about Milly and Mrs. Greely. He'd never opened up to Devon this way before. The man listened attentively, nodding or raising an eyebrow from time to time.

Garrett pulled into the parking lot in front of the jail and turned off the engine. "So what do you make of it?"

Drumming his fingers on the dashboard, Devon wrinkled his brow. "Do you believe God wants you and Savannah to raise this little girl?"

"Absolutely yes. No doubt in my mind."

Devon stopped drumming and faced him. "Then maybe it's time for you to take a step of faith."

"Like what?" Garrett pulled the key from the ignition and stared at him.

"What would you do if you were sure you wouldn't lose Milly?"

"I'd buy a house. Our apartment is too small to raise three children."

Devon smiled. "So what are you waiting for?"

Joy welled up in Garrett's chest. What was he waiting for? He took the steps into the jail two at a time with Devon on his heels and even gave a surprised George Burns a hug when they reached the meeting room.

"I know I got reason to be happy." A grin broke out on the big man's face. "But what are you so happy about?"

"You first."

"I'm finally getting out of this place in a week. My release came through." Mr. Burns pumped his fist in the air. "Not that this joint won't always have a place in my heart since this is where I met Jesus, but it sure will be good to be on the outside again."

Garrett grabbed his friend's large hand and shook it again and again. "That's wonderful. I'm so happy for you. You've served your time." Who would ever have thought he'd rejoice because Savannah's kidnapper was getting out of jail? But as sure as he stood here, Mr. Burns was a new creature in Christ.

"Your turn, Garrett. What are you happy about, brother?"

Garrett filled Mr. Burns in on Devon's advice on the situation with Milly. "I've put my life on hold waiting for that woman to make a move, but I'm done waiting. I'm taking a step of faith."

♠

Polly dropped her head in her hands, then peeked between her fingers at her father. He was seated across from her at a table in the dining room. "What are we going to do? The mines closed even sooner than you thought. We don't have the money to make the next loan payment."

"I'm trying to get a job with one of the other mining companies, but most of them aren't hiring." Father sighed. "I can't expect them to lay someone off to take me on. If only I could sell the house, we could use that money to make the loan payments."

"No one seems interested." Clenching her hands in her lap, Polly sniffed loudly, determined not to cry. Tears had been near the surface ever since that horrible day at the Fair. She'd wrestled for days about how to tell Charles she needed to stop all contact with him, certain it was best. Then he didn't call. Should she be relieved or sad? As time dragged on, to her dismay, she missed him immensely. She hadn't thought he'd give up so easily. How could she expect Charles to know what she wanted when she didn't know herself?

Polly drew a long shuddering breath. "I'd better leave if I'm going to get to Bible study on time. Savannah said she has something to tell me. I hope it's good news."

A chilly wind hurried her footsteps as she nearly ran to Mildred Young's house. As usual, her hostess had the door open almost before she knocked. Savannah scrambled from her chair to give her a hug. Polly clung to her friend. What would she do without these two?

"Come sit down and warm up with a cup of hot ginger tea." Mildred pulled out a chair beside Savannah and bustled to get the tea kettle.

Polly sat down and leaned toward Savannah. "What do you have to tell me? I could use some good news."

Savannah beamed and grabbed her hand. "Garrett and I have decided to buy a house."

Chapter 100

Polly's jaw dropped. "Buy a house? You've never mentioned buying a house."

"Garrett says it's a step of faith that we'll be raising Milly." Savannah patted her abdomen. "We'll need a bigger place when our new baby arrives."

Polly glanced at Mildred. "Did you know about this?"

She shrugged. "Nothing specific. Garrett mentioned once that he wasn't sure where they'd put everyone when the baby came."

Savannah leaned toward Polly. "There's more. Garrett wanted me to ask if your father still wants to sell your house?"

Polly clapped her hand over her mouth to shut off a squeal. "You're interested in buying our house?"

"We've always liked that house." Savannah took a long swallow of tea. "Ever since your family took me in when the boarding house burned, it's been like home to me."

How should she respond? She didn't want to pressure Savannah and Garrett by admitting her father's desperate situation but still... "Father is eager to sell our house since the Dye mines have closed."

"Garrett heard rumors from Dorothy at work. Why didn't you tell us?" Savannah reached for Polly's hand.

"I guess I was embarrassed." Polly stared at the floor.

"It's nothing to be ashamed of, Polly." Mildred tilted Polly's chin to look into her eyes. "Your family isn't the first and won't be the last to fall on hard times. How are things going at the hotel?"

Polly's sigh shook her whole body. She couldn't lie to her friends. "We're barely making our bills, let alone paying my mortgage. I should have bargained with the owner for a lower price."

"Polly, I can't believe you didn't tell us." Savannah's eyes blazed. "I thought we were your best friends."

"You are my best friends, but you had enough things weighing on you without taking on our problems." Polly sat up straight. "Anyway, it's not your problem. Don't you dare buy our house because you feel sorry for us."

Savannah squeezed her hand. "Garrett's interest in your house has nothing to do with the mines closing. I'm sure he'll get in touch with your father as soon as I tell him it's still for sale."

♠

Charles stepped out of the locomotive in Franklin and trudged toward the far end of parking lot. Another long weekend ahead. How could he call Polly again after their first date had ended in disaster? Still her red hair and green eyes were never far from his mind.

"Hello, Mr. Clarkson." A female voice called his name.

Turning, he recognized the trim, pretty brunette running toward him. She lived in Stoneboro, but when he groped for her name, he came up empty. "May I help you, Miss? You're from Stoneboro, aren't you?"

"I am. I believe you were the engineer on my train." The woman's friendly brown eyes drew him. He was so lonely. "I'm told there aren't any passenger trains to Stoneboro until tomorrow." She paused. "This is terribly forward of me, but I'm in a frightful hurry to get home—"

He stepped closer and cut in quickly to spare her the embarrassment of asking. "I'll be happy to give you a ride. I'm afraid I don't know your name."

"I'm Peggy Forbes." She paused, gasping for breath. "Actually, I believe you're my neighbor. I'm boarding down the street from you."

Down the street from him. Maybe there were other women who might be more receptive than Polly. "Let me help you with your bag, Miss Forbes." Charles reached for the small carpetbag.

She let him take it. "Thank you, Mr. Clarkson. You're so kind."

"I parked my car at the other end of the lot since I'd be gone for several days. I hope you don't mind walking."

"Not at all. I'm just so thankful for a ride home." Something like a sob caught in her throat.

Charles glanced at her, alarm rising. Surely he hadn't said or done anything to upset her. "Are you all right, ma'am?"

"My sister's been ill and has taken a turn for the worse." Miss Forbes drew a long, ragged breath. "Unless God intervenes, this may be my last chance to speak to her."

"I'm so sorry." Charles transferred her bag to his other hand, extended his free arm, and slowed his steps. "Here, take my arm. You must be worn out trying to keep up with me."

She swiped a tear from her cheek and grabbed his arm. When they reached the car, he helped her into the front seat and stowed her luggage. She looked his way when he slid into the automobile. His heart went out to her as she huddled close to the door, holding the collar of her coat against her neck. "Mr. Clarkson, I don't want you to think I'm a fast woman."

"Oh no, I wouldn't think that. You have nothing to fear, Miss Forbes."

"It's just that I don't really know you. I shouldn't have asked to ride with you." She reached for the door handle. "What was I thinking?"

He sighed. First he'd somehow managed to make Polly cry, now this woman was afraid of him. He really had a way with women. "Miss Forbes, please. I promise I won't lay a finger on you. You're safe with me. "

She let her hand fall into her lap, then muttered, more to herself than to him, "I'm too tired to sit in the station all night and I have no money for a hotel."

Charles started the car, careful not to make any sudden moves that might spook his passenger. For a moment, it had appeared she might be the answer to his loneliness, but now, the sooner he got her home the better.

Chapter 101

On Thursday evening Bob met Garrett and Savannah at his house on Broad Street. After a round of greetings, he thanked them for coming. "Why don't you have a look around?" He chuckled. "Polly said you wouldn't need anyone to show you the way."

"You're right." Savannah patted his arm. "I know my way around pretty well."

Their footsteps echoed in the nearly empty house as Bob dropped onto the window seat by the front door. He stared at the spot where Margaret's gray chair had been. Could he really sell the last place he'd lived with his precious wife? They needed the money and the memories of his brief time here with Lydia wouldn't be hard to leave behind. It seemed like a bad dream—a nightmare really.

He shook his head and focused on tuning into words and laughter from Savannah and Garrett who had disappeared upstairs. What impression did they have of this place now that it had been uninhabited for a couple of months? Would they still want to buy it?

Footsteps thundered down the stairs. He would know soon enough. Smiles on both their faces were encouraging. He stood. "So what do you think?"

"We'll want to make a few changes, but we think it will be perfect for our family." Garrett smiled.

Savannah gave a firm nod. "The little room off the bedroom will be a perfect nursery, and there's plenty of space for our other two."

"On the telephone, you said you're asking fifteen hundred dollars?" Garrett met his gaze.

"That's right." Bob jingled the house key he held. "I spoke to a couple of business men who are knowledgeable about real estate and they felt it was a fair price."

"Pa knows a bit about real estate, too, and he thought the price sounded right."

Lips pressed together, Bob nodded. "Good. Will you need to obtain a mortgage?"

"Savannah and I put money aside when we both worked and had no children. Pa said he'd loan us the rest. " Garrett stuck out his hand. "Do we have a deal?

Bob grabbed it and shook. "Indeed we do."

"Should I call to set up an appointment with Mr. Stranahan to draw up the contract?" Savannah smiled at Garrett and raised an eyebrow at Bob. "Or would one of you like to do it?"

"I'd be happy for you to take care of it." Bob rubbed his forehead. "We'll need about a week to remove the rest of our belongings."

"Of course." Garrett took a few steps toward the door. "We'll let you know when we have a closing date."

Bob remained by the window until Garrett and Savannah had driven away. Relief and regret battled for preeminence as he locked the door and headed for his car. Once inside, he leaned his head against the seat. Was this the right decision? Did they have a choice?

♠

Polly swept up crumbs from supper preparations and began pacing back and forth across the kitchen. Father had asked if she wanted to accompany him when he met Savannah and Garrett at the house. She declined, saying, "They don't need me trailing them while they make their decision. How embarrassing if they discovered some flaw that changed their minds."

"I don't think that's likely. They seem eager to make this transaction and get moved in before..." Bob's ears turned red and he coughed. "Before, you know, the baby comes."

Why did everyone have such a hard time discussing an upcoming birth? Some older women wore coats all summer to hide their condition. Except for her sadness that Will never had a child of his own, she wasn't sorry she had no children. How in the world would she have managed the hotel with a baby?

Of course, if she lost the hotel, that would be immaterial. She gasped. Where would they live? They couldn't very well ask Savannah and Garrett to give their house back.

A car pulled in behind the hotel. The engine puttered a few times, as Father's car always did, then died. Polly dashed to the door as his footsteps came up the back steps. "Father, you haven't signed papers to sell the house yet have you?"

"Not yet. We need a lawyer to draw up a contract. Why?"

She gasped for breath. "If you sell the house, where will we live if we can't make a go of it here?"

"I've already thought about that." Bob dropped into the chair at Polly's small desk. "We don't need a big house now that it's only the four of us. If we lose the hotel, we'll get a smaller place somewhere. I've had a hankering to move back to Franklin where I was raised."

"Yay!" Twila's cheer startled them as she skipped into the room.

Polly stared at her. "Why do you want to live in Franklin?"

"Last time we went roller skating in Stoneboro, I met a nice fellow from Sugar Creek." Twila's cheeks warmed.

"What was he doing in Stoneboro?" Father always worried about Twila getting involved with young men he didn't know.

"He came with Joseph Hood, the floor manager at the pavilion. He's from Franklin." Twila's eyes glowed. Her youngest sister was certainly old enough to date if she could find someone who met Father's approval.

"Don't start planning your life around him yet." Father's tone was gruff. "I haven't even met him."

Elsie sauntered into the room. "Who's planning their life?"

"No one." Polly came to Twila's rescue. "Father just mentioned he might want to get a place for us in Franklin if things don't work out with the hotel."

"So Savannah and Garrett are going to buy our house?" Elsie glanced from Father to Polly.

"It looks that way." Father's gaze roved over the faces of each of his daughters, as though seeking their approval, although the decision would be his. "It will help our finances since we can't depend on the mines for an income."

"While we're talking about the future..." Elsie took a deep breath. "I probably should tell you I'd like to go to business school in Pittsburgh in January."

Father's jaw dropped and Polly couldn't keep her own mouth closed. "In January?" She stared at her sister. "But what... what..." She stopped. It wasn't fair to ask Elsie what they'd do for a bookkeeper if she left. Her sister had never asked for the job.

And where would the money come from to pay for business school?

Chapter 102

The next day Savannah hung up the telephone, lifted Milly and planted a kiss on her rosy cheek. "We have an appointment to buy a house, Miss Milly! Are you excited?" The toddler's wispy red hair was silky to the touch as Savannah rested her cheek on the toddler's head.

Milly giggled. "Milly 'cited."

The door at the bottom of the stairs opened and Garrett ran up the steps. He engulfed them in a giant bear hug. "How are my girls today?"

"We are 'cited." Savannah grinned and lifted her face for his kiss. "Bob and Mr. Stranahan confirmed our appointment for next Thursday."

Sammy joined the group hug. "What kind of appointment?"

"An appointment to buy Bob Dye's house."

"Woo hoo." Sammy clapped and cheered. "That'll give a fellow some room to spread out."

He had never complained about being crowded, but he'd be eleven in April. Bigger boys needed more space. Savannah put Milly down and headed for the kitchen to start supper just as the telephone rang. Garrett reached for it. "Hello." There was a short pause.

"Well, hello, George Burns."

Savannah turned and stared at Garrett. Mr. Burns had never called her husband before. Something to do with getting out of jail? It was hard not to eavesdrop while she heated an iron skillet and buttered bread for toasted cheese sandwiches. Garrett's answers were noncommittal. What were they talking about?

"I see." Long silence. "I understand." Another silence. "Well, I'll need to talk to Savannah."

Her ears perked up. How did this involve her?

"Mama." Milly clung to her leg. "Milly eat?"

"Soon, Sweetheart. Very soon." She picked up her daughter and pulled a bag of potato chips from the cupboard. They were a family favorite although perhaps not the most nutritious choice.

Garrett hung up and stared at the telephone.

"What is it, Love? What did George Burns want?"

He bit his lip and shook his head. "We'll talk after the children are in bed." He glanced at Milly.

Savannah's stomach lurched. That didn't sound good. What could George need that they couldn't talk about in front of Milly?

♠

The evening dragged. Would the children's bedtime never come? On the other hand, did Garrett really want to talk to Savannah about his conversation with George? He pinched the lobe of his ear, a habit he'd developed since all the trouble with Milly started.

At last, Milly and Sam were both tucked in, stories read, prayers said. He and Savannah met in the hall outside the children's doors.

"Do you want a cup of tea while we talk, Love?" Savannah pulled his hand away from his ear and laced her fingers through his.

"No, let's just sit on the davenport." Garrett tugged her gently in that direction. "I don't know where to start." He plopped down on the couch with her beside him.

"How about at the beginning?" Savannah snuggled close.

Garrett sighed. "Before they died, Mr. Burns'

grandparents were staunch members of the Jackson Center Presbyterian Church where Reverend Greely pastors."

Savannah's eyebrows shot up. "What does that have to do with us?"

"George wants us to meet with him and the Greelys so he can apologize for kidnapping you and for the shame he's brought on the church by his behavior."

She gasped. "But Garrett—"

"I know. The timing couldn't be worse. The last thing I want to do is meet with Mrs. Greely, but how can we tell him no?" Garrett's head drooped. "He wants me to vouch for him, that he's a new creature in Christ, and assure them he plans to turn the tavern into a respectable establishment if the bank will loan him the money."

She drew away from Garrett and stared into space. "Why do I have to be there? Couldn't he apologize to me another time?"

"He thinks apologizing in front of them will convince them he's really sorry." Garrett tilted her chin in his direction. "What if this is what he needs to make a fresh start?"

"But what if this stirs things up with Mrs. Greely?"

He groaned. "I don't know. I just don't know. Devon is picking Burns up at the jail tomorrow, helping him buy a few groceries, then taking him to the tavern. George would like to meet with us and the Greely's at the church on Sunday afternoon."

♠

The locomotive engine chugged to a ragged stop on the Ashtabula branch railroad. Charles groaned. After notifying the telegraph operator to warn other trains of their position, he hurried through the passenger cars assuring the folks the problem would be fixed momentarily. He was pretty sure what the trouble was. Without hesitation, he grabbed a few tools, shouted instructions to his brakeman and fireman, and got to work. In minutes, the locomotive purred like a kitten.

He stood tall in his usual position, very much in charge

and completely in control. Everyone knew he was good at his job. It always pleased the other railroad employees to be assigned to his crew.

Scrubbing his hand across his forehead, he blew out a breath. Why couldn't he handle his personal life with the same competence as his professional one? Being decisive with the opposite sex had always been difficult. He still hadn't called Polly. An image of his mother flashed through his mind. She could strike fear to the heart of a grizzly with any man who attempted to take charge with her. Perhaps that had something to do with his difficulty in making decisions and being assertive when it came to women.

Regardless, it was time to take the bull by the horns and talk to Polly. His timidity was getting him nowhere. If he could "captain" a locomotive, surely he could take on one small, red-headed woman.

Chapter 103

The ride to meet George Burns and the Greelys in Jackson Center was a long, silent one. Garrett glanced at Savannah as she stared into space while opening and closing her handbag. Did she think he'd put George Burns' request ahead of their family? She told him she'd honor whatever decision he made. What if he'd made the wrong one?

"Savannah…" He hated the pleading note in his voice but he needed some reassurance she was okay with his choice.

She stared at her handbag a beat too long, then met his gaze. "I know you made the decision you thought was right. I'm not saying you're wrong."

It was as though she'd read his mind.

She sighed. "I'm just scared to death to meet with Mrs. Greely since they didn't respond to our letter."

"I'm not happy about it, either, Love. But I didn't see how I could tell Mr. Burns no." Garrett turned into the parking lot of the church where he used to meet with Jim Caldwell. If only it were Jim waiting for them instead of the Greelys. Their car was parked near the door, so they must already be inside.

George had arrived ahead of them, too, and came down the church steps to greet them.

Savannah hadn't seen George since that fateful day in Sandy Lake. Garrett squeezed Savannah's hand. "Are you okay?"

♠

Savannah froze in place. George Burns stood before her, tall and burly, shaggy black hair. Beads of sweat broke across her forehead. Suddenly it was fourteen years ago and his hands were tight around her wrists, dragging her from the street. She coughed and pulled out a handkerchief to wipe her face as the memories washed over her. *He may be a new creature in Christ but that didn't change her memories.*

Garrett had asked her a question. "What? Oh, I'll be fine." She gulped. "I was so scared of meeting Mrs. Greely, I didn't prepare myself for meeting Mr. Burns. Seeing him brings back that dreadful day."

He squeezed her hand. "Why don't you stay in the car for a few minutes?"

"Go say hello to him. I'll join you soon."

After a doubtful glance in her direction, he exited the car and shook Mr. Burns' hand. Savannah took three or four deep, cleansing breaths and whispered a scripture. *Your grace is sufficient for me.* Her pulse slowed and she got out of the car. *I can do this.*

She looked everywhere but at the man who had kidnapped her, then raised her gaze and gasped. Something was different about his eyes. His entire countenance had changed since she last saw him but especially his eyes. An inner glow had replaced the greedy sheen of lust. Her stomach settled and she shook his hand. "You're looking well, Mr. Burns."

He grinned. "Apparently jail food agrees with me. I'm gonna have to get used to eatin' my own cookin' again."

The church door opened and Reverend Greely appeared. "I thought I heard a car. Come on in. My wife is waiting."

Savannah grabbed Garrett's hand to steady herself as they climbed the steps with Mr. Burns behind them. *Oh God...*

"If you'll follow me, we'll meet in a Sunday school room downstairs." Reverend Greely led the way.

Savannah's heart pounded so loud, surely everyone must hear it. *Your grace is sufficient for me. Your grace is sufficient for me.*

And then there she was. Mrs. Greely didn't rise or make any effort to greet them, other than a slight nod when they entered the room. Her gimlet eyes widened as they swept over Savannah's very pregnant form. She half rose from her chair, as if to get a better look, then dropped back in her seat, something like a gasp escaping her lips.

Reverend Greely sent his wife a questioning look as he sat beside her at the long, wooden table. Savannah hung back, not wanting to sit directly across from her. Garrett indicated Mr. Burns should precede him, and seeming to sense her purpose, he followed, allowing Savannah to sit as far from the other woman as possible. Regardless, Savannah sensed Mrs. Greely's penetrating gaze never left her.

Savannah was so shaken she barely heard a word of the explanatory conversation that took place between Garrett, Mr. Burns and the Greelys until her husband turned to her. "Savannah, are you ready to receive George's apology?"

She straightened her spine and nodded. Mr. Burns' voice broke as he expressed his sincere regret for what he'd done. "I wish there were some way I could make it up to you, Sava—Mrs. Young."

"I appreciate your apology, Mr. Burns. God has forgiven me so much." Savannah's voice cracked. "I'm in no position to withhold forgiveness from you."

She kept her gaze on Mr. Burns, ignoring Mrs. Greely's snort and a muttered, "That's the truth" from Mrs. Greely.

When her former employer turned to the Greelys, Savannah squeezed Garrett's hand and slipped out to find the room which had replaced the outhouse. Mr. Burns' apology to them had nothing to do with her and she couldn't wait any longer. Some churches hadn't yet installed indoor plumbing but thankfully this one had. When she finished and stepped back into the hall, her heart lurched. Mrs. Greely was waiting for her.

The woman hissed like a snake, "Why didn't you tell me you were pregnant?"

Before Savannah could say a word, she continued. "Out

of the goodness of my heart, I gave our great granddaughter to you because I knew how much you wanted a baby. Now that Amanda's circumstances have changed, even though you're going to have a baby yourself, you refuse to give Milly back."

"The fact that I'm going to have a baby doesn't change the reality that Milly doesn't know any of you." A tear rolled down Savannah's cheek. "We adopted her in good faith that you would honor the adoption."

"My husband doesn't want me to take Milly from you but now that I have all the facts, I'll get her back if it's the last thing I do."

She'd never let Mrs. Greely have Milly. Unable to stay in this woman's presence a moment longer, she pivoted and almost ran to the Sunday school room.

Mrs. Greely was on her heels but didn't enter. Leaning into the doorway, the angry woman enunciated every word to her husband. "I'll. be. in. the. car."

Reverend Greely raised an eyebrow but said only, "All right, dear. I'll be out soon."

Savannah dropped into her chair as Garrett gave her a troubled look. She responded with a slight shake of her head. She would burst into tears if she tried to explain. He turned back to the conversation between the pastor and Mr. Burns concerning his plans to turn the tavern into a boarding house.

At last, Reverend Greely closed in prayer and shook hands with the men. "I'm sure today must have been difficult for you, Savannah."

You have no idea. But she only nodded as he continued, "You are to be commended for your forgiving spirit."

"Thank you, Reverend." She coughed. "Some things are harder to forgive than others."

The pastor smiled and patted her hand.

After they left the church, Garret and George Burns shook hands before Garrett gave him a bear hug. Mr. Burns stared at Mrs. Greely in the car for a moment, then turned back to them. "If there's ever anything I can do for you, you have only to ask."

If only there were something he could do…

Chapter 104

After saying goodbye to George, Garrett took Savannah's hand and led her to the car. He waited until the man was out of earshot. "What in the world happened with Mrs. Greely? She shot out after you as soon as you left the room."

He opened the passenger door, and Savannah dragged herself in. "I'll tell you on the way home."

As they drove to Sandy Lake, between tears and sobs, Savannah told him what had happened.

"Out of the goodness of her heart?" Garrett snorted. "Sounds like Mrs. G is re-writing the story."

"She is, but maybe Reverend Greely won't let her do anything." Savannah blew her nose and drew a long, shuddering breath. "He knows the truth."

Garrett tapped the steering wheel. "He's a good man, but this is his great granddaughter. I imagine his wife can make life pretty miserable if she doesn't get her way."

Savannah nodded. "I'm sure you're right. If we need a Christian arbiter to help us settle this, do you think Reverend Caldwell would do it?"

"I don't know if Mrs. Greely would agree to that. She might think he'd favor us since he was my mentor for so long."

After a long silence, Savannah squared her shoulders. "One thing, well maybe two things, we need to agree on is that no matter what happens, we will run to God not from Him in the midst of this trial."

"Agreed. What's the second thing?"

"We need to stay united and not blame each other regardless of the outcome."

♠

Polly stretched her weary legs in front of her and slumped into Mother's gray chair. Perhaps she could draw comfort by imagining her mother was here. Why did she sense a need for consolation when Sunday dinner had gone well with quite a few town folk coming to eat? Father and the girls had given their all, everyone working at fever pitch.

Why wasn't she excited and happy at the money they'd made which would help pay the mortgage this month? If she were honest with herself, nothing seemed to revive her spirits since Charles had disappeared from her world. Life stretched before her filled with nothing but work, work and more work. In her imagination, running a hotel had looked like fun. Little did she know.

The bell in the lobby rang and she jumped up. Her goal was to get to the front desk before a guest ever rang. Failed again. Mr. Tillson didn't look upset. "Hello, Mrs. Reiser. How are you?"

"I'm tired. It's been a long day with lots of hungry people wanting to eat." For once Polly was honest, instead of trying to pretend she was indestructible. She checked Mr. Tillson in, giving him his usual room, sensing his gaze on her.

"I have an idea." Her guest tapped his fingers on the counter. "Why don't I take you to Adda's restaurant where someone can wait on you for a change? Maybe you'd enjoy a piece of pie you didn't bake."

"Oh I couldn't. It wouldn't be appropriate." Polly shook her head.

"Why not?" Mr. Tillson's brown eyes challenged her. "Is there a law that hotel owners can't be escorted somewhere by a guest?"

"N…No, I guess not, but it doesn't seem right." Polly fumbled to find a valid reason.

Twila came to the sitting room door. "Go, Polly. I'll watch the front desk in case any guests arrive." She glanced at the clock. "Aunt Adda will be closing in an hour, so you'd better hurry."

Why not? Maybe an outing was what she needed. What harm could it do? She hurried upstairs to get her coat, shrugging into it as she returned to the lobby.

Mr. Tillson extended his arm to escort her to his car parked on Main Street. A gust of wind swirled around them. She shivered, and he drew her closer. An internal warning bell sounded. What did she really know about Mr. Tillson? But they were only going to Aunt Adda's.

He opened the door to his sleek, late model automobile, reaching into the back seat to grab a luxurious blanket which he tucked around her with a bit too much familiarity.

"I'm fine. Really." Polly drew back against the seat to put a little more space between them. The well-cushioned seat was more comfortable than she'd ever experienced in any other car. Life with Mr. Tillson wouldn't have many financial worries. Instantly, she was ashamed of herself. Not a good motive for pursuing a relationship.

♠

Charles grabbed his heavy winter coat and stepped into the unseasonably frigid temperature for November. Franklin set a new record low on Friday at twelve degrees and it didn't feel much warmer in Stoneboro tonight. He pulled up his coat collar. It was silly to go outside in this kind of weather but he couldn't bear to sit in the house another minute. It was almost enough to drive a man to drink. All week and through the weekend, he'd waffled back and forth about whether or not to follow through on his decision to call Polly. Now here it was Sunday evening…

He strode toward the house where he'd dropped Peggy Forbes on Monday evening. Had she made it home in time to talk to her sister? Should he stop to find out? The way she'd huddled next to the door, as far from him as possible, didn't give him much encouragement in spite of her friendliness when asking him for a ride home.

Women. Were they all experts at sending mixed messages or was he just exceptionally bad at reading the signs? With a deep sigh, he passed the house. Perhaps he was destined to spend the rest of his life alone.

Chapter 105

Savannah battled tears all week, Mrs. Greely's words ringing in her ears. *Now that I have all the facts, I'll get her back if it's the last thing I do.* She rarely allowed Milly out of her sight except when she slept. Not that the Greelys would attempt to spirit her away, but still… The only prayer she could muster was *Oh God, Oh God.*

If they hadn't met the Greely's at the church, maybe Mrs. G wouldn't have found out that Savannah was pregnant. If only Garrett hadn't… Every time she reached this juncture, she jumped back as though touching a hot stove. She'd been the one who said they needed to stay united no matter what happened. Blaming Garrett wouldn't change anything.

A gentle tap on the door alerted her to the time. Garrett's mother was watching Milly here during her nap while Garrett and Savannah met Bob Dye at Mr. Stranahan's office to close the deal on the house. Their step of faith would be complete.

♠

Polly walked up the steps to their house on Broad Street, her last time to walk through before turning her key over to Garrett and Savannah. She hesitated at the threshold, transported for a moment back to the day she'd first entered this house—to the chill of apprehension that had stopped her exuberant rush.

She bowed her head. What a journey to finally discover the reason for that bad feeling, as well as the solution. *You are so good, Father.* She whispered although the house was empty. The leaded window above the radiator had always been one of her favorite features, and she ran her fingers over it lightly. The image of her mother reading her Bible in her favorite gray chair overpowered Polly's senses, even to the memory of her mother's favorite lavender scent.

It remained with her as she trailed through the dining room where Reverend Lawrence had dispelled her fears that her family would fall apart as the Davis family had after Sarah died. *"Your mother was a wonderful person but the Bible says it's the power of God that holds everything together.* God's power had held them together and although they'd missed Mother terribly, the family had eaten many happy meals here after her passing.

She wandered on to the kitchen where her mother cooked for a relatively short time before Polly took her place. She'd recognized quickly that although she could do the things Mother did, she couldn't be the person she was. Nonetheless, Polly had done the best she could. By God's grace, she had kept her promise to her mother and helped her father raise the children. Would Mother have been proud of her?

Polly retraced her steps and hesitated at the door to Mother's sitting room which stirred memories of conversations with Kitt, her friend and former neighbor. Particularly the conversation they'd had prior to Kitt's kidnapping and other difficult ones. Although they seldom saw each other since Kitt's move to Ohio, they'd helped one another during those difficult years of attempting to become adults.

Her footsteps echoed as she climbed the stairs and relived her second-floor memories. The time they'd feared Twila had infantile paralysis and Savannah encouraged her. The day she'd discovered Sarah's diary. She entered the back bedroom, dropped to her knees and lifted the floorboard where the diary had been hidden. Only God had known how much Polly would need Sarah Davis' wisdom in the days ahead.

As waves of memories of her mother's passing threatened to overwhelm her, she replaced them with the happy days when this bedroom belonged to her and Will. Sweet times of newlywed love permeated her heart as she allowed herself to slip back in time. It was a luxury Polly didn't allow herself often because of the pain she experienced when reality returned.

Cars pulling up outside the house jolted her from her reverie, and soon voices and laughter spiraled up the stairs. With a deep sigh, Polly let go of the past and sprinted down the steps, willing herself to accept what she couldn't change. To whom would she rather turn over the key than to her dearest friend?

"Polly." Savannah grabbed her and they clung to each other. "We wondered why the door wasn't locked."

"I came to… well, to say goodbye to the house." Polly pulled the key from her pocket and held it out to Savannah.

"Say goodbye to the house?" Savannah glanced at Garrett. "You are as welcome here as you were when it belonged to you." She closed Polly's fingers over the key. "We're all family, you know."

"That's right." Garrett was nodding vigorously. "That goes for you, too, Bob." He wrapped his arm around the older man. "You gave Savannah a home when she had nowhere to go. We'll never forget that."

Father swallowed hard, visibly fighting tears as he returned Garrett's hug. "Thank you, Garrett. There's no one to whom we'd rather sell this house."

♠

Polly curled up in Mother's chair in the family living room after they returned to the hotel. She closed her eyes and propped her head on her hand.

"Tired, Florence?"

She opened her eyes to find Father standing in the doorway, gazing at her, a troubled frown on his forehead.

"Yes…no, I don't know." Polly shrugged.

"Sad about selling the house?" He plopped down across from her in a wing chair.

"Maybe a little, but it needed to happen." She closed her eyes again. "I'm sad that I won't have time to help Savannah move. The hotel takes every minute of every day."

After a short silence, Father sighed. "I know you're busy, Florence, but I think it's more than that. I'm worried about you."

Polly's eyes popped open. She stared at her father. "Why?"

"I think you're unhappy because Charles hasn't been around since your date didn't go well." Father leaned forward. "Why don't you call him?"

"It wouldn't be fair, Father. After what happened to Will, I can't get involved with another railroad man."

"Are you going to allow fear to keep you from having—"

"Stop. Don't try to talk me into something I'll regret."

The telephone in the lobby rang and Polly jumped up to answer it, happy for an interruption. "Hello."

"Hello, Polly." Charles' voice vibrated over the line. Her pulse sped up.

"I'm so sorry our first date didn't go well." Charles's deep voice croaked a bit. "I wonder if we could try again? Maybe go somewhere that wasn't special to you and Will."

She had gone against her instincts once and the result had been a disaster. Stiffening her spine, she cleared her throat. "Charles, I'm so sorry. To be honest, I miss you terribly. But I can't go through losing another man the way I lost Will."

"Couldn't we just be friends, Polly?"

Polly hardened her heart against his plea. "I vowed I'd never marry another railroad man. You're not asking me to marry you, but it just wouldn't be fair to lead you on."

Chapter 106

On Friday Savannah closed the cardboard box filled with summer clothes and blew a few strands of hair from her forehead. She'd become quite the expert on closing boxes the last few weeks. Her plan was to have Thanksgiving dinner in their new house. An ambitious goal since Thanksgiving was a week from yesterday.

She stood, rubbed the small of her back, and evaluated what still needed to be packed in their bedroom. Then walking to the door, she peered toward the kitchen. "How are you doing out there, Mother?"

"I'm doing fine." Garrett's mother climbed down from the step stool and joined Savannah. "I'm packing pretty much everything in the kitchen. You can eat meals with us for a couple days."

"Thank you. You and the ladies from the church have been amazing. A lot of them have helped pack. To be honest, I never thought they'd accept me like this because of my past."

"Sometimes people surprise us." Mother patted Savannah's arm and drew her into a hug.

"Everyone seems to want to help. Even Sammy and Milly have gotten into the act, packing some of their toys." Savannah glanced at the boxes lined up in Sammy's room. "Garrett frets all the time about how hard I'm working, insisting I not lift any boxes."

"He's right, you know." A frown marred Mother's brow.

"Why don't you lie down for a few minutes?"

"I'm fine, really. I just want to get finished." Savannah stretched and turned back toward their bedroom.

"This probably isn't the best time to be moving, but it would be hard after the baby arrives, too." Mother eyed Savannah pensively.

"Garrett carries and stacks boxes for me when he comes home at noon and in the evenings. And with you taking Milly sometimes, it's not such a hard task."

Mother smiled. "I bet Garrett has his hands full today."

"I'm sure." A grin tugged at her lips. Garrett had taken their active toddler to the church with him this morning. "Not sure how much polishing he'll get done on his sermon with Milly around."

♠

Polly opened the door to the room where Mr. Tillson usually stayed. He had checked out early today, so this was a good time to do some cleaning. A hint of his aftershave hung in the air, reminding her of their… Was it a date? He'd been a perfect gentleman except for hands that occasionally settled too close to areas usually considered off limits. Was it intentional? Maybe men expected women who'd been married in the past to allow more liberties.

Her dating experience was limited, having only seriously dated Garrett and Will. Mr. Tillson definitely leaned more toward the old Garrett's style. Her cheeks warmed, warning bells chiming again, but she tuned them out, wielding her dust cloth vigorously.

That done, she stripped the sheets from the bed Mr. Tillson slept in finding, to her alarm, that the task had taken on an intimate quality. Perhaps there were good reasons for hotelkeepers not to socialize with their customers. On the other hand, Terrence Tillson was the only man besides Charles who had expressed an interest in her lately. It had been heavenly to have someone cuddle her a bit and make her feel special. Her whole life revolved around meeting other people's needs.

She knelt by the bed, smoothing her fingers absentmindedly over the fresh pillowcase she'd just placed on the pillow.

"Polly—"

The voice was so unexpected that she shrieked and leapt to her feet.

"What are you doing?" Elsie stood in the doorway. "Why are you stroking Mr. Tillson's pillow?"

"It isn't Mr. Tillson's pillow. It belongs to the hotel." Polly avoided Elsie's eyes. "I just changed the pillowcase."

"Uh huh." Elsie's tone was skeptical. "Well, if you're done fondling the hotel's pillow, there's someone downstairs who wants to talk to you about booking a party."

♠

Garrett opened his eyes when the alarm clock's raucous summons sounded. Why was the alarm ringing before daylight on a Saturday? Ah, moving day. His parents, folks from the church, Bob Dye, Devon Black and George Burns would soon be here. Time to rise and shine.

Savannah stretched and groaned beside him.

"Why don't you rest a little longer, my Love? I'll get the children dressed so they can go with Mother when she comes."

"No, no. I'm getting up. People will be arriving before we know it." She leaned in for a kiss before throwing back the covers. "Probably our last kiss in this bedroom."

He chuckled. "We'll have lots more in our new bedroom, but let's have just one more here." Garrett drew her back and pressed his lips on hers. "As soon as you get dressed and eat breakfast, I'll take you to the other house. I want you out of here so you're not tempted to lift any boxes."

She groaned again. "You are such a worrywart. You don't expect me to stand around while everyone else is working, do you?"

"You can direct traffic." Garrett leaped out of bed. "Tell folks where to put the furniture and the well-marked boxes. Eventually, you can start unpacking things in the kitchen."

"Okay. I can do that."

Garrett smiled. "Good girl." She'd pretty much given up arguing with him since he'd gotten so bossy. He grabbed a blue denim work shirt and pants from his drawer—the last things in that drawer. "I'll send someone to move boxes for you in the kitchen."

The rest of the day was a blur—answering questions, shouting orders, making endless trips up and down stairs at the apartment or at the house, checking to be sure Savannah was following his orders. At last the apartment was empty. Pa helped him carry the pieces of their beds to their new bedrooms so they'd have a place to sleep tonight.

Ma trotted into the back bedroom, arms loaded with sheets, quilts, and pillows. "I unpacked some toys in the sitting room so Savannah could close the door, sit on the loveseat and keep an eye on Milly. She needs to rest."

"As soon as we get the sheets on this mattress, I'll make her lie down." Garrett grabbed a sheet.

Footsteps thundered up the stairs. "Papa!"

The urgency in his son's voice drew him, and he dashed through the nursery to the stairs. "What is it, Son?"

"Papa, come quick. Mama's sick."

Chapter 107

Garrett sped down the steps and raced to Savannah's side. "What's wrong, Love?"

"My back hurts something awful, and I'm having some cramps." Savannah's white face glistened with perspiration.

"I'll call Doc Cooley right away." Garrett turned toward the door.

"Wait. Maybe if I lie down, the pains will stop. Please?"

How he hated making these decisions. He swept her into his arms and headed for the stairs. "I'll take you up to our bed, and we'll ask Ma what she thinks."

He huffed and puffed with each step. Unexpectedly, Savannah giggled. "What's so funny?"

"I'm not as light as I used to be."

Garrett paused to catch his breath and cradled her against his heart, pressing his lips on her hair. "I wouldn't expect you to be."

"Cut out that mushy stuff, you two." Sam made a gagging sound behind them.

"Just wait, young man. You'll change your thinking about mushy stuff." Garrett finished the last few steps just as Ma appeared in the hall.

"What's going on?" Her brow furrowed.

"I'm not feeling so good—"

Garrett interrupted. "I think we should call Doc Cooley, don't you, Ma?"

"I don't even know what the problem is yet, Son. Let's take her back to the bedroom. Sammy, go find Grandpa and ask him to keep an eye on Milly, please."

After Savannah repeated her symptoms to Ma, Garrett waited for her response. Thank goodness, the responsibility for this decision now rested on her shoulders.

She frowned. "I believe the doctor would want us to call him. Maybe you've just overdone things today, but we should let him decide."

Savannah sighed as Garrett settled her on the bed and Ma fluffed her pillows. "All right, if that's what you think we should do. I hate to bother him."

Ma chuckled. "Have you ever known Doc Cooley to be annoyed about a house call?"

"I guess not, but my mother always acted like I was a nuisance if I got sick, so I guess that's how I expect other people to feel."

Patting Savannah's hand, Ma sat on the edge of the bed. "Remember when we said God isn't like your mother? Well, Doc Cooley isn't like her either."

Ma nodded for Garrett to go make the telephone call. He waited downstairs until the doctor arrived and greeted him at the door. "She's upstairs, Doctor."

Dr. Cooley shook his hand and then advised him to wait there while he examined Savannah. Sam came out of the sitting room as the doctor disappeared up the stairs. "Will Mama be okay?"

"I think so, Son. Dr. Cooley is checking on her."

Garrett kept peering at his pocket watch. Surely it had stopped. Time dragged, but less than ten minutes later, the doctor returned. "Is Savannah okay?" Garrett attempted to read his expression.

"I'm advising her to stay in bed, at least for several days. What she's experiencing could be false labor, but we don't want to take any chances. I'll check on her again tomorrow."

The doctor scrubbed his hand over his face. "She's

concerned about staying in bed when there's so much unpacking to do. I assured her other folks will help."

"Of course, that's the least of my worries. Thanks so much. What do I owe you?"

"You can pay me next time you come in, or I'll send you a bill. Try not to worry, young man." The doctor patted his shoulder and went out into the night.

♠

Savannah stared at Mother. "Do you think the baby is all right?"

"Dr. Cooley didn't seem overly worried. Staying in bed is just a precaution." Mother smoothed the quilt gently over Savannah's abdomen.

"I feel so bad that someone else will have to unpack our boxes while I stay in bed. How can I do that?" A frown puckered Savannah's brow.

"You just do it." Mother's kind eyes twinkled. "With Garrett and I standing guard, the harder thing will be getting out of bed. How are you feeling?"

"A little better, I think. My back is less painful and the cramping has slowed down." Closing her eyes, Savannah blew out a breath. "Mother, could you do something for me?"

"Anything, my Dear."

"Would you call Polly? She'll be mad if we don't tell her. You know how she is."

"Of course. You two are like sisters." Mother headed for the door.

Savannah concentrated on slow, steady breaths as Dr. Cooley had suggested. He said it would help her relax. As naturally as breathing, she began to pray. *Father, you know what's happening in my body. Please protect our baby. Don't allow the step of faith we've taken to do harm to our little one. Thank you for your protection, Jesus.*

A short time later, a car pulled up beside the house. Probably Polly. She hadn't wasted any time. Minutes later the door opened and closed and footsteps pounded up the stairs.

"Polly, you didn't have to come—" Her friend's face turned so white that Savannah sat up in alarm. "What's wrong, Polly?"

Polly crumpled to the floor and put her head between her knees.

"Mother, come quick," Savannah yelled as loud as she could muster and moved to the edge of the bed. Dr. Cooley had told her to stay in bed but how could she do that with her best friend passing out on the floor?

Polly must have sensed her movement. "Don't get up." Her voice was breathy. "I'll be all right."

Mother entered the room, puffing from her rapid ascent. She bent over Polly who had raised her head. "Are you okay?"

Polly nodded. "I'm sorry." Her voice dropped to a whisper. "Seeing Savannah in bed like that brought back memories of my mother in this room."

"Ah, Polly. I'm so sorry. I never thought…"

"Of course you didn't." Color was returning to Polly's face. "I'd have been upset if Mildred hadn't called. Are you feeling better?"

"I am, but the doctor says I have to stay in bed for now." Savannah wrinkled her nose.

"That happened to my mother too. You need to listen to the Doc. We'll all…" She stopped. "I was going to say we'll all help, but tomorrow is my busy day with community people coming for dinner. I hate it that I can't be here for you, Savannah. That hotel is like an albatross around my neck."

Chapter 108

George Burns walked up the steps into the church. Only a week since he met the Greelys and the Youngs here. He used to tell people the roof would fall in if he ever entered that church, but all that had changed. If he wanted to convince the Greelys he was serious about getting a fresh start, and he was, he needed to show up every Sunday. It's what his grandparents had taught him.

Mrs. Greely walked up the aisle ahead of him, talking real nice to everyone she met. She sat on a bench near the front. He chose a seat near the aisle and stared at the back of her head. Reverend Greely seemed like the real McCoy, but Mrs. Greely? He didn't know about her. Something odd about the way she dashed out of the room after Savannah last Sunday. And she definitely had something in her craw when she went and sat in her car. Didn't hardly seem Christian.

He pulled a hymnal out of the rack and stood up when Reverend Greely said to join in the singing. Later, he sat down and pulled out a Bible to look up the Scripture. First Corinthians, chapter thirteen. The reading was all about charity. George knew little about the Bible but his grandma had told him charity, the way it was used here, meant love. She said this scripture meant if you did all kinds of good things but you didn't have love, it was worthless.

His gaze was drawn again to the back of Mrs. Greely's head. He was no expert, but he hadn't seen even a tad of love in

Mrs. Greely's attitude toward Savannah. Shouldn't a preacher's wife show love to everyone? Or maybe he had it all wrong. When the sermon was over, Mrs. Greely came back and introduced him to everyone, more than implyin' she and her husband had helped him see the light.

Staring at the people who gathered around him, George set out to give credit where credit was due. "Do you all know Garrett and Savannah Young?" When some folks nodded, he told his story, how he'd kidnapped Savannah and how Garrett started visiting him when the prison chaplain moved away. "Can you imagine that? After what I done to the woman he loved?"

His gaze roved over the faces. "It was because of him I come to know Jesus. And Savannah forgave me too, even before I asked." Mrs. Greely's smile disappeared. "Them two are just about the best people I know."

When all his well-wishers walked away, Mrs. Greely glared at him. "If you knew what I know about Savannah and Garrett, you wouldn't think they were so wonderful." Her tone was low and filled with bitterness."

George smiled at her. "Why don't you try me?"

Mrs. Greely bit her lip. "Well… That is… they took something precious away from us and won't give it back."

"Ya mean they stole something from you?"

"Well, not exactly but…"

A conversation he'd had with Garrett awhile back occurred to him. "Are you talking about the baby they adopted?"

Mrs. Greely's jaw dropped. "Who told you that?"

"Garrett said they adopted a baby out of wedlock to spare someone public embarrassment and later the folks wanted her back." George cleared his throat. "He never told me who it was, mind you, but I'm guessing that baby might be the precious thing you're sayin' they took from you. Maybe a grand or a great grand."

"But you don't know the whole—"

"My understandin' is they took the baby out of the goodness of their hearts and adopted her a couple years ago. I can't believe you'd ask for the child back." He pointed a thick finger at Mrs. Greely. "You bein' a leader in the church and all, you should be setting an example for others."

"Gertrude, what have you done?" The church had cleared and Reverend Greely stood behind his wife. "What did you say to Savannah last week?"

His wife pinched her lips together. Reverend Greely glanced at George. "Did you tell her we want the baby back?"

Mrs. Greely's face turned almost purple. "They're going to have a baby of their own soon. Isn't that reason enough for them to give ours back?"

"Milly isn't ours, Gertie. We lost the privilege of claiming her because you didn't want the community to know our granddaughter was going to have a child out of wedlock."

He turned to George. "I'm sorry you had to be a witness to this. It shows that all of us are capable of sin. You've repented of yours and I hope my wife will repent of hers."

♠

Charles strolled out of the Presbyterian Church in Stoneboro. He'd walked to church this morning, needing time to clear his head. Ever since he talked to Polly on Thursday evening, he'd wrestled with what she'd said.

He couldn't promise her that nothing bad would happen to him. Only God knew his future. Even if he somehow convinced her to give him a chance, she'd never forgive him if… if… his fate should turn out to be the same as Will's. Still, there had to be a way. He couldn't give up on Polly.

Perhaps if he'd listened to the sermon this morning, God might have given him some divine direction. Instead, he'd been like a dog chasing its tail, trying to figure out what to do.

With a long drawn-out sigh, he lifted his eyes to heaven. *I give up, Lord. Maybe it's just not meant to be. If that position for an engineer is still open in Cleveland, I'm going to put in for a transfer. Maybe some distance will help me forget Polly. Maybe I'll find someone there to grow old with me.*

Chapter 109

Polly flopped down on her desk chair in the kitchen and propped her head on her hand just as Father entered. She had rushed down to see Savannah this morning, then made it through the busy Sunday dinner one more time.

"Have you eaten, Florence?"

She bit her lip. "I… I don't know."

"You have to stop doing that." Her father stooped and looked directly into her eyes. "Didn't you say you almost passed out in Savannah's bedroom last night?"

"That wasn't because I hadn't eaten. Or at least I don't think so. It was because of the memories of what happened to Mother in that room."

"Am I interrupting something?" Mr. Tillson's voice echoed across the empty dining room as he approached them.

Polly leapt to her feet. "I'm so sorry. You were probably out there ringing the bell for ages."

"Not that long. I heard voices, so I followed my ears." His contagious grin emerged.

"Florence, you need to get something to eat. I'll check Mr. Tillson in." Father stood.

"I tell you what, Polly. After I check in, let's you and me go to Adda's restaurant again. I arrived earlier this week, so we'll have plenty of time." Mr. Tillson smoothed down an unruly brown curl.

Polly stared at him, warning bells colliding with a desire to be treated to a dinner she hadn't cooked. "I'm too tired to change my clothes."

"That's all right. You look lovely just the way you are."

A tiny frown creased her father's forehead.

Mr. Tillson bowed Father's way. "I hope you don't mind me saying that, Mr. Dye."

His visible tension smoothed away at Mr. Tillson's disclaimer. "My daughter always looks lovely to me. It's up to you, Florence. Think about it while I take care of the check in."

It was unusual for her father not to object to her going out with someone he didn't know. Maybe he was desperate for someone to distract her from the funk she'd been in since Charles disappeared.

She stifled a yawn. Should she stay home and go to bed? That wouldn't be nearly as much fun as an evening out. She stood and removed her apron, then smoothed the skirt of her emerald green dress, tucked a few strands of hair behind her ear, and pinched her cheeks to add a bit of color. Going with Mr. Tillson without walking up two flights of steps to freshen up was tempting.

"You look fine, Florence." Her father had returned without making a sound, or maybe she'd been too deep in thought to hear him. "Mr. Tillson took his things up to his room, and I brought your coat in case you decide to go with him."

"You really think this is a good idea, Father?"

"You mean you going to dinner with a hotel guest? Did you feel safe last week?"

Polly couldn't quite meet his eyes. Safe wasn't the word. "We're only going to Aunt Adda's. What could happen?"

Mr. Tillson returned as a little frown puckered Father's brow.

"Are you ready, Polly?" He attempted to take Polly's coat from Father, who kept a firm hold on it.

"Florence hasn't said she wants to go."

"Of course I want to go." Polly patted Father's arm reassuringly.

This time he released her coat to Mr. Tillson. Their guest held it for her, a solicitous smile on his lips. "Let's be on our way then, and not waste any time." As they turned away from Father, Mr. Tillson's hand caressed her neck as she buttoned her coat.

After they crossed the veranda, he slid his arm around her, tucking his hand snuggly between her upper arm and her body. When she attempted to put space between them, it seemed to have the opposite affect. Yet the behavior didn't seem overt enough to justify a rebuke.

Stop being so old-fashioned, she scolded herself. The flappers she'd heard about would certainly have no problem with Mr. Tillson's behavior. Not that she wanted to be a flapper, but perhaps she needed to loosen up a bit. When her escort pulled the blanket from the back seat and tucked it snuggly around her, she didn't move away. Perhaps this was Mr. Tillson's way of showing how serious he was about their relationship.

And maybe this was the best way to erase the tender blue eyes and sweet smile that haunted her.

♠

Kicking and thrashing, Polly opened her mouth to scream but no sound came. How could she get away from this man who must certainly be part octopus? No matter how she tried, she couldn't escape his hands.

Waking with a start, she sat up in a cold sweat. The dream had been so real. Her breath came in short, harsh gasps. What was the matter with her? Her date last night with Mr. Tillson hadn't been *that* unpleasant. But apparently, judging from her dream, at some deep level she was a hopeless fuddy-duddy.

Polly sprang out of bed and made a quick business of getting dressed and making breakfast for her family and guests. Mr. Tillson had already left for work. She refused to dwell on her dream. After Twila left for school, Father and Elsie labored over the bookkeeping as Elsie trained Father to take over in January.

Polly grabbed her feather duster to go over the rooms of the hotel guests, starting with Mr. Tillson's.

As she swished her duster across his chest of drawers, something flew through the air and landed with a small clatter on the hardwood floor. She gasped. *Oh no, what if it was something valuable?* She squinted and dropped to her hands and knees, smoothing her fingers in all directions. The sun beamed through the window and glinted off a small shiny object.

She picked up the circular item, which appeared to be a solid gold band. Tiny words were etched inside, easily visible by the light from the window. *To my beloved husband, Terrance.* Her stomach churned and bile rose in her throat. Mr. Tillson was married.

Chapter 110

Monday morning Charles parked his car near the train station in Franklin. He jumped out and hurried inside, looking for the poster advertising the position for an engineer in Cleveland. Now that he'd made up his mind, he couldn't wait to make sure the job was still available. Thank God, the ad was there.

"This position still open?" He directed his question to the station agent.

"Far as I know. You interested?" The agent peered at him through the ticket window.

"Maybe." He scanned the information. The position was for a passenger train locomotive engineer which would mean regular hours, not that it really mattered. Pay would be a little higher than his present salary. He pulled a small tablet from his pocket and wrote down the contact person's name and telephone number.

The agent watched him. "I can telegraph the station agent in Cleveland now if you want."

Charles glanced at the clock on the wall. He had time before his shift. "All right. If you don't mind."

"Happy to do it."

The agent was courteous and swift. Charles gave him all the information, his full name, present position, contact information. In minutes, the man had set up an interview for Charles during his stop-over in Cleveland the next day.

Charles thanked him and walked away, his breath coming

in short puffs. This had happened so quickly. Green eyes, vibrant red hair and a musical laugh pursued him as he left.

♠

Polly stomped up the stairs to the third floor of the hotel, slammed the door to her room and threw herself on the bed. Mr. Tillson's ring was still clutched in her hand. Sobs shook her entire body. Sobs not of sorrow—she wasn't in love with the man, but of rage. How dare he treat her in such a familiar way, knowing all the while he was married?

A knock on her door. Swallowing her cries, Polly sat up and pulled out a handkerchief. She scrubbed her face. "What do you want?" Her tone was less than gracious.

"What's wrong, Florence? Why are you stomping and slamming doors?" A mixture of concern and irritation tinged Father's words.

He wouldn't go away until she answered. Her father was nothing if not persistent. "You might as well come in so I don't have to shout."

The door opened and he entered. After one look at her tear-stained face, he sat on the bed beside her. "Tell me what's going on." Tenderness softened his words.

Polly's face crumpled as she handed him Mr. Tillson's ring. He frowned. "Someone gave you a ring? Mr. Tillson?"

She snorted. "No, someone gave Mr. Tillson a ring. His *wife*."

Understanding glinted in her father's eyes. "So he's married."

"I found his ring when I was dusting."

Her father nodded. "I see. What are you going to do?"

"I'd like to tell him to get out and never come back, but I can't afford to do that. His money helps pay our bills." Polly shuddered. "I can hardly bear to think of taking his money."

"We're in a better position now that I sold our house."

Polly shrugged. "I'll talk to him tonight. When I'm through with him, he may decide to leave without me asking."

Polly stole frequent glances at the clock while she

worked. Would this day never end? Mr. Tillson's ring lay on top of her dresser. She would eventually use it to confront him.

She spent the day composing scathing words, followed by periods of fear-induced nausea. Would he come to her and ask about the ring? Would he even notice it was missing? The uncertainty of what lay ahead set her teeth on edge.

In the end she hid in the kitchen, asking her father and sisters to keep an eye on the desk and to serve the boarders their supper. When she finished preparing the meal, she went to her room. The rest of the family could clean up and wash dishes without her for once. If Mr. Tillson wanted to see her or get his ring back, he'd have to ask for her. It gave her a feeling of power.

Time dragged until at last Polly dug out her journal and attempted to write in it for the first time in months. She had barely dated her entry, *Monday, November 22, 1926,* when someone knocked.

"Come in."

Twila opened the door. "Mr. Tillson is asking for you." Her sister's dark brown eyes sparkled. "This is so romantic."

Polly restrained her snort. The last thing she needed was Twila asking questions. "Thank you. Tell him I'll be right down."

After one last glance in the mirror, she picked up the ring and put it in her pocket, then started down the stairs. What waited for her at the bottom? Where could they go to talk?

The come-hither glint in Mr. Tillson's eyes told her he hadn't missed his wedding ring. He was hoping to take up where they'd left off last night. "Polly, lovely as the flowers in the spring." His tone was smooth as silk.

When she didn't greet him or respond in any way to his syrupy words, his eyes clouded. "Aren't you glad to see me?"

"Tickled pink." Polly kept her voice devoid of emotion.

"Maybe we should go for a little ride. You've probably had a bad day." His face was a panorama of changing emotions, astonishment and irritation, quickly coated with solicitousness.

"Oh, I've had a bad day all right." Polly nodded for emphasis. "Your car might be the best place to talk." She ran up two flights of stairs, yanked her coat from the hook and rammed her arms in the sleeves, then stomped back down.

When they left the hotel and he reached for her arm, she glared at him. "Don't. Touch. Me."

"Polly, what's wrong? Why are you angry?"

She stopped in the middle of the veranda and stared at him, then spoke through gritted teeth. "Did you notice anything missing in your room?"

"Missing? I don't think so. What are you talking about?" It was obvious Mr. Tillson was clueless.

She reached into her pocket to give him his ring, then changed her mind. It would be better to do it in the car so people wouldn't hear her screaming at him on Main Street.

"Come on. I'll show you." She strode ahead of him and opened the passenger door, not waiting for him to catch up.

As soon as his door closed behind him, Polly handed him his ring, which sparkled in the light of the street lamp. "I found this today when I was dusting your room." Her tone was deceptively quiet.

A mask settled over his face, leaving it expressionless. "I thought you knew I was married."

"You thought no such thing." Her tone had risen a few decibels. "You *never* wore your wedding ring at the hotel."

Mr. Tillson shrugged. "Lots of men don't wear wedding rings."

"Lots of men don't *have* wedding rings, but you do." Polly pounded her fist on the dashboard. "You purposely deceived me."

He stared at her, then spoke in a low, gravelly voice. "You stole my wedding ring from my room. I could have you arrested."

"And I could tell your wife what you did."

Chapter 111

Savannah jumped out of bed. Dr. Cooley had told her she could be up by Wednesday if she didn't have any more cramps or backaches. Maybe this was how George Burns felt when he got out of jail. She laughed at herself as she dressed. She'd only been in bed for a couple of days, not years like Mr. Burns had spent in jail. Still it seemed like forever as she lay like a lump while everyone unpacked for her.

Garrett and his mother weren't happy about her wanting to have Thanksgiving dinner here tomorrow but hadn't completely squashed the idea. If everyone helped, there was no reason they couldn't eat at their new home on Broad Street. The cramps on Sunday night were now only a bad dream.

She restrained herself from skipping down the stairs, slowing her pace even more when Garrett's mother peered up at her. "Are you sure you should come down? I'm afraid you'll overdo."

"I'm fine, Mother. Really I am. Dr. Cooley said I could get up today. Remember?"

Mother furrowed her brow. "I know but— "

"Where's my little girl?" Interrupting might be the only way to derail Mother's train of thought. "And Sammy's home, too, right?"

"They're playing in the sitting room. Why don't you rest in there while I clean up the kitchen from breakfast?" Mother could be very persuasive.

"All right, that's probably a good idea. But I don't want you to overdo either." Savannah frowned and turned toward the door. "You've been working so hard to get us settled."

Mother laughed. "I'm fine. I've always enjoyed helping folks move. I had fun arranging your kitchen."

"All right, if you're sure."

♠

On Thanksgiving morning Garrett came into the kitchen where Savannah and Ma were preparing dinner. Turkey roasting in the oven tantalized his senses but didn't overcome his concern for his wife who was, as she said, *big as a barn.*

"Maybe you should sit down for a few minutes, Love?" He tried to soft-pedal his instructions since Savannah had grown a little tired of his bossiness.

"I haven't been working very long. I'll take a break soon. I want to finish this cranberry salad from your mother's recipe." Savannah tucked a few strands of hair behind her ear. Even in her oversized condition, his wife was still the most beautiful woman he'd ever seen.

He kissed her soft, rounded cheek and whispered, "You're gorgeous."

Savannah laughed out loud. "Oh yeah! If you like the extra-large size."

"I love you any way that you are, my Love." He kissed her lips. "What can I do to help?"

"You can set the table with our good china and goblets. Your mother will know where she put the things we don't use every day."

Finally, after a couple of rests on Savannah's part, everything was ready. His father arrived in time to give Garrett some pointers on carving his first turkey. It was also his first time to sit at the head of the table since they'd always spent holidays at his parents' home. Sam sat on his right, and Savannah on his left with Milly beside her. Pa sat at the foot of the table with Ma on his left beside Sam.

His heart overflowed with thanksgiving as he glanced

around the table at all the faces so precious to him, sitting in a home large enough to raise his family. It was a happy Thanksgiving, indeed. They all clasped hands as Garrett prayed from a joyful heart.

"Can I have some turkey, Mama?" Sam's question came almost before Garrett said amen.

"*May* I have some turkey, Sammy," Savannah corrected.

Sam screwed up his forehead. "You're asking me?"

Laughter flowed around the table as Savannah shrugged. "I'll give you a pass since it's Thanksgiving. Papa can hold the turkey platter while you help yourself."

Food and conversation flowed around the table in abundance, even Milly contributing with an occasional comment. "I like our new house, Mama."

Their step of faith had culminated in this Thanksgiving Day dinner. Would God honor it?

Pa put down his fork and clapped his hand to his forehead. "Oh for goodness sake, I forgot to give you your mail." He patted his pocket.

Garrett raised his eyebrows. "What mail?"

His father pulled a business-size envelope from his pocket. "When I stopped to get our mail yesterday, the post master gave me this. Said he's not really supposed to but figured you hadn't had a chance to get it, so busy with moving and all." He studied the envelope. "Probably church business. One of those stamped return addresses—Jackson Center Presbyterian Church."

Almost knocking over his chair, Garrett dashed to the other end of the table.

Pa handed him the envelope. "You think it's important?"

"Might be from the Greely's."

Savannah's hand flew to her mouth. "What if it's bad news?" She grabbed Milly's hand.

Making no reply, Garrett ripped off one end of the envelope. He pulled out a single sheet of paper, scanned the letter, then let out a whoop that could have raised the dead.

Savannah was beside him in a heartbeat. "What? What does it say?"

After a ceremonious throat-clearing, Garrett read aloud: *Dear Garrett and Savannah, I want to assure you that we will honor your adoption of our great granddaughter. You have provided her with a loving Christian home. What more could we want for Milly? I hope in time my wife will apologize for the agony she caused you both. I'm so sorry. God's richest blessings on you both. Reverend John Greely.*

Tears ran down Garrett's face as he dropped into his chair. "I was just wondering if God would honor our step of faith. What more could we ask to make our Thanksgiving Day complete?" He grasped Savannah's hand as everyone echoed loud amens.

"Does this mean Mrs. Greedy won't try to take my sister away?" Sam's serious face demanded an answer.

"That's what it means, Son."

Sam leaped from his chair and ran around the table to dance a jig with his mystified little sister.

When the celebration finally calmed down and plates were empty, Pa raised an eyebrow in Garrett's direction "One more thing. Did you hear Charles Clarkson is transferring to Cleveland in February?"

Savannah stared at him. "Who told you that?"

Pa winked at her. "Three guesses but I don't think you'll need more than one."

"Dorothy, of course. I wonder if Polly kno—" She stiffened. "Oh... Ow..."

Garrett leapt to his feet and rushed to her side. Ma was right behind him. He knelt beside his wife. "Savannah, what is it?"

Chapter 112

Dr. Cooley put his stethoscope into his black bag and tapped his foot, gazing at Savannah. "What have you been doing, young lady?" There was a twinkle in his kind eyes, but a layer of steel in his voice.

"Well..." Savannah coughed and then grasped her abdomen. "Preparing Thanksgiving dinner. Everyone helped."

"We tried to talk her out of it." Mother stepped toward the bed.

Dr. Cooley wagged his finger at Savannah. "I said you could get up if you took it easy. Cooking Thanksgiving dinner isn't taking it easy." He tilted his head and closed one eye. "We still have two months before we want this baby to be born."

"I'm sorry Dr. Cooley." Savannah blew out a breath. "I promise—"

But Dr. Cooley wasn't listening. He took out a prescription pad and wrote on it. When he finished, he handed it to her. "I'm prescribing bed rest until your baby is born. I wrote it down to make it official." Again, there was the mixture of the twinkle and steel.

"How can I take care of my two-year-old and cook for my family if I have to stay in bed?" Savannah groaned and clutched her back.

Mother grasped her free hand. "I'll help, and I know other ladies from the church will too."

"Hey, can I come in yet?" Garrett obviously wasn't

thrilled at being banished to the nursery.

Dr. Cooley had barely cracked the door when Garrett rushed in. "Is she okay?"

"We're hopeful that she and the baby will be all right. But we can't take any more chances." The doctor reached for the prescription Savannah held and handed it to Garrett. "She needs bed rest until the little one is born."

"Consider it done, even if I have to stay home to see to it." Garrett clenched his jaw.

♠

Polly bent over the beautifully browned turkey, wiggling drumstick and thigh. It was done. The aroma was tantalizing. Twila and Elsie were preparing the small dining room, decorating with little pumpkins and setting the table with their best china. They would eat around four o'clock.

She'd decided not to offer a Thanksgiving dinner to the public. A decision she didn't regret. She hadn't fully recovered from the battle on Monday with Mr. Tillson.

In the end, it was a draw. He wouldn't turn her over to the police if she didn't speak to his wife. Of course, she still came out the loser because he collected his luggage and sought lodging at the Hotel Homer or the Lake House in Stoneboro.

She shrugged. It was for the best not to have him around as a reminder of her error in judgment. Not having anyone was better than having a deceiver.

"Do you want me to carve the turkey?" Polly startled and turned to find Father at her elbow, treating her as he had all week like some fragile object.

"That would be nice." Polly pulled a large cutting board from the cupboard. "Seems like every time I turn around, you're right there."

"I'm worried about you, Florence."

"You worry too much, Fa—" The ringing of the telephone cut off her words. "I'll get it. You can start carving."

"Hello."

"Hello." Garrett's voice. "Savannah wanted me to tell

you she's back on bed rest."

Polly gasped. "What happened?"

Garrett filled her in on Savannah's latest setback as nausea rose in Polly's throat. "I'll be right there."

"You don't need to come. Savannah just wanted you to know."

"I have to see for myself that she's okay." Polly gulped. "Thanks for calling."

She flung the receiver and dashed to tell Father where she was going.

"You're leaving before Thanksgiving dinner?" Father's brows rose.

"The food is ready. You and the girls can put it in serving bowls and call the boarders to the table. I'll eat later."

Polly retrieved her coat and dashed out the back door. Sometimes she walked to Broad Street but not today. History would not repeat itself. She'd see to it.

When she walked into the back bedroom, Savannah was resting against three plump pillows.

"Polly, I told Garrett you didn't need to come. I just wanted to let you know what was happening." She stretched out her hand to take Polly's. Then a huge smile emerged. "But I'm so glad to see you."

"I had to see for myself that you're okay." Polly cleared her throat. "Too many ba—" She couldn't remind Savannah of the bad things that had happened here. "Never mind."

"Pull that chair over beside the bed, Polly, so I can be close to you." Savannah let go of Polly's hand. "I know this room brings back memories of when your mother passed away. That's why I said you didn't need to come."

"I'm sorry I reminded you, but someone should stay with you every minute."

"I'm all right, Polly. Fear is causing your imagination to run away with you."

This was the second person who'd mentioned fear. Polly set down the chair and one by one, unbuttoned the buttons on her coat. Was God speaking to her?

When Polly sat in the chair next to the bed, Savannah took her hand again. "Let's talk about something else. I suppose you know Charles Clarkson is transferring to Cleveland."

Polly's jaw dropped. "He's what?"

"Oh, I'm sorry. Dorothy has done it again. I assumed you knew." Savannah rubbed her forehead.

Closing her eyes for a moment, Polly sighed. "I haven't seen Charles since our date at the Stoneboro Fair." Her voice dropped to a whisper. "A week ago, he called to ask for another date, but I told him I couldn't see him again."

Chapter 113

Savannah patted her friend's hand. "Polly, Polly, my dear friend. Can't you see how fear is controlling your life?"

Polly bit her lip. "Father, tried to tell me but I wouldn't listen."

"Bring me my Bible, please." Savannah nodded at her bedside table on the other side of the bed.

Polly obeyed, then returned to her seat.

Paging through the well-worn book, Savannah stopped at Second Timothy and read verse seven. *"For God hath not given us the spirit of fear; but of power, and of love, and of a sound mind.* Fear isn't from God, Polly. And if it isn't from God, who is it from?"

"From Satan."

The words were so soft Savannah could barely hear. "What was that?"

"It's from Satan." Polly almost shouted the words.

Savannah nodded, then flipped to the Old Testament and read from the second verse of Isaiah twelve. *I will trust and not be afraid.*

"We always have a choice, whether to trust or to fear. Always. I'm not saying it's easy to make the right choice, but when I do, my life gets better."

Polly stood. "I'm sorry to leave so abruptly, Savannah. If you're okay, I have some serious thinking and praying to do. I've been so busy running the hotel that God and I are barely on speaking terms. I'm afraid Self is back on the throne."

"I'm fine, Polly. Garrett and his mother are taking good care of me."

Polly kissed Savannah's cheek. "I'll be back."

♠

Polly slipped in the back door to the hotel and tiptoed up the stairs. If Father heard her, he'd insist she join them for Thanksgiving dinner. Her hunger for time with her Heavenly Father outweighed her desire for food.

When she reached her room, she pulled her journal and Sarah's diary from a drawer in her bedside table. Next, she picked up her Bible and blew a fine layer of dust from it. "I'm sorry, Lord." How had she allowed so many days to pass without reading God's Word? No wonder she was miserable.

She grabbed Chartreuse, her fountain pen, from her bedside stand and put all the items she held on the bed. Then she plumped her pillows and settled herself against them. Maybe God needed to put her on bed rest for awhile until she got her priorities straight. She opened her journal, crossed out the old date and inserted a new one. November 25, 1926, Thanksgiving Day.

Father, are Savannah and my father right about fear controlling my life? It's obvious that I can't be directed by the Holy Spirit if I'm controlled by that powerful emotion. Mother told me long ago that if I lived my life in tune with your Spirit, your wisdom would become more and more available to me. Show me how. I don't want to be ruled by fear.

She put down her pen, picked up Sarah's diary and opened to the first page. She stopped at Sarah's second entry and stared at the page. *I am excited but also fearful.* Sarah had been fearful, too. Fearful of diseases that stole the lives of many Irish children in the United States.

Even though Sarah had said, *Only God could see me through the loss of a child,* fear prompted her to keep too tight a grip on her other children after those losses came. Instead of trusting God, she had attempted to keep her remaining children safe herself. She taught them by her behavior to put their trust in her, rather than in the Lord.

Picking up Chartreuse, she began again. *I too was controlled by fear from the first day I learned about the dangers of Will's job as a brakeman on the railroad. I didn't let it stop me from marrying him, but I allowed Satan to rob me of many happy moments. Then after Will died, instead of focusing on how you brought me through, I allowed fear to take a deeper foothold and made a vow never to marry another railroad man.*

I'm so disappointed in myself, Father. How many times since I became a follower of Jesus have I chosen fear instead of trust?

A tear trickled down Polly's nose and plopped down on the word *fear*, turning it into green blob. After blotting it with a tissue, she added, *What a mess I've made of my relationship with Charles Clarkson. I've driven away a good man who may have been in love with me. And it's too late. He's transferring to Cleveland in February.*

Another tear trickled down her cheek, but she swiped it away before it fell. Charles. She sat up straight. He hadn't moved yet. Was he alone on Thanksgiving Day? Maybe she could make amends by inviting him to join their family on this special day. She wouldn't blame him if he refused, but she would trust that if this was God's plan, Charles would say yes. Starting today, she would treat fear as an enemy and trust as her best friend.

She capped Chartreuse and picked up her Bible. Turning to Proverbs three, she read again words she had underlined in verses five through six. *Trust in the LORD with all thine heart; and lean not unto thine own understanding. In all thy ways acknowledge him, and he shall direct thy paths. Be not wise in thine own eyes: fear the LORD, and depart from evil.*

Someone once said if a person feared the Lord, in the proper sense, he didn't need to fear anything else. Laying down her Bible, she scooted off the bed. She had a telephone call to make.

Chapter 114

The sun had set and maybe this interminable day would finally end. Charles had forced himself to buy a small roasting chicken which he'd cooked and eaten at noon in honor of the day. It tasted like sawdust. Why had he bothered? They used to spend the holidays with Jane's family, but Charles sensed that his presence with them now was a painful reminder of her passing.

February and a new beginning couldn't come soon enough.

The telephone rang. There wasn't anyone he wanted to talk to—well, maybe one person, but she wasn't interested. He stared at the telephone. After the fourth ring pierced his eardrums, he picked up the receiver. "Hello."

Someone sputtered and coughed, then croaked, "Hello."

A crank call on Thanksgiving Day? "Who is this?"

"It's… It's Polly. I thought maybe you weren't home."

The one voice he'd longed to hear. No, he wouldn't allow himself to hope. "Oh, I'm home."

"I wondered if you'd like to come eat Thanksgiving dinner with us?"

Did she feel sorry for him? Was that what prompted this call? He'd make it easy on her. "I don't want to intrude."

"You wouldn't be intruding. It's just the boarders and our family." Polly hesitated. "Actually, they're already eating, but I made plenty."

She was inviting him after the meal had begun? Talk about a last-minute invitation. "Well…" What did he have to lose? He could go and tell her he was leaving in February. Put her out of her misery. "All right. If you're sure it's no trouble, I'll come."

"Okay, I'll be waiting for you."

♠

Polly put her hands over her burning cheeks. He hadn't seemed overjoyed to hear from her but he hadn't said no. She'd better prepare her family and the boarders.

As she headed for the dining room, her father called. "Polly, is that you?"

"It's me."

"Could you bring the pumpkin pies, please?"

"Sure." When she entered the dining room with the pies and dessert plates, everyone cheered. Her father smiled at her.

"How's Savannah?" Twila came to help her serve.

"She's doing okay, but Doc Cooley says she has to be on bed rest until the baby comes." Polly cleared her throat and glanced at her father. "I just invited Charles Clarkson to Thanksgiving dinner."

Father's jaw dropped. "You invited him *now*? We've already eaten."

"But I haven't. I thought he might be lonely."

Her father shrugged and shook his head. She didn't want to explain now. "He's on his way. I'll refill the bowls and platters while Twila serves the pie."

By the time Polly returned with replenished dishes, Elsie was clearing the dirty ones. "You and Charles shouldn't have to look at our dirty plates while you eat."

Elsie was doing something nice for Charles? She shrugged at Polly's puzzled look, then answered in an undertone. "Hey, if he can help you get over the blues, it'll be worth it."

Polly couldn't help chuckling. "Have I been that bad?"

"Oh yeah…" Elsie went into the kitchen just as Charles knocked on the back door. "I'll get it." Her cheerful words reached Polly's ears. "Hello, Charles. Come on in. Happy Thanksgiving."

Shaking her head, Polly headed for the kitchen. Would wonders never cease?

And then there he was. Her first glimpse of Charles in two and a half months. Her heart sped up. How she'd missed him. He was the only man besides Will who ever affected her this way. "Charles, I'm glad you could come on such short notice."

"Thank you for inviting me." Was his smile forced?

"Come on in. The rest of the folks are eating dessert, but I'll join you for the main course." Polly motioned for him to follow her to the far end of the table where she'd arranged the food. Everyone greeted him, and Charles sat across from her.

"Help yourself, there's plenty. I can't seem to cook in small amounts anymore."

Charles spooned food on his plate without looking at her. There was no sparkle in his eyes. What did she expect? Would her eyes sparkle to be in the company of someone who'd refused even to be friends? Maybe this was a bad idea.

Soon everyone had finished their pie and left the dining room except Polly and Charles. The silence grew oppressive. An apology. That's what was needed, so he'd know she was sorry.

"Charles—"

"Did you—"

They both stopped. "Ladies first." Charles motioned for her to continue.

"I wanted to say how sorry I am for hurting you…" Polly met his blue gaze. How much to tell him? "God's been showing me I've allowed fear to control my life. That's why I vowed never to get involved with a railroad man."

His eyes widened and his mouth formed an O.

♠

So what was Polly saying? And would she change her mind tomorrow? Charles stared at his plate and crossed his arms. On the other hand, last time they talked, she'd said she missed him terribly. He lifted his eyes and met her gaze for a long moment. "Are you saying you're willing to give us a chance?"

"I am. Father and Savannah both pointed out that fear was controlling my life. Turns out they were right." Polly's shoulders drooped. "I've been doing it for a long time."

"I understand. I have fears of my own." He reached for her hand.

"But maybe it's too late." Polly's green eyes darkened. "Savannah told me you're transferring to Cleveland."

He nodded. "I am. But we have a few months, and even afterward I can ride the train to Sandy Lake for my days off. Do you think I might be able to rent a room here for those visits?"

A smile peeked through the clouds that had gathered. "I'm sure you can. Do you have a buyer for your house?"

"Jane and I were renting so that won't be a problem." Charles finished his last bite of turkey and put down his fork. "Speaking of my house, would you like to come have a piece of pie with me there?"

"Well..." Polly giggled. "Did you bake it?"

"Are you implying I can't bake pies?" Charles pretended to scowl as he stood.

Polly joined him. "Can you?"

"Well, no. But I have my sources." He winked at her.

"I'll get my coat and tell Father where I'm going."

♠

Polly almost skipped down the stairs carrying her coat. Charles took it, held it for her, then tucked her hand through his arm as they left the hotel. She couldn't help comparing it to the few times she'd gone out with Mr. Tillson. With Charles, there were so sly moves leaving her guessing at his intentions as there'd been with Mr. Tillson. How could she have thought there'd be a future with him?

When they walked into the house Charles rented, he helped her remove her coat. "Polly..." He tilted her chin and gazed into her eyes. "There's something I've wanted to do since the day we met."

Polly melted at the love evident in his gaze.

"May I kiss you?"

She stepped closer and put her arms around his neck, her pulse pounding in her ears. With great tenderness, he slid his arms around her and lowered his lips to hers. Time stood still. His kiss was everything Polly could have hoped for. When he drew back, his eyes met hers. "Polly," he whispered, "I think I'm falling in love with you."

"And I with you. I was too frightened to let myself admit it." Polly rose on tiptoes to kiss him again.

How close she had come to missing the blessing of a relationship with this kind, good man. By God's grace she would continue to live out the positive aspects of Sarah's legacy while rising above her fears.

Epilogue
May 6, 1927

Polly sniffed the fresh scent of spring on the porch of Garrett and Savannah's house before knocking. Savannah always scolded her for not walking in but Polly respected their privacy.

The door opened and Savannah stood holding Polly's beautiful three-month-old namesake, Flo. She was a tiny replica of her lovely dark-haired, deep violet-blue-eyed mother.

"Happy Wedding day, Polly." Savannah drew her into the house and kissed her cheek.

"Thank you, Savannah, and thanks to you and Garrett for letting Charles and me get married here." Polly kissed Flo's chubby cheek, then held out her simple ivory wedding dress for Savannah's inspection. "This is the dress I finally chose."

Savannah tilted her head. "It's lovely and perfect for the occasion."

"I didn't want anything too fancy since Charles and I have both been married before, but yet, I wanted it to be special." Polly smoothed her hand over the silky material.

"And it is. You can go up to the spare bedroom at the top of the stairs to get dressed. Will Charles be here soon?" Savannah shifted Flo to her other hip.

"He will, and the rest of my family. Elsie is home from Business School; Twila, my brothers and their wives and Maggie and her family will all be here."

"Wonderful. And, of course, your father?"

"Of course. Did I tell you he found a small house in

Franklin for him and Twila to move into as soon as she graduates in June? Both of them already have jobs over there."

"That's wonderful. Do you still plan to sign the hotel over to Richard Ebbert in June?"

"I do. Charles and I decided that would be best. Mr. Ebbert will take over my mortgage. It's time." That upcoming transaction gave Polly great peace. She had run the hotel long enough to know it wasn't something she wanted to do long term.

"A few weeks ago, I rode the train to Cleveland with Charles to help choose a house to rent. He isn't in a hurry to buy." She started up the stairs. "I'd better get ready. Eleven o'clock will be here before we know it."

♠

The bridal march reached her ears, and Polly stepped back so Savannah could shepherd Sammy and Milly, their ring-bearer and flower girl, ahead of her on the stairs. She closed her eyes for a quick prayer. *Thank you, Father, for freeing me from fear and giving me another chance at happiness. I'm so grateful Charles didn't give up on me.*

When Polly reached the bottom of the stairs and stood in the landing doorway, her gaze met the love-filled eyes of her groom. He stood beside Garrett whom they'd asked to perform the ceremony.

The sun glinted through the leaded glass window, casting a rainbow across Charles' blond hair. It reminded her of God's promise at the end of Psalm twenty-three: *Surely goodness and mercy will follow me all the days of my life.* Was that God's promise to her?

Polly drew a deep breath as peace settled over her. Even if hard times came, by God's grace, she would choose to trust and not be afraid.

Author's Note

The Author's Note is my attempt to answer questions you may have about what really happened or what was fictitious in Sarah's Legacy Lived. Robert Dye (Bob/Father) did marry a second time on March 11, 1921. (His first wife, Margaret Humphrey, died on August 11, 1911.) Bob and his second wife only lived together a few years, but never divorced. The name of his second wife and her family have all been changed.

William (Will) and Florence (Polly) Reiser had a bungalow built in Stoneboro at the northeast corner of Franklin and Walnut Streets in 1921. J. Edward Sullivan was the contractor. The information about the tragic accident that took William's life on Valentine's Day, February 14, 1924, is accurate, as is the information concerning the Memorial service. (It is not known if William went by Will, Bill, or William. I chose to call him Will because there was another person named William in one of the earlier books.)

Beth Dye's character was based on Blanche Dye. Her name had to be changed for the series because Blanche Davis, who lived next door to the Dyes, was a main character in book one. The Dye children's careers, for those who pursued careers, are as indicated in this book.

Florence Dye Reiser sold the property in Stoneboro that she and William owned to Mr. and Mrs. C. E. Vogan on July 7, 1926, and bought the Central Hotel from them the same day. According to Isabel Dye, wife of George, the members of the

Dye family, who still lived at home, moved with Polly to the hotel. A newspaper article indicated Polly changed the name of the hotel to the Florence Hotel.

On November 18, 1926, W. J. & Mabel Gilmore (Isabel Dye's parents) bought Bob Dye's home on Broad Street for $1500 but, according to Isabel, never lived in it. She said since the Dye Coal mines had closed by 1926, she thought perhaps the Dyes had fallen on hard times and her parents bought the house to help them out. Perhaps the Dyes used the money to help pay the mortgage on the hotel.

On February 25, 1928, Florence sold the hotel to Richard A. Ebbert for $1 and other considerations. She then bought back the Dye home on March 27, 1928, for $1 and other considerations. The 1930 Census shows Polly living there with her father.

For the purpose of having a happy ending and to fit the scope of this book, I condensed some actual happenings, changing the true timeline. Polly did marry Charles Clarkson but not until May 6, 1936, so he was not involved at the hotel. (His first wife, Jane Throop Clarkson, died on February 13, 1934.) The 1940 census showed Charles and Polly living in Cleveland with Charles still employed as a railroad motor engineer. Charles' obituary said he was employed by the Pennsylvania Railroad for 43 years.

Please refer to the Author's Notes in books one, two, and three of the Sarah's Legacy series for a listing of those characters based on real people and those who are fictitious. The characters I've created (whether fictitious or based on real people) the conclusions I've drawn, and the story I've told are a work of fiction.

I hope you've enjoyed the stroll down memory's lane which the Sarah's Legacy series has afforded us, turning back the hands of time to walk the streets of Sandy Lake almost one hundred years ago. Catching a glimpse of this little town as it existed then is something I'd always wanted to do. Thank you for making the journey with me.

About the Author

Daisy Beiler Townsend wrote and published in magazines and periodicals such as Guideposts, The Upper Room and the Secret Place for many years.

In earlier years, she and her husband, Donn, wrote more than 100 songs and had a family music ministry and Christian Nursery School. Later, Daisy pursued certification as a pastoral counselor with the NCCA and ordination with the NCCC with whom she served for many years. Daisy and Donn were also missionaries to Japan with One Mission Society, with whom they are still affiliated, and led the Japan Prayer Initiative.

Researching the history of their home in Sandy Lake, PA, in 1998 led to beginning a historical novel inspired by the lives of former residents of their home in the late 19th and early 20th centuries. In 2014, Daisy published her first book, Homespun Faith, an autobiographical devotional, and then completed the first book in the Sarah's Legacy series in 2017, the second in 2019, and the third in 2020.

Daisy and Donn live in Pennsylvania and have three children and six grandchildren. Visit Daisy on Facebook, Twitter, Instagram or www.homespunfaith.com.